No Job
for a
Lady

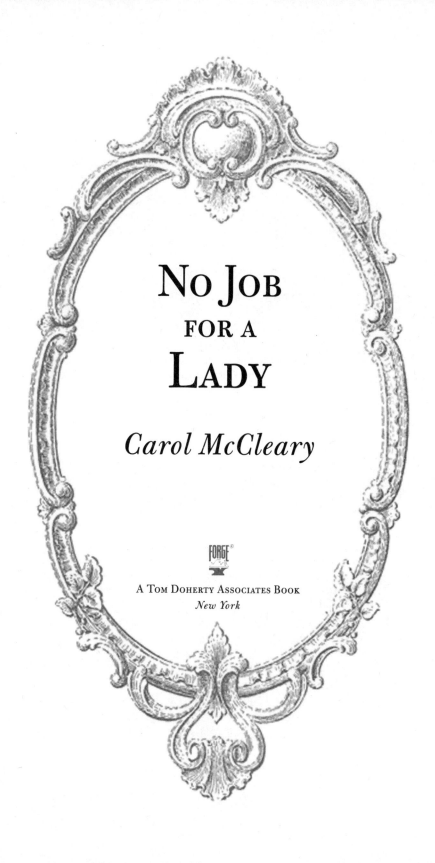

No Job
for a
Lady

Carol McCleary

FORGE®

A Tom Doherty Associates Book
New York

NO JOB FOR A LADY

Copyright © 2014 by Carol McCleary

A Forge Book
Published by Tom Doherty Associates, LLC
175 Fifth Avenue
New York, NY 10010

www.tor-forge.com

Forge® is a registered trademark of Tom Doherty Associates, LLC.

The Library of Congress Cataloging-in-Publication Data
is available upon request.

ISBN 978-0-7653-3440-4 (hardcover)
ISBN 978-1-4668-1105-8 (e-book)

Forge books may be purchased for educational, business, or promotional use. For information on bulk purchases, please contact Macmillan Corporate and Premium Sales Department at 1-800-221-7945, extension 5442, or write specialmarkets@macmillan.com.

First Edition: June 2014

Printed in the United States of America

0   9   8   7   6   5   4   3   2   1

MICHELLE MASHOKE-ANDERSON

a beautiful soul . . . warm heart . . . and very caring lady

you gave me hope in all aspects of my life

thank you

ACKNOWLEDGMENTS

With writing the Nellie Bly mysteries I have been able to meet many wonderful and fabulous people. But the *BEST* and *most wonderful surprise* was to be reconnected to my Very First Best Friend . . . *Pam Percy* . . . I never felt so lucky and happy to have her back in my life! It was the best gift Nellie could have ever given me.

And speaking of other beautiful gifts I've received . . .

The most fabulous girls to work out with in the world! Take a bow ladies . . . Sheila, Edie, and Darlene.

And I want to thank the girls at my favorite place, *Underground Café,* for always being so friendly and warm to me: Kacie Van Norman, Miranda Usselman, and Kasey Flewelling, and there is no way I can forget Carol DeCost, a Very Special Lady —*thank you, girls!*

An enormous thank-you to all the people who have picked up my books. I hope Nellie has inspired you.

And last, but not least in any manner, for this book would not be if it wasn't for Kelly Quinn, editor at Tor/Forge . . . thank you for being in my corner and watching my back. You are the best!

NELLIE BLY (1886)

The treasure which you think not
worth taking trouble and pains to
find, this one alone is the real treasure
you are longing for all your life. The
glittering treasure you are hunting for
day and night lies buried on the other
side of that hill yonder.

—B. Traven,
*The Treasure of the
Sierra Madre*

No Job

for a

Lady

PROLOGUE

1886

Teotihuacán, Mexico

The City of the Gods. A place so haunted by the bloodthirsty deities of ancient Mexico that the 200,000 people who populated it disappeared without a trace and no one dared take their place. The mighty Aztec emperors so feared its fierce spirits that they came once a year to offer a sacrifice in blood.

When I first saw the city, I stared in awe at the enormous stone ruins and towering pyramids, among the largest structures ever built by human hands, yet even in these modern times they call the Victorian era, no one lives here. Local villagers who come to an archaeological dig to work will not even spend the night. They call the main thoroughfare—a broad boulevard often wider than a football field, which runs over a mile through the heart of the city of stone and ghosts—the Avenue of the Dead.

Now I fear I know why.

Smothered by darkness, I stand in a netherworld beneath the ancient ruins, unable to move a muscle. Strange figures dart by as clawlike hands grope my body, pulling at my clothes. Try as I might, I don't have the strength to push them off. They dig into my flesh and I cry out in pain.

A sticky, smelly hand covers my mouth, suppressing any chance for help.

Chattery voices surround me, speaking in a strange tongue, as I'm being moved deeper and deeper into a void I fear I will never escape. Cold, damp, unstirred air embraces me. I feel as if I'm being prepared for sacrifice and there's nothing I can do.

As a murky black mist swirls around, my whole being feels as if it's suspended in a violent, twisting maelstrom. I have no control of my body—it is attached to me but not mine.

The hand leaves my mouth, but I don't scream. Something inside me warns not to let them know my fear.

The chatty voices disappear like ghosts fleeing in the night.

My eyes hurt as my vision starts to come back, blurred at first, then darting around as a wild animal trapped and looking for a way of escape. But there is no escape. I'm in a chamber that's coffin-black without a speck of light, not even the twinkle of a star. I can't see or hear anything.

I'm alone. Afraid to move.

I have been brought from the tepid night outside to a cool place that smells like earth. *A cave.* I'm sure of it. I don't dare take a step because I don't know what's around me. It's too dark to see anything. Not even my hand in front of my face. Am I at the edge of a cliff? Where would a step take me?

I feel as if I'm suspended in midair, but my feet tell me I'm on solid ground. I put my hands out to see if I can feel a wall, but I feel nothing. I wait, my heart in my throat, my mouth dry, breathing shallowly, in a place darker than night and quieter than a crypt.

Now I understand why the Aztecs feared the city built before the time of Christ and why the local villagers still do.

Stupid! I had been warned that, like Egypt, ancient Mexico has a history of mystery and magic, that its pantheon of violent gods were the most bloodthirsty of any that ever existed, possessing a bloodlust satisfied only by their worshipers ripping out hearts and draining the blood of sacrifice victims to satisfy the covenant with the gods.

Am I to be the next sacrifice to their gods?

My insistence on foolishly delving into ancient secrets that have been buried for more than a millennium have brought me to this place that must be underneath the city. The ancients who built Teotihuacán created colossal towering edifices aboveground, taller than a skyscraper, so there's no reason to believe they didn't put tunnels under their city. And this is where I've been taken.

But the blood covenant with the gods, shape-changing from man to beast to create terrifying creatures of the night, and barbaric cannibalism are just a very small part of the dangers I am about to face;

besides the ancient evils, there is a darkness of heart that permits even murder by "civilized" men who lust for ancient treasure.

To understand how I got into haunted caverns below a stone city that once rivaled ancient Rome in size and sophistication, I need to explain what took me from Pittsburgh, Pennsylvania, to Mexico against the advice of just about everyone close and dear to me.

My name is Nellie Bly. That's not my birth name, of course. I was christened Elizabeth Cochran but had to change my name when I got a job as a newspaper reporter, because reporting the news is not considered a ladylike career for a respectable young woman.

Not that I am in any way embarrassed by working in a profession with men who are considered uncouth by bankers and tradesmen. To the contrary, my own "profession" before a bit of audacious penmanship got me a reporting job was that of a factory girl. And I was lucky to work in a factory and earn my bread, because we live in an age where the only "careers" for "well-bred young women" are to be sent to finishing school by well-heeled parents so they can learn how to manage a house and please a husband.

Of course, if you were raised by a widowed mother along with a houseful of siblings, a woman's options, beyond the marriage bed, would be to obtain a job working in a factory at half the wages paid the man working next to you, or selling your body on the street until the Big Pox or some other noxious disease blessed you with an early death.

Getting a desk with the "boys" in the newsroom, those vulgar, mouthy denizens of the free press who dug out and reported the news, brought me five dollars a week, more money than I was making laboring long hours in a factory in a grimy city that has so many places of manufacture, you can get black lung from the sooty air.

I felt like Cinderella when Mr. Madden, the editor of *The Pittsburgh Dispatch,* told me that he wanted me to come to work at the paper after reading my letter to the paper objecting to an article that said women were fit only to be the helpmates of men.

Unfortunately, I soon learned that newspapers are not financed by what reporters write, but by the ads placed by businesses. An article in which I pointed out the sad state of workers—men and women— who toiled long hours for pay so low that they could hardly keep food on the table raised the ire of advertisers who employed such workers!

I was immediately assigned to the society page to report on weddings, teas, and the doings of people with more money than the good sense the good Lord gave them.

Chomping at the bit to do real reporting after I'd had an overdose of silly gossip, I asked my editor to give me a chance to be a foreign correspondent.

Heavens! I thought poor Mr. Madden was going to have a coronary. Being a foreign correspondent is *"no job for a lady,"* he told me flatly.

My rebuttal that neither was reporting silly gossip did not impress him. Which left me with a dilemma. I could either do society twaddle or find a man to support me in return for serving him in the kitchen and marriage bed. Neither option was acceptable.

I have always had the feeling that nothing is impossible if one applies a certain amount of energy in the right direction. If you want to do it, you can do it. You just have to work hard and smart.

Since the newspaper would not let me try my hand at reporting from a foreign place, I left my job and set out to tackle an assignment. I chose Mexico for the place from which I would send my dispatches because, as my librarian pointed out, it's not just a place that's wild and untamed, with sagebrush and bandidos, that borders our country, but a thousand miles south in the tropics are the remains of civilizations with striking similarities to ancient Egypt, from pyramids to hieroglyphics.

God help me!

Materializing out of the darkness like a wraith in the haunted cavern, Aztecs gods with huge eyes, gaping jaws, ugly, twisted, even demented features stand staring back at me. Each one is adorned in its own tall headpiece, cloaks of bright feathers, and shields befitting Aztec warrior kings. The feathers are long and brilliant—reds, greens, yellows, purples, oranges.

Only one of the inanimate creatures is not in feathers, and I stare at him with my heart racing. His back is to me, but I can still tell it is a man, not a god. He's almost naked, with strange gray skin that strikes me as *dead*—cold dead as gray marble, but without the shine and luster of polished stone.

He turns and comes toward me as I scream and scream.

Here would be a good field for
believers in women's rights. Let them
forego their lecturing and writing
and go to work; more work and less
talk. Take some girls that have the ability,
procure for them situations, start them on
their way and by so doing accomplish
more than by years of talking.

—"The Girl Puzzle,"
Nellie Bly's first piece,
published January 25, 1885,
in *The Pittsburgh Dispatch*

1

El Paso, Texas

I bite my upper lip, a terrible habit when I'm nervous. This time it's the long line for tickets at the train station causing the chewing. The ticket counter is an opening in an outside wall of the station house, leaving those of us in line to endure the cool of the evening as night falls. A line this long, this late, isn't a good sign.

The insane trip I set out on has already taken more than one wrong turn, and I don't need anything else to go sour. I spent four days traveling from Pittsburgh to El Paso, sitting and sleeping on hard seats. My body and soul ache at the prospect of hard seats for the final twelve-hundred-mile—three long days and nights—leg to Mexico City.

I want a Pullman sleeper berth and I am ready to fight for it.

A compartment all to myself would be even better. I need time to digest the fact that *I am going to Mexico alone.* I'm hoping that with a good night's sleep the sunken feeling in the pit of my stomach and overwhelming fear that I'm being quite foolish will go away. But I have a sick feeling that no matter how much rest I get, I won't be able to keep a bridle on my doubts.

What was I thinking! Well, as my dear mother says, when I act impulsively, I'm not thinking. For the first time in quite a while I, too, am questioning my good sense. It's just that when Mr. Madden refused to let me tackle a foreign correspondent assignment on the grounds that it was too dangerous for a woman . . . well, I became furious. What poppycock!

Like most men, he has little understanding of what women are capable of doing. And that brought us to butting heads because I'm too impatient to keep tackling the boring reporting assignments given to me solely because I wear petticoats.

Rebelling from being exiled to the society page, I set out to do something that no other female reporter has ever done: report news from Mexico.

Why Mexico? I had saved my pennies during my brief sojourn in the newsroom, but what little I had wasn't enough for reporting from "overseas." It would pay, however, for the seven days by train it takes to get from Pittsburgh to Mexico City, a journey of close to 2,500 miles.

Once in the Mexican capital, I would generate enough money to keep me going by sending articles back to the paper. I am certain Mr. Madden will not fail to publish the articles—even if he refused to underwrite the assignment, interesting stories about events in a land far away sent by a young woman of their community will excite the paper's readers.

My mother's elation at my abrupt success at going from laborer to newspaperwoman turned to shock and disbelief when I told her I would prove myself by reporting from untamed Mexico, a land of endless bloody revolutions, fierce bandidos, and wild Indians on the rampage.

Even though it is 1886, the West is not yet completely tamed, and I have read that Mexico is decades behind America in its own struggle to civilize itself. This makes the land south of us either fertile ground for exciting stories or a danger zone, depending on whether one is looking at the situation through my rose-colored vision or my mother's morbid fears.

I quit the paper, bade my few journalistic friends adieu, packed a bag, grabbed my mother, and set out to prove myself again. And as I said, at my own expense, something else that would never have happened to a man.

My mother insisted upon coming with me, of course, no doubt planning to poke with a hat pin any bandido who bothered me. She is certain that I will end up being kidnapped and having to make tortillas for a bandido chief—after I endured unspeakable things. And I must admit that her insisting upon accompanying me put the minds of my brothers and my editor a little more at ease, for they, too, were positive that I would be putting myself in harm's way.

Nevertheless, all this changed when last night on the train my mother got stomach problems.

To my dismay, there was no way she could continue. The poor dear had horrible stomachaches. At first, she couldn't stop throwing up. She was not in a dying state, just an uncomfortable, messy state. We figured she'd eaten something that didn't agree with her and by morning she'd be better, but she wasn't. Instead, she had a bit of a fever and just felt that icky, miserable feeling when one is under the weather—not wanting to move, just rest and sleep.

This left me in a pickle, for I felt responsible for her. A decision had to be made. Either I gave up my trip or I found a place for her to stay while I continued on. My mother hated to see me go on alone, but she knew how important it was that I complete what I had started. If I returned to Pittsburgh without having succeeded at my boast that I was capable of being a foreign correspondent, it would be with my tail between my legs and the only employment opportunity that of begging for my old job at the factory.

Before disembarking the train, I asked the porter, who was so helpful and kind when my poor mother became ill, if he knew of a place my mother could stay for a while. He gave me the address of an elderly couple who might rent us a room.

Thank goodness I was able to make safe and comfortable arrangements for her stay; otherwise, I would never have gone on.

I promised her once I arrived in Mexico that I would send letters every day so she would know how I was progressing—and that I was unharmed.

I am determined to prove myself come hell or high water. She knows how important this trip is to me, and no matter how crazy she thought I was in taking this trip, she also believed that it would be the only way for me to prove myself.

A shout from the ticket counter brings me back to reality: "Window closed; come back tomorrow morning."

"What?" I tap the shoulder of the man in front of me. "Are they really closing the window?"

He turns to me, a rather nice-looking man.

"Yes, I'm afraid so." He glances down at a railroad pocket watch, an item that reminds me of my own. When my father died, my mother gave me his watch, and it has been with me ever since.

"But why?"

"No idea. Maybe he's tired and wants to go home and eat. Can't blame the poor chap. Listen, I know you don't know me from a hole in the wall, but would you like to join me for dinner? I'm famished and wouldn't mind the company."

"I, uh . . ." I fumble, caught by surprise, not knowing what to say.

This is a first for me. I've never been asked out by a strange man. To the contrary, my life has been so occupied with helping my mother keep food on the table for my brothers and sister that I've had neither the time nor the inclination for courtship or even keeping company.

The first thing I can't help but notice is his height—I have to look up. He's tall, probably over six feet; his body hovers over my five-foot frame. I assume he indulges in sports, for he appears to have the build of an athlete. He's young, maybe five or six years older than my nineteen,* with striking green eyes that are framed in silver wire-rimmed pince-nez—another favorite of my dad's, except his glasses were gold. He's clean-shaven, which I prefer, and his hair—curly, dark brown—is not long, but not short, either, falling just below his ears. He's wearing a dark suit, giving him an eastern look, rather than the rough clothes of the westerners I see all around.

My mother claims I will fall for an older man because I worshiped my father, who died when I was six. He was prominent in our little community and became a judge. When not out tending to the horses, he wore suits.

"Cat got your tongue? It's just dinner. I thought you'd like the company. Frankly, I felt sorry for you because you appear to be a woman alone. A bit worried, are you, out in the world all by yourself?"

Well I'll be! What a turkey!

I square my shoulders. "I was concerned about getting a sleeper, not about traveling alone. I am quite capable of taking care of myself, thank you. And for your information, I'm not alone. I'm with my mother. Now if you'll excuse me, I must get back to her."

"Fine, have it your way." He starts to leave, but then turns back and tips his hat. "Good day."

He walks away, leaving me agitated—more at myself than at him. The invitation had been polite and my hesitation had annoyed or perhaps even embarrassed him. But he is also insensitive enough not to realize that I have a right as a woman to travel alone if I care to and that I am not hiding my head in fear. However, I also realize I am oversensitive about setting out alone, not only because of what it will do to my career if I fail but also about how it will shatter the high expectations of those who encouraged me.

* Nellie was actually twenty-two years old at the time of the Mexico trip. She lied about her age to maintain a "girl reporter" image.—The Editors

I have to admit that it probably would have been nice to have shared dinner with the gentleman. And he might even be heading in the same direction I am by train. But as usual, I've thrown caution to the wind and am doing it alone, going to a foreign country with a reputation of being wild and lawless, and with no one to lean on. No one to protect me or at least have for companionship and comfort, as my mother would have been. Oh, I am going to miss her sorely. Especially after I have turned down an invitation to dinner in this strange, rather wild, and backward town.

"Chin up, Nellie," I mumble to myself in the most confident voice I can muster, "you can do this."

One thing is for certain: Without a doubt, I will be here tomorrow at the crack of dawn to secure a private sleeping berth. Maybe I can sleep my way to Mexico and avoid the likes of him.

Once there, I will just take it day by day. I'll be fine.

In the meantime, I might as well head into the station building to wait. I'm not hungry and have crackers left over from lunch to nibble on. I want to be right here, even if I have to sit on a bench all night long. Besides, as much as I'd like to, I can't go back to my mother.

Since there was the possibility she might get better and try to continue on despite the fact she was weak and could relapse, I told her a little fib: I was leaving tonight. Right or wrong, I saw this as an opportunity of a lifetime, to experience traveling on my own, so I seized the opportunity. How could I pass it up?

Never before have I gone out of town all by myself, because it's not proper etiquette for a single woman to travel without a companion. Well, why is it proper etiquette for a man to travel alone? Once again, rules made by men. Why should they have all the fun? Besides, this is something I have wanted to do forever, and even though I realize this is probably not the smartest time to make this decision, being that I am going into a foreign country where I don't speak the language, I'm glad I'm doing it.

And without a doubt, I am scared.

But I can't, I won't let that stop me.

When I was five years of age, my father took me down to the stables to learn how to ride a horse. I was so scared. I didn't want to get on—the horse was a monster, even though it was only a pony—but my father insisted he wouldn't let the reins go.

Instead of giving in to my tugging and pulling to leave, my father knelt down and looked me square in the eyes and said, "Nellie, you'll never get anywhere in life if you don't face your fears. Worse, you will miss out on a lot. So hop on."

So here I am—facing my fear.

Tomorrow I will make sure to be first in line, before I lose my false courage.

2

Oh, no, I groan as I enter the station waiting room—men, women, children, and dogs, and stacks of baggage of all shapes and sizes are all about, so crowded together they appear to be one big, unwieldy mass.

The dim light of a large oil-lamp fixture hanging from the center of the ceiling falls with dreary effect on the scene. Some people are sleeping sitting up, lost for a while to all the cares of life; some are eating; some smoking; while a group of men are passing around a bottle occasionally as they deal from a greasy pack of cards.

The bench that I was determined to sit on till dawn is nowhere to be found. Every single one is completely occupied. It is evident that I cannot await the glimpse of dawn 'mid these surroundings. Even if I had planned on spending the rest of the night miserably nodding between sleep and wakefulness on a hard bench, I can't; there isn't even a squeeze-in space.

With a deep breath, I square my shoulders and leave, entering into the night again.

There are no inviting lights of hotels, and I have to wonder whether most travelers with a stopover at El Paso sleep on the streets.

A man with a lantern on his arm comes along and I ask directions to a hotel.

"They're all closed at this hour, filled anyway for sure," he says, "but if you can be satisfied with a room in a second-class guesthouse, my wife will put you up for the night at less than what a hotel would charge. Very clean, no bugs."

I am only too glad for any shelter and the thought of not sleeping with bed bugs for the night; well, to say the least, I am happy with his offer.

Without one thought of where he might take me, I follow the light of his lantern as he walks ahead of me.

I expect wood sidewalks, but instead there is just sand. The Texas border town is obviously not in a high state of building arts.

As we are passing a saloon, its double doors fly open and an old man in rough clothes, with a battered, dusty hat and a thick beard, comes staggering out, bumping into me.

"Jus' me and ol' Montezuma . . . we know where the gold's at," he says in a drunken slur, blowing alcohol breath in my face.

I move forward to get away from him. I have an extreme dislike for drunken men—they remind me of my stepfather, who got drunk regularly and became quite abusive—but the drunk takes ahold of my dress sleeve.

"Let go!" I jerk my arm out of his grip.

"Venus." He points his grimy, filthy index finger up. "The stars, they tell everything."

The doors to the saloon swing open again and three men come out. My guide also has come back, but he keeps a few steps away from us.

"Howard!" The younger of the men takes ahold of the drunk. "You old geezer, here you are."

"No," he says to me, as if it is a plea.

The young man, a cowboy by his dress, grabs the old man by the shoulders and steers him to the other two men, gents who look like nothing argues with them—not even the meanest bull.

Howard gurgles something indecipherable; all I pick up is the word *Montezuma* as he looks back at me with pleading eyes as the men pull him away.

"What are you going to do with him?" I ask, stepping forward, concerned because rolling drunks is a favorite pastime of thugs.

The young cowboy steps between me and the men hustling the old man down the alley next to the saloon.

"Sorry Howard frightened you like that, miss." He tips his hat and gives me a smile and a friendly look of concern.

He doesn't look much older than I am, but behind the smile he has the same hard edge as the other two. He's wearing a white Boss of the Plains hat made by Mr. Stetson, which is popular with cowboys. His mustache appears neatly groomed and his hair respectfully short, which I prefer, unlike the slightly longer hair on the man I met earlier at the ticket office.

He's wearing his six-shooter low on his left leg—a southpaw, something not too common. His whole appearance gives him the look of what they call a "gunslinger" in dime novels.

"I don't think he wants to go with your men."

The young cowboy gives a quick glance back. "Howard's fine, always a little ornery after having too much to drink. Hope he didn't offend you in any way."

"Drunks are always offensive, but no harm done."

"You sure? Howard has a tendency to mouth off and say crazy things—what did he say to you?"

"He's trying to get away from those men."

He glances back again in the direction Howard has been taken. "Like I said, he's an ornery coot who says crazy things." He gives me a grin. "You can just run along."

"Excuse me?" I look him square in the eye and stand my ground. "My feet take me where I alone tell them."

"I've gotta git," my lantern carrier says. His tone tells me he wants no part of the gunslinger, and he turns, hurrying away.

"Something's fishy," I mumble under my breath as I turn to leave.

"What'd you say?" the cowboy asks.

"Nothing."

"I thought I heard you say something."

"You heard wrong."

"Then I suggest you hurry along, or you're going to lose your friend."

He's right: My lantern carrier has wings on his feet.

"Wait!" I yell to him.

I don't go far before I can't help but glance back. The cowboy is rolling a cigarette and appears in no hurry to go back into the saloon—as if he is standing guard at the alley or making sure I do leave.

I know I should shrug the incident off, but it's hard for me when my gut tells me something is wrong. But robbing a drunk doesn't seem like a very likely motivation on the part of the three men, if for no other reason than they were better dressed than the older man—who didn't leave an impression of having much jangling in his pockets. Yet my gut says that the old man was frightened of them.

Walk away, Nellie; there is nothing for you in this. I hear my mother's voice in my head and I know she's right, as usual, so I reluctantly keep walking away and don't look back again. She has always claimed that I stick my nose in so many places it shouldn't be in that one day it's likely to get pinched.

What is wrong with me? I haven't even crossed the border yet and I'm already sticking my nose where it might get pinched. It's just that I hate seeing someone being manhandled. Having six brothers, I not only learned how to defend myself; they also instilled in me a desire to defend the helpless, though the fact the older man is boozed up doesn't particularly endear him to me.

Within a short time, through the sandy streets, we reach the place where there is but one room unoccupied. I gladly pay for it and, by the aid of a tallow candle, find my way to bed.

Relaxing as best I can on a cold-stiff mattress, I try to turn off my mind, checking off my encounter with the drunk and the gunslinger like it was a bad nightmare, but a puzzle keeps knocking on my head, wanting to be invited in. Finally, I realize what's bothering me.

The hats.

The cowboys all wore wide-brimmed Stetsons, but Howard was wearing a bowler, though it had been battered enough to hardly be recognized as one. And while Howard's clothes were that of a man who worked with his hands, they were strikingly different from the range outfits the cowboys wore.

All that meant is that the old man and the cowboys were not peas from the same pod. And what was Howard trying to tell me? Something about the stars and Montezuma? The Aztec emperor who's been dead for hundreds of years? Drunken talk that made no sense.

I wish my mother was here so I could talk this out with her. I need her common sense, for I know my imaginative and suspicious mind will weave a tale that will have little connection to reality.

I shake my head. I should bang it on the wall to get some sense into it, because I need to be up early and fresh. Tomorrow I am boarding the train for Mexico City and a grand adventure! I have to get to sleep.

Rats! All my logic is still not working, for I can't stop tossing and turning.

Frustrated, I get out of bed and go to the window. Maybe some fresh air will clear my mind of all this foolishness.

I'm about to raise the window, when I see a man standing below the gas-lit lamp on the street below, smoking a cigarette. He's wearing a white Stetson and—I'll be—he has a six-shooter strapped low on his leg. *His left leg.*

I'm sure he's looking up at my window, and I step aside so I can sneak a peek out.

Okay . . . and what does this mean? What's he doing out there?

I carefully peek back out again.

Yes—he is definitely there looking up at my window.

He takes a step forward and I jerk my head back in and press my body against the wall, my heart pounding.

Did he see me watching him?

"Get ahold of yourself, Nellie," I tell myself in a strong voice to calm my nerves. It's dark in my room, so I wouldn't have been silhouetted and easy to spot. Besides, what could he do even if he knew I had spotted him? I'm up here. He's down there. I'm safe.

I peek out again. He's still there, but now he's leaning against the lamppost.

I slip back into my place of complete darkness and try to take deep breaths to relax and think. Be logical. Think. Maybe he is waiting for someone. One of the other guests? When I signed the register, there were three names—all male. Good Lord, he might be staying here, because it might be the same three men who came out of the saloon.

No, that doesn't work. The man who rented me the room would have recognized them back in front of the saloon.

So why's the young cowboy, gunslinger, whatever he is, out there? A coincidence? Why not? I'm just being silly and paranoid.

I slowly look back out.

He's gone, yet the hairs on the back of my neck are still standing straight up. I lean back and bang my head against the wall. Darn it! I gave myself a good scare. And it all started because I stuck my nose into something.

I crawl back into bed. The morning can't come soon enough.

Tomorrow I'll board the train for Mexico City and leave behind the jabbering drunk and whatever schemes these El Paso cowboys have under their hats.

"Good riddance to bad rubbish," as my mother would say.

3

There were no drunks or cowboys outside the boardinghouse when I scurried out the next morning. I had, in fact, looked the moment I jumped out of bed.

Wanting to be the first in line to ensure getting a sleeper berth and knowing the reputation of Mexican trains for not watching the clock, I had a boardinghouse bowl of thin gruel boiled in water rather than sweet milk, then got myself to the southbound tracks an hour before I was scheduled to depart.

As I approach the ticket counter, I can't believe my eyes. There is already a line.

"But it's not even eight A.M. How can this be?"

"Do you always talk to yourself?"

I turn, to find the young gentleman who had asked me out to dinner last night in a rude manner.

"You again."

"Good morning to you, too." He tips his hat.

"I, uh, good morning." It comes out more reluctantly than I intend it to because a cat's got my tongue, again. I lied to him last night about traveling with my mother and now I will be caught.

"No need to explain. I know I have this charming effect on women."

"*Charming* isn't the word I was looking for."

"Ouch—you don't mince words. Well, not to worry, I've been told it's a big train. Hopefully, this will be the last we see of each other."

I start to reply, but then turn around and shut my mouth. It's rare that I walk away from someone when I should put him in his place. I don't like it a bit, but it's more important to get my sleeper, so I let it go.

Putting the man behind me out of mind, I take out my notepad and start penciling some thoughts about El Paso, the main portal to Mexico.

I am still at it when in a fog I hear *"Next . . . next . . ."*

"The ticket seller means you," the annoying man behind me says.

"I'd like a single sleeper, please."

"We only have a compartment for two left—husband and wife, mother and daughter, two people of the same sex—"

A door behind him opens and a man sticks his head out. "Jack, come here. Sorry, miss, he'll be right back."

I'm glad he was summoned. My mind is whirling. I need to think. What am I going to do? I want that sleeper. The thought of sitting up all the way to Mexico City makes me want to go collect my mother and go home.

"Are you going to take the compartment for you and your mother?" my shadow asks.

"My mother's sick," I blurt out. "I'm going on alone. I have to; my job demands it."

"What job is that?"

"I—I—" For some insane reason, unbeknownst to even myself, I don't want to reveal I'm a newspaperwoman, and my usual golden tongue is at a loss for words. "That, sir, is none of your business."

"I thought so."

"What do you mean by—"

"It means you're just trying to get sympathy, and that isn't going to work with me. I'm going to take the compartment."

"You can't take it. It's for two people."

"That's true, but"—he nods vaguely to the rear—"my, uh, traveling companion is back there catching up—"

"You're lying. You invited me to dinner last night when you didn't have anyone else to go with you."

"He's sick, too, and, frankly, having dinner alone was infinitely more entertaining than it would have been with you."

"You have a nerve—"

"Excuse me!"

The ticket seller is back.

"Husbands and wives don't get to argue in line. Now I have one last compartment to rent. If you two don't want it, step aside."

"We'll take it!"

4

Did I really say that?

I freeze for a moment, paralyzed by the impact of what I have just said. I have just claimed that this stranger is my husband.

I quickly shoot a glance at my "husband." He looks a bit amazed and about to spill the beans. I try to jar him into acquiescence.

"They're the last tickets—*dear*."

"I—I—" he stammers.

The ticket agent holds up his hands palms out as a signal for him to stop.

"Don't argue with her. It won't do any good; she's a woman. Twenty dollars, or step to the side."

I quickly put twenty dollars on the counter and grab both tickets after the agent makes a pencil mark on each of them.

"Let's go," I instruct my companion.

My knees are weak as we walk away. I acted completely audacious and now I have to face the man. I need to say something clever to get over this hump—*mountain*—I have created, but nothing comes to mind.

The truth is, I simply believe that if you want something, you must go full speed ahead. If I didn't have that attitude, I would not have gotten a reporter's job when I lacked both the experience and education required—and I would not have left after nine months as a reporter to establish myself as a foreign correspondent over the objections of my employer.

I have the tickets gripped firmly in my fist. I paid for them and they are both mine. But I have to deal with this man and I am used to getting my way. I will start with sugar.

"My mother will appreciate your kindness in getting her a sleeping berth. This trip has been so hard on her."

"You already told me that your mother is not traveling with you."

"She's feeling better and will—"

He lets out a loud guffaw. His coarse laugh is loud enough to attract the attention of those around us.

"I beg your pardon."

We stop and face each other. My tongue is still tied.

He shakes his head. Rather than angry, he appears to be perplexed. Even amused. "Such a little package of surprises you are. I'm not certain that you even have a mother, but if you do, I very much doubt that she would admit the relationship in public."

"How dare you."

"How dare I? You are the daredevil, madam. With reckless disregard for the truth as you plunge ahead. You're a funny girl. You won't have dinner with me, but you are willing to sleep with me."

"*Sir!* There's no call to be vulgar!"

"Look who is calling the kettle black. Lies flow off your tongue like Niagara." He smirks. "You should have just said that you wanted to share a compartment with me."

"That's not true. I'll have you to know I have no intentions of sharing that compartment with you. Here"—I reach inside my purse—"here's two dollars. You'll be able to purchase a seat for that."

"I get it. You use me as a tool to get yourself a comfortable compartment and then you throw me out like an old shoe." He turns his back to me and walks away, not even taking the money I offered.

I start to call him back but stop, worried that he is angry enough to cause a scene. Instead I watch him disappear into the crowd.

I feel horrible. He's right: I did use him for my selfish gain. My mother's sudden illness threatening to make me cancel the trip, and my career, and miserable nights on the train from St. Louis, have left me off balance.

So desperate to have everything go right, I'm out of control. I will have to rein myself in before I get into deeper trouble than I already am.

As for the man, I'll find him on the train and buy him lunch. There is no reason I should feel guilty. I didn't really cheat him out of a sleeping berth. I was in line before he was and was entitled first to what was available.

I will try to be in a charitable mood toward the man I have wronged, but I hear a devilish whisper in my head that says the best solution of all would be that he is unable to get a ticket because the train is sold out and thus I won't have to face him and eat humble pie.

5

Grateful that I have only one piece of luggage, I scurry off to board the train. With all the people boarding and few porters, it would be a pain trying to maneuver more luggage.

I decide to set down my carpetbag and wait for the crowd to thin down before boarding. No sense in getting trampled. Besides, I have comfort in knowing that I have a private compartment all to myself, so I won't even have to fight to get a window seat.

Even though I am still not over the trauma of having finagled my "husband" out of a sleeping berth, I am cheered by the fact that I don't see him. Maybe my wish has come true and he wasn't able to get even a bench seat on this one, or maybe he decided to wait until tomorrow for another train heading south. Either one works for me.

My mother would be mortified if she knew what I had done. I chuckle over what she would say if I told her that I got a train compartment by pretending a stranger was my husband. Besides being irked by the damage to my unsullied reputation, she would tell me that by trifling with a strange man, I had risked being murdered by the Servant Girl Annihilator,* who has killed a number of people in Texas, most of them women—damnable deeds done in the dark of night.

* During the years of 1884-1885, in Austin, Texas (population approximately seventeen thousand at the time), a killer called the Servant Girl Annihilator murdered eight people, of whom seven were women. "The murders were committed by some cunning madman who is insane on the subject of killing women" (*New York Times*, December 26, 1885). When the Jack the Ripper killings occurred in 1888 in London, there was contention that the Ripper may have been the Texas killer, and several cowboys were questioned by Scotland Yard. —The Editors

"What in heaven's name were you thinking?" is her customary rejoinder when I confess that I have strayed even modestly from her strict guidelines for feminine deportment.

My response that desperate times call for desperate measures rarely satisfies her fear that someday my impulsive acts will be too bold for my own good.

I stop chortling about how I put one over on the man as it occurs to me that he might be very angry indeed at me. I'm amused because I won, but he might be a sore loser. There is nothing he can do even if he wanted to. I have the tickets. But I look around again anyway, paranoid that he's about to descend upon me.

Down at the tail end of the train, a handsome carriage pulls up to a private railcar. A well-dressed man and woman descend from the carriage to board the railcar.

The man is dressed in a long black-tailed coat, with a top hat and cane; the woman has on a very large floppy black hat filled with lots of black feathers and a light black coat. I squint but still can't make out their features.

My interest is immediately roused. Private railcars are the height of luxury, comparable to owning a yacht. That gets me thinking: Could the occupants provide me with interesting materials for a dispatch? They have to be somebodies!

While I won't stoop to write boring news about society weddings and teas, we "unwashed plebeians" are all fascinated by the luxurious and often scandalous lives of the very rich, especially their excesses, so I will keep my eyes open. Who knows, the private car could be holding railroad robber baron Jay Gould himself, who put down a southwestern railroad workers' strike by hiring violent strikebreakers to beat the striking workers into submission. Clever devil that he is, he afterward boasted that he was able to hire half the working class to kill the other half.

Catching him with a mistress or ruining a secret business deal by making it public would not only make a dandy story and satisfy my sense of justice that he needs more than his nose pinched, it would guarantee my position at the newspaper.

A porter walks by, pushing a cart filled with luggage, and I stop him. "Excuse me."

"Yes, miss?"

"Do you know who that couple is?"

NO JOB FOR A LADY

He glances to where I am pointing. "No, but they must be people of great wealth and importance. It's all hush-hush; not even the crew's been told who they are. That's a real fancy private railcar they are boarding. Must be awfully nice to have so much money." He shakes his head and laughs as he moves on.

The whistle blows and the conductor yells, "All aboard! All aboard! Last call to board!"

I reach for my carpetbag, when a young man grabs it.

"Allow me." He gives me a boyish grin.

I let out a small cry of surprise. It's the young cowboy from the saloon, who later stood on the street and watched my window.

"What are you doing here? Following me?"

The gunslinger's grin gets wider. "No, ma'am. Looks like we just have tickets on the same train. Besides, if I followed you, I did it very quickly, because I got here before you."

"How do you know you got here before me?"

"After I bought my ticket, I saw you near the ticket booth, having a dustup with a gent. What was that all about?"

"Nothing."

"Didn't look like nothing to me."

"Looks can be deceiving."

I reach to take my bag from him and he swings it behind his back.

"Excuse me, but that is my bag."

"I'm gonna take it aboard for you. Is this all you are taking to Mexico?" He nods back. "My trappings are over there."

His gear is a rolled-up bedroll with a prairie coat and leather gloves thrown on it. Next to the bedroll is a saddle with chaps slung over it and a rifle on top of the pile. The leather saddle, like his clothes, is well broken in—which is why, I suppose, cowboys take their saddles with them.

"I travel a bit lighter than cowboys."

"So I see. My name's Harry, but my friends call me Sundance." He gives me a sly smile. "You met a couple of them last night. Not that you took much of a fancy to any of us."

Uh-huh. I almost ask him why he was spying on me last night, but I hold my tongue because I don't want to tip him off. If he was spying on me, I want to catch him at it.

Sundance has a look that shouts "bad boy" to me. It's his cockiness— the grin that says he's laughing at you and those bold eyes that seem to undress me. But he does it in a way that is both flattering and intriguing, unlike a crude masher.

He reminds me of the boys my mother has always told me you don't bring home to meet the parents. "There are the good boys," she says, "who dress proper and aren't wild. And there are the bad boys, who have a look to them and are always getting into trouble."

He's a cowboy, that's for sure, but there's something else about him that makes me wonder how much time he spends herding cows—as opposed to using that gun he keeps strapped to his leg.

He is dressed for range work—white wide-brimmed Stetson, red bandanna around his neck, checkered wool shirt, heavy denim jeans. His boots have pointed toes to help guide his foot into a stirrup and high heels to keep his foot from slipping through the stirrup.

I'm far from being a cowgirl, but I was raised around horses and have done quite a bit of horseback riding myself. Even won a few ribbons.

His clothes appear clean and have a dusty look that shows they are well-worn from days in the saddle. His low-hung gun could be slid out fast because it isn't strapped down.

I saw some cowboys working cattle on the plains during the train ride from Pittsburgh, but this is the closest I've been to one, other than the cowboys in the books I read as a little girl. The fictional cowboys fascinate me because they have interesting adventures—going into unknown territory and having to fight rustlers and Indians. They are nothing like the farmhands in my hometown of Cochran's Mills, Pennsylvania, population exactly 534.

I test the waters about what I saw last night.

"How's your friend Howard, the one you were helping back to the bunkhouse last night? He seemed a bit, uh, reluctant to go with your friends." My tone lets some puzzlement about his reluctance slip out.

"Oh, he's over there."

I follow the jerk of his head and there Howard is, in the flesh. He is easy to recognize, with his bowler hat and thick beard. He's boarding the next train car down, a gunnysack slung over his shoulder.

"He's with you. A cowboy?"

"Yep. But not exactly a cowboy. He's our cook, though he's hard to keep in line. If he's not about to get his poke cleaned by a lady of the night, he's running off to his first love, prospecting for gold.

"We were just helping him out last night. It's a written code between us cowboys—never leave a partner alone in that condition. Didn't want to see anything bad happen to him. That old coot knocks down more booze than a preacher guzzling holy water."

The train whistle blows again with the warning of departure.

"I think we'd better board if we want to make it to Mexico City." Sundance gives me that grin of his.

Once I'm aboard, he hands me my carpetbag.

I give him a smile and practice my Spanish. *"Gracias, señor."*

He salutes me with his fingers on the rim of his hat as he turns to go back and get his gear.

"My pleasure, Nellie."

I open my mouth to ask how he knows my name, but he's already slipped through the door.

6

W ho's the cowboy?"

"*What are you doing here?*"

It came out as a screech of horror. He's here! Occupying a seat in *my* compartment.

"Why don't you step in and close the door before people think you've seen a snake."

"I have!"

Slipping in, I slide the door shut behind me, then drop my carpetbag and glare at him. My temper rises as he chuckles.

"Nice to see you, too."

"What are you doing in my compartment? You have no right to be here. I'm going to call the conductor and have you arrested."

He shakes his head. "Apparently, you haven't looked carefully at the compartment tickets."

"What about them? Your name's not on them." I take the two tickets out of my purse as I speak. "I paid for them and—"

I stop and stare at the tickets.

"Ah . . . I can see your grasp of the situation spreading across your face like the illumination from one of Mr. Edison's newfangled lightbulbs."

There in bold print is an *H* on one and a *W* on the other.

"*H* for husband, *W* for wife." He smirks. "Mexico is a very religious country. As the ticket agent says, compartment ticket holders must be husband and wife or of the same sex."

"I will not be bullied. I will not share this compartment with you."

He shakes his head and shrugs. "I don't expect you to. Find yourself a seat on the train. Better hurry before they are all taken."

The train lurches forward and I grab the wall for support. We are already under way.

"Look," he says. "This is an awkward situation for both of us. I suggest we make the best of it. If we squabble, we will both be kicked off the train. I will pay my half of the compartment and we'll share it. There's room for both of us and even more privacy than there is in the corridor. And despite any judgment of my character by you, I am a gentleman."

He is right about more privacy, even if we share the compartment. Other than a couple of small compartments at either end, the berths in a Pullman are lined up down the corridor, one above the other in what is called the "open section." Modesty is secured by the sleeping clothes one wears and by a heavy black curtain the porter hangs in front of each berth.

The compartment has two sofa seats facing each other. There is not enough leg room between the two for people to face each other. Instead, one person sits at the end of a seat and the other person sits at the other end of the seat across the way. At night, the back from the sofa seats are used to fill the legroom to create the lower berth.

The upper berth is presently flat against the wall and ceiling above his head as he sits on a sofa seat. It is "made down" by being dropped into position by the porter at bedtime.

I chew on my bottom lip, trying to find a way out of the predicament, bringing more head shaking on his part.

"You really don't like to lose, do you? And it's obvious that you give no quarter and take no prisoners. Do you always get your way?"

"For your information, whatever slight progress I have made in this world has been the result of having to run twice as fast and twice as far as my peers. Now, sir, there are three contingencies to sharing this compartment. You forthwith pay me the ten dollars you owe, your deportment will never be less than the gentlemen you claim to be, and I get the lower berth."

The critical difference between the two berths is that the upper is as high up as my five-foot head-to-toe height. To get in and out, the porter provides a ladder at night and again in the morning.

He hands me ten dollars. "Agreed. Except you get the upper."

"Any gentleman worthy of his salt would give a lady the lower. Please consider the situation. Your long frame makes it easy for you to reach the top bunk, while my short, insignificant body makes it a horrendous task because I am not a monkey."

"That's why the porter has a ladder."

"I don't like being cooped up. I get claustrophobic."

"Madam, perhaps for a moment you might want to consider my point of view. You wanted a sleeper badly enough to connive to get it, using me as your tool. Next, you attempt to evict me. Failing at that, you wish to cramp my long frame into a small box while you stretch out below in luxury. May I ask—are you by chance the only daughter of a railroad or banking magnate?"

"I'll have you know that I earn my bread with my own hands and the only thing I have to do with railroads is buying tickets, while banks are where I store what few hard-earned pennies I have left after providing for basics."

He jumps to his feet and offers his hand, a more English than American gesture when it comes to a woman, but one that independent women like myself are pleased to accept.

"Watkins . . . Roger Watkins, New York City."

"Nellie Bly. Pittsburgh." It comes out as a grumble, but I give his hand a good squeeze. "Now, sir, I know you are a true gentleman and sportsman and will be gracious enough to resolve this matter with the flip of a coin."

"Good try, Miss Bly. . . . It is Miss, isn't it?"

"Yes."

"I would expect that to be the case."

My jaws go tight. Any goodwill that had momentarily risen between us is now dead as he deliberately tries to get my goat.

"My apology, Miss Bly. I'm sure you are not truly destined for spinsterhood. It just appears that way when you are so persistent." He gives me a once-over. "Are you, uh, on your way to Mexico to meet a husband?"

"Do I look like a mail-order bride?"

His shrug signals he might think that.

"For your information, sir, I am traveling to Mexico on important business. And maybe I'll even climb a pyramid or two."

"I hope—"

"Stop!" I tell him. "Wait."

I close my eyes tightly for just a moment and then open them.

"Darn, it didn't work. My mother says that if you close your eyes very tight and wish really hard, when you open your eyes again, unpleasant things will have disappeared." I give him a sour smile. "But you're still here."

Nellie's personal creed:

Determine right.
Decide fast.
Apply energy.
Act with conviction.
Fight to the finish.
Accept the consequences.
Move on.

7

A fine mess I've gotten myself into. How am I going to explain my sleeping arrangements if word gets out?

More important, why do I do these things?

It is only a short time before the train crosses the Rio Grande and into Mexico and everyone has to leave the train to have their luggage examined by Mexican customhouse officers. Standing in line for my turn, I have time to think and realize what a state of potentially embarrassing scandal and gossip my bold move to get a sleeper has placed me in.

An unmarried woman sharing a private compartment with a man! If my mother were here, she'd take a birch rod to my bottom, despite the fact I'm a full-grown woman. And my brothers—heaven help Roger Watkins if they were here. They'd tar and feather him and run him out of town on a rail.

Worse of all is the newspaper. If word of this gets to my editor, I will not find a job there when I return.

There is nothing I can do about it now except keep the cauldron from boiling over. I have deliberately not told Watkins I am a newspaper reporter. I don't know enough about him to expose that fact. For all I know, he might be a news reporter himself. Or use the knowledge to get his way with me.

Stop bickering with the man is a must. It's just that it's hard not to. Something about him raises my ire. I think it's that whenever I say yea, he says nay. The man appears determined not to give me an inch. I get the impression that there is a woman behind his attitude—perhaps one that left him at the altar, refused his overtures, or otherwise offended his manhood.

I will be spending a lot of time in the parlor car.

After clearing customs, I'm told the train will not depart for more than an hour. I return to the compartment to drop off my bag before heading for a restaurant near the station. I spotted my traveling companion returning to the train earlier.

He's camped out on the seat, smoking a pipe and reading a newspaper. His feet are extended across to the other bench, blocking my way if I had wished to take a seat. His only redeeming grace is that he has removed his shoes. There is a hole in the big toe of his sock. That establishes the fact that he is not married nor living with his mother.

Determined to be polite and gracious to avoid confrontation, I give him a smile and a gentle "Hello."

Engrossed in his reading, he barely nods his head and doesn't look up.

A man of few words.

I take a deep breath. My bag belongs under the seat he presently has his feet on—my seat. Thus I have two choices. I can get down on my hands and knees and attempt to slide my bag under the seat by slipping it under his legs . . . or I can ask him to get his head out of his blasted paper and remove his feet long enough for me to bend over and slip the bag under the seat.

To exercise either alternative, I must ignore his rudeness.

Submission to this man is just not in me. Neither is compromise.

I drop the bag on his extended legs.

He looks up, startled.

"Get your head out of that paper, your feet off my seat, and store my bag under the seat."

Without further ado, I leave for a restaurant to enjoy being as far away as possible from him.

"Uppity woman" follows me out the door.

I can't help but smile.

8

I find the restaurant recommended by the customs officer when I told him I wanted to sample good Mexican food. Strangely enough, it is run by Chinese.

Scribbles on the chalkboard that passes for a menu in the place tell me that corn, beans, and peppers are extremely important food items in Mexican cuisine, because it appears that about everything offered is some combination of those three food items, ranging from cornmeal to corn tortillas, refried beans to bean soup, along with peppers that seem to accompany everything that is offered. And all are offered at a very fair price.

As I'm sitting and studying the menu, someone hovers over me.

"Tolerate some company, Nellie?"

Sundance grins down at me.

"Please do. On one condition—how do you know my name?"

"Your name? It's the name on your luggage tag. Hope it's yours."

Why didn't I think of that? So much for conspiracies.

We order corn, beans, and peppers, of course, and he has beer served in a clay cup. As we chat, I get a surprise—he's from Mont Clare, Pennsylvania, a village that's a stretch from Pittsburgh, but not too far from Philadelphia. Mont Clare isn't much bigger than my own Cochran's Mills. He left home just four years ago to head out west on his own.

"Knocked around Sundance, Wyoming, for a while and that's where I picked up the handle Sundance. Easier to spit out than Harry Longabaugh."

"What are you cowboys going to do in Mexico?"

"Riding herd on some valuable head of cattle, horses, that sort of thing. Bring them back across the border from deep in Mexico."

"Don't they have Mexican cowboys to do that?"

"They do, but the buyer says too many prize bulls and Thorough-breds he's bought don't make it back when he hires local wranglers."

He asks me what I'm doing in Mexico and seems very impressed that I'm a newspaper reporter.

"A foreign correspondent at that. I've never met one of those."

I didn't volunteer that I hadn't, either. The food is dished up almost immediately. I really like the tortillas and beans, but Sundance says he's a meat and potatoes man. So is my mother. I'm sure she would hate Mexi-can food. I can already hear her complaining.

"Sorry old Howard bothered you," he says out of the blue.

"Oh, he's harmless, I guess."

"He is. Just has a habit of drinking too much and mouthing off. Did he tell you about his big claim?"

"No . . . he has a big claim?"

"All prospectors have one, or so they say. He was turning over rocks, looking for the shiny yellow, long before either of us was born. Howard's like all the others I've met. They work a little here, a little there, just to get a stake, because he's always looking for the big one. You know what I mean?"

"A pot of gold."

"The mother lode itself. Guys like Howard always think a deep vein of gold is just up the river a ways or over that next hill, but they never come back with more than a thimbleful of glitter. And they are always looking over their shoulder for claim jumpers.

"Brags that he got a lead to a big pile a while back after he married one of them Aztec women down south, though he probably just shacked up with her. Says she told him where a big pile of gold was before her broth-ers tried to scalp him. He tagged along with us as camp cook to get back down south to find it."

"From what I've seen of Howard, he needs the mother lode just to keep him in booze."

"If that ain't the truth. Suppose he told you about the pile he's always yapping about to us?"

I'm tempted to satisfy his curiosity and tell him what little Howard actually said to me, but I don't because it would probably just make him think that I know more than I really do.

"Howard never told me anything about his pot of gold. Is that why you followed me to dinner? To find out if he had? Are you a claim jumper, Sundance?"

Sundance chuckles and shakes his head. "Whoa, Nellie girl, grab the reins on that one. I was out to get some grub and saw you." He leans toward me and gives me a roguish grin. "I will confess, though, that you being the prettiest girl I've seen since I left Pennsylvania made me head your way when I saw you on the street a few minutes ago."

Vain that I am, a little flattery, and my suspicions fly out the window.

9

Before returning to the train, I exchange my money for Mexican pesos, getting a premium of twelve cents on every dollar.

Deciding not to deal with Mr. Watkins quite yet with my usual subtle charm, I head for the parlor car, where the seating is most comfortable and usually the least crowded because an extra fee is required for use of the car. The fee paid for a compartment entitles me to day use, but no one is permitted to spend the night there.

Now that we have crossed the Rio Grande and left behind the Mexican town of El Paso del Norte, our train slowly moves through small villages and I see for the first time women plowing fields while their lords and masters sit on a fence, smoking.

Oh how I've never longed for anything so much as I do to shove those lazy fellows off. Men! They seem to be the same worldwide. This will definitely make it in my first correspondence to the *Dispatch,* even though I won't be posting any letters until I reach Mexico City.

It is not long after I am seated that the train starts slowing down for the first stop. I have already been told that the train will be a proverbial milk train, stopping not only at sizable towns but also at many villages along the way to drop off goods and pick up passengers.

The stops will increase the time it will take to get to Mexico City, but I don't mind. The slower pace gives me an opportunity to see more of the land and its people and to acclimate myself.

I know the people in Pittsburgh will get such delight in reading about all the wonderful sights. And I will make sure to fill my letters with details about the food, clothing, way of living—everything and anything that not only educates them about Mexico but entertains them, too.

I can see the headlines: *MEXICO AND ITS PEOPLE BY NELLIE BLY.*

However, I can just imagine poor, dear Erasmus Wilson cursing me for sending my correspondence on blue-glazed paper, but it is all I have. Besides, he can only thank himself for this task of editing my work. It was my response to his article, "What Woman Was Made For" that landed me a job as a newspaperwoman.

After I had written a couple of newspaper articles back then, Mr. Madden had made dear Erasmus my personal editor to correct my rocky grammar. I must say Erasmus took it all in good stride and has been a good ally. When Mr. Madden reiterated for the umpteenth time his opposition to my heading for Mexico and on the day before I left said he would make no promise that my letters from Mexico would get into the newspaper, much less on the front page, dear Erasmus took me aside and whispered, "Don't worry, Nellie girl, you send them to me and they will appear, I promise."*

I just hope my articles will encourage Mr. Madden to officially make me his foreign correspondent. If they raise the readership of his newspaper, I know I'll have the job. One thing I have learned after becoming a news reporter is that publishers are as enthralled by the almighty dollar as everyone else.

My first impression of the Mexican country south of the border towns is that it is a bleak, arid landscape with rolling hills, about the same as a good deal of what I saw in Texas. I have been told that the southern half of the country is much greener than the northern region, going from subtropical to thick jungles. That is the part I am really looking forward to, the land of the Aztecs, with its ancient ruins and towering pyramids.

I can't wait to explore them. As a child, I use to daydream about digging for mummies and rare artifacts at ancient pyramids while fighting off evil men and wild creatures.

As I sit in the parlor car with its comfortable parlor seats, instead of writing in my journal as I had planned, I can't stop looking out the window, thinking about the mysteries of Mexico and the Aztec civilization.

It all seems too fantastic. I am finally going to be doing what I dreamed about as a little girl—tromping in the desert, looking for ancient relics and

---

* He kept his promise. Nellie's first article appeared in 1886, with her name in tall, bold type. For the next six months, they would get prominently displayed and other newspapers around the country would print her articles under the heading NELLIE IN MEXICO.—The Editors

hidden treasures. Mind you, I won't be hunting for artifacts or pots of gold, except for those that make interesting stories to wire home, but I am entering a world with a civilization as old as time and as completely different from that of Cochran's Mills and Pittsburgh as the moon and the sun are from each other.

I pull out a well-worn copy of an article about the Aztec civilization given to me by my librarian, Mrs. Percy. She gave it to me on one condition—that I would send detailed articles about the pyramids. It has been a lifelong dream of hers to climb one, but with marriage and children and a husband who refuses to leave Cochran's Mills, she gave up on her dream.

Besides my mother, Mrs. Percy was the only woman who told me to follow my dreams before I got married. In fact, I got the notion of making my mark as a foreign correspondent by reporting from Mexico from Mrs. Percy.

I told her I was tired of reporting high-society tripe—detailing the prices and latest styles in shoes, dresses, hosiery, lace, evening wraps, jewelry, handkerchiefs, even hairstyles, nothing that would help advance our society.

"Oh, but dear"—Mrs. Percy grabbed my hand and patted it, as if to comfort me—"you've done articles that have been very informative. Remember that one about E. H. Ober, the first woman to own and run an opera company. It was very insightful. It showed how women can work in the men's world of business and succeed. I'll tell you, it got many women thinking about how they could advance if they ignored what men said they could or couldn't do. Much to their fathers and husbands chagrin!" She laughed with delight.

She was right, but I had to point out to her that whenever I had done an article that raised issues about women—how they are treated and not recognized for their potential and not allowed the same benefits as men—Mr. Madden relegated me once again to doing insipid articles for the society pages. I was considering a trip to London, the financial and political hub of the world, to report on matters of international importance.

She listened soundly and then sagely pointed out that I would be lost in the crowded world of newspaper*men* in that distant city of millions.

"Don't you know that all the major newspapers in the world have correspondents in London? They say that most of the traffic carried on the great transatlantic telegraph cable that sits on the bottom of the ocean are the missives of reporters representing papers from New York to the Golden Gate."

She shook a skinny, bony finger at me. "No, London is out. You must go to where the competition is not so fierce."

I started to rebut, and she shushed me. "Choose your battles wisely, my dear. You want to make a mark in this world, get off the beaten path. That said, what would be your next choice?"

"Well . . ." I hesitated telling her, because whenever I thought about it, I thought it was completely insane. So with much trepidation, I blurted out, "Egypt! To report from the pyramids."

I thought her jaw would drop or at the least she'd howl with laughter, for the Land of the Pharaohs is halfway around the world, making it more expensive and impractical than even cosmopolitan London, which involves a mere five-day ocean crossing.

Instead, she stared at me with her jaw unhinged; her owl-like eyes behind big heavy black-framed glasses became wider. She started to say something and then appeared to gag on it, finally spitting it out as a whisper.

"Mexico."

"Mexico?" This time, it was my turn to be surprised. I couldn't believe she'd said Mexico. It made no sense to me whatsoever.

She shook her head vigorously and gave me a big, broad smile. "Yes! Mexico!"

"Good Lord, Mrs. Percy, Mexico! Why would I want to go to that place? From what I've heard, all it has is beans and bandidos."

"Pyramids, young lady, pyramids. Where do you think the biggest pyramids in the world are?"

"Egypt, of course."

Her eyes lit up with the delight of possessing superior knowledge.

"No! Mexico! The great civilizations of the Aztecs and Mayans left behind not only the largest pyramids but ancient ruins as old as those in Egypt and Greece. They are among the most fascinating in the world."

I have to admit I'm not as educated as Mrs. Percy, who attended high school. I was forced to leave school at the age of sixteen because of a heart condition.*

---

* Nellie never told the truth about leaving high school. She was embarrassed that it was because of financial reasons, not a heart condition. She had to leave school and go to work in a factory to help support her mother and siblings.—The Editors

However, I wasn't ready to believe her because that was not what I had been taught in public school and Sunday school. Egypt had Caesar and Cleopatra, the Ten Plagues, the Red Sea parting for Moses. Mexico had—had beans and bandidos, with deserts and sagebrush thrown in.

"That's because those books you were taught with were written by people from Europe or who had European ancestry," Mrs. Percy said. "The writers knew little or nothing about the great empires that lie to the south of us."

Once again, she shook her skinny finger at me. "Now, I'm not talking about the dry region of Mexico that lies along the border of Texas and other states. The Mexico of ancient civilizations lies more than a thousand miles farther south, in the center of the country. It would be an adventure just getting there."

She gave me a sly smile. "This is a keepsake of unfulfilled dreams." She opened up a drawer and took out an article, the one I now have. It speaks about how Mexico is an ancient place full of incredible ruins that date back to the time of Christ and even before; a land where high civilizations built great cities and pyramids that violated the very heavens, while further north, on the American plains, the native peoples were roving buffalo hunters.

Mrs. Percy went on to stress again to me that we don't appreciate the accomplishments of the great civilizations that had existed in the Americas before Columbus discovered the New World—the Aztec, the Mayan, and the Incan—because our eye for history was myopic.

"Shortsighted, that's what we are," she said. "Most Americans have European roots, including both of us, and it is our historical roots that we identify with. We ignore the fact that pre-Columbian Mexico has a history of accomplishments in science, medicine, architecture, and literature that rivals that of both ancient Rome and Egypt."

Ancient Mexico rivaling Rome and Egypt? It hardly seemed possible.

Our little library had only the one small pamphlet describing the Aztec Empire, which had been conquered almost four hundred years earlier by the Spanish, and she gave it to me.

To say the least, she stirred my interest. So much so that here I am on a train, rolling toward "ancient" Mexico.

And sharing a private compartment with a man I don't know.

Oh good Lord, if my mother finds out—I almost think I'd rather face the wrath of my brothers.

I stare back out the window and look in wonder at the groves of cacti, which raise their heads many feet in the air, their tops decorated with one of the most exquisite blossoms I have ever seen. My breath is taken away as I say it in my mind again: *I am on a train going to Mexico.*

Never in my wildest dreams did I ever think I would be doing this.

I just hope, pray, that I will somehow manage to experience the fascinating ancient glories of Mexico, because it is this enchantment I have come to report. The color and character of the modern country, as beautiful and interesting as it is, it's the remains of antiquity that interest me the most.

My attention gets knocked out from daydreaming by laughter coming from a group of men who are congregated around a woman, whom I can only see from the back.

She is wearing a big fancy red hat, with purple feathers all around it, almost like the lady that I saw entering the private railcar when we were boarding. It is not the same woman, though, because her hair is reddish, while the other woman had dark brownish hair.

I wonder who this woman is. Important or not, she must be pretty, because the men are hanging on her every word. It's amazing what a pretty face can do to men. I can hear my mother saying, *Nellie, first appearances are very important. People don't think about your intelligence when they first meet you. They look at your appearance—your face, hair, clothing, how you carry yourself, the wrapping, as your dear grandmother called it. Then if they like it, they will get to know you. Pity, but that's the way it is.*

And she's right. It shouldn't be that way, but it is. Looks first, brains second—that's if you want to attract the attention of a man.

This lady probably thinks she is the only woman in the car, and she'd be correct if it wasn't for me. It's easy to see that most of the occupants are American and Mexican businessmen, no doubt because of the extra fare required.

I toy with the idea of getting up and introducing myself to her, just to satisfy my curiosity as to who she is and what she really looks like, but decide against it. For the moment, I'm enjoying just sitting here and observing and daydreaming. It's much more fun than dealing with reality.

One thing I do notice about her is her laugh. It's hearty. It makes me think of a fun-loving barmaid. I like it. It's a laugh of someone with no pretense. I wonder if she is traveling alone. I seriously doubt it, but she might be someone to become acquainted with. It would be nice to have another woman to talk to.

"Look!" A man's exclamation breaks my attention.

Across the aisle, a young man takes his little boy and brings him to a window on my side.

"Look, Adam, cowboys."

The little boy squeals in delight.

The train is moving at a slow pace as we come up to two horsemen. Mexican cowboys! *Caballeros!* How wonderful.

They are the first real, live cowboys I have seen on the Mexican plains! I will never forget them. They are wearing immense sombreros, huge spurs, and have lassos hanging to the side of their saddles.

Even though I am not quite sure how they will respond, I jerk off my red scarf, stick my head out the window, and wave to them. From the thrilling and wicked stories I've read, I fancy they might begin shooting at me as quickly as anything else. However, I am delighted when they lift their sombreros in a manner not excelled by Pennsylvania etiquette and urge their horses into a mad run after us.

Such horses! What men on them!

The feet of the horses never seem to touch the ground. As the train picks up speed, we watch the race between horses of flesh and blood and our iron horse. At last, we gradually leave them behind.

I wave my scarf sadly in farewell and they respond with their sombreros. I never felt as much reluctance for leaving a man behind as I do to leave those *caballeros.*

I am bewitched by the land and its people; everything is so beautiful.

Between gazing in wonder on the cotton fields, which look, when moved by the breezes, like huge foaming breakers in their mad rush for the shore, I continue examining my fellow passengers. I'm amazed. I haven't even reached Mexico City and already I have fabulous ideas for my articles.

The train slows as it draws near what appears to be a modest-size town. As the train approaches the town, a large group of armed horsemen wearing sombreros and riding at a 2:09 speed leave clouds of dust as they stop and form in a decorous line on both sides of us.

Their hands rest on their holsters and none is smiling.

10

I lean across the aisle and ask a gentleman, "Do you know what's going on?"

"I have no idea."

"Maybe they're bandits and we are going to get robbed." I'm jesting, but his look suggests he doesn't like my idea. "I'm sure I'm wrong, but you must admit their presence is puzzling."

"On the contrary, señorita, they are here to protect us by keeping bandidos from attacking the train."

I turn, to find a tall, distinguished-looking man.

Close to six feet tall, he has thick black hair combed straight back, a long, slender aristocratic nose, and a pencil-thin mustache. His suit is a fine cut of worsted wool; his white shirt silk, adorned by ruby cuff links, has ruffles down the front to hide the buttons; his heavy watch chain is gold and encrusted with diamonds.

He appears very much to be a cultured and wealthy gentleman; his big brown eyes, below thick eyebrows, are framed by perfectly round glasses, while his long fingers appear designed for piano playing. His nails appear manicured, something you'll never see on the men in Cochran's Mills—or in the *Dispatch* newsroom.

"Don Antonio Rodriguez-Castillo, consul general of Mexico at El Paso." He slightly bows his head to acknowledge both of us. "Welcome to Mexico."

His accent is slight.

I rise and offer my hand. "*Gracias,* Señor Castillo. It is a pleasure to meet you. I am Nellie Bly, and this is gentleman is . . ." I look to the man who took umbrage at my comment about bandidos as the consul general gives my hand a slight squeeze.

He clears his throat. "Jack O'Brian, but if you'll excuse me, I have to join my wife."

"It is a pleasure meeting you, Señorita Bly."

"Señor Castillo?"

"Yes?"

"I'm normally not this forward, but would you join me for a moment? This is my first trip to Mexico, and I would love to learn about your country and any sights you think I should see."

"Of course, I would be honored."

He sits in Mr. O'Brian's seat, so we are facing each other.

"Are you traveling with family, señorita?"

I hope he doesn't notice my cringe at the question. "Not at the moment. I originally started with my mother as my traveling companion. But just before El Paso, she became sick from something she ate. It really put her under the weather. Poor thing couldn't travel any farther."

"And you didn't want to wait for her recovery?"

"I couldn't." Here comes one of my famous white lies, which just slides off my silken tongue. "I'm on assignment for *The Pittsburgh Dispatch* and have limited time."

I can't admit the truth because he'd think me a horrid daughter, but I made sure my mother was in good hands. And he's a man and wouldn't understand why a woman would accept the challenge of traveling alone to a foreign country. Seize the opportunity, Mrs. Percy said, so I did.

"*The Pittsburgh Dispatch* . . . a newspaper, señorita?"

"Yes, I'm their foreign correspondent." Another half-truth. I don't want to say the Mexico trip is self-assigned, because instead of him seeing me as a woman who has obtained a position usually reserved just for men, he'll view me the same as my editor does: an insubordinate female putting herself into danger by foolishly trying to tackle a man's job.

"Well, I must say it is an honor meeting you. I've never met a woman foreign correspondent . . . or even a female newspaper reporter, for that matter. I can assure you that there are no women reporting news in my own country. Your parents must be quite proud of you."

"My father has passed, but, yes, my mother supports my efforts. Thank you."

My father would have been proud of me, too, I'm sure, because it was he who put in my head that women are as capable as men. I slip my hand in my dress pocket and rub his gold pocket watch. He wore it every day, and now I do the same. It gives me comfort and a feeling of security, as if he is watching over me.

I find myself sitting a tad taller, besides blushing. I'm not use to a man complimenting me for being a newspaper reporter. Most men only register surprise, but some consider it a threat to their male status or an invasion of their territory. Even my brothers were mad at me. They said it wasn't a job fit for a lady and I would disgrace the family, even pointing out that if it was a proper job for a woman, I would be allowed to use my own name.

My mother and Mrs. Percy were the only ones who stood by me. In response to my brothers' objections, Mrs. Percy said, "Nellie, men do not know what's best for women. They think they do, but they don't."

"What features of my country are you planning to write about?" Señor Castillo asks.

Coming from a Mexican official, this is a loaded question. Stories of banditry and official corruption would appeal to the tastes of Pittsburgh readers, though I'm sure I'll gain their interest with colorful tales of the people and their food, but unless I want my dispatches to get me quickly tossed out of the country, or worse, I know better than to emphasize the negative.

"I'm open for anything that will interest my readers."

"Really? The preference of newspaper*men* I've known are to report about bandidos and notions of corruption in our government."

He must have read my mind—or my expression. And I caught his emphasis on *men* and the fact that I might attempt to imitate their negative reporting slant about Mexico. I need to defuse his concern that I will be just another reporter generating bad news about his country. It is time to be diplomatic.

"Actually, Mexico's colorful tales about how the people live is what really interests me. I will want to focus on the beautiful area and striking people of your land and culture. I know of no one back home who has been to Mexico, so they will be very interested to learn all about your food, clothing, customs—everything about your way of life. This probably would be boring to you, but not to North Americans."

"Yes, I quite agree. Mexico is a large country with many subcultures, ranging from people still living little different from their Aztec ancestors to those who race across the land as we are right now in what your own native people call an iron horse. As I'm sure you know, the heritage of the modern Mexican is mostly a mixture of European Spanish and indigenous Indian blood. Both bloodlines run in my veins and I am proud of them."

"As you should be. Even though my father was an American, his heritage is Irish, and he, too, was very proud of that."

"I can see, señorita, that you will be most evenhanded in your treatment of my people. Feel free to ask me questions if they come to your mind."

"Thank you, I will. I appreciate your confidence. I have to tell you, I am already falling in love with your food."

"Then perhaps you would honor me by joining me for dinner tonight? The daughter of a British friend is traveling with me. She's about your age, and, like you, she is experiencing my country for the first time. I'm sure she will enjoy your company. While the train fare is not considered a gourmet delight, I had the larder stocked with a few special items."

"That would be wonderful. I experienced a bit of Mexican food after we crossed the border, but it was prepared by a Chinese cook, so I'm not sure one can call that the real McCoy, even though I enjoyed it."

After establishing that I shall join him in the dining car at seven, Señor Castillo departs.

I beam with pleasure as I look out the window. I have barely crossed the border, and tonight I will be dining with a consul general of Mexico and enjoying authentic Mexican food. Maybe I can get him to invite me to his villa or whatever they call the homes of important Mexicans.

This could be the start of a very interesting trip.

11

So who was that Mexican guy you were talking to in the parlor car?"

Being immediately interrogated by Mr. Watkins, who is still sitting comfortably in my compartment, reading a book, when I enter, does not do my disposition any good. A credit to him, he removes his stocking feet from my seat.

I do a double take at the book he is reading—dark tales from Edgar Allan Poe. He seems the type who would be more inclined to read the Farmer's Almanac than a tale of mystery and suspense.

"Not that it's any of your business, but Señor Castillo is a very high-ranking Mexican government official. That we are involved in discussions of an official matter is all I am at liberty to say."

Let him chew on that one!

"I'm impressed. You have some discussions about the official nature of manure with that cowboy you were with?"

"You've been spying on me!"

"Excuse me, but I had to leave the train to eat, too, and saw you with him. Just curious. From the looks of how he carries his six-shooter, I wondered if you were going to hire him to evict me."

"Oh, would I love that. I just keep hoping that you'll be gone when I return, but you're always here, like a bad dream that keeps repeating itself."

He actually grins at my insult. "You were too busy talking to see me on the street or in the train. So, what does this *high-ranking* official do for the government?"

"As I said, I am not allowed to discuss it with anyone, especially someone I know nothing about."

"But I'm your husband . . . or did you forget?"

"My husband would let me have the lower berth. Now if you'll excuse me, I am going to freshen up."

"Good. Then we can have dinner together."

"Dinner? I'm sorry, but I have accepted a previous invitation. May I have my luggage?"

He bends down and pulls my carpetbag out from under the seat. "It's rather underfoot, isn't it?"

"It takes up much smaller space than yours."

"True, which makes me curious—most women take trunks and or at least three big bags. How did you manage to get everything in this little thing?"

He holds it up like it's a strange creature and I grab it out of his hands. Even the way he holds my bag annoys me.

"I don't like lugging around baggage and—and that includes you."

He gives me a sardonic grin. "Now why would you say that, especially since it is only because of me that you have this sleeper."

I start a reply but clamp my mouth shut. His statement is, unfortunately, true.

"Good," he says. "Now we are getting somewhere. Admitting the truth is cleansing to the soul, even if it was just the look on your face. So, dare I say we have a truce at hand?"

"Yes . . . if you give me the lower."

"No. What about dinner?"

"No. I already have dinner plans, and to answer your next question, which again is none of your business, yes, it is with that gentleman."

"I wasn't going to ask."

"Uh-huh." In a pig's eye. With carpetbag in hand, I open the door to our small washroom. It consists of a small metal sink with a hand pump for water and a mirror cabinet with enough room to store his shaving needs and an empty space for a jar of my skin lotion. The toilets are in the washrooms at the rear end of the car.

There is just enough room for me to squeeze in with my bag. I can't close the door all the way because there is no light inside. I leave the door ajar, just enough to get some light in, but blocking his view of me, even though I only intend to freshen my face.

Having been raised with brothers whom my mother and I had to constantly pick up after, I am surprised at how neat he is. His personal possessions are not scattered around the compartment, and the few in the cubbyhole washroom are neatly displayed. He has even taken a metal cup to hold his toothbrush and a tree twig. My father also used a twig to rub his teeth with, because he complained that brushes were constantly falling apart.

If Mr. Watkins wasn't so sarcastic, I might even be attracted to him, but there is something about him I can't quite put my finger on. He seems rather inquisitive about me, but I guess that's natural. I am curious about him, too. Under different circumstances, and if I wasn't so busy looking for stories, I wouldn't mind chatting and getting to know him a bit more in a friendly manner, instead of this inquisitional way.

I also have a feeling that he is not particularly fond of women. He is polite, no question about it, but he seems to take extra delight in refusing to abide by the rule of ladies first—especially when it comes to choosing a berth!

I wonder what happened in his life to give him such a negative slant about women.

"I'm surprised," Roger Watkins states when I come out of the washroom.

"About what?"

"How quickly it took you to freshen up. Most women take forever with their toiletry. When they come out, they basically look the same, except that maybe their hair is more combed, and not always for the better. Some women make their faces look like a clown's, with all that ridiculous stuff on their eyes and lips! Why do women wear such paint on their faces?"

For a moment, I am speechless. I've never heard a man ramble on and on about women, especially their attire. And what he just said to me, is it a compliment, or what?

"Well, I grew up with six brothers and I wasn't allowed much time in the bathroom. Besides, my mother doesn't believe in all that makeup. She says natural beauty is better. Unfortunately, I have neither natural beauty nor makeup."

"You are too hard on yourself. You're not a bad looker, except when you are jawing at me over the berths. And you have a smart mother. Shall we go?"

"Where?" is all I can say at the moment, for I am still flabbergasted at what he has just said.

"To the dining car."

"What? No. I already told you—"

"I know you have a dinner engagement. But, I, too, must eat, so I thought I'd at least escort you there. You never know what lurks between train cars."

"You read too many mysteries, and yes, I noticed your Poe book. And, no thank you, I do not need your protection." I square my shoulders. "I am an American girl who can take care of herself without the aid of a man."

"Fine. And speaking of Poe, listen to this: 'Take this kiss upon the brow!/And, in parting from you now,/Thus much let me avow—/You are not wrong, who deem/That my days have been a dream;/Yet if hope has flown away/In a night, or in a day,/In a vision, or in none,/Is it therefore the less gone? All that we see or seem/Is but a dream within a dream.'"

"I'm impressed. That is beautiful and very poignant. What's the title?"

"'A Dream Within a Dream.' It was published the year he died."

"How sad. Didn't Poe have a tragic life?"

"Drank himself to death."

"He also didn't have very good luck with women, did he? I suppose you haven't, either."

What made me say this, I have not a clue, but the minute it slipped off my tongue, I wished I could retrieve it, for the look on Roger's face made me want to crawl in a hole.

12

I leave feeling like a skunk. My wicked tongue made me say that. Unconsciously or maybe consciously, I was testing my theory that he had issues with women. Well, I guess I got my answer. Oh boy . . .

It is still too early for dinner, and I take a seat in a passenger car to do some more work on what will be my first news dispatch once I reach Mexico City and a post office.

The train starts to slow down and I glance out the window to see if we are going to be picking up anyone. I see no one except handsome horses doing something I haven't seen before. They are thrusting their heads into the water of a pond, "fishing" for grass that grows at the bottom. They stick their heads in until their eyes are below the water and then pull out a mouthful of grass.

As I stare at the horses, I think about Roger. Why did I have to make that comment about women?

I'm wicked, that's all there is to it. And I refuse to share bread with him—yes, I am being stinky. But I can't let it ruin my evening. I'm excited about having dinner with a Mexican diplomat, and nothing is going to spoil it. Somehow, later, I'll make up for my petty rudeness and all will be fine. I hope.

THE DINING CAR IS CLOSE to the front of the train, so I have to make my way through other cars to reach it.

"Oh no" slips out as I enter a passenger car.

I feel like I have entered the American West version of the den of Ali Baba and the Forty Thieves. Maybe I should have let Roger escort me.

The air is filled with smoke and sour smells of cheap tobacco, rotgut whiskey—and cowboys. Half a dozen cowboys, all dressed in rough range clothes pretty much like Sundance's, except his clothes are cleaner and he's had a razor to his face more often than the rest of these men.

A group are throwing cards into a hat, with the one who hits the target collecting the ante. Another cowboy blows on a harmonica while a man lies in the aisle, using his saddle as a pillow, his snoring adding to the harmonica tune. Joining the sleeping man in the aisle are the gear of many others—saddles, bedrolls, and rifles—making it a fine mess to navigate.

"Rustlers" is what my mother would call these gun-toting range hands.

Sundance looks up from cleaning his gun at the other end of the rail-car and does a double take when he sees me. He jumps to his feet, shouting, "Hey, you bunch of misfits! A lady's present!"

The cowboys react as if he had fired his gun. Cards get put away, hats are removed, saddles and bedrolls come off the floor, the poor snoring man gets a kick in the shin, and in seconds I am able to make my way as the sea of cowboys parts for me.

As I approach Sundance, I am unable to hide a big grin. His handsome, boyish face breaks into an even bigger grin as he removes his hat and makes a sweeping motion as if he is a cavalier.

"Miss Bly." He gives me a wink.

I feel like my cheeks are red-hot and all I can do is smile.

If there is one thing easterners believe about cowboys, it is that the men are gallant toward woman—most likely because there are not enough women to go around.

I decide to take a bold move. Turning back to the cowboys, I tell them, "You have again demonstrated that the American cowboy has more noble manners than the knights of the Round Table."

A cheer goes up.

As I turn back, a hand comes off the seating area to my right and grabs ahold of my skirt.

It's Howard, the old prospector whom Sundance and his pals hustled away from me last night in front of the saloon.

He grins up at me. "Gold," he says in a drunken slur. "Montezuma's own pile." He taps his head. "Them jaguars want it and I've got the map."

"Take your hands off her!"

A six-shooter appears as if it had jumped out of its holster in a blur and into Sundance's hand. The old man jerks back, letting go of my skirt.

Sundance no longer looks like a youth. His features are as hard as the steel of the gun he is holding.

"It's okay," I tell Sundance as I hurry along. "No harm, he's just drunk."

My voice has an edge to it because being touched again by this drunk brings back memories of my stepfather, who was free with his hands and his bad language. I will never forget his chiding, swearing at, and cursing my mother and us children—he even carried a gun and kept it loaded under the bed at night, threatening to shoot any of us if we misbehaved; many a time my mother became so fearful for our lives, she would take us out of the house and to a neighbor's. She scandalized the community by divorcing the lout. People had no problem with a violent, drunken man terrorizing the woman and children he was supposed to protect; instead, they condemned my mother for ridding him from the house and me for testifying in court about his gross behavior.*

A tall, stocky man with a large Stetson hat that almost hits the celling enters. He's also has a six-shooter in a holster strapped around his waist.

He tips his hat as he approaches me.

"Everything okay, miss?"

"Yes."

The cowhands are a rough lot, more hard-bitten than my dime-novel romanticized notions of cowboys. This man, who strikes me as the boss, appears to be the toughest, with a hard-case stare.

Howard curls up into a ball and Sundance puts his gun back into his holster. Everyone's personality changes.

The boss man reminds me of the horse ranch foreman my uncle had. They have that same walk—a jaunt that reeks of authority. If anyone disobeys them, well, they will only do it once, if they're smart. I never did like my uncle's foreman. He was mean and liked throwing around his authority, whether it was deserved or not. My dad called him a bully.

---

* October 14, 1878, Nellie's mother, Mary Jane Cochran Ford, filed for divorce. Only fifteen divorce actions took place that year in a county with a population of approximately forty thousand people, and only five were granted. Mary Jane's was one of those granted, thanks to Nellie's testimony and a letter she wrote to the judge about the abusive treatment her mother received from her stepfather. Her mother also did something unprecedented: She had the Ford name removed and went back to being "the widow, Mrs. Cochran."—The Editors

"Do we have a problem?" He addresses Sundance but looks down at Howard.

"No, sir, Mr. Maddock, everything is under control. Old Howard here just gets too excited sometimes when he's had too much rotgut. He's settled down now."

"Good."

I glance back just as I'm exiting the car to navigate the gangway. The boss man is leaning over Howard, talking. And it appears that whatever he is saying, it's making Howard agitated.

Moving between railcars with the train in motion is always a chore because the vibrating gangway between passenger cars is not covered, leaving one at the mercy of rain, wind, and the smoke from the coal or wood being burned in the boiler. I've heard there have been incidents of passengers falling while crossing from one car to the next, some to their death, even though the exposed gangway is only two short steps across—two windy and very shaky short steps across.

Before leaving Pittsburgh I read in the *Dispatch* that Mr. Pullman was introducing a new style of gangway between cars. He calls it a "vestibule" and will introduce it on the Pennsylvania Railroad later this year.

I pause on the gangway, my curiosity getting the better of me. As I look back through the small, dirty window on the door, Maddock's back is to me, but I get the impression he's still chewing out Howard, because the prospector is rubbing his hands and looking down.

He looks up for a moment, and I'm almost certain he sees me, as he expresses an emotion about the cowboys' boss man that I'm not expecting: contempt.

13

For reasons I don't fathom, the incident with Howard left a bad taste in my mouth. And it wasn't just his grabbing my skirt. He wasn't trying to be sexually offensive. All I know is I felt an undercurrent, a nasty undercurrent, pass among Howard, Sundance, and that foreman, Mr. Maddock—and Howard's mumbling about Montezuma's pile. Something I wasn't supposed to be a party to.

When Howard first bumped into me last night, he mentioned gold, Montezuma, and something about stars and Venus. Today, he's rambling about Montezuma and jaguars and a map. I wonder if he meant some sort of treasure. I will have to ask Don Antonio about that.

I enter the next car and am moving down the corridor in a brown study when a woman knocks me out of my deep absorption as she rises from a seat, steps in front of me, and boldly says, "How did you fair with the wild men?"

"Excuse me?"

It's the young woman from the lounge car, the one with the big fancy red hat with purple feathers all around it. She has a British accent.

"The cowboys." She points behind me.

I glance back and laugh. "Oh, them, they were fine—like knights of the Round Table, as long as you're a woman. Why? Did you have an unpleasant encounter with them?"

"No. I was going to attempt the crossing earlier, but they looked more dangerous than crocodiles on a sandbar. You're a braver woman than I."

I like her immediately. She has a certain openness and confidence that makes one feel welcomed.

"Actually, a rather interesting young cowhand named Sundance cleared a path for me, like Moses parting the Red Sea. Only he has a six-shooter rather than a staff."

"Oh, you must introduce me to him when you get the chance. We have absolutely no cowboys in the British Isles. So, Sundance kept all the other cowhands in line?"

"Yes, except for a drunken old prospector who can't keep his hands to himself. He jerked my skirt to tell me something about a map to Montezuma's pile. You wouldn't know if that is some sort of gold or treasure?"

"If I am correct, I think he means Montezuma's treasure. We must ask my uncle Don Antonio about it at dinner. I'm Gertrude Bell."

Unlike most women, she puts out her hand as an offer to shake, and I take it.

"Nice to meet you. You're Señor Castillo—Don Antonio's niece?"

"Not by blood. He attended university with my father and it's a title of affection we've given him."

My instant liking of Gertrude has grown. The handshake sealed it. Most women won't offer to shake and sometimes stare at me a bit offended when I put out my hand to them. Better yet, she has a firm handshake. My dad was a stickler on how to shake a hand. He never wanted me to shake hands like a fish—soft and wimpy—but to have a good strong grip. "Shows character, very important first impression," he said.

One of the first things I notice about Gertrude is her hair. It's this big, thick, curly mop of reddish—light auburn—hair that is untidy in a fashionable way. Her eyes are piercing green-blue and seem frank, honest, and inquisitive, but I also pick up a hint of confrontation—someone who likes a good fight. I've been accused of having the same look and temperament.

Her face is rather oval, with a good rounded chin, her lips bow-shaped, and her nose long and pointed, a bit sharp. Rather than great beauty, she radiates energy and a lust for life, as if the smallest things could interest her and bring great delight.

"Oh my, I'm sorry, I haven't introduced myself. I'm Nellie Bly. From Pittsburgh, Pennsylvania."

"I know. Don Antonio told me all about you. He said you're a newspaper reporter. How utterly exciting! I've never met a female reporter, though I've heard of one in London who covers the society page. Are you a society reporter?"

"I'm a foreign correspondent."

Gertrude gasps. "*No*. Nellie, that's so amazing. And they've sent you to Mexico? Don't they know how dangerous it is? Oh, this is so marvelous! I am so impressed. You must tell me—"

The look on my face has caused her to stop. I know my face is beet red, and I have to hold back tears.

"Nellie . . . what is it? What have I said to offend you?"

I pull her down next to me onto a pair of empty seats.

"I'm . . ." I hesitate, trying to get my composure. "I'm going to tell you the truth, but you must promise me you will keep it a sworn secret. Please, promise me this, Gertrude."

"Of course, I promise."

I believe her. It's those eyes—they don't lie. But where do I start? I can't just tell this obviously well-bred woman that I quit my job and headed for Mexico and am only pretending to be on assignment. She would never understand without comprehending that I haven't had the bed of roses I'm sure she's been raised in. I don't know how to tell a high-class British girl that I once worked in a factory and still keep her respect.

"I guess when my father died—"

"Oh, Nellie, I'm so sorry." She cups my hands. "I know how horrible that is. My mother died when I was three, so I have just a vague memory of her. However, everyone, especially my dad, says I'm a spitting image of her. I don't know what I would do without my father. He's everything to me. He's my life. When did your father die?"

"A long time ago. When I was six." I look down at my hands for a moment. "We were very close. To this day, I miss him terribly. Anyway, because of a horrible stepfather, whom, I am glad to say, my mother divorced—"

"Divorced! Your mother got divorced?" Gertrude looks at me not in surprise, but with more of an awed expression. "What a strong woman she must be. Good for her. I wish there were more women like your mother. So many wives are abused by men. It's terrible. So, what happened next?"

"Well, because of greedy people, my mother and siblings were left in a bad state of finances and I had no choice but to . . ." Once again I pause, deciding whether to tell her the truth or not—not because I don't trust her; it's just that I hate exposing this part of my life. I decide on the truth. ". . . to leave school and work as a factory girl to help put bread on the table. One day while waiting in line, I read a newspaper article that criticized women who earned their daily bread. This man had the gall to say women are abnormal—a *man-woman* if we worked in a man's field. Mind you! Utterly ridiculous."

"Quite so! The nerve of the man! I'm sorry, please continue."

"Well, every girl I spoke to was angered, but no one would or could say anything, for fear of losing her job. Forget that we worked just as hard as the men and never got a raise in pay, or, heaven forbid, promoted. We worked for ten cents an hour, while the men received twice that amount. All I could remember was my father constantly telling me that I should always stand up for myself. 'Men are not superior,' he'd say, 'even though they'd like you to think so. You are an equal, and never forget it. Do whatever you desire. Fight for your rights. You have only yourself to blame if you don't. And most important, remember there is nothing you can't do.' So, I sent the editor my opinion. Surprisingly, he not only appreciated my view; he offered me a job."

"Hurrah for you! Quite cheeky, I must say." She giggles, and that gets me laughing.

When we finally stop the merriment, her expression turns concerned. "Unfortunately, that columnist voices the opinion of most of the men on the planet. As my own father says, nothing will change unless you fight back. Good for you, Nellie. I, too, feel very strongly about that. So, tell me, you must fare quite well at reporting. I imagine newspapers trust only their finest reporters with foreign assignments."

I dodge the question, trying to avoid telling her I'm living a lie. "Fine, at first, despite the fact that my editor said my grammar and spelling are a bit rocky."

"Oh my word! You, too?" Gertrude laughs. "What a delight to hear someone else is a poor speller. My poor stepmum is always trying to correct my spelling and constantly tells me I will get nowhere in life if I don't learn how to spell properly."

"Well, he also told me my writing comes from the heart and I speak the truth, which is what he wanted, or so I believed, and I decided to make my sword my pen. However, when I wrote a story about the conditions of factory workers at local plants, I caused quite a stir. My editor was flat out told, by particular businessmen, that the paper would lose advertising if I continued to write about workers' conditions—especially those of women. The next thing I knew, I was attending silver-plate tea parties and weddings. So much for writing about the truth!"

"How ghastly! I have to attend several each year and dread them."

I bite the bullet and go on to explain how I tried to get my editor to let me become a foreign correspondent. "He said it was no job for a lady."

"Balderdash! The only jobs men know of for women are in the bed or the kitchen."

She spoke loudly enough for heads to turn, and we both scoot down in our seats and smother giggles.

When I am finished with my story, confessing that I was not sent by the newspaper to report, she gives me a big hug.

"I can't tell you how much I admire you, Nellie. I have the same feelings you do about avoiding spending my life as the helpmate to a man who has all the fun and adventures while I keep the hearth warm and the family nurtured."

"Then you won't tell your uncle?"

"He won't get it out of me even if they break my bones on the rack."

That sets off another wave of giggling like schoolgirls as we head for the dining car.

"So you're visiting from England?" I ask as we work our way through the train.

"Oxford. Studying history, my favorite subject. I'm on a short sabbatical to learn about the Aztec Empire. It's really an excuse to romp around some ancient ruins under a warm sun, rather than sit in a study and stare at winter's kill outside my window. Besides, my father says you get better knowledge by experiencing something firsthand." She stops and looks at me. "Now I have a secret to tell you. I want to become an archaeologist. I believe that if we know more about the past, we can advance better with the future."

"Gertrude, that's fabulous!"

"Not by man's way of thinking. Thank goodness I have my father. You and he are the only ones who know my desire. If my stepmother found out . . ." She pauses for a moment, as if she's thinking how to word her thoughts, something I am all too familiar with.

"It's not that she would object—she's all for causes and strong women, but she's still of the belief that a woman should get married and have children, first and foremost. Like the person who wrote that editorial that offended you, she believes a woman should be only her husband's helper when it comes to matters outside the home.

"Take this trip, for example—I knew that when I approached them about it, she would object, which she did, so I talked to Father first and had him in my corner." She checks the time on her pendant watch. "We must hurry. Don Antonio is quite the connoisseur of fine food and wine. He will have us both on the rack if we spoil his dinner."

I have complete trust in Gertrude. As my mother would say, "You're two peas in a pod," at least when it comes to men and life careers, so I'm tempted to spill the beans about my sharing a compartment with a man. I hold back as we head for the dining car and tell her instead about Mrs. Percy encouraging me to come to Mexico and the lack of resources available to study the country and ancient civilizations. I realize Gertrude probably knows much more about Mexico than I do, having studied it.

"You know a lot about the country and its history?" I ask, certain that anyone who goes to Oxford knows about everything. She's so lucky. I would have loved to have gone to college.

"A bit. We can get together tomorrow and I can give you some background materials for your dispatches."

Gertrude Bell

[Gertrude Bell was] the most brilliant
student we ever had at Lady Margaret Hall, or
indeed I think at any of the women's colleges. Her
journeys in Arabia and her achievements in Iraq have
passed into history. I need only recall the bright promise
of her college days, when the vivid, rather untidy, auburn-
haired girl of seventeen first came amongst us and took our
hearts by storm with her brilliant talk and her youthful confidence in herself and her belongings. She had a most engaging
way of saying "Well you know, my father says so and so" as a final
opinion on every question under discussion.

She threw herself with untiring energy into every phase of college
life: she swam, she rowed, she played tennis and hockey, she danced,
she spoke in debates; she kept up with modern literature, and told
us tales of modern authors, most of whom were her childhood's
friends. Yet all the time she put in seven hours of work, and at the
end of two years she won as brilliant a First Class in the School
of Modern History as has ever been won at Oxford.

—JANET COURTNEY, "Gertrude Bell, A Personal Study"
(Courtney, whose maiden name was Hogarth,
attended Oxford with Gertrude in 1886. The
article originally appeared in *North
American Review*, 1926, and the passage
above is quoted from the *The
Letters of Gertrude Bell*, 1927.)

14

Don Antonio rises to greet us in the dining room.

"Ah, I see you two have met." He gives me a smile and Gertrude a hug. "I must confess that this is one of the reasons I invited you to dinner, Nellie. I thought it would be nice for Gertrude to meet a young lady like herself, so she doesn't have to be bored on this trip with me."

Dinner is in a private area at the very far end of the dining car. Our table is elegantly set—embroidered linen, silver utensils, fine china. Vibrant pink roses fill a green vase that is the centerpiece.

I am relieved that Don Antonio has not dressed formally for dinner but has simply changed his business suit for another and that Gertrude has taken off her fancy hat. Her dress is almost as simple and as practical a travel dress as mine, but she has lace around the neck and pearl beading on the bottom of her sleeves that goes a few inches up the outside of each sleeve—these fine touches add a hint of glamour that I wish I could have.

Also, the curse of wanting to travel light meant bringing very little change of clothing. I'm just happy I don't look out of place. I don't want to look like a poor relative having dinner with a rich one. However, both Gertrude and Don Antonio are so warm and friendly, it really doesn't matter. Neither seems to have any pretense to them.

"Uncle, I see we have another place setting."

"Yes, guilty as charged."

"And whom did you invite?"

"A very nice young gentleman I met in the smoking lounge. He should be here any min—ah, here he is now."

Roger enters, and I am unable to hide the surprise and mortification on my face from Gertrude. Fortunately, Don Antonio is preoccupied with rising and shaking hands with Roger.

She starts to say something and I shake my head.

As Don Antonio makes introductions, I force myself to put on a cordial, if not pleasant, face—or at least one that doesn't make it appear I consider Roger akin to an ax murderer.

"This is my adopted niece, Gertrude Bell, and Nellie Bly, an American news reporter from Pittsburgh, Pennsylvania. Ladies, Roger Watkins."

Roger smiles and utters a platitude about the pleasure of dining with beautiful women. He gives no clue that he knows me.

After Roger is seated, Don Antonio says, "Roger is studying Mexican history under a professor at Columbia University whom I knew when I was an attaché at our consular office in New York. It appears, Gertrude, that Roger is also taking a leave of absence from book studies to experience history firsthand."

"I don't blame you." Gertrude gives Roger a smile that is so warm and friendly, he looks ready to drool. I can see now why those men in the parlor car were hanging on her every word. "One can take only so much of burying one's head in books. Did Don Antonio tell you there is a great deal of Mexico's history still lying in plain sight?"

She doesn't wait for a response. You can't miss her excitement about the subject, because her voice goes up an octave. "Just think! Most of the meat off the bones of the great civilizations of Greece, Rome, and Egypt have been scraped clean, but Mexico's ancient and medieval history has barely been touched."

She throws up her hands with excitement. "We might discover something astounding at an ancient site because so little attention has been given to its colorful history."

I can't blame Roger for liking Gertrude and giving her a big smile. One that, I might add, he's never offered me. But admittedly, I've never been that pleasant to him—for good reason. I am a bit surprised that he is studying history. I never attended college, of course, but I tend to think of students in general as more mild-mannered and bookish than how Roger strikes me.

"I'm hoping that one of my experiences with history will be climbing a pyramid." He looks at me just as he is finishing the comment.

Uh-huh.

"That tops my agenda, too." Gertrude grabs my hand. "Nellie, you must join us! It would be wonderful. I think not only that you'll enjoy yourself, but also that it might provide interesting material to send to your newspaper."

"Yes, why don't you, Nellie?" Roger says.

I concede that I'll consider it and resist the temptation of saying that I'd jump at the opportunity to go to the top of a pyramid with him if it gave me a chance to push him off.

Don Antonio raises his crystal champagne glass.

"A toast. Thank you for joining me and my niece tonight. And may I say, it's not often I've dined with two university scholars and a female newspaper reporter."

I notice he emphasizes the word *female*. One day, I hope being a reporter and going to college will be considered the norm for women.

"I also admire you for traveling alone, Nellie. Few women would travel unescorted, let alone to a foreign country where most people don't speak their language. Gertrude also made the trip from London to El Paso by herself, over the objections of her family. I suspect you two are the harbingers of a new age of independent women. Not that all men would agree with the advent of women who are decisively independent. Roger, being young yourself, I would be most interested in your opinion on the subject. How do you feel about it?"

"I wouldn't dare venture any negative opinion about independent womanhood, lest one of these young ladies scalp me with a steak knife. Besides, I am all in favor of women realizing their full potential."

Gertrude and her uncle think his reply is clever, but I think he's hiding his true feelings—no doubt he feels a woman's realm shouldn't extend beyond the kitchen and bedroom.

"I was raised by a single mother who showed me what a woman is capable of doing and taught me to respect a woman's ability to achieve many of the things that are reserved for men." Roger then addresses me. "Certainly going from a factory girl to a news reporter is a great accomplishment."

How does he know I had worked in a factory? I give him a smile and a nod. "Thank you. As far as traveling alone, I believe that if you are polite, respectful, and considerate of a country's customs, no matter where you go, or what the language, people will reciprocate kindly. Respect and kindness are a universal language."

"Well said, Nellie." Don Antonio smiles at me. "You will find my people most helpful and considerate to strangers, especially señoritas."

I need to divert the conversation away from myself before a can of worms opens. "I'm sure I will. Now, Don Antonio, for my readers, I would really like to hear your evaluation of the tension between the United States and Mexico that is being reported."

"Mexico wants to be a good neighbor and trading partner with your country. That is the goal," he replies.

It is an intentionally diplomatic statement and gives little insight into the real problems. I let it pass, knowing he would not want to be quoted as saying anything controversial, especially about the war between the two countries. In addition to the United States taking undisputed control of Texas, which had already broken away from Mexico several years before the war, we took nearly 900,000 square miles from Mexico, which now makes up a lot of America's West and Southwest, including all or part of California, Nevada, Utah, New Mexico, Arizona, Colorado, Oklahoma, and Kansas.

Even though the war ended nearly forty years ago, it cost Mexico over half its territory, and I don't care what he professes, that had to have left a bad taste toward Americans with his fellow men, making it a sore subject even today—one, I'm sure, he wants to avoid.

"But let us talk about something more enjoyable," Don Antonio says.

The diplomat offers a champagne toast to independent women.

I have to admit that because of my stepfather turning from Dr. Jekyll into Mr. Hyde whenever he had what my mother called "demon rum," I have an aversion to the very notion of imbibing anything stronger than sarsaparilla. However, the champagne goes down nicely and tickles my nose. I'm surprised to find I like it.

I thank Don Antonio for the pleasant new experience. "I've never had champagne before. It's quite delicious. I don't feel like I'm drinking liquor, it's so smooth and refreshing. Does it always tickle one's nose?"

"Yes," Gertrude says, "but Uncle Antonio says it does that only to beautiful women. Isn't that true?"

"Absolutely. And tonight I have proof that I am right, for two beautiful women are at my table."

Unlike Gertrude, who appears comfortable with her uncle's compliment, I find myself looking down into my champagne glass. I don't do well with compliments, unless it's about my work; then I am just proud.

The incident with the prospector has me curious, and I describe how I first had to wade through a sea of cowboys.

"There's a man with them whom one of the cowboys referred to as a prospector. He was a bit inebriated, to say the least, and he started mumbling about something called 'Montezuma's pile' and that he's got it. Gertrude believes he might be referring to a legend about Montezuma's treasure."

"*Sí.*" Don Antonio leans back and shakes his head with a chuckle. "I cannot tell you how many times I have heard a similar story, often from a miner or prospector who claims to have found Montezuma's gold or at least a map leading to it. Each one told me I would be a very rich man if I grubstaked them, as *norteamericanos* call supplying money to a prospector."

He refills our glasses with champagne. I already feel warm and pleasantly light-headed from the first glass, but I can handle it, I'm sure, as I have a strong mind that alcohol cannot take control of.

"Montezuma was the Aztec emperor at the time of the conquest. The Fates bestowed upon him the misfortune to reign at a time when the Spanish arrived armed with strange weapons and astride great beasts we call horses. However, the tale of this misfortunate emperor and his treasure begins much earlier.

"At the time of Christ, the largest city in the western hemisphere, the center of a powerful empire and a metropolis that rivaled ancient Rome in size, was about thirty miles northeast of the current site of Mexico City. As a matter of fact, it is a place that all three of you should see. It is the largest site of archaeological interest in all the Americas and has two magnificent pyramids, the Pyramid of the Sun and the Pyramid of the Moon. The pyramid dedicated to the sun god is only a hair smaller than the Great Pyramid of Giza in Egypt. The edifices are a beautiful sight to behold—breathtaking, I must say."

"Are the pyramids still standing? Can you climb them?" I ask.

He gives me a smile. "Yes, you can climb them. The larger one is taller than a skyscraper and has stone steps that go all the way to the top. I commonly refer to the city as 'Teo' for short, but its name is Teotihuacán. That, of course, is not Spanish, but Nahuatl, the language of the Aztecs. It might surprise you, but the Aztec tongue is still spoken in many rural areas. In that language, Teotihuacán means 'City of the Gods.'

"No one knows the real name of the city or even the name or culture of the civilization that built it. It is one of the world's great ancient mysteries. We don't even know why this largest city ever built on the American continent before Columbus was abandoned by its people, who left behind not just pyramids that violate the very heavens but also other temples and structures. The ruins have been ravaged by time, but those that remain are awe-inspiring."

Listening to the diplomat, I am amazed and confounded that such magnificence from the past lies so close to my country and that it is so ignored in our history books.

"Teo became a ghost city," Don Antonio says, "not only because its own people abandoned it nearly a thousand years before the Spanish conquest but also because the city struck fear in those who came there. Even the mighty Aztecs, whose powerful legions terrorized any kingdom that resisted its power, so feared the city that they never occupied the site. They sensed dark magic at the huge pyramids and temples along the broad boulevard that we call 'the Avenue of the Dead.'"

"Dark magic? Is that because of the human sacrifices the pre-Columbian civilizations practiced?" I ask.

Don Antonio gives a sigh. I sense it is the diplomat in him wanting to avoid a negative subject.

"No. All the Mesoamerican civilizations conducted blood sacrifices to the gods. The ancient gods of Mexico were a terrifying, bloodthirsty lot and the civilizations that came after the fall of Teo believed not only that the city was the home of these fearsome deities but that the gods had destroyed Teo because its people had not carried out the blood covenant to their satisfaction."

"What is the blood covenant?" I ask.

"Uncle, please let me explain; it's in my studies, and I've always wondered if the facts are correct. You know how things can get altered when put in a book, even by scholars."

Gertrude has such excitement in her voice, it just draws you into whatever she says.

"Please do, my dear."

Her face lights up and she makes sure to look at each of us. "The ancient Americans believed that the gods kept powerful forces like storms and volcanic fire from destroying them. The gods also provided the sunshine, rain, seed, and everything else needed to grow crops. They also believed that the gods required blood as their reward for these services. The gods needed blood to stay strong and protect the people."

"So the blood covenant," says Roger, joining in, "was the promise of the people to supply blood to the gods in return for services. A contract between mankind and a pantheon of gods."

"Exactly," Don Antonio says.

"How does Montezuma's treasure fit into the scheme of things?" I ask.

It's Gertrude who answers. "The gullible emperor was taken captive by Cortés, not in battle, but when Montezuma permitted the Spaniard into the Aztec capital city with his army. Montezuma was repaid for his hospitality to the Spanish by being made a prisoner in his own palace.

"Even before he was held prisoner, Montezuma gave Cortés and his men an unimaginable amount of gold and silver in the form of sculptures of animals and other treasures. The riches meant little to the emperor, but all these incredible gifts only made the conquistadors want more."

"I'm not surprised," Roger says. "People always want more; they are never satisfied."

"So true," Don Antonio murmurs. "The conquistadors imprisoned Montezuma, looted his palace, and terrorized the city, torturing and killing women, children, and men—whoever stood in their way or threatened them. I say this despite the fact that I am proud of the Spanish blood that runs in my veins."

"That's horrible," I say.

"That's life," Roger replies.

I give him a quick look. He definitely has a caustic view of the motives of people, but probably an accurate one, at that.

Don Antonio continues. "Eventually, the Aztecs rose up against Cortés and his men. They even attacked their emperor, stoning him to death when he stepped onto his palace balcony to address them."

"Why?" I ask.

"They blamed Montezuma."

"But didn't they all welcome Cortés?"

"Yes, but they were rightfully angry. Montezuma had a huge army but didn't use it to defeat Cortés because he believed the Spaniard fulfilled the prophecy of a god returning to claim his empire. After Cortés's men committed atrocities in the city, the Aztecs rebelled against the Spanish and their *indio* allies. The bloody battle raged through the night as Cortés's army was driven out of the city. So many men were killed, it's said one could walk across the city's canals on the backs of the dead.

"The decisive battle did not take place in the Aztec capital, which Mexico City was later built atop, but . . . where?" Don Antonio pauses and smiles, directing the question at Roger, the scholar.

The question appears to catch Roger off guard. "Where? Why don't we let Gertrude answer that. I'm sure it's an important piece of historical information she found in her studies."

"Otumba," Gertrude states proudly. "Cortés had retreated there to regroup."

"Yes," Don Antonio says, "and this is where we return to Teotihuacán and Montezuma's treasure. Otumba is near Teo. Cortés may have even had lookouts on the pyramids, keeping watch for the Aztec army."

"Cortés won the battle at Otumba?" I ask.

"Yes, he won the battle and others, but Otumba was the one that truly broke the back of the Aztec Empire."

"I assume that Montezuma's treasure refers to the emperor's vast wealth," I say. "But if Montezuma was dead before the last battles were fought, how could he have buried his treasure?"

"He didn't. And your assumption is incorrect. Montezuma's treasure does not refer to the emperor's personal horde of jewels and gold, but to something even more valuable."

15

I don't understand," Roger says. "There's a well-known legend that Montezuma left a hidden treasure and that there are those who seek it even today."

"*Sí,* so the tale goes. But like so many stories of treasure maps, more gold has changed hands acquiring the so-called maps than the treasures they are supposed to lead to. You must remember not only that Montezuma was dead by the time the Aztecs were defeated but that the greatest treasure of all, according to Europeans, was not in Montezuma's palace."

I put in my opinion. "Gold is how we value treasure."

"Exactly. And in terms of how Europeans value wealth, the single most valuable thing in the Aztec Empire was a large solid-gold disk dedicated to the sun god. It sat atop the Pyramid of the Sun at Teo. And it vanished immediately after the battle at Otumba."

"Who took it?" I ask.

Don Antonio shrugs. "No one knows, but one thing is certain: It was not the Spanish. The disk was taller than a man and is said to have weighed thousands of pounds. Cortés had no equipment to move such a heavy object quickly and he had only a few horses. Besides, he was preoccupied with the final battles to subdue the Aztecs and capture their capital."

"The Aztecs didn't have beasts of burden, either. There were no horses, donkeys, or other beasts of burden at all in the New World before the conquest," Gertrude adds. "So how did the Aztecs move such a heavy object?"

"With the same techniques they used to get the disk to the top of a pyramid over two hundred feet tall. The pyramids themselves are composed of thousands of great blocks of stone, each weighing tons. And like the Egyptians and other ancient societies, they had almost endless labor available and clever ways of moving enormous objects. Sadly and amazingly, what they did with their hands we now require large pieces of complex machinery to do," says Don Antonio.

"So it's most probable that the Aztecs themselves moved it to keep it from the Spanish," Roger says.

"*Sí.* There is no doubt that many individual treasures were hidden after the fall of the empire by wealthy *indios.* And later, many an Aztec nobleman had his feet held over a hot fire to make him reveal where he had stashed his treasures. But the legendry treasure that has been sought since the conquest, the one referred to as 'Montezuma's gold,' is the gold disk of the sun god."

"It wouldn't have gone far, would it?" Roger asks.

"Señor?" Don Antonio looks at him, puzzled, as do I and Gertrude.

"Well, it just stands to reason when getting something that big down from the top of a pyramid, you have the help of gravity. But once it's on the ground, moving it would be much slower. With a war going on and all, it just makes sense to me that it was hidden somewhere in the vicinity of the pyramids. At least that's my uninformed opinion."

"Sounds reasonable." I clap my hands. "What an interesting story."

"Isn't it?" Gertrude says. "And people still believe it to this day."

"What do you think, Don Antonio?" Roger asks. "Is the treasure still out there, ready to be found when the right rock is turned over?"

"Who knows, señor. I only wish my Aztec ancestors had left me a map. The problem with old tales about treasures is that they never seem to be found, although on rare occasions a lucky farmer digs up something of value that was hurriedly buried as the Spanish advanced."

"But isn't there evidence that supports the fact that Montezuma's treasure exists?" I ask.

"What evidence are you referring to, señorita?"

"Well, first of all, if the gold disk existed it would be worth a king's ransom. Is that correct?"

"For a certainty. The golden disk appears in pre-conquest Aztec codices—books of picture writing, hieroglyphics."

"And it's true that the Spanish didn't find it?"

"A certainty. Cortés had over five hundred soldiers, all of whom were as greedy for treasure as he was. This much gold could not have been kept secret. And although the conquistadors each got a share of the treasure, the lion's share went to the king in Madrid. Cortés's entire small army would have ended up on the rack, and then the hangman, had they cheated the king out of the biggest Aztec treasure of all."

"And I assume that an Aztec or any one suddenly possessing great wealth after the conquest would have been highly noticeable to the Spanish. The fact that it was there, then gone, and that no one knows what happened to it, seems to imply that it is still out there somewhere."

"Very well put, Nellie." Don Antonio gives me a smile. "And, if you are interested in finding it yourself, I can assure you that when you venture out on to the streets of Mexico City, a street peddler will offer to sell you a map that shows the location of the treasure.

"In my opinion, it will remain hidden for eternity because those who know its location are long dead. For sure, the Aztec nobleman who directed its removal and hiding would have had most of the laborers killed after they completed the task, thus eliminating most who knew the secret. Frankly, it is one of those legends that excite treasure hunters much more than historians."

Food interrupts our discussion. To my surprise, there are no refried beans, tortillas, or peppers. On my plate is brandied goose, accompanied by creamy mashed potatoes and asparagus hollandaise. In Cochran's Mills, they'd call it "French fixin's."

Don Antonio picks up on the confusion that my face must be revealing.

"Ah, señorita, you thought you would have an authentic Mexican meal, did you not?"

"Well, yes, I did."

"Actually, what you are having *is* an authentic Mexican meal. French food is very common in Mexico, more so than it is north of the border, except for Louisiana perhaps. It was introduced to our culture literally by cannons and muskets. It's only been about twenty years since my country was occupied by French troops. Do you know about our history with the French?"

"A little. I believe a European prince, Maximilian, was placed on the Mexican throne due to the machinations of Napoléon the Third and a group of Mexican leaders."

"Yes, and while the emperor was disposed of by a firing squad, the taste for French cuisine, at least by the more affluent of our citizens, remained."

Helpless, I throw up my hands in surrender. "And I have already developed a fond taste for corn tortillas with beans, cheese, and peppers."

They all laugh.

"Don't feel bad, Nellie," Don Antonio says, "beans and corn are the basic foods of most of my countrymen, but frankly, it is the food of the common people. Those with a higher level of lifestyle dine more frequently on meat and potatoes with baked bread. You'll find tortillas and beans in the marketplace rather than in restaurants."

My mind is spinning about the story of the golden disk of the sun god all the way through a Mexican dessert—a creamy, rich orange-scented custard with a golden syrupy topping of caramelized sugar. I can't wait to get back to my journal and jot down the whole tale. But before I send it in, I will get one of those treasure maps Don Antonio mentioned, so I can include it in my story.

However, there is one more potential story I hope the diplomat will contribute to.

"Don Antonio, do you know who the people in the private car at the end of the train are? A porter told me that they are people of importance."

He pauses for a second, just enough to tell me he knows something but is not going to reveal it.

"Not really. Unfortunately, being a consul general of Mexico does not make me privy to everything."

"Really?" This comment comes from Gertrude, heavily seasoned with doubt.

"Yes, my dear, contrary to your belief, I am not kept in the loop of everything. And, of course, there are matters I am duty-bound to keep secret."

"Are we talking about that millionaire horse buff, Frederic Gebhard, and his lady, Lily Langtry?" Roger asks.

"Lily Langtry!" comes from both Gertrude and me.

"I can't believe it." I turn to Gertrude.

"Wouldn't that be fabulous?" Her face shows the same excitement as is on mine. "She's so beautiful, not to mention her clothes—they're stunning. And what a life she leads—famous actress, mistress to Edward, Prince of Wales . . . well, was—"

"What happened?" I ask.

"Sarah Bernhardt, another famous actress, came along and whisked him away. Gossip is that Prince Edward was getting tired of Lily spending his money and one night at a dinner party, Edward said to her, 'I've spent enough on you to build a battleship,' whereupon she tartly replied, 'And you've spent enough in me to float one.'"

"Gertrude! Shame on you," Don Antonio snaps.

"Well, it's true; at least that's the gossip. And people say that she doesn't worry about what people think of her, not even our future king. She says and does as she pleases."

"How do you know it's them?" I ask Roger.

"Their trip to Mexico was in all the New York gossip columns, even though they tried to keep it hush-hush. But it's hard to keep the whereabouts of a couple of their magnitude secret, though no one knows why they're visiting Mexico. There was speculation that it's to acquire some prize horse, that being his passion."

"And Lily's," Gertrude adds. "She's became quite involved in the sport of Thoroughbred horse racing."

"Interesting." Don Antonio dabs his napkin to his lips to hide a grin before taking another sip of his champagne.

I can tell by his pretense at lacking interest that he knew all along who the occupants in the private railcar are. Her visiting Mexico would cause a sensation that he could not afford to ignore.

My mind is already wondering how I can devise a way to meet them.

16

Something Roger said at dinner presses at me, but there isn't any conversation between us as we make our way back to our sleeper. I kept my mouth shut in front of the others, but it nags at me and I'm having a devil of a time holding my peace until we are alone.

Some cowboys are still playing a game in which they fling cards into a hat, but half of them are snoozing. The ones awake silently make way for us. Neither Sundance nor the drunken prospector with the treasure map are in sight.

Roger isn't saying a word, which suits me fine right now, but the moment we reach the privacy of our compartment, I will jump on him for answers. Ever since he complimented me on going from a factory girl to a reporter, it's been gnawing at me. How did he know that?

I am very interested to hear his answer and I want to be facing him so I can read his eyes as he lies to me. He thinks that because I'm quiet, I didn't pick up what had to be a faux pas on his part.

He's in for a surprise. I am going to drill him about how and what he knows about me. And more important, who he is. He says he's a New York university scholar, but that would make it a long reach to know anything about a Pittsburgh newspaper reporter.

By the same token, if he is a reporter, he could well have heard of me, because female reporters are so rare. And if that is the case, he has some reason for keeping me from knowing; otherwise, he'd simply say so.

His being a reporter is not what's bothering me. It's not like I'm following a hot lead on a story that he might steal. It's that he might have heard about the impetuous girl reporter who ran off to prove she can be a foreign correspondent. Revealing that I'm not actually on assignment from a newspaper, but trying to prove myself, will close "official doors" like Consul General Castillo to me—not to mention that it would be terribly humiliating.

Once in our little sleeper compartment, Roger starts to bury his head back into his book, but I snatch it out of his hands.

"Hey! Give me that."

"Not until we talk."

"I was afraid of that. You were too quiet coming back. I knew eventually you would want not just the lower berth but my scalp as well before this trip is over with. Well, you can have my scalp, but not my bed." He tilts his head forward, offering me his neck. "Go ahead, cut it off."

"How did you know I had worked in a factory?"

"A factory girl? Ah, my comment at dinner."

Just as I thought—he's stalling to conjure up a lie. I can see the wheels turning in his head. He didn't realize he had slipped up.

"I heard about you through a friend."

"A friend? I work for *The Pittsburgh Dispatch,* not a New York newspaper."

"This may amaze you, but news from the *Dispatch* is not limited to Pittsburgh. The paper's read throughout much of that region. My friend happens to have family there."

"Really. If that's true, why didn't you tell me you recognized my name when I told you it?"

He pulls a face and gives me a narrow look, almost squinting, as if he is trying to figure out who and what I am.

"Who do you think you are? A prosecuting attorney? I don't have to answer your questions."

"Mr. Watkins, you can answer my questions, or I'll have you put off this train."

That causes a temporary speech impediment for him.

"What?"

"I will tell Don Antonio that you have attempted to molest me. That will not only get you put off the train; Mexican men are so chivalrous, they will probably hang you from the nearest cactus."

He gapes at me for a moment, once again dumbstruck, and then shakes his head. I can't tell if he is scared or amused.

"You're not a woman. You're a devil in petticoats."

I give him the most charming smile I can manage at a time when I want to strangle the truth out of him.

"Roger . . . dear friend . . . I've had to fight very hard in this *man's* world to achieve what slight success I've achieved. Tonight, I found out you are hiding information about me. Whatever you have up your sleeve, I want to make sure I cut off the head of the snake now before it bites me. *Comprende, amigo?*"

"*Sí, señorita.* Now, Nellie, dear *paranoid* girl, I didn't know *who* you were until I put two and two together when Don Antonio said you were a newspaper reporter. I then realized you must be the girl my friend Sarah told me about. She, too, is quite an ambitious young woman, and she admires you." He gives me a tight, sardonic smile. "She said she'd like to be just like you, but of course she would probably change her mind if she met you."

I don't know if he's putting a shine on me. There is nothing like a bit of flattery to get across a point, even if he ends it with a cut. But I'm not comfortable with the explanation, though it is possible. News that a young female had been hired at the *Dispatch* had been reported far and wide in the state and had stirred the ambitions of many young women, but fear of being exposed as a fraud keeps the short hairs on the back of my neck up.

"Why do you look like a hanging judge devising punishment?" he asks.

"I haven't decided if you are telling the whole truth."

"Why would I lie? What's the point? You're right about one thing: Your mother must be quite an independent woman. It shows in you."

"I want the truth, not compliments, Mr. Watkins, but thank you. Now, next question—"

He puts his hands up. "No more questions. You know what?" He pretends to squint at me, as if he's trying to get a peek at my secrets. "You're acting awfully suspicious—like you have something to hide. What did you do, Nellie? Rob a bank on your way out of Pittsburgh?"

Boy, did he hit the mark on that one. But a good offense is the best defense. "That rope they string up mashers with is getting short. I suggest you tell me who you really are."

"*Who I really am?*" He rubs his chin as if in great thought. "Well, my mother and father, the Watkins, named me Roger, which is how by coincidence I call myself Roger Watkins." He throws up his hands in surrender. "Look. This animosity is getting us nowhere. You're in Mexico to do stories. I'm here to learn its history firsthand. Why don't we be friends?"

"Hmm."

"Hmm what? I don't understand why you're not satisfied with this wonderful private compartment. This is paradise compared to having to sit upright for days on hard seats."

"The problem is that there is always a snake in paradise."

17

It's nearly bedtime, but I want to jot down some ideas for my articles. Roger goes back to reading his book and I sit across from him, making notes about what I have learned since I last recorded my reflections in the parlor car.

Cowboys are modern knights, a bit dustier perhaps, and I suppose they bathe as infrequently as the armored men on horseback did.

The world of the Aztec and Mayans existed mostly on one crop: corn. But they fed their gods blood in order to get a good crop.

Most Mexicans are rather poor and eat a great deal of corn and beans, while the wealthier class prefer French cuisine and champagne.

And you can easily buy a map leading you to a lost treasure of Aztec gold, but you will find only fool's gold where X marks the spot.

I like the last item best, but it is so far-fetched that I decide I will mail more serious articles to the *Dispatch* before venturing into the fanciful. I like the tale of the "weeping tree" Don Antonio told us just before we left dinner: After the Spanish massacred a large number of Aztecs they thought were plotting against them, Cortés, his army, and *indio* allies had to fight their way out of the Aztec capital. They suffered many dead and wounded men, and two-thirds of their stolen treasure ended up in the lake surrounding the city as they retreated across the causeway leading to dry land. After the battle, Cortés sat under a tree and wept— most likely for the loss of treasure rather than for his comrades, Don Antonio said.

They called the battle Noche Trist—the sad night. And the tree is called the Weeping Tree. It now stands on the grounds of an old chapel and gets many visitors because it is said that on certain nights you can hear the tree weep and that the next morning water will be at its base—tears from the long-dead Cortés.

The news about Lily Langtry and her wealthy lover being aboard is sensational news, but it is also a story I will try to add interest to by enclosing an interview with her. I have never met or interviewed anyone as famous as the great actress, and it would be such a thrill. Now I just have to figure out how. Another thing to add to my list of things to do.

So far, the best part of this trip is that I have made a new friend, Gertrude Bell.

I feel as if she understands me and thinks what I am doing is the right thing, unlike it being crazy or naïve, as my brothers and Mr. Madden think. It's nice to have someone in my corner, especially since I don't have my mother with me—she was my ally. Now I feel like I have made one with Gertrude.

I add more rambling notations about the manners and mannerisms of the people I've seen only from the train so far. The *indios* and their clothing appear surprisingly fresh and clean, despite the lowly way so many have to live and work. Along the gutters by the railroad, they can be seen washing their few bits of apparel and bathing.

When I asked a Mexican gentleman in the parlor car earlier about these people, who seem more primitive than many city dwellers, he said many rural people have not assimilated into modern society and that the poorer ones live rather primitively. The homes of many of them are but holes in the ground, with a straw roof. The smoke creeps out from the doorways all day and at night and the families sleep in the ashes. They seldom lie down, but sleep sitting up, like a tailor, strange to say, but they never nod or fall over.

With that description and the one of the Mexican horsemen who charge up at every stop to guard the train, I am very satisfied. I haven't even made it to Mexico City, and already I have quite a bit of interesting material for articles. This has to help me get a permanent position as foreign correspondent for the *Dispatch* when I return—it just has to, or this insane trip I've embarked on will be a waste of time. I can't let that happen.

I'm anxious to experience something sensational to report, besides Lily Langtry. I guess it would be too much to ask for some bandidos to rob the train without hurting any of us. Crazy thought, I know, but I can't help wondering how often the train does gets robbed as it works its way across the great arid area of northern Mexico. Towns and villages are usu-ally few and far between, so there would be many excellent places to stop and rob the train.

I jot down another brief notation: Roger? Was he telling the truth when he said he learned about me from a friend? I don't see a motive for him to be secretive. However, I'm beginning to believe he's being secre-tive as to who he is. Tonight at dinner, he cleverly avoided answering Cas-tillo's question about where the final conquistador battle took place. However, it is possible he just didn't know and was embarrassed. I would have done the same—but I'm not a university-level scholar of history.

Then there is Sundance. Why is he so interested in knowing what Howard said to me that night?

Another question comes to mind because Roger seems to know each time I speak to the cowboy: Could Roger and Sundance know each other? No, that's impossible. One is a cowboy, the other a scholar.

"Are you about done writing in that journal of yours?" Roger gets up from the seat and stretches. "I'd like to retire."

"Yes." I close my journal. "You can call the porter to make up our berths."

"What were you so eagerly writing about?"

"That is—"

"None of my business."

I give him a narrow look. "Are you sure you are not a reporter trying to steal my thunder?"

He rolls his eyes. "I'm beginning to suspect that you are an egomaniac. A paranoid one, at that."

AS WE STAND IN THE CORRIDOR, watching our berths being prepared, I'm surprised that the porter is not the same one who has been taking care of our needs since we boarded the train. Instead, it's one who helped serve us in the dining car.

I especially noticed him at dinner because he seemed to hang around, as if he was listening to our conversation. More of my egomaniacal para-noia, I guess.

He also stands out a bit from the conductor and other porters because he is what Don Antonio and others refer to specifically as an *"indio,"* a designation given to Mexicans whose bloodline has not been mixed with

European blood. The other train employees I've seen are "mestizos," like Don Antonio, a name denoting people whose bloodline is a mixture of indigenous blood—Aztec, Mayan, and other cultures—and European blood, mostly Spanish.

The *indios* in general tend to be shorter and smaller of build than mestizos, but, like their American Indian cousins, they appear strong and toned muscularly.

"What's bugging you?" Roger asks.

"Why do you think something's bugging me?"

"You're staring at that porter the same way you stared at me when you thought I was stealing your thunder."

"Have I told you what I like about you?"

He brightens up. "No. Do tell."

"Nothing. Absolutely nothing."

"That's too bad. Because I think you're all right. Quite an impressive young woman, in fact. An inspiration for women, my friend says."

That gives me pause.

"Ah," he says, "there's that look."

"What look?"

"The 'can it be true?' look. You gave the same sort of look at your glass of champagne tonight before you took the first sip. Your eyebrows crinkle and your nose slightly twitches."

"I don't know."

"What don't you know?"

"If you are just shining me on."

"Here we go again." He gives me his coy smile. "Imagining me as an enemy."

"Not an enemy. More of an annoyance."

"You like me, don't you?"

This is another remark from him that stops me in my tracks and leaves me speechless.

"I can tell," he continues, "by the way you rag on me. You're basically shy with men and unsure of their motives. You hide it by taking the offense."

The porter interrupts whatever cruel and cutting retort my wicked tongue is forming.

He gestures at the ladder he has set up so I can climb up to the top bunk. *"La escalera."*

"He's letting us know he will be back for the ladder later," Roger says.

The Pullman car doesn't have ladders for every upper berth because they would take up too much space in compartments and corridors, not to mention having to store them all day. Which means anyone in an upper is stuck until the porter makes his rounds in the morning, unless they are in physical shape to climb down or ring for a porter to come with a ladder.

"Don't you think he's a strange little man?" I ask as we go back into the compartment.

Yes, I am avoiding answering the question as to whether I like him, because I can't think of a response.

"Who?"

"Our porter. Well, he's not our porter, to speak of."

"I never really took notice of him. Didn't know we had a specific one. Besides, what difference does it make?"

"None. Just that he was also one of the waiters who served us at dinner."

"And?" Roger rolls his hands as if to say, what does this mean?

"I don't know. He doesn't appear to speak English, but I would swear that in the dining car he was trying to listen to what we were saying in English."

"Maybe he's trying to learn the language."

"Maybe." Still, I'm not convinced. "Any chance you've changed your mind and will be a true gentleman and give me the lower berth?"

"No."

"How about drawing cards? High card gets the lower."

"No. You told me you grew up with six brothers."

"So?"

"No doubt you learned a lot about cards from them." He jerks his thumb at the upper. "Good night, Nellie."

Lying awake, I question my feelings about Roger. Is he right? Do I like him? No, that's not possible. However, I have to admit he raises two emotions in me; annoyance at his often superior male attitude, making me wonder if, in fact, he had a relationship with a woman that went sour; then, in contrast, I do find him rather attractive physically. Not that I would ever think of doing anything about it. I have to save myself for marriage, because a sexual encounter would most likely bring pregnancy.

Which makes me wonder how women like Lily Langtry manage to keep from getting pregnant when they have so many sexual relationships. I've heard other young women talking about the methods they've used, ranging from putting a vinegar-soaked cotton pad in their private parts to the man using a sheath of rubber tubing managed by Mr. Goodyear. And I've heard of the many times it didn't work and an unwanted pregnancy occurred, destroying a young woman's life and that of a child because the man couldn't or wouldn't marry the unfortunate girl.

With a sigh, I close my eyes and listen to the sound and feel of the train's steel wheels rolling on the rails. I've heard people complain about how this keeps them up, but it doesn't bother me. Instead, I thank my lucky stars that I've had the good fortune to make this trip. There has always been a bit of travel fever in my blood and now I'm finally doing it.

I've never had the opportunity to see the world, and this trip to Mexico, commenced with little planning and even less money, is my first real "travel" experience. Up to now, a trip from Pittsburgh to Philadelphia to see the Liberty Bell has been the extent of my traveling experience, and always with a companion.

Now I am alone and in a few days I will be able to climb pyramids and trample through jungles.

Mrs. Percy will be so happy for me.

18

Oh Lord, Lord, I wish my head would stop spinning.

Lying in the upper berth, I'm being punished for enjoying Don Antonio's champagne too much. Or, as my mother would say, for imbibing demon rum. The fact that it was snooty French champagne would not affect her characterization.

Never have I felt like this. My poor head has been spinning ever since I lay down. And I must admit the creaks and groans of the train as it gets its second wind going up a grade haven't helped. So much for thinking my mind is stronger than the champagne.

It finally stops swirling and I'm starting to feel like my head and body are one again, which is good. But now I need to relieve myself, which is bad—the washroom with the toilet is at the fear end of the train.

Why couldn't they have squeezed in a toilet in our little washroom?

Still, it makes no difference where the toilet is, because I am encased in the upper berth of a moving train. Up a creek without a boat or a paddle, or whatever it's supposed to be. In my case, it's without a ladder.

There's a cord that when pulled rings a bell at the porter's night station at the other end the car, but if I do this, it will wake people up and down the car, who will greet me with their grumbles as I hurry, red-faced and embarrassed, to the toilet.

Would wake up Roger, too, though his snoring is quite loud, and if that's any indication of how soundly he's sleeping, he's dead to the world. Still, I don't want to chance it, for I would be humiliated, having him know that I have to get up to relieve myself. It's a private matter, although there seems to be no shame involved when a man gets up in the middle of the night to do his business.

This leaves me with a very big problem: getting down. It's going to take some agility to manage it without stepping on Roger's face. And I will have to leave a warm blanket for the cold. The coals in the stove that heat the whole car have died down and won't be replenished and fired again until its wake-up time, leaving the night air very crisp and chilly.

As I lie in my tiny sleeper, debating what to do, a news article I read about the great actress Sarah Bernhardt comes to mind—she sometimes sleeps in a coffin. Right now, I feel like I'm lying in one, and it's a creepy feeling.

If I was less sensitive about my personal bodily functions, I would wake up Roger for help. And I have another factor that is causing me pause: I didn't bring a robe. I climbed into the upper berth and pulled the curtain closed before changing into my nightclothes, exactly what I would have done had the berth been in the public corridor.

Even though my woolen nightgown is long and thick, a proper lady should not be seen in her nightgown—no matter how shapeless it is to satisfy a woman's modesty.

Having brought only a single piece of luggage, there wasn't room for a robe, and I had more important items to take—my jar of face cream and writing materials. Sacrifices had to be made, but right now I am regretting it.

Well, nature calls and I must get down.

Refusing to be the one known as the girl who woke everyone up in the dead of night by calling for a porter, I peek outside the curtain to see what I am up against.

Great . . . it looks like a cliff for a runt like me. From my bunk looking down, it is extremely awkward and dangerous. If I were taller, it wouldn't be so bad, but being only five feet tall, this is not looking good. Damn Roger.

I take a deep breath and roll over onto my stomach to get into position to drop off the edge. I pray I don't land on Roger's head or, worse, slip and go crashing down and injuring myself.

Carefully positioning my body so I can slide my legs off the thin mattress, I get my feet to land on the very edge of the armrest of Roger's bunk. Because his curtain is drawn, I don't know exactly where his head is, but judging from his snoring, it can't be far from where my feet have landed. Wonderful.

If his temperament is anything like my brothers when woken from a dead sleep, I'm in trouble. They are bears when woken unexpectedly.

With my left foot on the armrest, I lower my right foot—oh no, I can't stretch far enough to hold on to my berth above and place my foot on the floor.

"What the—" comes from Roger.

"Noooo!" I lose my balance, start to fall forward, desperately pull back, and my hand slips off the berth and I pitch forward, falling like a rock into the lower berth, landing on top of Roger, chest-to-chest.

I push back, but his arms instantly come around and pull me to him. His lips meet mine and I feel an electrifying bolt shoot through me all the way to my toes.

I surrender to the kiss, to his strong arms embracing me.

The spell breaks as he grabs a handful of my nightgown and starts to pull it up.

I jerk away, pulling myself free, and step back, getting my feet and emotions in balance.

"You have no right to do that and you will not speak of it—period!"

With that proclamation, I quickly exit into the corridor and try not to think about his lips on mine, his body pressed into me, knowing that I should hate him for seizing the opportunity to steal a kiss, but I don't.

As expected, the public corridor is dark. The only light is a dim oil lamp on the wall at the far end, where the porter sleeps upright in a chair and the washroom is located. The door to the short open-air gangway that leads to the next car is after the washroom.

The porter's chair is empty and there's no sign of him. So much for my ringing for the ladder; it would have gone unanswered.

About to step into the washroom, I hear a *thump* and my attention is snapped to the dirty glass window on the gangway door.

A face is crunched up against the window.

It's Howard, the prospector.

He's slammed up against the door, with his face pressed against the small window. It's hard for me to see through the window, which is fogged by years of smoky coal flumes, but his features are startled and his eyes wide.

He suddenly jerks back and I see over his shoulder a strange aberration that has appeared to have grabbed him from behind. My view through the dirty window is blurred, but it looks like a fawn-colored creature with the features of a beast is pulling him away from the window.

The hand of the creature holding Howard from behind comes around, grasping a hunting knife.

I scream and scream as a flurry of struggle takes place and they drop from sight.

I can't see the whole gangway through the window and can't make out what happened to them, but a couple of steps left or right on the gangway would send them falling off the train.

I grab the emergency cord that signals the engineer to stop the train by pulling it downward, but my hand is stopped by someone behind me.

19

W hat's going on?" Sundance has a grip on my arm. "Why'd you
scream?"

"He was attacked!"

"Who?" He quickly scans the area, then looks back at me like I am
crazy. "What are you talking about?"

"Howard! Your friend was attacked out there." I gesture at the door
to the gangway and spin around, jerking my arm out of his grip and grabbing the emergency cord. He tries to stop me again, but it's too late, as I've
pulled it down.

"We have to stop the train!" I shout at him. "He was thrown off."

Sundance rushes to the door. People who have been awakened by my
screaming have gathered behind me and are now yelling for answers.

"What's going on?" a man yells.

"Is she all right?" asks a woman.

I want to answer them, but I am glued to watching Sundance. He has
opened the door and is peering out. After what seems like an eternity but
is only seconds, he comes back to me.

"Nellie, no one is there."

"They must have fallen off."

I push by him and open the door to check out the gangway. With no
overlap between the cars, the gangway is open to the elements. I try to see
if there is blood on the floor, but I can't see anything—it's too dark.

It's just a couple of steps to the next car, and the door to that one is
closed. I lean out and look back in the direction Howard and his attacker
must have landed when they went off the train. All I see is night and the

desert terrain next to the tracks slipping by. The train has not stopped or even slowed down.

"Why didn't they stop the train?" I ask no one in particular.

"Why should they stop the train?" a passenger asks me.

"A man went off. He was being attacked by a creature."

"A creature!" The poor passenger backs away in horror as other passengers gasp at my proclamation.

"What creature?" Sundance asks.

"I don't know. It cut his throat."

"A creature cut his throat?" Sundance says. "I didn't see any blood out there. Nellie, you're making no sense."

"I'm telling you, a creature—"

"What's going on?" the conductor shouts in heavily accented English as he comes running down the corridor. He's obese and it's hard for him to run, breathe, and talk at the same time. His face is all red. Behind him is the porter who prepared our berths and served us dinner.

"Why isn't the train stopping?" I ask.

"Stopping? Why should it stop?"

"I pulled the cord. A man was attacked. He was thrown off the train."

"A man was thrown off the train!"

"Yes! A friend of his." I gesture at Sundance. "He was attacked by a creature."

"A creature!"

"Yes . . ." I feel faint and helpless and begin to sway.

Sundance grabs my arm to steady me. "Nellie, they can't stop the train. We're going down a grade."

Roger rushes up to me. "What happened? Are you all right?" He looks at Sundance. "Did you hurt her?"

"Hell no! I found her standing here, yelling like a banshee."

By this time, the aisle is completely filled with people in bedclothes. They're jabbering and staring at me like I'm a lunatic.

"I knew it." A man steps forward, his wife by his side. "She's the one."

"She's the one what?" Roger asks.

"The one who started rumors that we're going to be robbed by bandidos." The man accuses me with a short, fat, stubby finger.

"What? What are you talking about?" I ask.

"That's correct," his wife says. "My husband told me she started a rumor about bandidos attacking the train. Later, we saw her gushing champagne with a diplomat. Disgraceful behavior for a young lady, if you ask me."

"But—but—I—I—" I sway dizzily and Roger steadies me.

"Look at her. She's still intoxicated," the wife says with disgust.

Roger, Sundance, and the others stare at me with questions in their eyes. Unfortunately, she's right. The champagne has made me queasy.

"You don't understand!"

A deep, icy chill envelopes me and I break out in a sweat. I'm the only one who saw anything. There is no evidence in the gangway, not even a drop of blood. And I'm not really certain as to what the thing was behind the man. But Sundance was there, too.

"You saw it." It's a demand to Sundance, not a question.

"Saw it?" He shakes his head. "I'm sorry, Nellie, I'm sure you saw something, but I didn't see anything."

"What did you see, Nellie?" Roger asks.

"That drunken old prospector who cooks for the cowboys was on the gangway. I saw him through the window and then . . . I don't know what it—it was, but something strange was attacking him. Then both went off the train. I think. I'm not sure."

Roger interrupts an angry outburst from the conductor. "There's a simple answer to all this. Let's see if this cook-prospector, or whatever the devil he is, is still on the train."

20

I know what I saw.

It's morning and I am reassuring myself after the fitful night I spent running over and over in my mind's eye what I saw, and occasionally peeking out between the crack in my curtain to see if the creature that attacked the prospector has decided to come back to get rid of me.

Naturally, the train never stopped.

Roger and I are at breakfast with Don Antonio and Gertrude, who whispered to me just as we sat down, "Let's talk later."

I gave her a little smile in agreement. I really need to talk to her. I feel like the train leper—no, make that the object of the cruel curiosity people display when staring at a circus freak.

No mention has been made about the events last night—yet. But I am certain the consul general wants to discuss it and assure himself that nothing negative about his country will flow from it into an article by me. I feel as if there is a time bomb under my chair that will explode when the subject comes up.

Roger has not mentioned the matter, either, though I expected to be confronted with it the moment I climbed down from my berth. He no doubt avoided the subject out of pure fear that I would become irrational and attack him with the only potential weapon I brought on the trip, a large jar of face cream I cannot live without.

No mention was made, either, of the way he took advantage of me when I lost my balance.

A man joins us, Jack Thompson. He's about forty and the bulge hanging over his belt is well developed and no doubt still in its infancy.

"Señor Thompson is a farm equipment salesman from El Paso," Don Antonio tells us.

Hearing the men talk about the hay reapers and threshing machines that Thompson sells to the more prosperous Mexican farmers doesn't help take my mind off last night's incident.

All I keep thinking is that there is one vindication for my tale: A search was made, at Roger's and my insistence, for Howard. *And he is missing.* But that didn't settle the matter in the eyes of anyone but me. Seeing a "creature" had been too much for anyone to swallow—even me.

"He still can't be found?" I ask Don Antonio.

The question pops out of my mouth when Thompson pauses for a moment about how a reaper bundles and binds hay.

This creates a longer pause and everyone looks at me.

"Sorry. I'm afraid it just slipped out of my thoughts."

"Yes, he is still missing," Don Antonio says. "Another search was made this morning at my insistence. I even had the top of the entire length of the train checked. He would have to be smaller than a mouse to keep hidden."

The consul nods his head to Thompson. "Señor Thompson has an interesting theory about what occurred last night. He has been kind enough to join us this morning to share it with us. It appears to explain a great deal."

"No one doubts you saw the old-timer go off the train," Thompson says in a condescending tone that I personally want to smack. "But his pack is also missing. And that indicates he jumped ship."

I already knew this. The fact his belongs were missing and that he had been acting paranoid about people trying to get his "treasure map" left the impression his exit had been voluntary. To everyone but me, that is.

Don Antonio taps his coffee cup with his spoon to signal a waiter that it's empty. He appears to choose his words carefully as he speaks to me. "Señor Thompson and I believe that the man planned to jump the train right at the moment it peaked the hill and started its descent. That way, the train would have been barely moving and it would have been an easy jump."

"And why would he do that—voluntarily?" I ask.

"To get away from the cowboys who he thought were going to steal the treasure map he constantly rattled on about. He had joined them as a cook and talked about the map and soon began to express fear that the others would steal it. The foreman of the cowboys, Señor Maddock, says the old gringo had threatened to leave the train before and had been kept from going at every stop because he had been given advanced wages."

The sequence of events had a ring of truth to it, but I'm not going to be bullied by a show of authority. I saw something strange and I'm not backing down from it. I shake my head. "I don't know—"

"Paranoia, ma'am," Mr. Thompson says. "It rages like a fever with gold hunters, and for good reason. There is always someone after their grubstake or jumping their claim. I've dealt with prospectors before. Have grubstaked a number of 'em myself, though I've yet to see the color of gold in return. But they're all the same. Think they've found the mother lode and sleep with a gun in their bedroll because they're convinced some-one will steal it."

"So you think he jumped off to go and seek or protect that Aztec trea-sure he was always mumbling about?" Roger asks Thompson.

"That's about the sum of it. Let me ask you this. How do we account for that bedroll and gear he carried in a big fawn-colored sack being gone, too?" He gives me a contrived sympathetic look that makes my jaw tighten. "And I think you'll agree with me that it's unlikely any, uh, any nonhuman thing managed to traipse down a train aisle to steal his posses-sions after all the ruckus you caused."

I stir, uneasy in my chair, antsy, my anger rising, ready to launch. "And the creature I saw? The *nonhuman*. This you believe is a figment of my imagination? Better yet, perhaps my frail female constitution couldn't take a second glass of champagne with all the excitement of being in Mexico?"

"Actually, señorita," Don Antonio says, smiling with great charm, his tone silky, "we do think that you saw something that any of us would have thought freakish. Is that not true, señor?" He looks to Mr. Thompson.

"What happened is clear as a bell from where I sit. Sundance helped us figure it out last night by doing a little test. Look behind you."

I turn around, to find Sundance with a fawn-colored bedroll slung over his shoulder.

"You think that's my creature?"

"Quite, as our young friend from Britain might put it," Thompson says. "Anyone looking through a dirty window in the dark could easily believe it to be something not human. We borrowed that from another cowboy because it's very similar to Howard's bedroll."

"It could be mistaken for an ugly face in the dark," Roger says. "It was dark and the window is so dirty, you can hardly see through it anytime."

Gertrude starts to say something, but she clams up when I glare at her.

I also clamp my trap shut. I know when I am defeated. And to be honest, deep down, in a tiny recess of my reasonable mind, I have some doubts myself as to what I actually saw. However, I know it wasn't that silly bedroll. But was it a creature? And did I see fear on the man's face . . . or his face twisted in that drunken sneer I'd seen before?

Sundance is waiting for me when we leave. He takes off his hat and gives me his charming, boyish grin.

"Just trying to help, Nellie."

"Thank you. But next time you see me being lynched, please don't whip the horse out from under me.

Roger gives me a look as we pass on. "That should make him feel guilty."

"I hope so."

21

I ditched Roger after breakfast, telling him I was going to take refuge somewhere where I wouldn't be stared at.

He assured me that the incident had already been forgotten, but I shrugged that off—it was still burning fresh in me, so I was sure there were many others who hadn't forgotten.

I gave the porter in the last car a coin to deliver a note to Gertrude to meet me there.

The last car of the train is an older passenger one with hard wooden bench seats in need of repair, making it the least occupied. Gertrude obviously wanted a private meeting, and there was too much chance that her uncle would catch us huddled in the parlor car.

She pats my hand as she sits down next to me. "You poor thing. What a horror you've been through."

"Actually, I think the prospector had it much worse. I appreciate your uncle's having taken time to create a sequence of events in which I save face."

"You don't accept the wrinkled bag theory?"

"Not unless champagne affects one like opium and I was hallucinating. It's just . . ." I shake my head. "I know what I saw wasn't human but also wasn't wrinkled cloth."

She bites her lower lip. "Nellie, I'm going to tell you something, but please don't write about it in a story to your newspaper. Don Antonio would be very upset if he knew I had spoken to you about it."

"What is it?"

"Did the creature you saw remind you of anything?"

"No, I've never seen anything like it. And I got only a brief glimpse of it through a dirty window in the dark."

"Could it have been a mask?"

"A mask? Yes, I suppose it could have been. It was rather feline, like a cat—maybe a mountain lion."

"How about a jaguar?"

"A jaguar? I don't know. They look rather like big cats, don't they? Like cougars, what we call mountain lions?"

"Yes, similar to your mountain lions, but bigger. Jaguars can weigh several hundred pounds. They are quite fierce animals. To the ancient Mexicans, jaguars were not just kings of the jungle but also sacred beasts with magical powers."

It's obvious she is trying to tell me something but is having a hard time getting it out.

"Gertrude, what are you trying to say? That I saw a jaguar last night? Because if that is so, they are wandering around on two feet and slicing people's throats with big hunting knives."

"Maybe . . ."

"Maybe? Now you're sounding like me."

"Hear me out. Don Antonio told us that after the Spanish conquest, many Aztecs hid their treasures. But that's not all that happened. A resistance arose, a secret society devoted to driving out the Spanish. It never created a major revolt against the invaders; instead, the members operated as assassins who attacked Spaniards, most often at night along lonely roads."

"Sounds like other assassination cults in history. Wasn't there a Jewish group around the time of Christ that killed the Roman invaders of Israel?"

"The Sicarii. What the Romans called 'dagger men.' Judas Iscariot might have been a member. During the Crusades, an Islamic group of assassins, the Hashshashin, arose to attack Christian leaders. It's where we got the word *assassin*. The secret Aztec group had the same purpose—to drive out the enemy that had enslaved its people.

"They were known as the Cult of the Jaguar because they worshiped the jungle beast as their god of war. They even dressed as jaguars when they attacked the Spanish. The garb was based upon preconquest elite Aztec warriors known as Jaguar Knights. The Jaguar Knights were considered the toughest warriors in the empire and also acted as personal guards of the emperors.

"Don Antonio says we will see street entertainers dressed as Jaguar Knights performing for tourists in Mexico City. He says the Cult of the Jaguar has significance for the *indios* today because there is still deep rooted resentment and even hatred over the way those with pure *indio* blood are treated as second-class citizens by the rest of Mexican society."

"That's why you want to know if the thing I saw could have had jaguar features. Good Lord, are there people running around wearing jaguar masks and killing people?"

"Well, I don't know if I would go that far, but for certain, jaguar masks exist and have a lot of symbolism."

I chew on her information for a moment before asking, "Did your uncle suggest that some Cult of the Jaguar members could have killed the prospector?"

"Not at all. In fact, I learned about the cult from my history studies at Oxford." She shoots a glance around and leans in closer to whisper. "When I mentioned it to Don Antonio this morning, he became rather agitated. He hates anything that reflects negativity on Mexico. Your being a news reporter has made him redouble his efforts to keep a lid on anything that doesn't reflect well on the country. I think that's why he had Thompson at breakfast—to convince you that you hadn't really seen anything worth reporting."

"It wouldn't make any sense anyway. Howard was a down-on-his-luck prospector, not a Spanish grandee enslaving *indios* on a hacienda. There wouldn't be any motive for cult members to attack him."

Gertrude glances around again before speaking in a conspiratorial tone. "Nellie, this seems incredible, but Don Antonio said something this morning that I found stunning when I broached the subject of the cult. He said that many people believe that the cult members were, or are, the keepers of the disk of the sun god."

"No! Do you realize—"

"Of course. Your prospector claimed to have a map identifying where the disk is hidden."

"Not just that, Gertrude. It means something else."

"What?"

"If it is worth killing for, it probably is the actual map to the treasure."

"You're right. No one would kill him for one of those maps you buy off a street corner."

I jump up from my seat to leave.

"Where are you going?" She grabs my hand.

"To tell Roger and everyone else on this train that I am not crazy."

"Nellie, you promised not to say a word to anyone."

"Oh, you're right." I flop back down in the seat and cross my heart. "A promise is a promise. And I will keep it. I'm sorry. All I could think of was that now I wouldn't have to endure those looks. But, hey, if I told this story about the jaguar, I'd probably be put in a straitjacket. It's bizarre. I mean, could this really be true—that some ancient cult killed poor Howard?"

"I don't know what happened to the man, but you haven't heard the most bizarre part yet."

"Good Lord, what you've told me already has left me gasping."

Gertrude smiles. "This is the best part. In Europe, we have legendary beasts called werewolves, shape-changers who turn from human to beast."

"We have them, too. They start growing hair when it's a full moon. I'm almost afraid to ask, but are you going to tell me that the man was attacked by a werewolf?"

"Close. Part of the legend of the Cult of the Jaguar is that certain high priests of the cult acquired the ability of shape-changing."

"From man to jaguar?"

"Yes. Were-jaguars."

"Were-jaguars." I shake my head as I repeat the word. It not only has a strange ring to it but it conjures up so many weird thoughts in my already overworked imagination, I'm afraid my head will explode.

"The tale goes," Gertrude continues, her tone revealing that she is relishing the gory details, "that the high priests used magic mushrooms and drank the blood of sacrificed victims to accomplish the change. When they changed form, they didn't become four-legged jaguars, but walked on two feet as men while taking on some of the features and the strength of the great cat."

"And all of this is true? You read this in a history book?"

"Well . . . not quite a history book. It's a collection of the mysterious and magical folktales of Mexico."

"Ah. I see. And I thought an Oxford scholar would be at least slightly less whimsical than I am."

She jabs my shoulder with a forefinger. "To quote my history master, 'Folktales are history disguised as literature.' But I am also not advocating that you saw a were-jaguar attacking your friend—either the mythical beast or someone with a mask. But you have to admit that the link is interesting and provocative."

That is an understatement.

My head swirls as I try to digest the strange tale and the attack on the old prospector.

"I can't imagine why anyone would wear a mask to attack the man. It's a mere accident that I was even there at that moment to see it."

I bend over and hold my head in my hands. "I don't know what to think." I look back up to Gertrude. "I love a mystery and magic and the occult, but making a link between what I saw and an ancient murder cult is too far a reach even for me. Maybe it was nothing more than the bag on his shoulder that I saw."

"And maybe you'd better hope that whatever you saw isn't still on the train."

22

Try as I might to doze off, it's another night of no sleep. When I close my eyes, my imagination goes wild and I get flashes of that strange face I saw. Then the face forms into a bedroll, all twisted out of shape, and I'm standing in a room with people laughing at me as I cringe with humiliation.

I'm oversensitive, I know. My mother says it's because I always want to win, to be the best. Rather than reliving last night's humiliation, I need to focus on this moment and the rest of my trip and return home. I'm a good reporter and will make it as a foreign correspondent. I need to stick to the wonderful people and interesting things about the south-of-the-border culture I see all around. And heed my mother's advice about reining in my imagination and sticking my nose in places where it doesn't belong. The old prospector no doubt was making a fast getaway from the train and I probably frightened him with my screams as much as thinking I was seeing some kind of creature scared me.

Hell and damnation! I can't just lie in the bunk; my mind won't let my body rest. There is no avoiding it: Sleep is escaping me and I might as well get up. Thank goodness last night Roger was gracious enough to lend me his robe and never asked for it back.

I slip quietly down from the upper berth, this time managing to do so without falling on top of him. I make a little noise, but with that snoring, the train would have to derail to wake him up.

There is empty seating at the front of the car. As quiet as a mouse, I make my way to it in the dim light and take a seat. I am at the opposite end from the washrooms where I had witnessed the incident, and that suits me fine. However, it has the same dirty-windowed door that leads to the gangway to the next car, but the window has less impact on my nerves and imagination.

Once seated, I stare out the window, listening to the rolling thunder of the steel wheels on the track, watching sandy mounds and cactus slip by. The moon is full and bright and I watch a flock of ducks rise in dark clouds at the approach of the train and move off to a more secluded spot to be alone and not have their sleep disturbed. I wish I could join them.

All I want is peace and quiet—to think and try to sort out what happened, to get a handle on Gertrude's incredible tale of were-jaguars and the scenario Thompson came up with and had Sundance reenact.

Nothing my mind conjures up erases Howard's terrified expression that I observed through the dirty window. Or the grotesque face of the thing that had a grip on him and slid a knife across his throat.

How could I have imagined that? It's too vivid in my mind, and the hairs stand straight up on the back of my neck every time I think about it. That tells me more about what I saw than other people's theories.

Good Lord—what would Don Antonio say if I insisted that it was a were-jaguar that attacked the man and that I would report it as such in the first missive I sent from Mexico City?

It doesn't take much imagination to conclude that he would declare me persona non grata in Mexico and have me taken off this train and put on the next one back to El Paso.

Oh my God! I smother a laugh of hysteria. What would they say in the newsroom at the *Dispatch* if I told them I got thrown out of Mexico because I saw a mythical man-jaguar kill someone—a werewolf with a cat's face? I can just see Mr. Madden's expression, and my poor mother would have me institutionalized for my own protection if Mr. Madden didn't beat her to it.

I lean back and close my eyes. Maybe I can get some sleep and discover this was all just a bad dream when I awake. Wouldn't that be lovely!

Bam!

I'm woken by a loud slamming noise and I sit straight up.

Staring at me through the dirty window of the door to the gangway is the porter who made up our berths. His features are twisted with shock and surprise. He then slowly, almost mechanically, slides to the side, moving away from the window.

There is a movement beyond him, as if someone else is on the gangway, too, but it's too dark for me to see who or what it is—all I see is a shadow, a silhouette of someone.

The porter disappears from the gangway window and I catch the flash of his white uniform as he flies by my window.

I jump up, letting out a scream that could be heard back in Cochran's Mills—a long, agonizing, piercing cry.

Stumbling, I get to the emergency cord and collapse down to my knees. Somehow, I force myself back up and grab the cord and pull and pull and—

Nothing.

No horrific screech of locked steel wheels skidding along steel tracks.

No sudden violent stop that sends passengers and luggage flying.

Nothing as I pull the cord again and again.

The train continues rolling smoothly along.

I let go of the emergency cord and it dangles loosely next to me. It's broken. The engineer in the locomotive all the way at the front of the train didn't get my signal. But plenty of passengers heard my screams.

Passengers have gotten out of their bunks. After their first excited exclamations, they grow silent and stare at me, like a lynch mob.

The man who accused me of spreading rumors about the train's being robbed steps in front of his wife to shield her from me.

"She's dangerous!"

23

"You will not be put off at the next stop," Don Antonio tells me in his calm, diplomatic, reassuring voice, "regardless of what the conductor told you."

Despite his cool, calm diplomatic veneer, I am certain that I will be facing a firing squad or at the very least be set off the train at any of the small watering holes we are passing, now that I've admitted seeing the porter airborne outside my window.

He shoots a glance to Gertrude, who avoids his eye, just as she has been avoiding mine.

Thank you, Gertrude for coming to my aid, I silently convey to her with a small, helpless grin. How I had managed to jump out of the frying pan and into the pot or into a fire, or however that expression goes, is beyond me. At the moment, I am unable to defend myself and barely able to present myself at the breakfast table. I refused to go to breakfast when Roger asked me to, and it wasn't until I got a message—a command—from Don Antonio that I made my way to the dining car—not without a few stares and glares from my fellow passengers.

"I have taken care of it. But, my dear, you must promise me that you will not ever, under any circumstances, even if your life depends upon it—"

"Pull that cord. Or scream. I promise. I will not pull the cord. I will not scream. Even if I am being murdered. But—"

"No ifs or buts. You will not do anything to disturb the passengers or crew of this train. Is that understood, young lady?"

I hang my head. I have no defense. I am guilty as charged. But . . .

"I just don't understand. The porter—"

"I have told you there is *no* porter missing."

He did tell me. And I refused to take his word this morning, just as I refused to take the word of the conductor and went on a search myself, speaking to all the porters on the train about their missing comrade, in a futile attempt to establish that he did indeed exit. All I got from them were head shakes, shrugs, and rolling eyes when I asked them to confirm that one of their members had been an *indio* who was now missing.

"But he was the only *indio* porter I saw on the train. I can't believe no one else saw him."

I am so frustrated, I could *scream*. I just don't understand how no one on the train could remember the only obvious *indio* porter. Gertrude did say that people don't remember waiters and porters.

She's right, which is why even she didn't notice we had an *indio*-looking porter on the train. I am aware of it because I am actively studying people for my article. And it didn't help my case when the regularly assigned porter for our compartment claimed to have prepared our berths—and Roger didn't deny that it was this man.

But even if passengers don't particularly remember porters, how about the man's fellow porters? Wouldn't they know if one of their own was missing?

It occurs to my paranoid mind that in this poor country, which universally operates off a system of *mordida,* it wouldn't take much to get porters to forget about a missing porter. But not only can't I come up with a reason for that; I don't think they would have a conspiracy of silence to protect a killer.

Turning over the coin, the *indio* porter wasn't always around. He seemed to have taken the place of the regular porter who turned down our berths and that of another porter in the dining room, but he didn't appear to do either job on a regular basis. Could he have passed around bribes to be permitted aboard to spy on people?

So who was this *indio* porter, what happened to him, and why has everyone conveniently forgotten he existed?

I tried this line of reason on Don Antonio for about three seconds before his eyes grew wide and I saw myself on a train northbound in their reflection.

I glare at Roger, who has been listening quietly as he puffs on his pipe. Like Gertrude, he avoids my eye, and my ire.

"Roger, how could you not remember that the porter who made up our compartment last night was an *indio*?"

"What?" Don Antonio asks. "What do you mean—'our compartment?'"

Oh crap.

Here are buried cities older than Pompeii, sculptures thousands of years old, hieroglyphics for the wise to study, and everywhere the picturesque people in their garb and manners of centuries ago—and all this within a day's travel from the city. Surely in all the world there is none other such wonderful natural museum.

—NELLIE BLY,
Six Months in Mexico

24

Leaving the dining car, I hurry away, refusing to talk to Roger or anyone else as I escape the meeting with Don Antonio. I'm fleeing my big mouth and the look of shock on the faces of both the consul and Gertrude when they discovered I'm sharing a compartment with Roger.

I am also annoyed at Roger's failure to recall the ethnicity of the porter who prepared our berths—especially when I had pointed out to him that the porter was not the one who had greeted us originally.

I can excuse the failure of the porter's not being particularly noticed at dinner—as Gertrude pointed out, one doesn't notice people serving you. Not, at least, if one happens to be used to being served. But I can't excuse Roger.

What I need to do now is get to our compartment before Roger, change my clothes, pack my carpetbag and find someplace on this train I can stay until we get to Mexico City. If I never see Roger again, that will be fine with me, and if that means sleeping one night sitting up, so be it, I will. And Gertrude—why didn't she make eye contact with me or her uncle until my slip of the tongue? What is she avoiding?

If only my mother were here. None of this would have happened. I really need her to steer me away from the crooked roads that my impulses take me. Well, what's done is done. I just need to keep my nose clean for one more day. Once we arrive in Mexico City, I shall go my way and they will go theirs. What a relief that will be, as I'm sure they feel the same way. However, I will miss Gertrude.

———

THANK GOD I GET TO the compartment before Roger. I wonder where he went. Oh well, what do I care? And I decide not to pack my carpetbag. Why should he have the comfort of the sleeper? Besides, he's the one who should be feeling like a jerk. Maybe the fact he has soiled my reputation will finally motivate him to leave the compartment.

To my relief, I find a seat in the last car, where there seems to be no one who recognizes me as the infamous screamer. The terrain outside changed overnight from arid to green as we entered the Valley of Mexico. We are a thousand miles from dusty desert border towns and now the world is becoming subtropical.

The rolling hills outside don't show it, but we are high above both the Pacific Ocean to the west and the Atlantic to the east, where dense jungles lie. It's amazing. We are over seven thousand feet above sea level, nearly a mile and a half high, with the peaks in the distance towering nearly three miles.

It's hard for me to comprehend the elevation, but central Mexico is atop a great plateau sounded by high mountains, some of which are volcanic.

I jot down a note to put in my first article about Mexico City that the metropolis sits nearly a mile and a half high, higher than any mountain east of the Mississippi River. It's pleasant to think about something else, and I feel my body starting to relax—a little.

The train starts to slow down, its aching metal bones making rheumatoidlike sounds.

There is no village in sight and no guard of horsemen galloping to us. I wonder why we are stopping. It's still early in the morning and the fog hasn't lifted. The air is warm and moist.

With the fog and the humidity, I feel as if I have entered a different world—a lost world, strange, yet beautiful. And it was once exactly that before Europeans destroyed the indigenous civilization and imposed their culture upon the land.

This is all so amazing to me. I am entering the region of the country where the Aztecs had their great civilization, as had the *indio* societies that came before the Aztecs and left incredible relics of their grand past.

"Excuse me, miss."

I look up from my journal, to see a man with his wife, I presume. "Yes?"

"We don't mean to bother you, but do you know if we are going to be seeing the Mayas soon?"

"Mayas . . . no, the Mayan civilization is hundreds of miles south. This region we are entering was dominated by the mighty Aztecs, whose armies marched and conquered like Roman legions."

"Really," the wife says.

They appear interested, so I continue, giving them a combination of what I picked up from Mrs. Percy, Gertrude, and Don Antonio.

"Yes. Before them came the golden Toltec civilization, with its mythical god-king Quetzalcóatl. And preceding the Toltec was an even greater civilization, which built an incredible city called Teotihuacán, which, according to the Aztec language, means a place where the gods were born. No one knows anything about the civilization, despite that fact it was the largest city in the Americas before Columbus arrived. Its towering pyramids left an indelible imprint on the valley and all the cultures that followed."

The man smiles at me. "You do know quite a lot about the Mexican culture. Are you a student?"

"Wait." The wife stares at me. "Aren't you the young lady who has been stopping the train?"

We hear the screech of wheels as the train starts rumbling to a complete stop. It appears to be in the middle of nowhere, or at least it seems that way. With the landscape blurred by fog, if there is a town, we can't see it, and that stirs murmurs of concern from passengers about bandidos.

"I didn't do it!"

25

I get up and go out onto the gangway to get away from the other passengers and find out why the train has stopped in the middle of nowhere.

A mule train is approaching, emerging from the fog like a centipede on its multiple legs. The passengers who are also wondering why we stopped will be relieved to know we are about to take on cargo, instead of being attached by bandidos.

The train makes one last jerking motion and I almost go flying off the gangway, when a hand steadies me.

It's Mr. Thompson, the farm equipment salesman, who instructs others on what I see—and don't see.

"Best be careful, missy. Never can tell what will happen if you lose your balance."

"Thank you."

I try to sound sincere, but I know the smile I give him is not. His supposed words of care seem more like words of warning, like if I'm not careful, something horrible is going to happen to me. I really don't like this man. There's something about him that irritates me, besides the fact that he managed to convert a duffel bag into a beast.

Maybe it's the question that has been buzzing in my head since he had his theory demonstrated: *Why* did he even get himself involved? What ax is he grinding by making me look like an idiot?

It's also the way he looks at me. Not as a man looking at a woman, but like a dog staring at a bone with meat on it, and wanting to sink his teeth in.

Some men are that way—they don't see the woman, just her body parts. Hopefully, he saves his amorous attentions for ladies of the night, who at least get paid for being treated like a piece of meat.

The air is damp, but it's refreshing after being in a train car that is heavily laden with the smell given off by burning candles, a woodstove, and the exhalations of my fellow passengers.

As I wander toward a railcar into which cargo from the mule train is being transferred, I hear an angry male voice with a German accent shout, *"Dumme esel!"*

We had Pennsylvania German neighbors when I was young, people erroneously called "Dutch." I know enough of their language to understand that he is calling a donkey stupid.

As I come out of the clearing, the German speaker is about to raise a whip to swat a donkey. A Mexican laborer, what I've heard called a "peon," is pulling the donkey's reins. The stubborn animal has its front hooves planted and isn't cooperating, a not uncommon attitude with donkeys, especially if they've been overloaded.

In a strange way, I have always felt an affection for the stubborn beasts, which are smaller than their cousins—horses and mules. My eldest brother constantly tells me I'm as stubborn as a donkey. Especially when I wouldn't listen to the people who told me it was too dangerous for a woman to travel to Mexico alone.

"Stop!" I yell at the man with the whip.

The startled man snaps around to face me.

"Don't you dare strike that poor animal! How could you even think of whipping him!"

The European stares at me, obviously at a loss for words, but only for a moment, then says in perfect English, with a slight accent, "Madam, this poor animal, as you describe it, is an ornery, cranky four-legged devil who has valuable property on him. He also happens to be the only one of the pack animals that has stopped short of the train."

I sense a bit of humor in his explanation, but that just annoys me, because I realize he's not taking me seriously.

"How would you like to have someone slap you with a whip?"

He grins and appears to translate my remark in rapid Spanish to the laborer, who breaks out laughing.

"Depends who's slapping," the German replies, addressing me this time. "And I suppose I would deserve it if I was being ornery for no reason."

"Perhaps, sir, the reason for the stubbornness is that the poor creature is a small donkey that is carrying the same heavy load as the other animals—which are mules."

Mules are, of course, much bigger than donkeys because they are the offspring of the mating of a horse and a donkey.

"Pardon me, but you are not correct. He is not overloaded; he is cantankerous. And frankly, madam, it is none of your business. You should return to the train and your knitting, caring for your husband, or whatever occupies your time when you are not making accusations against strangers."

The man is rude and insufferable.

"Seeing an animal whipped for no reason is the business of all human beings, and I will not permit it."

He laughs. He has the gall to stand there and laugh at me. I am sorely tempted to grab his whip and use it on him.

"Getting my cargo aboard the train is my business." He waves his hand as an invitation for me to try my hand at moving the donkey. "Since you believe there is no good reason to whip the beast, perhaps you'd care to talk to it. Do you speak jackass, by any chance?"

"Interesting that you should ask that. As a matter of fact, I frequently find that I am able to communicate much more intelligently with four-legged ones than the two-legged jackasses I encounter much too often."

"Please," he says, taking the reins from the worker's hand and offering them to me as he bows, "be my guest."

Little does he know that he is dealing with a girl who was raised with horses, mules, and donkeys.

"With pleasure."

I take the reins and turn to face the donkey. His big brown eyes, surrounded with long black lashes, stare back at me. How could anyone hurt such an adorable creature? I know they are tough, but they have to be. They're small, and other animals would push them around if they didn't stand their ground. Being small myself, I can relate to that.

I learn forward and first give him a kiss on his forehead and then blow in his ear. It's a trick my father taught me. He shakes his head, snorts—and moves. I blow in his ear again and he continues to move forward. Once we are at the train car, I hand the reins back to the worker, but not before taking a peek at the cargo—they are loading heavy crates with stone objects from the pack animals and unloading picks and shovels and other digging equipment.

I get only a glance at the goods, so it's hard to tell, but it makes me think the German is a prospector. I'm tempted to ask him facetiously if he has the copy of Montezuma's map, but I decide not to be flippant.

The German laughs aloud and shakes his head in disbelief as the donkey lines up for his turn to be unloaded and I give the sweet thing one last kiss on his forehead for good luck.

I'm able to get a good look at the German, now that my temper is not colored by his arrogance. He is perhaps in his mid-thirties, a rugged man, his clothes dusty, his hat sweat-stained. He is slender of build, his face weathered and deeply tanned. An attractive male, one might say.

"You have won the day, madam." He takes his hat off and makes a bowing gesture. "I will concede to being a four-legged jackass if you'll tell me what you whispered in that creature's ear that made him move."

Oh, am I tempted to say something smart, but I hold back.

"I just blew in his ear. Works every time. You should try it." I give him a little curtsy. "Good morning to you, sir." And I leave him to his animals and merchandise—whatever it might be.

26

For the first time in quite a while, I feel good. I had fun with the donkey and the man and I find myself in a happy spirit, oblivious to my surroundings as I think about happier days when I skipped behind my father as he cared for our animals.

The rustle of something moving through the bushes causes me to pause and I look around, wondering if it's another pack animal. It's hard to tell because the bushes are shrouded in fog.

The fog takes on a more sinister feel as my paranoia kicks in about who—or what—is lurking in the bushes.

"Stop it, Nellie," I mutter aloud; "you're being foolish." And I start to move on. That's when I hear movement in the bushes again, only this time louder and more pronounced—something that is moving slowly in the brush, then stops.

"Who's there?"

Nothing.

Ready to bolt or scream, or both, I try to keep myself from panicking, because I know better than to cause another disturbance. I realize it's stupid to be worried about a noise in the bushes. If this were home, I would assume it was a deer or a cow—something harmless. Instead, I'm keeping a rein on my fear and standing my ground for no other reason than I don't want my overworked imagination to send me running to the train, screaming, with my tail between my legs.

Never being one good with directions, even on a clear day, I look for the dark outline of the train and move toward where I think it's at, hoping I'm right. It strikes me that I know zero about the four-legged predators in

Mexico and that in those bushes there could be an animal looking for a meal and that if I don't hurry, I might be it.

As I walk at a brisk pace, the noise comes again.

I've had it. I spin around, praying it's one of the German's laborers leading a donkey. Instead, a hideous face, buried in the fog and shadows of the bushes, confronts me with a hostile glare.

Without thought, I whip around, pick up my dress, and run as fast as my feet can carry me toward the dark wall ahead, which, thank God, turns out to be the train. I fly by passengers who have gotten off to check out the terrain. Just as I reach the steps, I turn around.

There is nothing behind me but fog and a few people.

My poor heart is racing and my breathing is trying to catch up with it as I grab the hand support and step up on the gangway. Once safely inside, I go straight to the compartment. Roger is there, his head in a magazine.

I plop down across from him.

He doesn't even look up, but says, "Why are you breathing so hard? And please don't tell me you saw something like that creature again."

The man is incredible! If I weren't a lady, I'd smack him on the side of his head.

"As a matter of fact . . ." Thank goodness my brain catches up with my tongue before I blurt out that I had been pursued by a strange beast. Since he already thinks I'm crazy, I lie. "I nearly stepped on a snake."

"Hmm."

What did I see? I got a good-enough look to know it was a face. But not a human one. And it wasn't the same as the face I saw behind the prospector.

I'm beginning to wonder about how much of the mystery and magic of Mexico is of the black arts. That thing in the bushes was something grotesque, the stuff of nightmares. It was the face of an animal. A jaguar? Maybe. Like the other face, it had a feline look. However, knowing that it was the face of an animal wasn't the only thing that shivered me to my bones.

The most soul-wrenching thing of it all is that I could make out enough of the dark shape to which the head was attached to know that it wasn't a four-legged beast.

It was half human, half beast.

In a strange way, seeing this *thing* in the fog made it clear to me that what I saw the night Howard was killed was an inanimate mask—the attacker's face was lifeless.

What I saw outside the train was made of flesh and blood.

Blood. That thought shivers me. I've heard more about and thought more about blood in the past couple of days than ever before. Mexico's ancient gods must have bathed in the stuff.

Leaning back, I close my eyes and concentrate. Okay, girl, you've seen a murder committed by someone in a circus mask. Now you've seen a creature of the night that looks like it came out of a nightmare. What do you make of it?

"Will you do me a favor, Roger?"

He stumbles out of his reading trance. "What?"

"This trip to Mexico has taken on many interesting facets. If I give you the name of the hotel where my mother is staying, would you wire her if anything unfortunate happens to me?"

How much I would like to
paint the beauties of Mexico in colors
so faithful that the people in the States could
see what they are losing by not coming here. How
I would like to show you the green valley where the
heat of summer and blast of winter never dare approach;
where every foot of ground recalls wonderful historical
events, extinct races of men and animals, and civilization older
by far than the pyramids. Then would I take you from the table-
land to the mountain, where we descend into deep canons that
compare in their strange beauty with any in the world; the queer
separation of the earth, not more than 100 feet from edge to edge of
precipice, but 400 feet deep. More wonderful still is the sight when
the rainy season fills these gorges with a mad, roaring torrent.

Then would I lead you to the edge of some bluff that outrivals
the Palisades—and let you look down the dizzy heights 500 feet
to the green meadows, the blooming orchards, the acres of
pulque plant, the little homes that nestle at the foot of this
strange wall. Then further up into the mountains you
could see glaciers, grander, it is claimed, than any
found in the Alps.

—Nellie Bly, *Six Months in Mexico*

27

The City of Mexico is simply called "Mexico" by the country's inhabitants, which fits, because when we get off the train, we see no city.

"It doesn't make any sense," I tell Roger. "They should have the train going straight into the city."

He doesn't respond because he knows it is not a statement of great import, but a meaningless observation created by my frustration as to what I see as bureaucratic malfeasance.

I have been aware since I got on at El Paso that the train would stop short of the city, but I still feel the need to complain. The government simply has not extended the rail system all the way into the city. That leaves the passengers with the necessity of hiring transportation to complete their journey.

It's hot and humid and starting to get sticky. That and the fact that I had another restless night with dreams of half-human creatures with jaguar features attacking me has left me in a less than my usual even temperament.

My nocturnal struggles even woke poor Roger, which is a miracle in itself. He banged his head when I let out a yelp for help. Fortunately, the sound had not traveled any farther than the bottom berth, or Don Antonio would have had me make my way to the railhead by shank's mare.

Our last dinner had been slightly awkward. Don Antonio, always the diplomat, had not shown any sign that Roger and I had been invited only because Gertrude had requested it, but I'm reasonably certain that was the case.

Everyone made polite dinner talk and never broached the subject about the prospector or Roger and I sharing a compartment—which was fine with me. Mostly, Gertrude chatted about how she is going to learn how to speak Arabic and challenge male domination in the world of travel and exploration, especially in Egypt and the Holy Land, where she has friends in the British Diplomatic Service.

The two men made insipid listening responses, leaving me to wonder what they really thought of women with lofty ambitions. I hope she will be able to make her dreams come true, as well as my own.

I was relieved when Gertrude offered to play a game of chess after dessert. I really didn't want to be alone, but I also didn't want to talk, making the concentration required by chess perfect. And she tutored me in Spanish, which helped fill in the empty holes in our conversations.

I suspect she was too polite to bring up my sleeping arrangements with Roger, and I was in no mood to share. It was hard enough not to confide in her about what I had seen outside. If I started talking about it, I would end up telling her about the man-beast and lose whatever credibility I had left with her—if I had any left. I was sure she was miffed at me for not confiding in her about my "relationship" with Roger and, worse, was questioning my morals.

Of course, no one questions the morality of Lily Langtry, who has had a host of lovers. The rules of morality for women don't extend to making love to kings and millionaires.

Before we parted, I was surprised when Gertrude gave me a genuine hug and took the name of my hotel, with a promise between us to get together. I had assumed she had written me off as a tainted woman.

I hate promises like that because they rarely get fulfilled, especially when traveling. Besides, I'm not sure how long I will be in the city, because I don't know where stories will take me or how much free time, if any, I will have.

I have to shake off all the strange things that I've encountered and get to work. Nothing is going to stop me from achieving that goal. Not even jaguars or people who look like jaguars.

And I have the issue of my mother—I mustn't keep her waiting too long. She promised to stay put until I sent for her, but, knowing her, after a few days she will be antsy and try to make her way to me. However, with so many weird things happening, I waiver between wanting the comfort of her company and praying that she stays put—I wouldn't want her to encounter the dangers I have. I would never forgive myself if anything happened to her.

Roger breaks into my brown study. "It's hopeless. We're going to be stuck here awhile."

Dozens of public coaches and a few private ones are lined up at the entrance to the station; all the public ones are being swamped.

"Well, be prepared to do battle."

"What does that mean?" he asks.

"We will have to wait for more to arrive, but I have learned from experienced travelers to the city that one must be prepared not only to get a coach but to make sure one is treated fairly."

"And how do we get treated fairly?"

"When a public coach procures a permit, they are graded and marked. A first-class coach carries a white flag, a second-class a blue flag, and a third-class a red flag. The prices are, respectively, per hour: one dollar, seventy-five cents, and fifty cents."

"I would imagine that the cleanliness and comfort are directly related to the price paid."

"Yes. And while the rules are meant to protect travelers, this doesn't always work, because the drivers are very cunning."

"You don't say." Roger gives me a grin. "Sounds like every livery driver I've encountered in every large city I've been in."

Ignoring his sarcasm, I continue. "I was told they'll remove the flag and charge double prices, even though they can be punished for it. And as you've guessed, one does not want to take a third-class rig, because they are unreliable and filthy. Anyway, you're right: It will be a while before we can try and elbow our way aboard."

"And how do you know this?"

"Because there were rumblings among the passengers that a lesser number of coaches will be available because they have been requisitioned by the military to convey troops."

Roger puts his luggage down and sits on it. "Perfect. Well, we might as well try to make ourselves comfortable, since we are resolved in having to wait until the carriages return after dropping off loads. And considering it's an hour over and back, we, my dear Nellie, will be here for a couple of hours." With that, he pulls his hat down over his eyes.

"How can you be so nonchalant?"

"I have come to accept in life that there are times when I can do nothing to alter the undesirable, so why get my feathers ruffled? It won't speed up the carriages. You might want to try it. It might make you a bit less . . . tense?"

"Oh, so now you are a philosopher and critic! I am not tense. But as you sit back and ponder the meaning of life, keep in mind that you're a student of ancient history—you don't have to worry about competition and deadlines, because everyone you deal with is dead."

I turn and pace back and forth. Me—tense? The nerve of him. What has he done? If I waited for things to happen, I'd be nowhere. But now that I've let him know I won't take his guff, I have to admit that he's right in this instance: Nothing can be done but wait, even if I'm antsy and it will drive me nuts.

To bide my time, I lapse into my favorite pastime when I'm forced to wait—watching people.

They are like little worker ants—all scurrying around in a crazy but orderly manner. Some are gathering up their luggage, others waving good-bye to fellow passengers or saying hello to those who have come to pick them up, while some, like us, appear to know it's hopeless to try to get immediate transportation.

My attention is drawn to the freight car at the rear of the train. The German gentleman who tried to whip the donkey is standing by a mule train that appears ready to take on a load. I didn't realize he had stayed aboard.

What really piques my interest is that Thompson, the farm salesman, and Maddox, the cowboy boss, have gathered together with him and are talking like they know one another, unlike strangers who have bumped into one another in a train yard. It's their body language. "Old home week," my mother would say. Sundance is also engaged in their conversation.

Hmm . . . now all I need is to have Don Antonio join them.

Interesting—I'd love to be a fly on one of their hats and find out what they have in common.

"There's a seat on that one!"

28

I spin around, to find Roger, bag in hand, running for a stagecoach.

Before I can react, he has thrown his bag up to the man riding shotgun, who, in turns, tosses it atop the already-large pile of bags and trunks on top of the coach.

Roger climbs aboard, slipping through the open door and onto a seat as I grab my carpetbag and make a mad dash for the rig.

Roger slams the door behind him and leans out the window, holding up his hands up in a gesture of helplessness. "Sorry—last seat."

I am too much of a lady to repeat here what I say under my breath, but the word describes Roger's ancestry in a vulgar fashion.

From Roger's raised eyebrows as he leans out the window to look back at me, I know he got my meaning loud and clear.

With bag in hand, I am ready to explode like Mount Vesuvius as I breathe in the dust created by the coach's wheels. First, he took the bottom berth. Now he takes the last seat on a coach, stranding me for hours. If I ever get my hands on him . . .

Once again, he has demonstrated that he is not a gentleman and definitely shown his dislike of, even contempt for women. I understand and am forced to accept that men have many privileges not accorded to women, but one of the counterbalances of that right is that a man has the duty to stand so a woman can have the last seat on a bloody coach!

"*Nellie!*" Its Gertrude, leaning out of a carriage window and waving at me as it approaches.

This is not any ordinary conveyance, but an elegant carriage emblazoned with brightly polished silver trim, a coat of arms on the door, crimson velvet cushions that the driver sits on, and drawn by two handsome black Thoroughbreds.

As the carriage comes to a halt, Don Antonio steps down, tips his hat to me, and gives me a short bow. "Señorita, *por favor,* please permit us the pleasure of your company for the short journey into the city."

"*Mucho gracias!*" I'm so delighted I could hug him. He's a real gentleman.

Getrude laughs. "My tutoring didn't help much last night, it's *muchas gracias,* Nellie."

"In whatever language, a million thanks," I tell them, grinning as I climb aboard with Don Antonio's gentlemanly assist.

I let out an "Ooh" as I sink into the seat.

"Is anything wrong, señorita?" Don Antonio asks.

"No, not at all. These seats, the leather is so plush and soft . . . it's like sitting on a cloud. I'm sure the queen of England doesn't put her behind on softer material."

Gertrude laughs. "Oh, I'm sure she does."

"Well, I'm just so pleased for being rescued, I could be riding in a cart and loving it. But this carriage is amazing. The wheels make little, if any, noise on the ground and the clippety-clop of the hooves of those fine steeds sound like the soft tap of a ballet dancer's slippers to my ear. It's all so beautiful."

I don't add that Don Antonio's carriage lives up to the reputation of the capital city's priding itself on having the finest private rigs in the world. Teak-trimmed, with what looks like enough silver to mint a dollar for everyone in Pittsburgh, is how I will describe it in an article.

"Thank you," Don Antonio says, "but take a look over there." He points to another carriage, which is even grander than his.

"Wow!" is all I can say, for that carriage is ostentatiously laden with so much gold and silver trim, bandidos would salivate over it. However, the two people boarding it really grab my attention.

"That is Lily Langtry and her playboy lover?"

"Yes. She is *muy bonita,* very beautiful."

"Ah, like most of the rest of the men on the planet, I see my uncle is drawn by her beauty." Gertrude gives him a smile of tolerance.

"I confess you are correct. She radiates that divine magnetism called charisma, which inspires people to pay to see her onstage."

"Yes, but don't you think that her exquisite dress helps?" Gertrude doesn't wait for his answer. "Look at her black satin dress. It's so beautiful, it would make an ugly duckling shine. It's embroidered in both silver and gold and bestrewn with jewels, definitely from Paris. All for a short carriage ride into the city. No doubt she will change the moment she arrives at her hotel. However, did you know, Nellie, that just about every dress she wears is black?"

"No. I wonder why. Is she in mourning?"

Gertrude laughs. "No. Black is considered very elegant and slimming. And with just the right touch of jewelry, it's exquisite. Oh my . . . look at her hat. It's what fashion designers are calling a 'home rule' bonnet. It's the newest rage. They have no strings and no crown. Hers is the newest look, no crown at all, only an opening bordered with a wreath of roses so her hair can show. She's always right in fashion."

"We have a proverb about fashion," Don Antonio says. "If the fool did not go to market, the damaged goods would never get sold."

I point at a man behind Lily Langtry. He hasn't gotten in the carriage yet and is talking to the driver. "So that's Frederic Gebhard, the wealthy New York socialite and man-about-town whom Roger told us about. He's quite dapper, but not an especially handsome brute."

Dressed in a top hat and double-breasted frock coat, his clothing shouts New York or London. Behind the magnificent rig they are boarding is another one, which is being loaded with a mountain of trunks.

"They don't travel light."

"It's Lily Langtry," Gertrude says. "What would you expect? My friends at Oxford will be surprised when I tell them I saw the immortal Jersey Lily in Mexico, of all places. You know she had to leave London after a scandal erupted when her husband threatened to name the Prince of Wales as her lover in a suit for divorce."

Now, that is interesting information to put in an article.

"They've come to Mexico because of their mutual interest in horse racing," the consul says, revealing he knows more about their presence than he admitted earlier. "Gebhard owns Eole, the long-distance runner that has won most of the mile-and-a-half to three-mile races."

"Are they keeping their identities secret so as not to drive up the prices of horseflesh?" I ask.

"No doubt that is one reason. In addition, it is likely a fear that bandidos might take special interest in them, perhaps even attempt a kidnapping. Her visit to the city is meant to be kept secret, but it will cause much attention anyway. The carriage that puts to shame my own poor rig is loaned to them by *el presidente* himself."

That doesn't surprise me. I'm sure they will also be wined and dined by the country's president. Being one of the most beautiful and famous women in the world does come with some privileges.

"This is going make such a great dispatch," I say, unable to contain my excitement. "Even the fact about them riding in President Díaz's coach. My editor will be so pleased. Lily Langtry and Frederic Gebhard in Mexico City. Never in a million years would I have expected this. How exciting."

"Señorita, I must ask you to hold off conveying the news of their presence in the city until they have returned back over the border."

"But—"

He holds up his hand to stop my objection. "It's both for their safety and the fact that they are here to make purchases of very fine horseflesh and are keeping their true identities under the rose for the moment. It would not be fair to take advantage of my knowledge about their activities."

"Because the request is from you, mum's the word until I know they have returned to the States."

I will keep my promise, of course, but I am still a red-blooded reporter, and what I didn't reveal is that I will try, naturally, to get as much information as I can about the newsworthy actress and rich playboy while they are here so that I can really relay, after they leave the country, some stories that will make Mr. Madden realize I know how to get top-of-the-line stories.

We come across a stagecoach that's had a wheel come off, leaving the coach body precariously leaning. Half a dozen frustrated passengers are standing next to it, including Roger.

As we sweep by on our heavenly cloud of a carriage, Roger catches sight of me and gawks.

I give him a small, sweet smile in return but am careful not to utter his name nor give him a wave, for fear they will stop and let him aboard.

Don Antonio notices my look. "Spot someone you know?"

"No, no one of importance."

MEXICO CITY GRAND CARRIAGE
(*Six Months in Mexico*)

29

El presidente's grandiose carriage is pulling away from the curb when we arrive at the Hotel Iturbide.

"They're staying at my hotel!" I grin at my companions. "Maybe I'll have the room across the hall from them."

Don Antonio chuckles. "Not likely, señorita. They have taken the entire top floor for just the two of them. The rooms they don't occupy will be kept empty to ensure their privacy."

"Considering the number of trunks I saw, they probably need rooms just for their wardrobes." I give a quiet laugh. "Unlike mine, which can fit on three hangers."

"Nellie, you are going to have to tell me or, better yet, show me how you do that. I could never be without my hats and dresses. It's something I must learn." Gertrude gives a sigh. "Clothing is a weakness of mine. One day, I am going to have to get that habit under control, especially if I plan to go to Egypt. No more fancy hats and dinner dresses. They will have to be practical and durable, and you are the perfect person to help me, Nellie!"

Before I can say anything, Gertrude continues her diatribe about her fascination with Lily Langtry's clothes. "Can you imagine what her gowns must look like? They must be gorgeous! All of my evening dresses would look like wilted flowers in comparison. Uncle, I must go shopping!"

This time, Don Antonio gives a big laugh and shakes his head. "Didn't you just say you were going to control yourself? Your mother warned me. We shall see." He nods his head at the hotel entrance. "Nellie, did you know that the hotel was once the palace of Agustín de Iturbide, who set himself up as emperor of Mexico after the revolution that threw off the yoke of Spain. Before the revolution, we were a Spanish colony called New Spain."

"He also faced a firing squad, like Maximilian, the Austrian arch-duke whom the French set on the throne years later," Gertrude adds.

Don Antonio gives a deep sigh. "I'm afraid my countrymen are not gentle toward royal despots."

"Wow. I'll try to remember that if I'm offered the throne."

Gertrude finds my comment amusing, but I think Don Antonio doesn't. I just get a forced smile from him.

"If it's all right with you," Gertrude says, changing the subject, "I'll send you a chit later to see if we can arrange to do some sightseeing together."

After agreeing and thanking them profusely, I am out of the carriage and into the hotel, shaking my head no to a bellman who wants to carry my one little bag.

The hotel is an incredibly imposing building of the Mexican-Spanish style. The entrance takes one into a large, breathtaking open court or square that is filled with flowers of various brilliant colors in clay pots; vines with purple, pink, and yellow flowers twisting and climbing up pillars that seem to reach to the sky; while scattered about on sea blue tiles are round wrought-iron tables and chairs, with colorful cushions, for the hotel guests.

I've stepped into paradise. It's a perfect place to relax and be creative. I could just stay put in this courtyard and write mystery novels.*

All the rooms are arranged around this court, opening out into a circle of balconies.

I already know that the lowest floor in Mexico is the cheapest. The higher up one goes, the higher the price. The reason for this is that at the top one escapes any possible dampness and can get the light and sun and avoid the noise from the streets below. I had reserved a mid-level room.

The reception area is crowded as I make my way to the check-in desk and a clerk who speaks good English.

"Your hotel is very busy," I remark as I fill in the registration form.

"Very. Many people have come to the city for Día de los Muertos, the Day of the Dead celebration. You are familiar with that tradition?"

"No, not at all. Please tell me."

"It is a day in which we pay tribute to our dead so they know they are

* Nellie did try her hand at writing mysteries. After racing around the world in seventy-two days several years later, she received a contract from a publishing house to write three mysteries. In 1889, she wrote *Mystery of Central Park* and two other books that have been lost in time.—The Editors

still in our hearts. The families of those who have passed go to the grave-yard to share the joy of singing, dancing, and merriment with loved ones they have lost. There will be gifts for the dead, too. Toys will be brought for *niños,* flowers for *mujeres,* and perhaps a little tequila for the *hombres,* no?" He laughs.

His laughter is so contagious, I can't help but join him, but after hav-ing French champagne, I would have to disagree with him about women receiving flowers. I think they should have champagne instead.

"The friends and family who have gathered in the graveyard will eat and drink and enjoy themselves, often until dawn, to acknowledge their departed ones."

He points to a ceramic doll on the fireplace mantel shelf. The doll is dressed in a very pretty bright blue-and-purple evening gown. I do a dou-ble take as I realize that the doll is a skeleton.

"She's a skeleton!" bursts out of my mouth.

"*Sí.* You will see *esqueletos,* skeletons, everywhere you go in the city. It is quite a sight. Some tourists like it, others not."

Great. Just what I needed. First, blood-thirsty were-jaguars and now bony dead people who would frighten the wits out of the Headless Horseman of Sleepy Hollow.

He checks my registration information. "You are fortunate that you have a reservation, señorita. So many people are in town for the festivities, you would find it difficult, if not impossible, to find a suitable room."

He glances around to make sure he is not overheard. "Señorita, you would be amazed at what a rat-infested hovel people without reservations will be doomed to occupy."

"Do you have a reservation for Roger Watkins?" I have no idea why I ask this, because Roger and I had already established we were staying at the same hotel one night when we were being civil to each other and hav-ing a pleasant conversation.

The clerk checks a long sheet. "*Sí,* señorita. A *norteamericano,* arriv-ing today."

"He's asked me to cancel it for him."

I am breathless as I head for the stairwell. What makes me do these things, I have no idea. Mother says it's the devil taking control of me for his own devious work. I say tit for tat.

Let him eat cake! And sleep with rats.

30

My room has a redbrick floor. It's large but has no ventilation except for the glass doors that open onto the balcony. There is a little iron cot in the corner of the room, a hard chair, a table, a washstand, and a wardrobe.

Very uninviting and very uninspiring. Nothing like their courtyard—which is a loss leader, no doubt.

The washroom with toilet and tub is down the hall and shared by all the rooms on the floor.

It all looks so miserable—if not for the glass doors to the balcony, I'd feel like I was in a prisoner's cell. I am beginning to wish I were back home. Good thing my mother isn't here—she would be complaining like the dickens.

Right now, I am so envious of Lily Langtry. If she doesn't like her room—*her whole floor of rooms*—*el presidente* will probably move out of the Presidential Palace so she can use it. No question that rank has its privileges. And as I keep getting reminded, so does beauty and fame, both of which I fall very short of.

Since there is nothing I can do about it, I am going to go outside and enjoy the beautiful day and see this wonderfully strange and exotic city.

Even though I am immediately assailed by sights, sounds, and smells that seemed muted when I was in the carriage, as I exit the hotel into the crowded street, I decide that instead of seeing the city at carriage level, I am going to walk and see it on foot level.

Egad! The desk clerk wasn't kidding. Skeletons are everywhere—walking on the street, hanging in shop windows; being sold as candy, dolls, toys, and costumes and masks in stores and by street vendors.

The Day of the Dead in Mexico is a wonderful idea. I rather like the whole concept of paying homage to those who have gone before us, not just as a mournful occasion but also in a happy way—to celebrate their lives, remembering the joy and good things they brought us.

However, their hideous skeleton costumes do remind me a bit of Halloween, the eve of All Saint's Day. Halloween is my favorite holiday, but I think I prefer the Mexican version of raising ghosts, because although it has a religious aspect, Halloween is filled with maliciousness and mischief, not good cheer, as I would like it.

Día de los Muertos is going to be perfect for one of my articles. No one I know of celebrates the dead in this manner, and when the people in Pittsburgh read about this, they will be intrigued, though I know they won't like the idea of remembering the dead with song and joy rather than in dark, gloomy homage. Most of my readers will call it sacrilegious.

Besides the spooky festival atmosphere, I am surprised by how much utter wealth and dismal poverty stand side by side on the streets. From the clothing people wear, there appears to be the very rich and the very poor, with very few of the large number of middle class one would expect to find on a busy street in Pittsburgh.

It's interesting that they don't seem to turn up their noses at one another, either; the half-clad Indian has as much room on the Fifth Avenue of Mexico City as the millionaire's wife. This is quite refreshing. I like it.

I am also struck by the fine figures these people present. There are some really beautiful girls among this lower class of people. It's common to see women's hair three-quarters of the length down their backs and incredibly thick and silky smooth—like black velvet. I have to fight the urge to touch it, it's so beautiful. They often wear it loose, but more frequently in two long plaits. Wigmakers would find no employment here. The men also wear long hair with heavy bangs.

There is one thing that the poor and rich, men and women, appear to indulge in with equal delight and pleasure—cigarette smoking. My impression is that no spot in the city is sacred from smoking. On the railway cars, up and down the streets, in shops, restaurants, even in a church I step into, everywhere smokers are to be seen—men and women, young and old, poor and elite, smoking.

Policemen also occupy the center of the street at every termination of a block, reminding one, as one looks down the streets, of so many posts.

They wear white caps with numbers on them, blue suits, and nickel buttons. A medieval-looking mace now takes the place of the sword of former days.

Another thing that really impresses me is how Mexican politeness extends to even those among the lowest classes. In all their dealings, they are as polite as a dancing master. The moment one is addressed, off comes his poor, old, ragged hat; he'll stand bareheaded until you leave him. And they are not only polite to other people but among themselves, as well. One poor, ragged woman is trying to sell a broken knife and rusty lock at a pawnbroker's stand. "Will you buy?" she asks plaintively. *"No, señora, gracias"* ("No, thank you") was his polite reply.

I spot a man walking along with an open coffin on his head, from which is visible the remains of some child. In an instant, all the men in the gutters, on the walks, or in the doorways have their hats off, and remain bareheaded until the sad procession is far away. The pallbearer, if such he may be called, dodges in and out among the carriages, burros, and wagons, which fill the street, as the drivers lift their hats, but the silent bearer—the father, I suppose—moves along, unmindful of all.

As I pass along where a new building is being erected, my attention is drawn to the body of a laborer who has fallen from the building. He is lying on the sidewalk; a white cloth covers all of the body except his sandaled feet.

"The Virgin rests his soul" and "Virgin Mother grant him grace" are prayers spoken from his kind who pass by as the policeman commands the body to be carried away.

Seeing a "meat express" coming down the street makes me wish I had taken another route. An old mule or horse that has reached its second childhood serves for the carrier for the meat—a long iron rod, from which hooks project, is fastened on the back of the beast by means of straps. Slabs of beef hang on the hooks, uncovered, leaving it exposed to the mud, dirt, and flies of the streets, as well as the hair of the animal.

Men with two large baskets that hang over their shoulders from poles, one basket in front, one behind, follow behind. The baskets are filled with meat. The men have their trousers rolled up high so that the blood from the meat dripping from the reed baskets will not soil them, but instead run down their bare legs.

A tailor standing in front of his shop realizes I am a tourist and explains that the contents of the baskets are the refuse from the cow, which most people will not eat. It will be sold to the poor. "They will be as happy to get it as we are to get a fine steak off the flank," he says.

This information still doesn't whet my appetite; if anything, for the moment it has made me vow to give up eating meat.

The street is as crowded with men being used as pack animals as it is with mules. In fact, men seem to be working as pack animals, with cages of fowl, baskets of eggs, and bushels of roots and charcoal strung over their shoulders.

"Like mule trains, the peons come from the mountains in droves of from twenty-five to fifty, carrying packs that average three hundred pounds," the tailor tells me.

I doubt these Mexicans, who are typically smaller-built than *americanos* of *el norte,* can carry that much weight, but from what I can see, I would not argue if someone told me they were able to lug on their backs close to their own weight.

Hucksters cry out their wares and all goes as merry as a birthday party, and the streets and parks are thronged with men and women selling ice cream, pulque, candies, cakes, and other dainties. They carry their stock on their heads while moving, and when they stop, they set it on a tripod, which they carry in their arms.

It's quite amazing how all the care in the world vanishes as I walk down the street. Music from a Mexican band is superb; even the birds are charmed. They add their little songs. All this, mingled with the many chimes that ring every fifteen minutes, makes the scene one that is never forgotten. The rich people promenade around and enjoy themselves, similar to the poor.

The water carrier, *aguador,* is one of the most common sights on the street. They suspend water jars from their heads, one in front, one in back. Around their bodies are leather aprons to protect them from the water, which they get at big fountains and basins located throughout the city.

As I continue to wander around the city, I find a street on which there are no business houses or even shops serving that evil-smelling brew— pulque. It has nothing but coffin manufacturers.

From one end of the street to the other, you see in every door men and boys making and painting all kinds and sizes of coffins. The dwelling houses are old and dilapidated and the street narrow and dingy. Here the men work day after day, and never whistle, talk, or sing, as they go at their hewing, painting and gluing with long faces, as if they were driving nails into their own coffins. It is, of course, called Coffin Street.

I am sorry I have no picture of it to send back to Pittsburgh, so people could see the coffins piled up to the ceiling; a little table sits in the center, where the workman puts on the finishing touches, after which they are placed in rows against the building by the sad-visaged and silent workers to await a purchaser.

Near this somber thoroughfare is another street, where every other door is a shoe shop, the one between being a drinking house. Many of the shoemakers have their shops on the pavement, with a straw mat fastened on a pole to keep off the sun. Here he sits making new shoes and mending old ones until the sun goes down, when he lowers the pole and, taking off the straw mat, furnishes a bed for himself in some corner during the night.

Every street is very irregular, narrow in some places, wide in others, and as crooked as the path of a sinner.

What is also of unfailing interest to me are the names of these streets.

In the City of Mexico, streets and store signs and names of the different squares are not named and numbered like ours. Instead, every square is called a street and has a separate name; the same with all the stores and public buildings.

No difference how small, they have some long, fantastic name painted above the doorway. I cannot refrain from taking my pad out and writing down these names of some of the strangest and most peculiar ones to tell my readers. A restaurant is called the Coffee House of the Little Hell, and a grocery store the Tail of the Devil. Paris Boot and the Boot of Gold are both shoe stores. The Red Sombrero sells silk hats. The Surprise, the God of Fashion, the Way to Beauty Is Through the Purse, and the Land of Love are dry-goods stores kept by Frenchmen. Temptation, the Reform, the Flowers of April, the Sun of May, the Fifth of May, the Christmas Night, and the Dynamite sell pulque at a *laco* a mug to the thirsty natives.

The street names also honor all the saints ever heard of or imagined— the Joint of God, the Sad Indian, the Devil, Street of Bitterness, Intense Misery, a Sot, the Shutting up of Jesus, Bridge of the Holy Ghost, and many others equally.

In a weak moment, I ask a seller on the street of a Good Death if what it says on the little tinseled charm on beads he has—that it will keep away the devil and bring good luck to the wearer—is really true. I know by his answer that I have met George Washington, Jr. "*Sí* señorita, I cannot lie."

I finally leave the amazing sights and sounds and head back to the hotel. With the sun so bright in this subtropical city and the air so thin because the city's elevation is so high, I am getting tired and ready for a nap.

Everything has gone along beautifully today, starting with my triumph over Roger in getting a luxurious carriage ride.

It's devious of me, but I can't help but chuckle as I envision the look on Roger's face when the clerk tells him his reservation has been canceled.

My only regret is that he probably will find a room elsewhere, or, worse, that he'll end up in a royal suite at a better hotel!

MEXICAN FAMILY
(*Six Months in Mexico*)

31

When I open my room door and step in, I find *Roger on my bed*.

"Wha—what—"

The door slams behind me as I stand frozen in shock. He's sprawled on my bed, smoking a pipe, with his head on my pillow, but worse than that, he's stripped down to a sleeveless undershirt, pants, and bare feet, reading a newspaper.

He takes the pipe out of his mouth and grins as he looks up.

"Had a hard day, dear?"

"You—you—you're finished, kaput!" I wave my hands wildly like a steam propeller. "I'm going to have you arrested. You'll spend the rest of your life in a Mexican prison making tortillas for big hombres."

Spinning around, I grab the door handle and jerk the door open.

"Better ask Mr. Madden if that's a good idea."

I freeze in place and let out an involuntary gasp. With my hand still on the doorknob, I turn around slowly.

That obnoxious, annoying grin of triumph is spread across his face.

"My friend in Pennsylvania contacted the *Dispatch* to let them know their star *foreign correspondent* is progressing well on her assignment. Funny thing, though . . . it seems that Madden, the paper's editor in chief, complained loudly that—"

With a bang that could have been heard by Lily Langtry in the heavens above, I send the door flying shut. Mustering all the strength and courage my five-foot frame can muster, I step forward, ready for battle.

"I will not be blackmailed."

"And I will not sleep in the gutter. That's what my sleeping arrangements became when you played your little joke."

"I—I'll talk to the clerk."

"I already talked to three clerks and the manager. *El presidente* would have been next, but then I realized I had this room."

"But you can't have my room. Where will I go?"

"Madam, there is a place where I would love to send you— unfortunately, I would definitely end up in that Mexican prison you keep threatening me with if I let my anger control my common sense. As for sleeping arrangements, this room is larger than the compartment we shared on the train."

"I will not share this room with you. It wouldn't be decent."

"Not decent? This big room?" He stares at his pipe as if it will answer the question on his face. "But the little train compartment was?"

"We were traveling. Men and women sleep in separate berths in the public area of Pullman cars. The compartment wasn't that far removed, and in case you don't remember, we had separate beds."

He sits up and puts his feet on the floor and taps tobacco out of his pipe into an ashtray on the nightstand beside the bed.

"I am not going to argue with you. You have once again created an intolerable situation." He smirks. "I'm beginning to wonder whether you are managing things so we are thrown together."

I let out a wounded animal's cry. "I would rather share a room with a snake than with you."

"No one says you have to share the room with me." He shrugs and again gives me his nasty smirk. "There's always the street."

"This—this is outrageous! Insane."

"No. Just not to your liking."

For the first time in a long time, I don't know what to do, what to say. I am a trapped animal, held at bay by strong chains. It makes no sense.

"Where will you sleep?" I ask.

He looks at the cot as if seeing it for the first time and then gestures at it with his hands. "Why, I'm going to sleep right here."

"But there's no place for me."

He grins. "You don't really believe I wouldn't think about your comfort, do you? I had the maid bring you bedding."

He indicates two blankets and a pillow stacked on the washstand.

He waves his hands at the floor. "Pick any spot you like."

There is murder in my heart. Rage. My breathing becomes labored. I can't see my face, but I know it has gone from white to red and now it must be a deep purple. If ever in my life I've been ready to strangle, mangle, or slice and dice a human being, this is the moment.

He recognizes the danger and speaks quietly. "Don't do anything hasty. Just remember, if Don Antonio finds out you lied about being a foreign correspondent, you can say adios to Mexico. And your career. Now this arrangement isn't perfect; I admit that. But it will work—for both of us. You'll see, just like on the train."

I swallow hard and think fast, my head nodding up and down as if it has springs on it. "I'll take the cot—"

"Sorry. Deal breaker."

"You can't expect a woman to sleep on the floor. Why, there'll be bugs on it."

He stares at the floor beneath his spread-out feet. A cockroach is crawling along it.

"I see what you mean."

He lifts a bare foot and stamps down, smashing the roach, then twists his foot to make sure the bug is really dead. He looks back up at me.

"You can use your hands or your feet. They squish real easy either way."

32

All night long, I lie on a hard floor, jerking awake repeatedly, keeping an eye out for spiders, scorpions, and whatever else they have in Mexico that stings or bites. Never have I welcomed a morning with such aggravation and fury.

As quickly as possible, I get out of the room, fleeing from Roger; otherwise, I fear I would have committed bodily harm as he nonchalantly lay in bed, starring up at the ceiling, smoking his pipe, after he had a peaceful night.

For certain, everyone in the reception area can hear my teeth grinding as I head for the front entrance and storm out into the street. Even the doorman turns away to avoid making eye contact as he holds the door open. Smart man.

I'm as angry at myself for letting Roger get the best of me as I am at his conniving and rudeness. Our relationship has degraded to pure blackmail—and I am the victim!

What awful luck! There are thirty-eight states in our great nation. The odds of bumping into someone who knows someone else who knows my editor has to be almost nil.

Regardless of how I slice it, the bastard has discovered my charade and can make demands of me at will. I'm doomed.

Since the moment I finagled a sleeping compartment for two so I could avoid sleeping upright on a hard seat for days, I have had nothing but bad luck, ill fortune, poor karma, everything that evil spirits can throw at me. In hindsight, I would rather have ridden on the roof of the train than be subjected to that man's whims.

Not knowing what to do or where to go, I wander aimlessly down endless streets, turning here and there, not really caring if I get lost or what time it is. I hate this helpless feeling.

Exhausted, I stop and take a deep breath. What am I doing? Here I am in this lovely, exotic city, and instead of enjoying it or giving it the concentration that is needed for writing articles about its colorful streets and people, I'm too caught up with my anger. This will get me nowhere.

I take another deep breath. "Move forward Nellie." I've never been one to cry over spilt milk—waste of time. Let him think he's won or at least has the upper hand. The real war has just begun. I've never been a quitter, nor given in to men. Roger has a lot to learn.

With my strong, in-control attitude restored, I soak up the atmosphere of the city, jotting down my impressions in pencil on a small tablet I carry, not at all concerned about how far I've ventured from the hotel, for there will always be a taxi available to get me back.

My one misgiving about leaving the hotel in such a rush is that I forgot Gertrude might contact me and arrange a time for us to meet. Hopefully, she didn't plan anything for today. I'm enjoying this time to myself.

As I trudge along in a neighborhood that is poor and much less crowded than the heart of the city, where I started, I feel a bit light-headed—probably because the day is quite warm and the air thin, making one feel giddy.

Giggling young girls start to dance around me, pulling at my skirt. Knowing they are just having fun, I let them lead me into an alley that opens into a much smaller square. It appears deserted, but I am suddenly surrounded by Mexican men, and the dancing girls are gone.

"What is it? What do you want?"

No answer comes from them. Instead, the men stare at me, strangely silent, their features impassive.

I don't like this at all.

They are dressed in the straw hats, white pants, and shirts typical of peons. Their features are expressionless, telling me nothing. I have no clue as to their intent.

Panic starts to grip me.

A young girl carrying a bouquet of flowers abruptly appears in front of me. She shoves the flowers in my face, violently shaking them, sending a powder at me.

To avoid the stuff, I put my hands in front of my face, but I know I've breathed in the dust, because I can feel my lungs burning.

I feel faint. As in a slow-motion dream, I find myself falling, soaring downward, as if I am a bird that has lost its wings, diving straight down into a bottomless black pit.

33

Murky black mist swirls around, gripping me. I spin with it, moving slower than the strange pandemonium that surrounds me, my vision distorted, my mind fouled.

I am no longer soaring downward without wings; instead, my whole being feels like it's suspended in a violent, twisting maelstrom. I have no control of my body—it is attached to me, but not mine.

Strange figures dart by as clawlike hands grope my body, pulling at my clothes. Try as I might, I don't have the strength to push them off. They dig into my flesh and I cry out in pain.

A wet, sticky, smelly hand covers my mouth, smothering any chance that a cry for help would be heard.

Chatty voices surround me, speaking in a strange tongue, as I'm being moved deeper and deeper into a void I fear I will never escape. Cold, wet dampness embraces me. I feel like I'm being prepared for death and there is nothing I can do.

The hand leaves my mouth, but I don't scream. A wave of courage inside stops me, gives me hope, telling me not to let them know my fear.

My eyes hurt as my vision starts to come back, blurred at first, then darting around as if I am a wild animal trapped and looking for a way of escape. Nothing comes into view except different shades of darkness. I realize I'm in a chamber of stone and mortar, some sort of concrete monster that has me entrapped in a murky hell.

Grotesque faces appear around me. Some are masks, others are animalistic—*faces of jaguars.*

I don't have the power to scream as my heart races out of control. A flash of fiery light—a torch—blinds me, and I close my eyes as voices in the strange language shout at me, saying things that I don't understand.

My eyes blink open again and the fire is gone, but I see another light ahead of me. I jerk forward, taking a step, trying to move out of the nightmare.

A strange force of panic and terror arises inside me and I scream and run like a wounded animal toward the light. The closer I get to it, the more it blinds me, but I keep running, stumbling forward.

As I burst out into bright daylight, I hear voices, exciting voices, not that awful chattering I was surrounded with. I try to run, but mostly stagger toward the voices. People—normal, everyday people jabbering in Spanish—gather around me.

Slowly, the dense mist in my mind is starting to clear, and I force myself to breathe deeply, to get life back into my body, but my knees buckle as my mind slips back into that dark, ugly void, and I feel myself freefalling.

34

F raulein . . . Nellie . . ."

I open my eyes and squint, trying to make the blurred features come into some kind of defined shape.

"Don't move."

The command is accented, but it's not a Spanish one.

I try to push the person hovering over me away.

"Lie still."

A wet towel is laid on my forehead.

"You passed out from the sun and might have hit your head when you fell."

I know exactly who is hovering over me, giving me instructions. I recognize the voice and the blurry countenance, but I just can't unite them together into a coherent thought. I close my eyes and slip back into the black void; only this time, it's not threatening.

ROGER IS IN THE ROOM when I arrive back at the hotel.

He takes one look at me, and jumps off the cot, tossing aside the newspaper he was reading.

"Good Lord, what happened to you? You look—are you all right?"

I don't have to be told that I look like something the cat dragged in.

"I passed out on the street. The sun, the food, the altitude, whatever. I was taken to a hospital."

"You poor thing. Here, lie down. The cot is yours."

"No, thank you." I grab my blankets to curl up on the floor.

"No, please, take the cot. Tell me what happened."

"That's about it. I passed out, and next thing I knew, I was at a hospital. The doctor said I was dehydrated. Do you mind if I freshen up?"

He leaves, again showing concern, wanting to know if he can get me anything. I am surprised. This is not the Roger I have learned to hate.

I slip off my dress and stand at the washbasin in my petticoat. I didn't necessarily have to send him out to keep him from seeing me in undergarments. I was raised with brothers and, like many women, in a pinch I don't consider it indecent to be seen in undergarments as long as the clothing hides my flesh and my shape.

I sent him out because I needed more time to think. My mind began racing with thoughts as soon as I got my senses back, and I need to sort them out.

The person who aided me on the streets, or at least supervised the aid given to me, was the man with the German accent and pack animals from the train. He and a woman took me to a nearby hospital in his carriage. The woman, the wife of a shopkeeper near where I fell, stayed with me until I saw the doctor. The German left before I had enough of my mental faculties back to thank him for his aid.

There was little wrong with me, and the doctor was probably right when he advised that I sorely needed liquids. But as soon as I had my wits back, I took a taxi to the police station.

It took a while to get a police officer who spoke enough English to have even a rough idea of what I was saying. I tried to explain that a girl had done something with a bunch of flowers to make me lose my senses.

When I told him about hideous creatures staring at me, he said, "*Sí,* señorita, many skeletons."

"No, they weren't Day of the Dead costumes," I told him, though I'd seen enough bones on the street to haunt my sleep for a long time to come. "Jaguars or people dressed as ones."

I didn't know how to say *were-jaguars,* and maybe that was for the better, for he clamped his mouth shut and looked away, pressing his lips together. I'm sure he had to smother a laugh.

"Perhaps they were going to rob you," he said, "and this foreign hombre, the one who helped you, stopped them."

I asked to speak to his supervisor, but it was useless. He translated for the senior officer, who listened and then simply nodded and tapped his head.

"*Sol,*" he said, again tapping his head.

Sunstroke.

When I arrived back at the hotel, I was as confused as I had been at the police station. I honestly don't know what to think. Had I been watched? Followed from the hotel until they saw an opportunity to ambush me? But why? Was there actually something deliberately put in the flowers that took my mind? Opium or something like it that robs one of one's senses? Or did I faint because I really did have a reaction to flower pollen, dehydration, and too much sun?

What about the beastly faces—or was my imagination fed by what I saw on the train?

I sit on the edge of the cot with my head in my hands, trying to make some kind of sense out of it all, but all that keeps flying at me are more questions: Where did the German man fit in, and how did he happen to be there at the right time?

Mexico City is not a small town. But he miraculously appeared when I fainted. I don't swallow that. Yet, what motive would he have had to have followed me? And then come to my rescue?

Mother's words of warning blare in my head: *Venture to where you are not wanted and you will get hurt. And you don't have nine lives like a cat.* Mother hates it when she says "Curiosity killed the cat" and my retort is "Satisfaction brought him back."

We haggled over my impulsiveness like children, but I'd better get satisfactory answers, or maybe Mexico will be the end of this kitten.

Since no answers are coming to me, I lie back down on the cot. I might as well get some much-needed sleep.

It seems like I had just closed my eyes when I'm awakened by knocking on the door. It's a bellman with flowers and a note with "Please Respond" written on the envelope.

> *Hope you feel better. Will you dine with me at eight? Hotel dining room.*
>
> > *Traven*

I write "Yes" on the note and give it back to the bellman. As I shut my door, I almost open it again to call him back. What am I thinking? I have no idea who Traven is. I just assumed that he's the German donkey man who came to my aid. Well, dinner in the hotel is a safe bet, even if he turns out to be an ax murderer.

I'm glad he contacted me, for I had been pondering how to contact him and thank him, and get some answers. I wonder if he is staying at this hotel.

A soft tapping comes and the door slowly opens. Roger sticks his head in.

"Nellie?"

"It's okay; come in."

He slips in and closes the door behind him. "I ordered a pitcher of fresh lemonade from room service for you. You need to keep fluids in you in this warm climate. It'll be up shortly."

"Thanks."

"And"—he holds up his index finger to emphasize his proclamation—"I have given a hotel clerk a large gratuity to find me a room anywhere in the city so that you can have this one all to yourself."

"Afraid you'll be murdered along with me?"

His face falls, and I am slammed with instant guilt. I don't know why I say these things.

"I'm only joking, Roger."

"Uh-huh." He notices the flowers.

"They just came. I think they're from the man who came to my rescue after I, uh, fainted."

"Who is he?"

"A German who got on the train when we stopped about an hour outside the city. He loaded goods onto the train from pack animals."

"I remember him. Nice of him to send flowers."

"He invited me to dinner, too."

"Hmm."

He takes off his shirt, tosses it aside, and sacks out on the cot. It's not hard to see he is peeved. Why, I am not sure. He can't be jealous?

"That's so nice of you." I try to heal his wounds. "For the room and the lemonade. And the cot."

His eyebrows rise and he gives me a puzzled look. "The cot?"

"Yes, you did offer me the cot."

"And I'm sure you enjoyed it, but you appear well now. Maybe your friend Traven has a spare cot."

"*You bastard.*" More of my description of his persona is interrupted by a knock on the door. My lemonade has arrived.

"Come in!" I snap at the door.

The door opens and Gertrude steps in.

"Nellie, darling, I'm so glad—" She stops cold and stares wide-eyed.

I'm in my petticoat and Roger is lying on the cot, decked out in his undershirt.

"I—I—" she fumbles, and backs out, closing the door behind her.

I howl something completely unladylike as I rush to the door. Opening it, I yell at Gertrude's back as she hurries down the corridor.

"Wait! I have an explanation!"

She stops and turns around slowly.

"I . . . I . . ." It's one of those rare moments when I am at a loss at what to say, so all I do is smile and say, "I'll explain later."

She grins and shakes her head. "I can hardly wait to hear what you dream up. Don Antonio is downstairs. We heard about your incident and came over to check on you, but you seem to be fine."

"Thank you. I'll be down in a moment."

I shut the door and turn back to Roger. "You almost did it."

He cocks his head and stares at me. "Did what?"

"Got me to like you. Fortunately, once again, you showed your true colors."

35

"You had us greatly concerned," Don Antonio says when I am seated at a corner table of the hotel café, where lunch is served.

The café is closed, but the consul general is important enough to get the three of us a table and refreshments.

Gertrude gives no clue that she has discovered once again that I am a fallen woman. To the contrary, from the glint in her eye and small, secretive smile, I do believe her opinion of me as an independent woman has risen to new heights.

"I was notified by the police department, but that word came only a short time ago," Don Antonio tells me.

I explain what happened, giving them the short version: I fainted from the sun and dehydration. I don't know what the police told him, but I hope it wasn't any more than what I offered, because I fear that Don Antonio will escort me to the train station and give me a one-way ticket to El Paso if he believes I am fantasizing about being attacked by bizarre mythical creatures from Mexican history.

It's evident from his rather official tone that I am on probation. If he knew what Gertrude knew about my "morals," he'd have me on that train pronto.

"How is your room?" Don Antonio asks. "Is it comfortable? The city is crowded, but I could—"

"It's okay, Uncle," Gertrude says, interrupting him. "I saw it. Very comfortable." She gives me a smile.

Damn—damn—damn. I know she's only trying to help, but I would have complained about the room, in the hopes of getting one where I didn't have to sleep on the floor.

He draws on his cigar and eyes me narrowly through the smoke. "The note from the chief of police said you were hallucinating when you arrived there from the hospital."

Taking a deep breath, I try to keep my voice calm and not reveal my panic as I give him a version of the truth. Not knowing how much he knows puts me in a bad spot. If he catches me in a lie, I'm doomed.

"I'm so embarrassed. All those stories about strange creatures on the train. I'm not exactly sure what I told the doctor or the police, but I think the heat and not being used to this high altitude affected me. I'm sure they got an earful of hallucinating gibberish."

I hope I was vague enough not to excite his interest further on exactly what I did say.

"I can understand that," Gertrude pipes up. "It was a really strange journey—that old prospector going missing and all that. Then there're all the walking horrors on the streets as the town gets ready for the Day of the Dead. It's completely understandable. I think we should get together tomorrow, Nellie." She turns to her uncle and gives him a loving smile. "You'll give us a list of nice things to see, won't you, Uncle?"

"Oh course, my dear." He smile and nods, but there is something in the way he stares at me with half-closed eyes that makes me nervous.

"Great! You get a good night's sleep, Nellie." She gives me a wink. "We'll meet up in the afternoon. I have a commitment for lunch, but I will come by about two."

I let out a little sigh and tell them truthfully, "All I want to do for the rest of my time in Mexico is see the many wonderful things the country has to offer and share them with my readers."

It isn't just a little bit of sugar for Don Antonio. The truth is that I have no intention of getting into any more messes, and I decide to cement this by taking a bold step.

"Would you do me a great favor?" I ask Don Antonio. "I am so thrilled about what I've already seen, especially the delightful festival honoring the dead that's coming up, would you mind reading my first article before I wire it to my paper?"

I am so pleased with myself for figuring out a way to reassure him of my good intentions so I don't get thrown out of the country, I grin like a banshee.

"Of course, señorita. It will be my pleasure. In fact, it will be my honor to assist you with *all* your articles. I will instruct the post office that your transmittals must all come through me first."

Now I've really done it. Me and my big mouth.

36

As I reach the bottom of the hotel stairs at dinnertime, the man who tried to whip the donkey and who came to my aid on the street is waiting.

"Fräulein, what a pleasure it is to see you again."

He kisses my hand.

"Nice to see you, too . . . when I'm not lying on the ground."

He chuckles. "The sun, the water . . ."

I groan. "If I hear about the sun or anything else one more time, I will run out of this hotel screaming."

He stares at me, speechless, and I give him a smile to break the ice I've created. "*Guten Abend,* Herr Traven."

"Ah, I see you also speak German. You are a woman of many talents." He smiles and takes my hand as we head for the dining room.

"Thank you, but I must warn you, I speak very little of your language. *Muy poquito,* as the Mexicans would say. Where I'm from, we have German-speaking neighbors who are called Pennsylvania Dutch. Don't ask me why they're called Dutch. From Deutsch, I guess. It's from them I have picked up a few phrases. Very nice people. And they don't whip their animals."

"Are you ever going to forgive me for that moment of frustration?"

"It's the donkey's forgiveness you should ask for."

"Good enough. After we have dinner, I will find a jackass and beg for absolution."

"There may be one right here in the hotel I could introduce you to." I am thinking of Roger, of course.

We are seated before I ask him a question that's been puzzling me. "I'm curious. Is Traven your first or last name?"

"Both. It keeps things simple."

It always intrigues me when people are vague about their names. This usually means they have a good reason—often connected to avoiding the police. I'd like to know what his is.

"No. I'm not on the run from the police."

"You read minds?"

"Only through a person's eyes. I saw the thought churning in your brain."

"And what is a gentleman from Germany doing with pack animals in rural Mexico?"

"I'm an archaeologist, conducting a dig. And you are in Mexico for . . ."

"I'm a foreign correspondent for *The Pittsburgh Dispatch*. But I'm sure you already knew that."

"Yes. I heard about you on the train."

Oh great.

"I can see your mind working again, Nellie. In answer to the question in your head, yes, I heard that you are a hysterical woman who was seeing things because she had too much to drink. Champagne, I believe. A good vintage, I'm told. But I also heard that the American man—someone called him a gold prospector—you saw go off the train actually was missing."

"Then you must have also heard that because of my fragile female constitution, I suffered such severe mental trauma that I was imagining strange creatures that attack and kill people."

"Something of that nature. But after verbally dueling with you over a donkey, I don't believe you are any more fragile than anyone else who witnesses traumatic events."

I sit back as if I am relaxed, but I can't help but tense up. I don't know how to take him. He's not taunting me. To the contrary, I get the impression that he's opening the subject for discussion. There is something behind the dinner invitation besides inquiring about my health after the incident today. But I don't know where to direct the conversation, because I know almost nothing about him. I don't want word to get back to Don Antonio that I talk incessantly about Mexican creatures from nightmares.

"I want to thank you for your assistance today. I don't know what would have happened if you hadn't come along."

NO JOB FOR A LADY

"You would have been all right. Not speaking the language fluently would have posed something of a problem, but Mexican people are generally quite helpful and would have gotten you to the hospital. But I was happy to be in the area. Fortunately, the artifacts I brought from my dig are stored near where you fainted."

Well, that answers one of my questions. I suspect he knew I was going to ask how he happened along; otherwise, he wouldn't have offered the information.

The waiter arrives and converses in Spanish with Traven. This is fine with me because it gives me a breather. Things are moving too fast. I have no idea if he's telling the truth about his being in the area when I passed out, but I also have no reason to doubt him . . . except that it is a coincidence. And I don't like coincidence.

They stop conversing and Traven looks at me. "He recommends foie gras, salad nicoise, roasted quail with cherries, garlic *pommes frites*—"

"*Frijoles con queso, cebollas,* and tortillas. With salsa," I add.

Traven purses his lips and nods. "Beans with cheese, onions, tortillas, and salsa."

The waiter gives a worried look and rattles something off to Traven.

"He wants to know if you're certain—"

"Yes. Tell him I'm a peon at heart."

He does—at least I understood that the word *peon* was used in his statement to the waiter.

The waiter leaves, shaking his head.

Traven chuckles. "He has to speak to the chef. But I can assure you they will accommodate you. However, I have to warn you—they won't have your selection in the kitchen unless it's left over from lunch served to the staff. They probably will send someone to the marketplace to get your dinner."

Oh my, I hope he is wrong. One of the first things I noticed when I went out today was that on almost every street corner, women were on their knees, mashing corn between smooth stones, making it into a thick batter, and finally shaping it into round, flat cakes. I was shocked when they spit on their hands to keep the dough from sticking. They fry the tortillas in a pan of hot grease, kept heated by a few lumps of charcoal.

I love tortillas, but, like eating a chicken leg, I don't need to know how it got to the table.

What also amazed me is that both the rich and poor buy and eat the street-made tortillas, unmindful of the way they are made. But it is a bread that Americans must be educated to. Many Americans surprise the Mexicans by refusing even a taste after they see how they are made. When one elderly tortilla lady offered me one, I couldn't refuse. With that look on her face, I felt like I was insulting her. To my surprise, it was delicious.

"What brings a German here to Mexico and not to Egypt to dig up the past?"

"In my case, a lust to experience life in many directions. I was a deck officer on a steamer, but I jumped ship in Alexandria and met an archaeologist at a hotel. He invited me to go up the Nile with him to Luxor and a dig in the Valley of the Kings. I believe the main reason for the invitation was because of security. I know how to shoot a gun.

"As you probably know, most practical archaeology is learned in the field rather than in the classroom. I discovered I liked digging up the past and learned quickly on the job. But I soon found that the Egyptian field was too crowded with university archaeologists being financed by wealthy collectors and rich museums. It takes wealthy backers to dig in Egypt, because the fees paid to the government are high and digs normally take years. The progress is counted in years because the easily found artifacts have long since been removed. Years on a single dig to find a few artifacts was too slow for me."

"Then why are you still an archaeologist?"

"It got in my blood. I relish restoring the past, finding objects built by human hands a hundred or a thousand years ago and still in good condition. When I handle relics, I sense a little bit of the maker in them.

"I heard from other Europeans about how free and open Mexico is, and their colorful history is not well known. So I decided to give it a try. And I'm very glad I did. There are still political and bureaucratic bottlenecks to deal with, but the fees are minimal compared to those in Egypt and there's little competition."

He shrugs and gives a slight look of frustration. "That was five years ago. It's still a struggle, but there are some wealthy collectors of Mesoamerican artifacts, and I have made a connection with one."

"And who is this wealthy collector?"

"Ah, Miss Bly . . . It is Miss, isn't it?"

"Yes, and will stay that way for a while longer. I'm busy building my career."

"Smart woman. I also am too busy building my career to consider other pleasures."

"You're avoiding my question."

"No, just not answering it."

"And why not? A man of means is helping you uncover the past. I'm sure he would appreciate some publicity, giving him credit for using his money for some good."

Traven shakes his head. "No, archaeological digs are a cutthroat business. Where to dig and who will pay for it are trade secrets that are fiercely guarded and defended. It's a treasure hunt and is as closely guarded as a pirate's treasure map."

"Or an old prospector's one."

Here I go again. It just popped out, but I could see from his face that I had hit right on the nose the reason he invited me to dinner.

37

My peon's dinner is served on silver plates and looks fit for a queen. And it is delicious. The chef added a sweet corn tamale that is delectable.

However, my comment about the prospector hung over the meal like the proverbial "skeleton at the feast," adding a sprinkle of suspense to the dinner because neither of us addressed the remark, letting it dangle in front of us but just out of reach.

We both had custard for dessert, he a French crème brûlée and I the Mexican flan with caramel poured over it.

When the plates were cleared, Traven suggested a spicy chocolate drink made from cacao that has peppers added.

"Mexico produces the finest chocolate drinks in the world from its cacao trees. It's an ancient drink that predates the conquest. They say Montezuma drank a couple dozen cups a day."

"Maybe he should have given Cortés a cup of it with some hemlock sprinkled in."

"All right, you win."

"What have I won?"

"That I have to volunteer information before you do. You deliberately avoided following up with your comment about the prospector, waiting to see if I would crack first."

"Isn't that why you invited me to dinner? To pump me about what I know about Howard, the prospector, treasure hunter, camp cook, whatever he is or was, and his map to Montezuma's hoard?"

"In my defense, I am only half guilty. I invited you to dinner because you are an attractive woman and I wanted to know more about you and the challenging career you have chosen. And I wanted to know more about the prospector."

"Why are you interested in him?"

"Isn't it obvious, Fräulein? He was a treasure hunter. I am a treasure hunter. That is what an archaeologist does—he seeks buried treasure, though not for the same reasons as those who hunt only for precious metals. If Montezuma's treasure does exist, it would be a great archaeological find."

"I've been told that you can buy a map like his, if he really did have one, for a peso on the street."

"True, and I've been offered ones that appear so genuine that only the fact there was no treasure where they showed proves they are frauds. No, it's not the map that first caught my interest, but the jaguar."

"Really? Well, you are the first to have any interest in that subject. The consensus is that I was hallucinating. Too much champagne."

"I believe you saw a were-jaguar."

I almost choke on the chocolate drink. Besides Gertrude, he is the first person to just blatantly say the word, and he wants to talk about it. This is both interesting and puzzling, but I'm cautious about launching into the subject, saying things that might get back to Don Antonio. The subject isn't really settled in my mind, either. The fact is, I've seen two different creatures—one was an obvious mask and the other I don't know how to describe except that it was infinitely more frightening.

"Nellie, I'm not suggesting that you saw some mythical beast of the night."

"Than what are you saying?"

He proceeds to tell me pretty much what I had already heard from Gertrude—that the Cult of the Jaguar was formed to drive out the Spanish after the conquest and that from it grew legends about magician-priests who could shape-change into the big jungle cats.

"In Nahuatl, the Aztec language, the priests able to transform into jaguars were magicians called *nawals*. Many people believe *nawals* still exist. Mexico is still very primitive in most rural areas, with people having some beliefs not much different from those of their Aztec ancestors."

"Do you believe these shape-changing magicians really exist?"

"I've seen ones villagers claim are *nawals*, but I've never seen anyone change shape from man to beast. But as I said, there are plenty of people in this country who do believe it, more than you'd find in Europe, where many people believe werewolves exist."

"Are you telling me that a *nawal* killed the prospector?"

"Someone killed the prospector. You saw a struggle. And accusations that you had had too much champagne are nonsense. No one wants to believe you saw a creature, because they would have to admit there actually is a spirit world where things they don't understand exist." He hesitates. "As for who attacked the man . . ." He shakes his head. "I leave open the possibility that there are things I've never seen that can only be described as bizarre, but I also only acknowledge what my five senses tell me. The only transformation from man to jaguar I've seen has mostly been accomplished by street entertainers."

" 'Mostly'?"

We are already speaking in a low tone, and he lowers his voice even more to a very confidential note.

"Mexico has not been kind to its rich archaeological treasures. Like Egypt and other poor countries with a glorious past, it has permitted foreigners to come in and take them."

He has dodged my question, but I let it go for the moment. He obviously doesn't want to address it yet. "Like someone taking the Liberty Bell from America or the Magna Carta from England?" I ask.

"No, not at all. The historical treasures of rich nations are not just guarded; they are protected from thieves, negligence, and the ravages of the elements. That isn't the case in nations where most of the people are desperately poor and the preservation of artifacts takes bread from them. In this country, it's not unusual for a farmer to break up an ancient monument containing irreplaceable artwork to build a rock wall.

"And before you pass judgment on me and archaeologists around the world who find ancient artifacts and ship them home, keep in mind that most of those irreplaceable, often priceless relics wouldn't survive if they were not removed and safely stored in museums and private collections outside the poor country where they are being battered."

There's logic to what he's saying. But in a perfect world, the rich people and institutions would build museums in the poor countries to shelter the antiquities. That way, people could see their own glorious past and maybe get a spark of pride from it. However, I don't want to antagonize him with my egalitarian ideals when he hasn't finished telling me about bloodsucking creatures of the night, so I nod my head in vague agreement.

"I apologize," he says. "I didn't mean to go off on a tangent, but this is something I have been struggling with ever since I got involved in archaeology. Are you familiar with the concept of *mordida*?"

"No."

"*Mordida* means 'bite.' It's a bribe given to a public official, like a judge or tax collector, to avoid fines and taxes. A system of that oils the wheels in this country and most other poor countries. In the case of antiquities, we pay the bite to get permits granted so we can excavate ruins and ship out what we find."

I wouldn't be surprised to learn that Don Antonio gets *mordida*. If Traven's rich "angel" is an American, it's almost certain that Traven is shipping the relics through El Paso. They wouldn't get through if Don Antonio gave it a thumbs-down.

"We don't take everything. Only the best," Traven continues. "I can see from the look on your face and the way your hands are wringing that napkin that you are considering strangling me for being a thief of history. But please take into consideration that what I don't save will probably end up on the rubble pile of history."

"I understand. You are a great humanitarian who is saving the history of Mexico by sending it to a rich foreigner who will show it only to his family and close friends, none of whom, I presume, is Mexican or has even visited the country. Is that about the sum of it?"

"Fair enough, Fräulein. Without the sarcasm."

"So what does the money bite and saving history's relics have to do with an old prospector and were-jaguars?"

"May I give you some advice before I respond to your cross-examination? Don't even think about entering the diplomatic corps. I suspect you would start more wars than avoid them."

I can't help but laugh, not a "ha-ha," but nice laughter of relief. "You're right, Traven. I'm tired. And achy. I feel as if I've been put through a wringer. I apologize."

"Fair enough. But you still think I'm a scoundrel. Perhaps you should come out to Teotihuacán and see for yourself the state of preservation of Mexican antiquities."

"Maybe I will."

"Let me know if you decide to come and I will make the arrangements. In regard to the prospector, I would greatly appreciate if it you would tell me exactly what you saw. I heard only the barest details on the train."

"Because no one believed me."

"Exactly. In return for taking the trouble to educate me, I will share information with you."

"Fair enough." And I go into all I remember to describe what I saw that night.

"And you're certain it was a face, not a bag on his shoulder?"

"Absolutely. But it might have been a mask."

"That's what I am wondering. I take it you haven't seen the performers who portray Aztec Jaguar Knights for the tourists in the main square. You should have a look and see if there is any similarity."

"I'll do that. I also saw something else. After I defended your donkey, when I was going back to the train, someone was watching me."

"Someone dressed as a jaguar?"

"I don't know how to put it, but there was something, someone . . . scarier, more chilling. More like . . . like . . ."

"A man-beast."

"Yes. At least not an obvious mask."

"That is what I want to share with you." Traven looks at me intently. "I told you we get official permission to remove antiquities by paying *mordida* to officials. But there are some elements of society that want to stop us."

"The Cult of the Jaguar?"

"Perhaps. I haven't seen what you saw on the train or outside the train, but I have been having trouble at the dig. Workers have been scared off. I've had to hire guards. And rumors are swirling. There are claims that were-jaguars were seen."

He shakes his head. "After years of digging at a number of different sites in the region, this came up suddenly after I relocated to Teotihuacán a few months ago."

"Maybe you're close to something that somebody wants to protect."

"If that's the case, they know more than I do. Teo is the largest and most important archaeological site in Mexico, but most of its relics are too large to move."

He stares at me for a moment. "You keep nodding your head and pursing your lips as if you're mulling over something—what?"

"Try this on for size. You think the old prospector really did have a map because there was no reason to kill him unless he did. And you're wondering if that map showed Montezuma's treasure as being in Teo. And if he said something about Teo to me."

"Did he?"

He deserved an answer for helping me on the street, and I gave it. "No. But I have one more impression. You're wondering if you're going to be murdered by zealots who want to keep the country's antiquities from being stolen by foreigners. Besides the fanatics dressing up as were-jaguars to scare off your workers, you're worried that they might come around one day and have you make a blood sacrifice."

I sure know how to say things that bring a conversation to a complete halt.

38

I stop at the front desk to speak to the night clerk after parting from Traven and getting my hand kissed again. I like the way Europeans treat women, though I've heard they often behave more chivalrously toward other women than toward their own wives.

Even though our conversation ended abruptly, I was able to ask Traven if his hotel, which is up the street from mine, had any empty rooms—I was thinking maybe I'd get lucky and find a room for Roger. No such luck. As far as he knew, the hotel was full up.

"Where can I find information about the Aztecs, Montezuma, and antiquities that predate the conquest?" I ask the clerk. "A library won't do. I can't read Spanish."

He ponders the question for a moment. "Museo Azteca."

Ah. An Aztec museum. Perfect. Why didn't I think of that? If tourists go there, someone must speak English. He writes down the address so that I can give it to a cabbie in the morning.

"*Gracias.*"

Usually, I would bounce up the flights of steps, but tonight I'm bushed. I still feel like I've been put through a laundry wringer and every ounce of energy I had has been wrung out—again.

I'm not surprised, yet I'm disappointed to find Roger still in residence, asleep on top of the covers with his clothes on when I enter. A book on his chest indicates he'd been reading before dozing off.

I hold my tongue and refrain from saying something caustic about his earlier promise to find another room even if he had to sell his body on the streets. Those weren't his exact words, but the thought reflects my own feelings as to what he should resort to in order to get out of my room, if he is a gentleman.

"Message slipped under the door." He nods at a pink envelope atop the blankets I will use again to sleep on the hard floor.

"You're awake."

"Brilliant deduction."

I ignore his sarcastic remark and pick up the envelope. My name is written on the top of fine stationery in an elaborate swirl. "From Gertrude," I mutter to myself.

As I slip the note out, my eye goes to the bold signature at the end of the short note before I even read the contents. I gasp.

"What's the matter?" Roger bolts up on the bed. "You all right?"

"Lily Langtry."

"What about Lily Langtry? You look like you've seen a ghost. Did she die?"

"She's inviting me to lunch."

He stares at me for a moment, as if he's unable to grasp what I said. Then slowly and mechanically, he says, "Lily Langtry invited you to lunch."

"Lily Langtry invited me to lunch."

It's unbelievable. I check the envelope and note again in case I made a mistake. No question. It's signed with her name. And the stationery must have cost a pretty penny. It has to be from her.

"Why?" Roger asks the question, but it is the same one buzzing in my head, except his tone implies that she has contacted me about scrubbing her floors rather than about my being a newspaper reporter.

"No doubt she found out that I am also staying in the hotel," I say haughtily, "and wishes to have me interview her for an article. People in Pittsburgh are quite familiar with the who and what of London, Paris, and New York."

"Well, I would think so. I'm sure that Nellie Bly of *The Pittsburgh Dispatch* is known all the way to . . ." He grins. "The city limits?"

I'VE NEVER BEEN ONE to be in a sweet disposition when I wake in the morning, especially when I've had broken sleep. This morning, I'm in a particularly foul mood. I had been asleep only a couple of hours when I felt something much larger than a cockroach sitting on top of me.

When I struck a match from the box I keep next to me to check on crawling critters, I found myself staring into the shiny eyes of a gray mouse. He probably was more scared than I was, but I sent him flying.

Had it been a rat, I would have marched downstairs and slept on a lobby couch if the clerk couldn't find me a room, but I was raised on a farm, and house mice I can handle. However, that little mouse spiked up my adrenaline and getting back to sleep was impossible. Instead, my mind kept running my conversation with Traven over and over through my head. It didn't set right with me. And neither does an invitation from one of the most famous and glamorous women in the world. Why does she want to have lunch with me?

The sarcasm from that bastard snoring on the only bed in the room hit home. It would be a cold day in hell before a woman with her international stature gave an interview to a girl reporter from a newspaper known far and wide . . . in Pittsburgh.

Some game is being played—cat and mouse. Or is it jaguar and Nellie?

It started on the train with a man being killed and then tossed off by what appeared to be a creature of the night. And it followed me to a gruesome attack on a cobblestone street in Mexico City. Now an invitation arrives that both excites and thrills me.

In all honesty, I should be dizzy with pleasure at the prospect of interviewing Lily Langtry, and I am—if I just knew what the invitation is for. I don't think one of the world's most famous actresses wants to talk about were-jaguars with me. Montezuma's treasure would be another thing. Being rich and having everything never keeps people from wanting more.

To quote Shakespeare or someone else wordy like that, methinks that there is a game afoot here and I am a pawn about to be the sacrificial lamb.

Or . . . maybe I am just being paranoid and the woman actually does want some publicity about her Mexico trip. Maybe she doesn't know that Pittsburgh is not a hub of the universe.

And maybe I am kidding myself.

Instead of puttering around leisurely in the morning, which I normally do to bring life back into my mind and body, I quickly get up and hurry out the door before Roger wakes up. Not only does his presence put me in more of a sour mood but I may strangle him.

39

A cabbie deposits me in front of a building that looks more like a palace than a museum.

The outside walls are thick masonry, but they are a unique and stunning reddish color. The main entrance and portal are done in a grayish white stone, as is the central balcony. The elaborate portals are Baroque. But what interests me most is that the columns rest on clawed feet that have above them netherworld lionlike stone faces that appear to leer up at anyone who enters.

Squatting down, I examine the not quite human faces to see if they have the jaguar features I've been encountering.

"Buenos días, señorita."

I look up, to find a tall and lanky elderly gentleman with bushy white hair that is pulled back in a ponytail.

"Buenos días, señor. Uh, *hablas Inglés?"*

"Far too little now that we get occasional *norteamericano* visitors," he says with only the slightest accent, "but I spent some time in Texas. Forgive my manners." He politely gives me a hand to help me up. "I have not introduced myself. I am Francisco Guerrero y Torres, curator for this museum."

"A pleasure to meet you. I'm Nellie Bly." I choose not to tell him I'm a newspaper reporter, out of fear that it would put him on guard and make him less inclined to speak uncensored.

"What brings you to our museum, Señorita Bly?"

"The love of history. I'd like to increase my very inadequate knowledge of Mexican history prior to the conquest. I was told your museum holds some of the finest pieces of Mexican art."

I hadn't been told anything of the kind, but I hope my compliment will open the door. His answer surprises me.

"Then you must allow me to give you a personal tour."

"I'd love that. What are these creatures at the foot of the columns? Are they jaguars?"

"No, jaguars are the jungle cats only of the New World. These are not Mexican, but European. They are called chimeras. You probably best know them as gargoyles. The creatures were designed to frighten away evil spirits so they wouldn't enter a building. Protectors, you might say."

He points at a symbol on the wall of the entrance. "However, this is definitely Aztec."

It appears to me to be a drawing of part of a head, but without a face. Very plain and simple, it looks as if a child could have scribbled it.

"As you know," he continues, "the Aztecs used picture writing. This is the name glyph of Montezuma the Second, the emperor who thought Cortés was a returning god. The symbol shows a crown, nosepiece, ear spool, and speech scroll. When it appears in print or on a wall, you know it is the emperor's name."

The museum entryway opens to a Spanish-style courtyard that is large enough to fit the Cochran's Mills house I lived in until I was six. It is two-storied, with the rooms of the upper level set back from a wide balcony with a black wrought-iron railing. The balcony is supported by the columns of a veranda that runs the length of the ground floor. Brilliant red bougainvillea interlaced with fragrant white jasmine covers the veranda railing and races up the columns.

The courtyard is paved with light gray tiles that have a brownish tint. In the center is a fountain where a stern Neptune is attacking a sea monster with his three-pronged spear as pink and white water lilies float on the pond's surface.

The only evidence that we are in a museum rather than in the home of an aristocrat are stone edifices of the past that are lined up in front of the veranda all the way around the courtyard.

At first glance, it is obvious that the relics of a grand past have not been treated well by man or time. They are chipped and broken, not unlike the archaeological treasures I've seen in books from other civilizations. But even though the pictures I've seen of the Venus de Milo in Paris show both of her arms broken off, the Aztec warrior nearest me looks worse for wear even though he's missing only one hand. With many chips and dirt and dust still encrusted, he conveys the impression that he had returned battered from a battle he didn't fare well in.

Broken pieces of what had been statues of people, animals, and creatures from nightmares are rather haphazardly scattered about. There is neither order nor serious care given to any of these relics. Quite sad, but I suppose the fact that they have been taken from farmers' fields and brought within the museum walls are the most that can be done in this poor country.

The courtyard, fountain, and building itself all have something of a look of abandonment—that at some time in the distant past, they became dilapidated as the ordinary upkeep was ignored by the owners. Yet still, there is a tattered but elegant beauty to the mansion, like a rose pressed between the pages of a book and forgotten.

"The museum occupies only the courtyard and some rooms on the ground floor," he tells me as I look around. "The second floor is the residence of the family who own this grand house. They are the descendants of the conquistador who built it after the conquest. As a warrior of the conquerors, he shared in some of the great wealth Cortés and his small army of Spaniards gathered. Many of the conquistadors or their descendants built fine houses like this in the city or on the vast haciendas they were awarded.

"The house has been passed down from generation to generation, but times have changed and they can no longer afford the upkeep, so they are letting us use the bottom half. Fortunately, a few of my countrymen still treasure their glorious history enough to generously pay the rent."

From the state of the maintenance and the lack of care given to the antiquities, it is pretty obvious that the donors are either not that rich or not that generous.

The curator reminds me of a priest trying to keep alive an old church whose parishioners have abandoned it. I notice a donation box near the entrance. On my way out, I will put some pesos in it.

As we walk down the row of antiquities, he waves his hand in a gesture that takes in the entire place.

"As you can see, diminishing fortunes over time have left the place needing much repair. It would take *mucho dinero* to bring it back to its original glory." He chuckles. "The kind produced by a prosperous silver mine, not a museum, no?"

"I don't suppose many museums are moneymaking endeavors."

"Wealthy *norteamericano* and *alemán* museums are serious collectors of the archaeological treasures of my country. So are wealthy private collectors."

I recognized *alemán* as the Spanish word for German. "By serious collectors, I assume you are talking about rich foreigners buying up your antiquities?"

"Stealing them is a more accurate description, señorita. It's a battle to get pieces into this little museum before they are put on a train to the United States or on a ship to Europe." He gestures at the stone edifices. "These are ones I won the race with. But so many others, often the very finest antiquities, leave the country, with custom officers looking the other way."

He rubs his thumbs and fingers together in a universal gesture of money. "*Mordida*. The curse is not just of Mexico but of all the countries of Latin America."

Bribery of public officials certainly isn't unknown in the States, but *mordida* appears to have been made a part of the national culture here—so much so that's it's done without affecting one's conscience.

"If I wanted to sell some of the finest pieces in here to foreigners, I could indeed build a proper museum. But for what purpose? I would have lost some of our history that no money could replace."

"Is the archaeologist Traven one of those removing historical artifacts from the country?" I already know the answer, but I'm curious about his opinion of the man.

"All archaeologists are thieves."

Well, that's a blunt reply that says little. "What made you take on what must be a thankless task of preserving your country's physical history?"

Being a person who is driven to accomplish something of importance— something that makes a difference, especially for women—I always wonder what the fire is in the belly of others who take on extraordinary tasks.

"I started working for a foreign archaeologist some years ago. I had been a schoolteacher, but I knew little about the amazing history of my *indio* ancestors. However, besides my own language, I spoke English and Nahuatl. The *indio* tongue helped not only in dealing with workers, many of whom know little Spanish, but also in reading the hieroglyphic word pictures of the Nahuatl-speaking Aztecs.

"I grew angry as I watched so much history Mexican children would never know disappear because the only evidence of it was being exported to faraway lands." He grimaces with distaste. "I was more disgusted with the greed and corruption of my own people than with the foreigners'.

"They didn't care that these pieces of history belonged to all of us—those alive today and to our descendants a thousand years from now. It is the duty of every generation to preserve our cultural treasures and pass them on so future generations can admire and, more important, learn from them."

"So you started a museum, a vault to store them in so they would be safe, and began gathering pieces."

He chuckles. "The road was a bit more twisted than that. At a foreign archaeologist's dig, we came across a particularly fine specimen of Quetzalcóatl, the Feathered Serpent." He walks me over to a motif that appears to come off a wall. "This snarling snake is an example of the god, but the piece we found was a statue of its head several feet tall and in fine condition. That night when the piece was sitting on a wagon waiting to be carted to the train station for a trip across the border, I got on the cart and drove it to *el presidente*'s palace here in the city."

"What a wonderful story! And I imagine that was the first piece for your museum. May I see it?"

"I'm afraid not. I was arrested for theft. But, señorita, some good did come out of my rash act. The piece never left Mexico, though it also has never seen the inside of a museum. It now protects the doorway to *el presidente*'s hacienda." He shrugs philosophically. "But my effort attracted the attention of several wealthy people who have since helped me save more pieces of our history."

Another man, younger than the curator, enters.

"Ah, señorita," the curator gives me an apologetic smile, "my assistant José is back. I have an important matter that requires my immediate attention. José will finish the tour of our house of antiquities. Your pardon, *por favor*." He turns to José before leaving. "Show Señorita Bly our collection."

"My pleasure. This way, señorita."

José's breath smells like tacos and beer. While Torres is dressed in a very simple manner—loose white cotton pants and shirt and sandals, similar to how I've seen peons dressed for church—José's hair is unkempt, as are his clothes. No doubt a person of José's questionable character is all the museum can afford.

"Is there something in particular you would like to see, señorita?"

"Yes. Montezuma's treasure."

"Ah! When you find it, call me. I will help you carry it."

"For the museum?"

"Of course." He grins. "After I buy a grand hacienda and the finest horses in all Mexico, all in the line of the battle stallion Cortés himself rode into battle."

"Actually, there is something I want to see. A were-jaguar."

I watch his face as I speak. His eyebrows go up, but his features reveal little—he has too much beer in his belly to show any more emotion than an intoxicated smirk.

To my surprise, he says, "Come, I will show you."

He takes me into a room filled with more statues that have either a missing finger, arm, leg, foot, head, heads, or all of these—and with chips all over them. None is in perfect condition, but like a child with a defect, that makes them all the more beautiful.

I follow him over to a green stone head.

"This is your were-jaguar."

The hair on the back of my neck goes straight up and my right knee starts shaking. The features are not those of the circuslike masks that I've been told street entertainers wear.

It's not a mask at all.

Rather, the shape of the head is pretty much human—or at least humanistic. No one would confuse the features for those of an animal. Heinous, for sure. Something from the dark side of nature, or more likely some dreaded other world. But the animalism to be found in it is subtle—square lines of the jaw, fat lips above teeth that are not fangs yet are meant for more ripping than what people can do. And the eyes: The almond-shaped eyes don't stare; they pierce. They entrap me, locking me in a stare-down with the stone entity.

I've seen the creature before—in the fog, after I chastised Traven about the donkey. And now I'm certain I saw the same creature or its brother yesterday after my mind was robbed by what I still believe to be a mind-stealing opiate.

"Ugly, no?" José says.

"I don't know if I would call it ugly. It's not pleasant to look at, that's for sure. Monstrous, perhaps. Like the werewolf, it's neither really man nor beast, but a miscue by nature."

He nods as if he understands what I am talking about, but I think I have rambled beyond his comprehension of English.

"José, what can you tell me about were-jaguars?"

"They are creatures of the night left over from the days of our Aztec ancestors. *Indio* magicians eat mushrooms and turn into the creatures during the hours of darkness. They drink the blood of children and flay their skin like Xipe."

"Xipe?"

"An Aztec god who skinned himself alive in order to be reborn. Aztec priests used to skin some sacrifice victims and wear their skin. The lucky ones just got their hearts ripped out."

"I've been told the Aztecs killed thousands every year. I can't help wondering how the people felt when they walked up those pyramid steps, knowing that their hearts were going to be ripped out."

"They had joyous thoughts because of dream dust."

"What's that?"

"It's a powder mixed together by *indio* magicians. It makes a person helpless but happy."

"Helpless and happy . . ." Those neck hairs rise again as I feel angry and puzzled. "How was it applied?"

"The murals I've seen show a priest shaking the dust in the face of a victim before the person starts up the pyramid stairs."

"A priest or a little girl with a bunch of flowers."

"Señorita?"

"Nothing." I smile thinly. "Just thinking aloud."

As we walk along, he tells me about various relics, but my mind is churning. Dream dust. Were-jaguars.

"Here is Montezuma's treasure."

His words jerk me out of my concentration. "What did you say?"

"This is called a calendar round." He points at a round stone with markings. "It was used by the Aztecs to tell the date, as we would use a calendar. The most famous one is said to be made of solid gold."

"On top of the Pyramid of the Sun. And it disappeared."

"*Sí*, señorita. And I have a map that shows you where it is. I will sell it to you for a mere five pesos." He laughs at his own joke.

"What about the Cult of the Jaguar? Do you know about that?"

The pleasant alcoholic buzz he'd been glowing with suddenly disappears. He straightens up and glances around.

"I don't know what you mean."

Uh-huh. I pull five pesos out of my pocket. "I'll take some information instead of the treasure map."

He licks his lips. "I . . . I don't know."

I count another five pesos into my hand. "The Cult of the Jaguar."

I hold out the money and he grabs it and puts it in his pocket.

"You must not tell my uncle."

Well, that explains how he managed to get this job.

"I won't tell your uncle."

He shoots a look around to make sure we are still alone. "No one talks about the cult."

"Are they afraid?"

"Afraid?" He shrugs as he contemplates the question. "Perhaps. Mostly, it is taboo because it will bring bad luck. Some say the cult doesn't exist. Others say that it is still here, willing to murder to protect Mexico."

"What do you say?"

"Me? I say nothing." His voice drops to a whisper. "If you want to know about the Cult of the Jaguar, you will have to speak to La Bruja."

"Who is La Bruja?"

"A witch."

"Are you serious?"

"They say she is a *nawal,* a priestess of black magic who is able to shape-change. That's why they call her La Bruja. You understand? It means the witch?"

I hadn't understood, but I get it now.

"Her real name is Princess Doña Marina."

"Is she a real princess?"

Another shrug. "Who knows? She says she's a descendant of Aztec royalty and named after the famous Doña Marina. You know who that is?"

"Tell me."

"Doña Marina was an Aztec girl sold into slavery and given to the Spanish upon their arrival. She was not only able to learn languages quickly but was very intelligent, too. Cortés called her a princess and used her as his interpreter. She was not actually a princess, though she might have been of the minor nobility.

"She warned Cortés of plots against him by *indio* leaders who claimed to be his friends. They say that without Doña Marina, Cortés would have been murdered by *indio* chiefs who pretended to be his allies and the conquest would have failed."

"How do I find this Doña Marina? La Bruja."

"It's not possible, señorita. No one with good sense would seek her out."

"No one has ever accused me of having good sense. So how do I contact her?"

"I honestly don't know. I have heard she lives somewhere near Teoti-huacán."

"Do you—"

He backs away, shaking his head. "No, señorita, that is all I have to say. I know no more. *Nada.*"

Stuffing pesos in the donation box as I race out, I hurry to the taxi I have waiting. I want the cabbie to take a circuitous route back to the hotel and I don't want to be late for lunch with the fabulous Lily Langtry.

As he pulls away, we go by a luxury carriage also in front of the museum. I'm sure there couldn't be two exactly alike, so I'm certain it's the one loaned to Gebhard and Langtry by *el presidente*. The rig sits by the curb, empty except for the driver, who is asleep.

Lily would be back at the hotel, still engaged in the hours of preparation I'm sure she goes through whenever she appears in public, so Gebhard must be paying a visit to the museum.

I wonder . . . was the urgent matter the curator had to attend to a visit by the American millionaire?

Here to make a donation?

Or make a purchase?

AZTEC GOD
(*Six Months in Mexico*)

40

José watched as his uncle escorts the *norteamericano,* Frederic Geb-hard, to his fancy coach.

He had not heard what the two men were discussing, but neither his uncle nor the wealthy foreigner appeared to be in a good mood when they walked by him on their way to the carriage.

The money the young woman had given José is burning a hole in his pocket, but his hopes to sneak out and visit a cantina are squashed when his uncle intercepts him as he prepares to leave.

"Get in here," Torres snaps.

The bad humor José noticed about his uncle when he was with the foreigner is almost volcanic as he follows him into a room.

Torres whips around to confront him. "What did you say to the woman—the reporter?"

"Reporter?"

"Yes, you idiot! She is a newspaper reporter. What did she ask you about?"

"Many things." José is scared now. He knows he has repeatedly tested his uncle's patience with his behavior and laziness. "But nothing of im-portance."

"Tell me exactly what she asked about."

"About Aztecs. Sacrifices. Dream dust—"

"She asked about the dust? You never volunteered it?"

"No, Uncle, I swear upon all that is holy, she asked me. I told her only that it's a legend and no one knows for sure if it even exists."

José can see that Torres doesn't believe him.

"What did you tell her about the jaguars?"

"The jaguars?" José shakes his head. "Nothing, I told her nothing."

The blow hits José across the side of his head without warning. His head is spinning and he staggers to his left, falling over a large stone relic of a frog god.

"Don't ever lie to me again. Now get out of here."

41

As my carriage makes its way down cobblestone streets, I think about what the assistant curator told me about how sacrifices were conducted in the days of the Aztecs.

Dream dust . . . so that is what I experienced. Knowing from firsthand experience what this does to a human—making you dreamy and feeling like you're no longer attached to your body—I can imagine how easy it would be to have people stand in a long line that stretches out from a pyramid, waiting to be led up the stone steps to a slab at the top where they would have their hearts ripped out . . . and not put up a fight.

Closing my eyes, I imagine an Aztec priest dressed hideously in the skin that had been flayed off of someone earlier, bending over another victim, holding a sharp knife high in the air, then plunging the dagger down into the victim's chest, slicing it open so the priest can pull out the helpless victim's beating heart while he is still conscious.

Oh my God. Those Aztecs were not gentle creatures.

What I find most interesting is how cleverly they kept the victims from rebelling.

Dream dust—shake a little in their face and the victims are in nirvana. Instead of kicking and screaming, they go peacefully to their slaughter. How despicable! They were tricked into believing they were in some wonderful place, when they were really in hell—which is where I landed after the girl shook the powder in my face.

My carriage comes to the Zócalo, the city square that is the heart of Mexico City. Before the conquest, this spot was also the center of the Aztec capital, Tenochtitlán. A grand cathedral of Christendom now sits where a pagan pyramid once stood. Not far from it is the palace of Cortés, where the Spanish governors of New Spain, the name given to Mexico by Spain during colonial times, held state and which later heads of the nation of Mexico used as their White House.

Today, I have not come for history. However, later I will follow up and do an article about this famous square. Right now, I am here to see a performance that I've been told occurs for tourists every day.

Looking off into the distance, I spot a circle of people watching two men in animal costumes fighting with swords. Good. This is what I have come to see.

With hand signals and mixed words of Spanish and English, I get my driver to move closer so I can have a better look. The swords are wood, with elaborate designs etched on them. The two fighters are dressed in cloth costumes of jaguars.

Gertrude told me that they represent Jaguar Knights, elite warriors who were the best of the Aztec fighting units. And that members of the Cult of the Jaguar also dressed as the knights when the cult was formed to drive out the Spanish and protect Montezuma's treasure.

So who are the street performers imitating—the knights or the cult members?

As we get even closer, I fixate on the masks.

Oh my word. Cold chills race up and down my spine as I watch them. "A goose walked over my grave," my mother says when she gets the shivers. Not because the crude masks are scary, but because they're exactly like the one I saw on the train when Howard was shoved off with his throat cut. So much for the wrinkled bedroll theory. And they bear no similarity to the features of the thing I saw later, outside the train. Interesting.

"Go to the hotel," I tell the cabbie, motioning with my hands to keep moving when my command isn't understood.

Sitting back in my seat, I realize I don't know any more now than I did before I saw the street performers. But it's clear that somebody was playing a game on the train—a deadly one, at that. And I don't know the rules or even the other players.

One thing I can see through the haze created by the manipulations is that there was something almost theatrical about the attack on Howard, the prospector. Staged—like the show behind me. But now that I'm positive the attacker wore a mask, I know the hands behind the murder are very human.

Now, if I could just be as sure about what I saw outside the train.

As I lean back in the carriage, trying to clear my mind for my luncheon with the incredible Lily Langtry, my imagination starts running wild again, this time adding a couple more characters to the scenario.

If I'm right, her lover, Gebhard, was at the museum. There is nothing wrong with that. He might be interested in the museum—a donor. Still, too much of a coincidence for me, and I don't like happenstances—like my being there researching were-jaguars and things that go bump in the night when Gebhard conveniently showed up. No, I don't like it.

Like coincidences, unanswered questions are something I hate.

With luck, I will find out what he was doing there when I have lunch with his famous lover.

42

Pickles! I'm late. This is not the right way to make first impressions, especially with someone as singularly unapproachable as the Jersey Lily.

My carriage barely comes to a stop at the front entrance of my hotel as I'm paying my driver and dashing out. I rush by a group of people who are standing around, as if they are waiting for someone in front of the hotel entrance. As I hurry across the lobby, a woman is coming down the stairs—or I should say that she is moving with such elegance that she seems to be floating down.

Lily Langtry—the Jersey Lily.

She catches my eye and I throw up my hands and silently mouth, Sorry I'm late, and get a dazzling smile in return as I rush to meet her at the bottom of the stairs.

Her preference is for black dresses, and this one is simple. The material is satin, with pearls sewn around the neckline which is vee-cut, not showy, just enough to entice any man. It's formfitting but not tight, just snug enough to show her curves. Since it is sleeveless, she has a soft white cotton shawl draped on her shoulders. From about her knees down, the dress flares a little but stops about two inches above her ankles.

She's wearing a thin gold bracelet around her left ankle. It gives her a very attractive, if not sensual, look. I've never seen a bracelet worn that way before.

Her hair is gently piled on top, with little curly pieces slipping down on her soft white porcelain face, which makes her large oval eyes stand out.

No wonder men fawn over her.

"With your bubbling enthusiasm, you must be Nellie Bly, the young reporter I've heard so much about."

"Guilty as charged." Also guilty of beaming at the compliment—at least I hope it was a compliment.

"Shall we go? I have a carriage waiting for us. I hope you don't mind, but instead of being cooped up in the dining room, I thought it would be much more delightful to have a picnic lunch while we see the Floating Gardens."

I'm so excited at meeting a real celebrity that she could have told me we were having lunch at the dog pound and I would have been thrilled.

As we exit the hotel, I realize now why the people outside are standing around—they're waiting for her. Obviously, word leaked out that she would make an appearance at this time.

They swarm around Lily, and I'm very impressed with how she handles them: She's polite and friendly, making each one feel she's noted his or her presence, even if it's just by the briefest flash of a smile or wave of a hand.

One Mexican man, clearly quite wealthy, from his clothes, gives her a bouquet of white lilies and begs her to marry him. "I own a silver mine," he tells her. "I will pave the way to the church with silver dollars for you to walk upon so your feet never touch the ground!"

Lily throws him a kiss. "Oh, darling, if only I wasn't already spoken for."

And we are off.

It is not *el presidente*'s carriage that has enough gold and silver trim to supply a mint, but one that is only slightly less extravagant, also with seats that are so soft and cushiony, I feel like I'm floating on a cloud. We have not only a driver but also a footman, who stands at the back of the carriage.

I'm in Cinderella's coach and loving it. It's amazing how riding in such an exquisite coach can make one feel like royalty. I can't wait to tell Mother.

"I apologize for the crowd," she says. "Unfortunately, a lack of privacy is the price of my modest fame. That is one reason why I wanted to go to the Floating Gardens rather than sit in the hotel dining room, being stared at like a fish in a bowl. No one will know me there. Oh my good-

ness, I forgot to ask you if you've already been there. . . . I just assumed
you hadn't."

"No, I haven't. This is perfect, because it's one of the sights I want to
see."

"Wonderful."

The actress looks fondly down at the lilies now lying by her side and
smiles softy at them. "That was sweet of that man to give these to me."

She gently touches them and then looks at me. "I wonder where he
got them. They're Jersey lilies, the symbol of Jersey and the source of my
nickname. Sir John Everett Millais did a portrait of me and named it
A Jersey Lily, and it just took hold. Did you know that the island of Jersey
is just off the coast of Normandy, France?" She doesn't wait for an answer,
but continues. "It's the largest of the Channel Islands and a British Crown
Dependency, which we are very proud of. I had happy times there with
my brothers."

"How many brothers do you have?" I ask.

"Six, all older, except one, and he's my favorite. Do you have any
brothers?"

"Yes, as a matter of fact, I, too, have six, and my favorite is also the
younger one. I think my brothers taught me more about how to survive in
this world than my sisters."

"Very true, and I assume you mean in this *man*-orientated world."
Her laugh is delicate. "Being the only girl, I became very tomboyish. My
poor teacher couldn't handle me, so they let me study with my brothers.
It's amazing how much more they teach boys than girls."

It sounds much like my own upbringing. "How did you become an
actress?"

"Oh"—again she laughs—"by mistake through my friends Oscar Wilde
and Sarah Bernhardt. They talked me into it. And I've had a nice run.
I've been on the stage mostly in Europe, of course, but I've been on tour
in your country also and, I'm happy to say, very well received."

"My librarian, Mrs. Percy, had the pleasure of seeing you in *As You
Like It.* She is going to be thrilled when she hears I've met you, as will my
mother and everyone in my town."

"Where are you from? And please tell me how you became a newspaper reporter. I've never met a female reporter. I'm very impressed."

I can't help but blush. As Roger rudely pointed out, I'm known only to the city limits of an inconsequential town, but here I am, receiving a compliment from a woman who is rich and world-famous, beautiful and talented, and who has kings and rich playboys as lovers. She has the world at her feet.

Thrilled that she is interested in me, but afraid I might bore her, I quickly tell her about my hometown, how my father died suddenly, about my mother's remarriage to an awful man, all of which left her in horrible financial straits and forced me to give up my schooling to work in a factory—which, strangely enough, led me to my job as a news reporter, despite my brothers' feelings that reporting is a man's job, not a woman's.

"I'm not surprised your brothers were against it," she says. "Even though my brothers love me dearly, they would be furious if I ever tried to enter their or any part of the male work world. You are a brave woman, Nellie."

I don't know what to say, which is so not like me. Instead, I just smile and blush, again. However, what I am thinking is that I'm not fortunate enough to have her beauty and talent, so I have no choice but to use my brain—it's all I have.

She seems to be reading my thoughts, for she says, "For some reason, men have thought me beautiful, and I decided to use it to my best advantage. It started when I first came to London. As they say, I was 'brought out by my friends.' They took me to the theater, where, unbeknownst to me, a painter, Frank Miles, saw me and was smitten by me. So much so, he set out to discover who I was.

"Miles went to all his clubs and visited his artist friends, declaring he had seen a beauty, and he described me to everybody he knew, until one of his friends met me. He reported back to Mr. Miles, who came and begged me to sit for a portrait.

"I consented, and when the portrait was finished, he sold it to Prince Leopold. From that time on, I was invited everywhere and made a great deal of by many members of the royal family and nobility. After sitting for Frank Miles, I sat for portraits by Millais and Burne-Jones, and now Frith is putting my face in one of his great pictures.

"Men," she says, laughing, "they're so predictable. They will do just about anything for beauty, especially if other men have shown interest. My dear friend Oscar believes beauty is the most important thing in life. For some reason, possessing it makes them feel superior to other men."

She laughs again and claps her hands. "I can't believe how I am rambling on. Do you do this to everyone you meet? Make them confess, like they are in church?"

"Only people with fascinating lives."

"Well, I can't say how fascinating my life has been, but I personally am pleased with the knowledge that one of my ancestors is the infamous Sir Richard le Breton."

"Who's he?"

"One of the four knights who murdered Saint Thomas Becket. He delivered the final blow that chopped off his head. They believed their friend Lord William died of a broken heart after Becket refused to permit him to marry."

"Oh . . ."

She gives that delightful spontaneous laugh again. "Don't fret about it. Becket was more political than saintly. The Pope made him a saint to annoy the king."

As the carriage makes its way to the famous Floating Gardens, we spot the oddest sight: a slaughter shop. The stone building looks like a fortress. Around the entrance are hundreds of tired-looking mules on which men are hanging meat. Only one wagon is being loaded, but as I learned during my walk on the street two days ago, after rubbing the bony sides of the pack animals, the meat is just as palatable as when hauled in carts.

The carts are built like a chicken coop and elevated on two large wheels. On each side of the coop and lying in a large heap on the bottom is the meat. Astride the pile sits a half-clad fellow, and in front, on the outside, sits the "bloody" driver.

Trudging along in a string of about forty are men with baskets filled with the gory refuse, from which the blood runs in little rivers, until they look as if they have actually bathed in gore.

Having gotten a dose of it on the street, I am not as shocked and disgusted as Lily.

"Oh my . . . what a dreadful sight." Lily looks aghast. "Almost spoils one's appetite for lunch."

43

When the carriage reaches its waterfront destination, we alight and are instantly surrounded with boatmen, neatly clad in suits consisting of a white linen blouse and pants.

Each clamors for us to try his boat, shouting in Spanish and English. The crowd is so dense that it is impossible to move. As there is no regular price, we have to make a bargain, so we select a strong brown fellow, who, although he presses close up to us, has not uttered a word, while the rest have been dwelling on the merits of their boats.

We go with him to the edge of the canal to look at his little flat vessel covered with a tin roof. White linen keeps out the sun at the sides, and a pink calico cloth edged with red and green fringe covers very flat seats.

The bottom is scrubbed very white and the Mexican tricolors float from the pole at the end.

"Let's take this one," Lily says. "Don't worry about those hard seats."

She signals the footman, who rode at the back of the carriage, and he comes running with large, soft, comfy cushions.

I ask the boatman his price. "Six *norteamericano* dollars," he replies.

She is willing to pay without question, but I say, "No, no, it's too much."

After much debating and deliberating, he sets his price at one dollar, which I accept and insist upon paying, since Lily has provided the land transportation and picnic lunch.

The Floating Gardens, La Viga, is the prettiest sight I have yet seen in Mexico. Sunday is market day, and the waters are crowded with boats containing goods being taken into the city and manufactured items being sent out.

Some boats are packed full of fresh vegetables; others contain gay-colored birds, which the boatman says the *indios* trap in the mountains and bring to market here. Many boats are packed with exquisite flowers from stem to stern, all but where the boatman stands with a long pool to push the vessel through the water.

In many boats, work is being done en route: While a man pilots his boat over the glassy waters, the ever-busy woman aboard weaves wreaths, making bouquets from the stock before her.

Such roses! As I inhale their perfume, I recall kind friends at home and wish they were here with me. There are daisies, honeysuckle, bachelor's buttons, in a variety unknown in the States. And the poppies! Surely no other spot on earth brings forth such a variety of shade, color, and size. They are even finer than the peonies in the States.

As these boatfuls of flowers pass us, the *indios* look at us with pleasant smiles and we answer with cheerful salutes.

We see that people along the banks have decorated their simple straw huts with long plants, which contain yellow and red flowers. Our boatman tells us that they plait them at the top in a diamond shape, and not only put them on their homes but use them to decorate the pulque shops and stretch them across streets as a communal decoration.

The most disagreeable sight is the butcher at work. Scattered along the shoreline are large copper kettles filled with boiling water. I gag as a man holds a little brown pig down with his knee and cuts its throat, while another holds a small bowl in which he catches the blood.

When I turn my head, in that split second, I have a flash of my body lying on a white stone while an Aztec priest with a jaguar face hovers over me, holding a long, curved knife; the priest is covered in blood, lots of blood.

"That is a ghastly sight." Lily rubs goose bumps on her arms. "Wish we didn't have to see that."

Unfortunately, farther up, we see the first work completed. On sticks, put in the ground around a large charcoal fire, are the different pieces of pork roasting.

"Look." She points to very large drooping willows along the bank that are crowded with men, women, and children.

The men are nursing the babies and smoking the pipe of peace, while the women are washing their clothes. They are not dressed in the height of fashion by our standards, but what would be the extreme full dress of their own class.

"Isn't it wonderful," Lily says. "The women seem so happy and cheerful and contented, as though they are queens. They are even dressed in what must be their Sunday clothes, and all they are doing is laundry."

I suspect that the women on the bank washing clothes by hand are probably thinking how wonderful it would be to be cruising by in a well-shaded boat.

Lily looks back at them for a moment, as if there is something about their simple existence that she has missed in her own life.

"Ready for lunch?" she asks. Before I answer, she grabs the picnic basket that was taken from the trunk of the carriage and put on the boat by her footman.

I am rather expecting potato salad, beef sandwiches, and pickles, which is what we would have taken to a picnic back home, but then Lily lifts up the white linen cloths that are protecting the food, French food—small pieces of pastries and breads with vegetables on top and different-colored cheese spreads; pastry puffs and baguettes; fruit salad; cucumber cups; chicken tarragon sandwiches. Then she lifts the last cloth.

"Surprise!" She laughs with delight and claps her hands as she reveals bean and cheese wrapped in tortillas. "When the dining room manager came to my suite to discuss the picnic menu, I told him you would be my guest, and he told me about your preference for simple peon food. I hope you don't mind having champagne. I know it's not quite the drink of the common people of this country, but I think champagne goes with everything. Don't you?"

"Yes." I am thrilled. Mexican food and champagne on ice—what could be more perfect?

As she pours me a drink, which I now know not to gulp, but to sip slowly, I ask if the boatman can share our lunch.

"Of course!" Lily insists that he stop and join us and that he also have a glass of champagne and her gourmet French food.

The boatman tells us he has never tasted such food. His hearty thanks, good appetite, and humble, beholding words between mouthfuls do me a world of good.

White we eat and watch some virile *caballeros* and the flirtatious se-ñoritas frolicking along the shoreline, the reporter in me makes me ask Lily a blunt question.

"I hope you don't mind my asking this, but why did you invite me to lunch? Please don't get me wrong; I've very glad you did, but I'm puzzled. I suspect you have more requests for interviews than you can accept."

"You are a smart girl." Lily looks at me in a way that makes me believe she really means it. "So, I am going to tell you the truth. It was Frederic who put me up to inviting you to lunch, but I must tell you I'm glad he did, because I'm very pleased to have gotten to know you. Not only are you delightful but you remind me of myself when I was your age—determined and wanting the world. Do you mind my asking your age?"

I shake my head no as I quickly swallow my food. "Nineteen."

Lily looks up from the rim of her champagne glass. "Nellie, my dear, you definitely are a true woman, but I'll let you in on a secret. You can't fool a woman about age, especially me. I'm a professional. Correct me if I'm wrong, but I'd say you are around twenty-one or twenty-two."

I just smile.

"Not to worry. It's our secret. I'll let you in on a secret of mine. Frederic thinks he's older than I am."

After we stop laughing, I ask her, "Why did Mr. Gebhard want you to spend time with me?"

"Frederic has never had the best of relationships with reporters, and your being a reporter has him worried. He fears you will reveal to your paper that he is buying prize stallions descended from Cortés's warhorses, while claiming they are ordinary Thoroughbreds to avoid customs duties. That, my dear, is how the rich get even richer, cheating on taxes and paying people to help them do it."

My mother would say that greed is universal.

"Also, I would not appreciate the negative publicity generated by such a story. So . . . may I assume that this is our secret and you will not reveal Frederic's scheme to your paper?"

I think for a moment. Not because I plan to, but only that I find it interesting how the rich are always trying to pull the wool over everyone's eyes all the time.

"You assume correctly. I promise not to utter a word about seeing you or Mr. Gebhard. I came here to report about Mexico and its people; that is all."

"Thank you, Nellie, I really appreciate this."

This gives me a window of opportunity, and I decide to take it. I've been dying to know why Mr. Gebhard's coach was at the museum and if she was there and why.

"Lily, this morning I went to the museum, and as I was leaving, I saw that really fancy coach the Mexican president has loaned you and Frederic."

I pause for a moment because I know I need to word this right, in order to get her to tell me. "I didn't see you, and I was wondering whether Mr. Gebhard was there because he shares my interest in Aztec artifacts."

"I wasn't there and have no interest in the objects. And you are correct. It was Frederic. He has the finest collection of Aztec artifacts in the world and is thinking of donating some pieces to the museum."

Her neutral tone gives me the feeling that Lily isn't telling me the truth—or at least not the whole truth. But I'm curious as to whether Mr. Gebhard is the "trade secret" rich man who is supporting Traven's work.

"Then Mr. Gebhard must know Traven. He's an archaeologist I met on the train."

"Of course, darling! Don't you find it odd that he goes only by Traven? The man's so secretive. I've done my best to find out why, but he's mum. Tell me, what are your plans for tomorrow?"

"I'm thinking of going to that ancient city called Teo—something." I wasn't really, but I threw it out to see what reaction I would get.

"We're going there and I was going to suggest you come along with us. We'll see Traven when we get to Teo. Why don't you join us?" Not waiting for a reply, she continues, all excited. "I insist. *El presidente* is loaning us a stagecoach. It's much too dusty for an open carriage. You will find it more comfortable than riding in a hired coach with those hard seats they all have. And the road to the place is infested with bandidos. You'll be much safer with us. We'll have an armed escort."

I'm amazed. Everyone and everything appears to be pointing me to Teo. I have to wonder whether La Bruja is using some of her occult powers to lure me there.

"It's settled," Lily says, without waiting for an answer. "You're going with us."

"Señoritas," our boatman says, "the Floating Gardens. There." He points ahead. "La Viga is about six to twelve feet deep and thirty feet wide. The trees you see lining it on both sides are willow and silver maple trees. It starts from Lake Tezcuco, about eight miles from the city, forms a ring, and goes back to the same source. Look." He points to an area in front of us. "There are the Floating Gardens. They are just above the Custom House."

Lily gestures to where he is pointing. "Isn't that solid land?"

"No, señorita. With your permission, we will take a canoe and go in among them."

We climb from our boat into an even smaller dugout. Wading in the

water, he pushes us under a low stone bridge, at the risk of being be-
headed. We salute the owners of a little castle built of cane and roofed
with straw and go on, in high anticipation, to see the gardens.

I feel like we are entering into some secret fairyland, for in blocks of
fifteen by thirty feet the gardens are nestled, surrounded by water and rising two feet above its surface. The ground is fertile and rich and anything
will grow in them. Some have fruit trees, others vegetables, and some look
like one bed of flowers suspended in the water.

"This is absolutely breathtaking." I am in awe. Never have I seen anything so pleasing to the eye. All around in the little canals through which
we drift are hundreds of elegant water lilies.

"May we take some?" I ask our boatman.

"*Sí.*"

Eagerly, we gather them with a desire that never seems to be satisfied,
and even when our boat is full, we still clutch ones that are "the prettiest yet."

On the solid part of some of the gardens, cattle and horses, sheep and
pigs are tied to trees to save them from falling into the water.

The quaint little homes are some of the prettiest features; they are
surrounded by trees and flowers, and many of them have exquisite little
summer houses, built also of cane, which command a view of the gardens.
The hedges, or walls, are all of roses, which are in bloom, sending forth a
perfume that is entrancing. The gardeners water their plots every day, the
boatman tells us.

They fasten a dipper on the end of a long pole and with it they dip up
water and fling it over their vegetables in quite a deft and speedy manner.

"Do the gardens really float?" Lily asks me.

"No, they don't anymore. They are stationary, according to my librarian, Mrs. Percy."

"Nellie, please do not spoil the pretty belief about them by telling me
the truth."

"The gardens did originally float. Mrs. Percy says they were built of
weeds, cane, and roots and were banked up with earth. The Aztecs had
not only their gardens on them but also their little homes, and they poled
them around whenever they wished. They're now rooted, but that doesn't
make them any less marvelous."

We bask in the sun as our boatman pulls us through the gardens.

Scattered around in front of some of the homes are wooden crosses
with cotton cloths tied to them, and I ask our boatman what they're for.

"They are believed to prevent storms from visiting the land. The theory is that after the wind has played with the cotton cloth, it is unable to blow strong enough to destroy anything."

Along each side of La Viga are beautiful *paseos,* nature pathways and horse trails bordered by large shade trees. The boatman tells us they form some of most beautiful carriage drives in the city.

"This is one of the things I wanted to see," Lily says. "Look at all of the ladies and gentlemen on horseback." She looks back at me. "Did you know this is also one of the favorite places for racing? Frederic hopes to come back here before we leave Mexico. Are you fond of fine riding?"

"Yes, as a matter of fact, I have won some ribbons."

"That's fabulous! Once I tell Frederic about your love for horses, he will forget that you are a reporter."

"Lily, look!" I point to two young fellows who are racing their horses bareback. What a fabulous exhibition.

My happy mood is suddenly quenched when I spot the tanned hide of a jaguar hanging up to dry on the wall of a cottage. The reality of what I experienced yesterday comes back and smacks me in the face. I turn my head so that Lily can't see my features turn sour.

THE FLOATING GARDENS
(*Six Months in Mexico*)

44

When I arrive back at my room, there is a note from Gertrude and a surprise: Roger is gone. Vanished without a trace.

Gertrude's note is on the washbasin, but no message from Roger. Nothing. Nada. Not even a scribble letting me know that he has vacated and wishing me luck on my reporting, or inquiring how I feel after being attacked by nightmarish creatures on a public street two days ago.

He has simply taken his luggage and slipped away like a thief in the night. The only evidence in the room that he ever existed is a lingering scent of his cherry-scented pipe tobacco, and my annoyance at the affront. The one thing I hate more than being confronted is being ignored.

I sit down on the cot—now my bed—and pout. The fact he has made a quick and silent departure irks me no end. How dare he? He doesn't know it, but he filled the void of my absent mother, despite being my unwanted traveling companion and verbal adversary for days. I was thoroughly annoyed that he forced himself upon me in the train and at the hotel, but he was company. And he has no right to sneak out without a word, depriving me of another opportunity to kick him out. Especially after all we have been through together.

Outrageous and completely thoughtless—typical of Roger.

A dark thought occurs to me: He's gotten a superior room. A suite all to himself, leaving me with this rat- and roach-infested hovel. It would be just like him.

I stare around the room. It's empty. I can't boast to him about my day with the Jersey Lily and the invitation to go to Teo.

No question about it, Roger is a scoundrel, leaving me like this.

It's tough being an independent woman and keeping up a brave front without a man when bloodthirsty things from centuries past have raised their ugly heads, so it was nice to have his company at a time when things that go bump in the night were bedeviling me.

I hate to admit it, but he really wasn't that bad in many ways. For one, he has a sharp mind—a character trait that is on the top of my list of what I would like in a husband. I liked that he often won the battle of wits between us. It showed me he isn't a wimp.

Then there was that kiss on the train. It was an accident—no more than a brush of lips. And even though there was no passion in it, and I may have been stirred up a bit by it, it was meaningless.

So why am I acting this way?

Because it excited me at the time. My face got flushed, my heart beat rapidly—a natural and harmless reaction. Besides, he's rather attractive in body. But I certainly wouldn't have shared a train compartment or hotel room with him had he been someone I felt I could not trust or was repulsed by.

Angry for my feelings about him and realizing that he doesn't share them, I pace back and forth from the door to the cot, hoping that I will meet him one more time so that I can give him a piece of my mind.

"Men! They are nothing but trouble."

As I crunch up my hands in frustration, I feel Gertrude's message get all squished up. In my ranting about Roger, I had forgotten all about it. I quickly open it and smooth it out to read.

Nellie dearest: So sorry to have ignored you. Been busy with Don Antonio's clan. We are going tomorrow to Teotihuacán with Langtry and Gebhard. Would be lovely if you can join us. Do try.

Your friend,
Gertrude

Teo. Again.

Everybody wants me in Teo.

Is there some sort of cosmic force drawing me to Teo? I've gotten an invitation from everybody but La Bruja. But then again . . . maybe she's the one stimulating all the invitations.

She is a witch, after all.

Maybe I could get her to use her powers on Roger.

45

Ah . . . the life of the rich and famous. I am so grateful to be floating on a cloud again, this time over the bumpy road to Teotihuacán. Left to my own limited resources, I would have been bouncing on hard seats in a grimy public coach.

El presidente's stagecoach is a Concord, a vehicle so comfortable that Mark Twain described it as a "cradle on wheels." Rigged in a four-in-hand fashion so a single driver can handle the four big horses pulling it, the Concord also has a suspension system that consists of leather straps underneath, which cause the body of the coach to swing back and forth, far preferable to the jarring, up-and-down bouncing motion of the springs used in less superior rigs.

My description of this particular coach as a "cloud" is more accurate than Mr. Twain's baby cradle, because the interior seats are nothing like the hard leather ones in the public conveyances we have back home, Concord or not.

As with the town carriage the president provided for Lily and her lover for city use, this stagecoach is heavily endowed with teak from the tropical jungles of the Far East and precious metals from the mines of Mexico.

A loaded wagon drawn by two mules trails behind us. It's filled with travel trunks, many times bigger than my small carpetbag, and two large wardrobe trunks, which not only have room for hanging clothes but have drawers, as well. I'm sure my entire wardrobe back home would fit into just one of these mammoth wardrobes.

As I observed at the rail station the first time I saw Lily, a world-famous actress doesn't travel light.

The trek to Teo, which is about thirty miles from Mexico City, is accessed on what we'd call back home a beaten path, rather than a road.

The coach holds six comfortably, and that is its manifest today. The seating is vis-à-vis, three of us on each side.

Across from me is Don Antonio, the Jersey Lily is to his right, and man-about-town Frederick Gebhard sits next to her.

I have the window seat, with Gertrude to my left. Mr. Thompson, the farm equipment salesman I met on the train, is beside her. He gives Gertrude and me a smile that makes me rethink my desire to make the trip to Teo. He started antagonizing me the moment I saw him this morning.

"So nice to see you again, Miss Bly," Thompson said when had we gathered in front of the hotel to board. "Heard you've been getting too much sun and seeing more bloodsucking were-jaguars!"

He gave a good laugh and I gave him a smile, while I wished I could have kicked him in a most delicate area. I haven't forgiven him for insinuating that what I observed on the train was the result of an overactive imagination and my delicate female constitution. His little joke at the hotel was rubbing salt in a still-raw wound.

I would have thought that a farm equipment salesman would be an odd bedfellow for a high government official to have invited to share the coach with the famous actress and her paramour, but it is soon apparent that the "farms" that Thompson sells to are those vast holdings called haciendas and that his work brings him into contact with the owners and their horseflesh because he sells tack. And as I catch bits and pieces of their conversation, it is obvious he was invited along to give Gebhard some tips on where to find the best horses.

Another surprise is the more familiar faces from the train—the cowboys and their foreman, Mr. Maddock. They are the security escort Lily alluded to. I thought she meant Mexican troops.

"I asked the ranch hands to come along to Teotihuacán," Don Antonio says after we are under way. "The hacienda with the cattle they'll be herding back to Texas is in the area, so I asked if they would accompany us. They will come in handy if bandidos decide to pay us a visit."

The mounted cowboys form a double column far enough to the rear to keep from eating too much dust. They also have a heavy-duty wagon drawn by big workhorses, but it's not even half full with their gear.

"Rightly considerate of you, Don Antonio," Mr. Thompson says.

"We wouldn't want anything to happen to these pretty ladies." He pulls out a cigar to light but puts it away when Lily gives a smile and a "Please."

Just before we got moving, Sundance came trotting by my window and gave me a big cocky grin and a wave of his hat.

"I see you have an admirer," Lily teases me.

"I understand you also have a westerner for an admirer," I reply.

I am referring to the notorious Judge Roy Bean, the Texas "hanging judge," who hands out hard justice from his saloon in a small Texas town, coincidentally called Langtry, near the Pecos River. Bean is known to be an ardent admirer—a worshiper—of Lily, so much so that he named his roughneck saloon the Jersey Lily.

"So I've heard." Lily gives her hearty yet so delicate laugh—I wonder how she does that. "I know nothing about the man except that he is said to administer justice in an ironfisted manner. I like the American West and have traveled from coast to coast on the rails. Someday, I will stop at Judge Bean's saloon and pay him a visit."*

While the two men discuss the bloodline of Mexico's horses, including the greatest prize of all, the bloodline of the horses of the conquest—descendants of the thirteen horses Cortés brought over from Spain—I mention to Lily and Gertrude that Mrs. Percy, my librarian, believes there are many similarities between the Aztec and Egyptian cultures.

"Unfortunately, books about Mexico are not on the purchase list for our little library," I add, alibiing for my own ignorance.

"Well, in truth, there aren't that many books that deal in depth with the Mexican civilizations anywhere. They're hard to find," Gertrude says. "And your librarian was right. Most Americans and Europeans fail to recognize the incredible accomplishments of Latin American and Asian cultures because their education is directed toward Europe and the Mediterranean.

"If they thought about it, they would realize that the Mesoamerican civilizations, like the Aztec, Mayan, and Incan, had accomplishments as great in science, medicine, language, and art as those of the ancient Egyptians, Babylonians, and Romans."

"You are quite the history scholar," Lily says. "And I must say it's fascinating. Do tell us more."

---

* Lily kept her promise, but Judge Roy Bean had passed away before she paid the visit.—The Editors

"Yes, Gertrude, please continue," I say. The more I know about the history, the more chance I will have of deducing what the current crop of neo-Aztecs have up their sleeves.

"Many of the similarities between the Egyptians and the forebearers of the Aztecs and Mayans are obvious. Both built great civilizations dating back to before the time of Christ. They built pyramids, with the largest and third largest in the world being here in Mexico. They wrote in word pictures called hieroglyphics, developed complex cities with sewage systems, practiced medicine as a high science, and built roads linking large cities.

"There are many similarities with the Romans, too. As did the Romans, the Aztecs brought their drinking water down from distant mountains via aqueducts. And like the Romans, Aztec legions conquered a great empire and demanded tribute from the conquered."

Gertrude rattles on about the accomplishments of the civilizations that had flourished for thousands of years south of the border. She is a storehouse of knowledge. I confess that I am not a "book learner," as she obviously is. I tend to pick up my information from seeing and listening, which only works as long as I have someone like Gertrude or Mrs. Percy sharing the knowledge they've gained from the written word.

Gertrude stops to makes sure the men are engaged in their conversation before speaking to us in a confidential manner.

"It's not just the history of the medieval and ancient Aztecs and Mayans that's intriguing. There is something else about those civilizations that is still alive today."

Gertrude shoots another glance at the men, who are discussing the bloodline of warhorses that died over three hundred years ago. Their discussion has become quite lively as they argue about the best ways to keep from being cheated by fraudulent claims.

In a lower tone meant only for Lily and me, she continues. "They say that there is both dark mystery and magic in the ancient ruins at Teo. Some of it is due to the wrath of the gods that the Spanish trampled upon when their armies conquered the land."

Lily smothers a giggle. "You're joking. You don't really believe that, do you?"

Gertrude gives us a mischievous grin. "One of my professors makes an annual trip to Mexico to study the vestiges of the late, great civilizations. He warned me not to make light of the pantheon of Mesoamerican gods. They were a bloodthirsty lot, with a most vindictive and violent nature. He says the people believe that the gods were vanquished from the cities where the Spanish destroyed the temples but that they still haunt the great ruins, like those at Teotihuacán and Chichén Itzá."

"Gertrude," says Don Antonio, interrupting, "those are the bedtime stories told to children.

"Yes, Uncle." But full of mischief, she slips in another comment. "Wait until you see the grotesque Feathered Serpent in Teo."

She then goes back to more history: The tops of the pyramids are flat because the Aztecs built temples on top to use for worship. Egyptian pyramids are pointed because they were used only for tombs for their pharaohs.

"Besides having a written language expressed in hieroglyphics, the Aztecs and Mayans made paper, printed books, and were among the finest astronomers of the ancient world."

Lily claps her hands, as she is inclined to do when she is excited. "Yes. Do you know anything about those people who live in the Utah desert, the ones with many wives—"

"Mormons," I say.

"Yes, that's it, Mormons. They believe that people from the Near East came to America before the time of Christ, a people whose written language is called 'reformed Egyptian.' Wouldn't that explain why the Aztecs and the Egyptians were so similar? If the Mormons are right, the Aztecs and Mayans came from Egypt."

None of us has an answer, but it is an intriguing concept. And like me, Lily is obviously attracted to the mysterious side of Mexico.

"Teotihuacán is a true mystery city," Gertrude says, despite Don Antonio's wish for her to stop. "The city was built almost two thousand years ago. At its height, it had a couple hundred thousand people. But this is the really strange and eerie part."

I can see from the grin she is suppressing and the sparkle in her eye that she is deliberately teasing her uncle by pursuing the conversation on the forbidden subject.

She speaks in a low stage whisper, as if her uncle, sitting a few feet away, can't hear her. "No one knows who built it or who occupied it. Better yet, no one knows why it was abandoned. Was it war? Famine? Violent weather? What would cause an enormous number of people, the entire population, to abandon their homes and temples? Why would no other peoples for almost a thousand years before the Spanish arrived occupy this amazing city with its towering edifices?

"The one known thing is that the ghost city so frightened the Aztecs that not only did they refuse to live in it but the Aztec emperor would come to Teo once a year and leave gifts for the gods."

"Blood," says Thompson unexpectedly, interrupting. He ignores a frown from Don Antonio and goes on. "He brought big barrels of blood taken from sacrifice victims, because that's how the Aztecs got favors from the gods—by ripping out the hearts of thousands of slaves and prisoners of war to feed to the gods so the gods would do them favors. Didn't do a bit of good, did it, when Cortés came with a few hundred soldiers and frightened millions of them into submission? Where were their gods then to protect them?"

"You are not being fair to the Aztecs." Don Antonio is perturbed. "It is true the Spanish scared them, but it was their superstitions that brought them down, not their abilities as warriors. Unfortunately, they thought Cortés was a god, as their legends said a god would return much the way it appeared to them that Cortés did.

"Don't dismiss the fighting prowess of my *indio* ancestors. As Gertrude said, like the Romans, they were conquerors who demanded tribute from a conquered city. As long as those in the city satisfied their demands, they were left alone. But if they refused, an Aztec legion would descend on them, killing or enslaving everyone in the city, and then raze the city.

"Blood ran like a river down pyramid steps by the time they got through ripping out the hearts of the vanquished. If the person sacrificed was a warrior captured in battle, the Aztec warrior who made the capture ate the victim's heart."

"That's awful," Lily says.

Don Antonio shakes his index finger at Lily. "Only if you are on the losing side, señorita."

46

As we come over a rise, we get our first glimpse of the ancient city sprawled out below in the distance.

The sight takes my breath away. A porthole into an incredible period of history has been opened and I am stepping into it.

Lily gives an exclamation of amazement. Even the rich playboy from New York appears moved.

"It's remarkable." Gertrude sits on the edge of her seat, looking out the window. "I've read about it, seen drawings, but I didn't realize how incredibly stunning it actually is."

The large size of the ancient city is a also surprise. I had expected some scattered ruins. Instead, a long, broad, straight boulevard runs down the center of what had obviously been the heart of a great city. The thoroughfare looks to be over a mile long. About as wide as a football field in the beginning, the roadway, in places, is several times that wide.

Teotihuacán is a metropolis of stone, the one building material of the ancients that manages to resist most of the ravages of time. That is all that is left of the city, but the survivors are colossal and magnificent.

No matter how much I've heard from others about how enormous and incredible the edifices of pre-Columbian Mexico are, and how similar many of them are to the towering monuments along the Nile, I was not prepared to look out the window and see a vast complex capped by two pyramids, the larger of which has a base of more than twelve acres and is taller than a skyscraper.

There are many large stone structures with sets of steps, maybe a couple dozen at first glance. Any structures or additions to the pyramids and temples not made of stone have been swept away by the ravages of

time, while the enormous pyramids themselves appear, to my untrained
eye, to be unaltered, though I know they once had temples atop them.

"Avenida de los Muertos," Don Antonio tells us in regard to the broad
thoroughfare that runs down the middle of the stone city. "The Avenue of
the Dead. But you must understand that so little is known about the city
that we neither know the real name of the street or even the actual name of
the city itself. Teotihuacán is the name given by the Aztecs, who believed
that the gods who created the world resided here. And the name of the
avenue comes from the Nahuatl word for 'place of the dead,' not in refer-
ence to a burial place, but what they sensed about the city."

The ancient city is much more mystical and majestic than I ever imagined. I feel as if I am stepping back in time to a place filled with beauty,
heartache, war, destruction, and explosions of creativity—and buried secrets.

I now appreciate Traven's love for archaeology.

The ruins of what Don Antonio tells us were temples built before the
time of Christ line most of the boulevard. About two-thirds of the way
down the street is the colossus that ranks as one of the largest man-made
structures on earth: the Pyramid of the Sun.

"Pirámide del Sol," Don Antonio says with pride in his voice. "Over
two hundred and thirty feet high."

"Almost twice as high as the tallest building in the United States," I
tell them. "The Home Insurance Company building in Chicago is only
one hundred and thirty-eight feet."

"The largest pyramid in the world is in Cholula, southeast of Mexico
City," Don Antonio says. "The second largest is the Great Pyramid at
Giza, in Egypt. The sun god's pyramid is a hair smaller than the big
Egyptian one, making it the third largest in the world."

He points at the far end, where the boulevard runs up to a second
pyramid. "Pirámide de la Luna appears from our vantage point to be as
tall as its sister Sun, but that is only because it is on higher ground. It is
actually quite a bit shorter than the sun god's monument, being about
one hundred and forty feet, just slightly higher than the building Nellie
spoke of."

"The ruins are spectacular," Gertrude says, "even after being ne-
glected for over a thousand years since the city was abandoned. But can
you image what the city must have looked like when it had a couple hundred thousand people in it and was spread out over miles?"

"Can you imagine the labor it took to build the city?" I ask, exposing the factory girl mentality in me. "Not just those who designed it and the artisans who made it beautiful and unique but the vast army of laborers it must have taken."

"Using only primitive stone tools to cut and carve the finished stone," Gertrude puts in. "They had not developed the ability to mine and process bronze or iron."

I let out a sigh. "I am so envious of Traven. To explore and unravel the past of a great civilization."

Gertrude gets misty-eyed. "That is what I want to do."

"Which is?" Don Antonio asks.

"Explore ancient cities. The unknown. The mysterious. Perhaps even go to places no one has ever been."

"Or at least where no woman has gone," I have to add.

"Your father would not approve," Don Antonio says.*

Gertrude turns to me. "How many men approved of your being a reporter?"

"Only the editor who took a gamble and hired me."

"It frightens me," Lily says.

The comment comes out of the blue and catches us by surprise.

She slowly shakes her head as she stares fixedly at the city. "There is something not evil, but . . . but otherworldly, as if it really were built by gods from the heavens rather than mortals. No wonder this ghost city so frightened the Aztecs."

I understand how she feels. I sense a spiritual essence, as if the ancient gods were not all vanquished by the conquering Spaniards. It's easy to imagine how it frightened the mighty Aztec warlords and their emperors.

Like them, I feel the presence of the bloodthirsty gods.

I just wish she hadn't called it a "ghost city."

* He was right: Gertrude Bell's father did not approve. But she went on to become one of the greatest adventurers in history and literally helped found two nations. See page 287. —The Editors

47

This is so exciting," Gertrude says after we pile out of the carriage and walk over to where tents have been set up for visitors.

She leaves me to supervise the unloading of her luggage, which is a trunk and a valise, while she speaks to her uncle about getting us a tour of Traven's dig. My baggage does not need much management; I just have the coachman hand the carpetbag down.

The tents for guests, tourists, or whatever they call us, are set up in a circle like a wagon train taking a defensive position against attacking Indians. That suits me fine, because the tents are all within shouting distance of one another. Chocolate brown and caked with dust, they remind me of army tents, and the relationship is confirmed when I look closer and see faded Mexican army insignias on them.

Having learned that most of the country runs on the fine art of bribery and corruption à la *mordida,* it's not hard for me to assume that while the tents are "rented" to guests by locals here at Teo, somewhere in the food chain is a general whose troops are now sleeping on the ground. Not exactly honest, but as I've discovered on this trip, all's fair in love and money.

A Mexican woman is giving instructions to workers as to where luggage goes, which is the clue to which tent my head will be lying in tonight. I already know that Gertrude and I will share one.

There are two large tents. The trunks and wardrobes of the rich and famous are taken to one, while Don Antonio's luggage goes to the other. Thompson gets a small one all to himself and I follow Gertrude's luggage to another small one. There are more tents and, I suppose, more visitors to the site.

Sundance and the other cowboys head to a stand of trees to set up camp. I heard Don Antonio tell the foremen that his men are to keep their hands off their guns and go easy on the beer, tequila, and women.

As I go by the small tent next to ours, its door flap is half open and I get a whiff of tobacco, which stops me dead in my tracks, and I find myself staring at the opening. My heart picks up its beat; my breath becomes shorter.

Cherry-flavored pipe tobacco.

It's a very popular favor of pipe tobacco. I'm sure my father smoked it. Walk into any smoking lounge on a train and you will smell it. Some of the boys in the newsroom favored it, though the pleasant smell was usually overwhelmed by pungent cigar stink. One of my brothers even smokes a cherry blend. There is nothing unique or distinguishing about it. But my feet are frozen and I can't take my eyes off the half-open tent door.

I have an irresistible urge to step over and pull the flap back and stick my head in, but I find my feet not cooperating.

What if it isn't Roger? Or he is lying on a cot, not fully clothed, or, worse, another woman is in there with him?

As I ponder my next move, the flap is jerked open and I nearly jump out of my shoes.

"You!" I snarl.

"Well, bless my britches, it's the girl reporter in the flesh."

"You fol—" I start to tell him he followed me, but it is obvious he'd gotten here ahead of me.

"You have once again gotten lucky. There are two cots in here."

I hear a gasp. Gertrude is approaching us. She's staring at me wide-eyed with surprise—and glee.

"I see you've made other lodging arrangements," she blurts out as she flies by with a sound that is either giggling or gasping.

I stare, speechless, as she disappears into the tent assigned to us.

Roger smirks. "Can I carry your bag in?"

"You—I'm going to—"

He grins and takes a puff of his pipe and blows smoke at me. "Missed me, haven't you?"

Bewildered and befuddled, I retreat. I don't know what it is about the man that causes my tongue to get tied when it is usually so liquid and even slippery when I need to make a point.

I storm into the tent and confront Gertrude.

"Don't you think for one moment that I—"

She shakes her head and holds her hands over her ears.

"What are you doing?" I ask.

She smirks and rolls her eyes. "My dear, if you are going to tell me that your arrangements with that man for the past days—*and nights*—are not an example of your being a sexually liberated woman, I don't want to hear it. Nellie, I admire you immensely for what at the very least has the appearance of scandalous behavior."

She smothers another giggle. "Please don't spoil it by giving me a perfectly reasonable explanation that proves that you are just a nice girl with unsatisfied passions like the rest of us."

Her rather frivolous take on Roger and me actually works out perfectly. A truthful explanation that would satisfy her would necessitate exposing a can of worms.

"Good enough, think what you like. Think the worst, if that pleases you. What did you find out from your uncle?"

"Traven is excavating at the Temple of Quetzalcóatl, the Feathered Serpent. Don Antonio says he'll talk to Traven about showing us the dig, but we aren't just to wander over or even wander around by ourselves. There are spiders bigger than your hands, along with snakes and scorpions."

"I'll take nasty crawling creatures over ghosts and vengeful gods."

Gertrude laughs.

What she doesn't realize is, I am dead serious.

48

The cots in the tent have so many lumps, it makes the hard pads at the hotel seem fit for the princess who felt a pea through a stack of mattresses. Even the lumps have lumps.

Besides the two iron cots, a small wood table with a washbowl on top is the only other piece of furniture. No well or creek is in the vicinity to get water to freshen up with.

"Rain barrels outside," Gertrude says. "Don Antonio said if there are rats or snakes in them, just toss them aside. He also said that the facilities are considered luxurious compared to most sites of archaeological digs. I think he's trying to dissuade me from a life of travel and adventure."

Rats, I could deal with. Snakes, I will scream.

There is neither soap nor towels, but we no sooner notice the lack thereof when the woman who was supervising the luggage removal comes in and sets down both.

"Señoritas," she says, and leaves as quickly as she entered.

"Ah" is all I can say as I test a mattress. "It feels like it's stuffed with scratchy hay. What do you want to bet that Lily and her beau will sleep on goose feathers tonight?"

"Probably one that she brought in that mountain of luggage that followed us like the supply wagon of an army."

We leave the tent to take a walk down the Avenue of the Dead before dinner. Gertrude confirms that we are not the only visitors at the site.

"Don Antonio said to hire one of the young boys who come clamoring to be tour guides. He says their versions of the history of the ruins will be more fantasy than fact, but they know the places to stay away from because they're unstable or have a nest of snakes."

Walking toward the ruins, we see Thompson and Sundance. They are deep in conversation, with Mr. Thompson seated on the remains of a stone pillar. He appears to be doing all the talking, and Sundance doesn't look a bit pleased. Rather agitated, in fact. Unfortunately, they are speaking too low for me to eavesdrop.

"Your cowboy friend seems a bit annoyed."

"I don't think it's smart to ruffle Sundance's feathers. He's the youngest of the bunch, but the other cowboys seem to step lightly around him."

A few more words are exchanged and then Sundance slaps his hat on and leaves Thompson, who stays seated and pulls out a little black book and begins to write.

"Ladies." Sundance tips his hat and gives us a thin smile, not his usual cocky, friendly grin, as he stamps by with tight jaws.

Gertrude glances back at the cowboy. "That definitely was not a good conversation."

What does the cowboy have going with the farm equipment salesman that has gone sour? I wonder.

A group of young boys runs up to us, each clamoring away about how he can give us the best tour of Teotihuacán. It reminds me of the boatmen at the Floating Gardens.

One boy in particular stands out to me. It makes no difference that he's short and skinny. There's a strong look of determination in his face, a glint in his eyes, and a liberal use of his elbows to make his way to the front. And unlike the other boys, who appear to know only a few words of English, he utters a whole sentence.

"I will give the lovely señoritas a fine tour of Teotihuacán."

Gertrude nods her agreement that he's our choice, and I ask, "How much?"

"Ten pesos."

"One."

"Five," he counters.

"Fifty centavos," I snap.

Cutting my original offer in half stops him cold.

"No, señorita, one peso, *por favor.*"

"*Bueno,* but you will be paid at the end and then only if we are satisfied."

Gertrude whispers to me that I've gotten the hang of negotiating "in Mexican."

"Oh, you will be more than satisfied," the boy says. "I know all the history." He stretches his very gaunt four-foot frame tall and proud. "I learned the history from the *alemán* hombre."

He gestures up the broad boulevard, in the direction where I assume Traven is at his dig. He tells us his name is Juan.

Gertrude asks, "Did you learn your English in school?"

"No, señorita, here. No go to school. Must help my mother get food for the little ones."

Oh my God. "Five pesos," I tell him. "But you still have to earn it."

The boy is astonished at his sudden raise in pay.

Gertrude shakes her head. "Nellie, I take back my compliment about your negotiating skills."

She's probably right. No doubt he's a little hustler and a fraud, but when he said he left school to help his mother, my heart ached, for I, too, had to make sacrifices to help my mother get food on the table.*

Excitedly waving his arms like a symphony conductor putting out a fire, Juan says that the wide boulevard, the Avenue of the Dead, was crowded with people during sacrifice days. He gives us rather exaggerated but entertaining tales about how sacrifices were conducted and the bloodthirstiness of the crowds.

These ruins are not a place that many individual tourists would come to, but we pass a small group from Germany and one from Britain.

"Don Antonio says they don't talk to one another," Gertrude says, nodding her head at them. "Which is the state of the world, since the two countries are competing to be the world's greatest military power."

She goes on to tell me that her father says that someday America will be a world power. "But that will take a few lifetimes. First, you have to conquer your own Wild West."

While the boy is walking ahead, leading us to a ruin, Gertrude and I talk about my "sunstroke." I tell her only what I said to others, because I'm not sure yet if I can trust her not to tell her uncle that I'm running around claiming there is an Aztec murder cult thirsting for my blood.

"I heard you had dinner with Traven," she says as a passing remark, but I feel she wants to know more. "Rather interesting man, one name and all."

---

* Nellie left school at age sixteen because of financial problems, though after she became famous, she claimed she left because of a heart condition. Her plan had been to become a teacher.—The Editors

"True enough. Did he tell you I asked a million questions about his work?" I want to see if he told her we had discussed were-jaguars.

"Actually, Don Antonio told me about the dinner." She lowers her voice so that the boy wouldn't hear. "He also said that Traven is strapped for cash and may have to give up the dig."

"No. Tell me."

"He said Traven got a wire weeks ago saying his sponsor would no longer support the project because he'd gotten so little out of it. Don Antonio said Traven was in a fine state. I don't know if it's the case, but maybe that's one of the reasons Frederic Gebhard has come to Teo. Apparently, he has some Egyptian pieces but has never collected any Mesoamerican artifacts."

"Really?" That puzzles me, because Lily had told me the opposite. "Are you sure about that? I thought he had a significant collection of Mexican pieces."

"No, Gebhard would have had to get a permit to export the pieces across the border."

"And Don Antonio is the one he would have to get the permit from?"

"Exactly."

Gertrude goes off to see something Juan is rattling on about as I wander a bit in deep thought.

So Lily lied when she told me Gebhard had a collection of Aztec pieces. But why? She doesn't seem like the type to lie. Perhaps she was simply repeating what Gebhard had told her. And it may well be that he had gathered a major collection without getting a permit. So far, I have learned that money can buy anything in Mexico, including public services.

Lily's invitation to lunch with her had been a puzzle from the start. She said Gebhard had asked her to talk to me about keeping a lid on their presence in Mexico, so that it didn't drive up horse prices or expose his cheating. Yet they did nothing to hide their arrival. By now, every newspaper in Mexico City will have carried the story. Which means the story will be sent back by American foreign correspondents in the city.

I am jarred out of my brown study by a man who startles me. He is suddenly there as I walk next to the stone wall of a temple.

"Sorry," I stammer.

He has a large mustache in the style of many Mexicans and is dressed as a peon would be, with a wide straw hat, a simple cotton shirt and pants, and leather sandals.

"Señorita." He holds out a female doll. It's a crude thing, made of straw and clothed in a simple dress.

"No, no bueno."

"La Bruja," he says, shoving the doll at me.

"What? What do you want?"

"La Bruja," he says again, pushing the doll at me.

I slap it away. "Get away from me!"

"Nellie? You all right?"

I hear Gertrude's voice from around the corner as the man says something in Spanish. He talks fast and the only words I recognize are *La Bruja*. He shoves the doll at me again and I back off, pushing it away.

He drops the doll at my feet and runs, disappearing behind a wall.

Picking up the doll, I realize it's holding a rolled-up piece of paper. I pull the paper from its grip and unfold it, revealing a simple message.

La Bruja. 8. Here.

I hear the crunch of shoes and slip the message in my pocket.

"Are you all right? It sounded like you were yelling at someone."

"I'm okay. Just . . . there was a man, tried to sell me a doll. Sorry, he startled me."

Juan stares at the doll. "La Bruja . . ." he whispers.

He spins around and runs away like a banshee out of hell.

"Juan!" I yell after him, but he's gone.

Gertrude stares at me. "Why'd he run?"

"Maybe he saw a snake."

49

Dinner is in a communal dining hall, a large tent with the sides rolled up to let in a breeze. As we sit down for dinner, I find myself paying no attention to the chatter around me, because my mind is focused on my quandary.

A message from La Bruja to me? Literally a command that I meet with her tonight.

How does the infamous witch even know that I exist? Or that I'm in Teo? And how did she know what I looked like in order for her messenger to single me out for delivery of the doll?

Most important—what is the purpose of the invitation? This question is the sticking point, along with whether she really expects me to meet with her all alone in some ancient ruin that I'm sure has snakes and maybe even things that go bump in the night.

Obviously, she knows me better than I know myself, because that is exactly what I am thinking of doing. With one caveat. At eight o'clock, it will not be really dark. Close, but Don Antonio says that visitors often stroll up the Avenue of the Dead after dinner and even go up one of the pyramids to get close enough to enjoy the night sky. The ruins where I am supposed to meet the woman will have people around—I hope.

Why all the mystery? A doll with a note. Obviously, the doll is La Bruja's calling card. One look at it by little Juan and the kid almost jumped out of his sandals as he made a getaway.

If she was aboveboard and had nothing to hide, she would have either come to the camp and introduced herself or sent me a simple message to set up a convenient time for a meeting in a civil place—during daylight.

Of course, she wouldn't be called a witch if she weren't sneaky and didn't have a pocketful of tricks, would she?

I thought about asking Gertrude to come, but with her, it always goes back to those questions that she will ask and that I don't want to answer. And I can just imagine what Don Antonio would do to me if I caused some harm to come to his dearest old friend's daughter. That would definitely be the end for me on two counts, because I would never forgive myself if something happened to her and because I am hopelessly entangled in intrigue.

Wondering who gave the witch my particulars, I take stock of my dinner companions.

Everyone is here—the actress and the playboy, the consul general, the farm equipment salesman, the German archaeologist, the intelligent girl from Oxford, and me, the pretend foreign correspondent. Oh yes, and there is the historian from New York whose neck I would like to wring.

Still puzzled by this strange request, I slip out the mysterious note to look at it again for the dozenth time.

"Love letter from one of your many ardent admirers?"

To my chagrin, Roger has come over and is sitting himself down across from Gertrude and me. He nods at the note, which I quickly slip in my pocket.

"An invitation to a treasure hunt." I don't know why I said that. Maybe to get his goat. Stupid, of course. He would be a perfect companion for my meeting with the witch. The only thing stopping me from asking is my pride and pent-up anger toward him.

"Really. Want company?"

"When I do, Mr. Watkins, it will be with a gentleman of integrity, intelligence, and impeccable manners."

"Good heavens, Nellie, what a bore a man like that would be," Gertrude puts in. She smiles at Roger. "So nice to see you again."

"The pleasure is all mine."

My right foot is tapping a mile a minute and I start tapping the table with my fork. "I wish they would hurry up and serve us." I am trying to change the subject and keep from blurting out something to Roger in public that I might regret, but I am also hungry.

Being served to each guest is a delicious-looking concoction of grilled, freshly slaughtered goat, onions, peppers, and garlic. It smells savory and I can't wait to dig into it. I've never had goat and am looking forward to experiencing something new.

It's served with bread baked in an outdoor oven. And the bread smells heavenly, too, just like my mother's loaves. I really like tortillas and beans, but after having them for several days, I'm ready to try something different.

A plate of the goat dish goes down in front of Gertrude and another is placed before Roger. My stomach juices gurgle with anticipation as I get a whiff of the pungent goat feast.

A plate of beans, cheese, and onions with a tortilla on the side is set in front of me.

The boss lady who tells all the laborers what to do smiles down at me.

"Special. For señorita."

50

There are times when I have had to tread unknown territory to get ahead, whether it was showing up for the interview at the *Dispatch* after sending a letter scolding the paper or defying the gods of newspaperdom to run off to Mexico to pursue a dream of being a foreign correspondent.

At those times, and others, when I face the unknown with dread and apprehension, I just tell myself to bite the bullet and keep moving forward. I do it with dogged determination, executed by taking one hesitant step, then another and another, until I have accomplished my goal.

As I set out this night in a haunted city almost as old as time, to speak to a witch, who frightens the wits out of a very smart street boy, about bloodthirsty were-jaguars, I just hope tonight I will succeed—at least in staying alive.

However, my reluctant feet seem to be telling me that I should revise my theory of facing every challenge with grim determination, that sometimes the best defense is to run like hell in the other direction.

Not recruiting Roger to come along exposes one of my weaknesses. I'm not a team player, even at the best of times. I tend not to listen well to instructions from others, but learn best by going out and banging my head, sometimes until sense is pounded into it. And I hate asking for favors.

My tendency to be a loner and the fact that I am too proud or stupid to ask for a favor aren't setting well with me tonight as my imagination runs wild when I pass ancient carvings of the unimaginable horrors of human sacrifice.

Unfortunately, it occurs to me that the dirt my feet are treading upon was once trod on by people who got in line to get their hearts ripped out as gleeful crowds roared for more blood for the gods.

Charming thoughts, girl.

Torches of a group of tourists climbing the Pyramid of the Moon at the far end of the boulevard are visible, but no one else appears to be about.

Great. About what I should have expected. I am all alone.

The crunching of steps comes from behind me, and I swing around, but no one is there—at least no one I can see, not that I can see much. There is just enough moonlight to take the edge off the darkness, but without exposing much detail.

Keep moving, girl.

Since I have come this far, I might as well go the rest of the way. Just a few more steps and the witch will be here and I will get answers and be able to go home. All very logical and reasonable. Except logic and reason fade as I trudge on alone in the dark night.

What was I thinking? I wasn't. And am still not. Plain and simple. Most people do crazy things for the almighty dollar, or treasure of gold in this case. I do it for the story.

I expect she speaks English or has a translator, for a couple of reasons—it's unlikely she would have set up a meeting unless she knew we could communicate, and in the note she sent, the word *Here* was written in English. I just hope I am right.

No one is at the ruins when I arrive at the spot where I met the doll bearer.

"Hello?" I say, loudly enough to be heard, but not enough to wake any vengeful gods.

My foot starts tapping impatiently, nervously, as if it's trying to tell me something. I fidget for another moment, when suddenly the doll man materializes in the faint moonlight without a sound. He startles me and I let out a little yelp.

"Señorita" is all he says. Then he motions at me with his hand to follow him as he turns in the direction from which he had come.

Forcing my reluctant feet to move, I follow, my throat dry, my heart racing. My body seems to be telling me something to which my mind is stubbornly not paying heed.

Thick subtropical foliage begins immediately behind the line of ruins, and I follow the doll man into it. There is no trail, at least none I can discern in the dark, but he still moves rather quickly, and I have to do the same to keep up.

I'm only a short distance into the thicket when alarm bells go off in my head again and I stop in my tracks.

This is insane! Turn around and go back!

Swinging around, I see a dark figure coming toward me. I can't make it out, but it must be a man. Or beast?

How did I get myself into this?

The doll man says, *"Señorita. ¡Andale!"*

Hurry up I do, following the doll man. He is human, at least, and I haven't the faintest idea of what's behind me.

A glow in the foliage becomes visible in the direction he's taking me. Torches or a campfire, I'm not sure.

We finally enter into a clearing where a circle of torches on the outer edge is creating a shadowy haze. There is just enough light so I can see that men dressed as peons, similar to the doll man, are the torchbearers.

In front of me is a woman sitting in a very large chair. A guard stands on each side of her. I take in a sharp breath. The two guards flanking the woman as if she is a queen are dressed in crude Jaguar Knight costumes, similar to what I had seen at the Zócalo in the city, and on the train.

The "knights" are holding broad wooden swords that look like the obsidian-edged swords shown in Aztec motifs. Obsidian is a volcanic glass that creates a super-sharp edge, enabling the wielder to whack off a head with one swing. These wooden swords probably have the same head-whacking edge as the Aztec ones did.

The woman's features are fanned by flickering torchlight and shadows, but I can make out just enough of her face to see that it's painted in wild shapes and colors.

"Buenas noches, señora. I hope you speak English." And I hope she doesn't hear the jitters I hear in my voice.

"Where is the map?" The woman's voice is heavily accented, but I get the gist of it.

"The map?" I know exactly which map she is asking about, but the question catches me by surprise. Why is she asking me about the map? If these are followers of the ancient cult protecting Montezuma's treasures, don't they know where the disk is?

Why does everyone keep thinking I know where the treasure is?

"I don't have the map."

"The golden calendar round belongs to the sun god. It must not be disturbed. I will stop you and the other gringos from stealing it."

"I don't disagree with you, but I don't have the map." It's pretty clear that she isn't a keeper of the secret and is lusting after Montezuma's treasure herself.

"You're lying. You must give us the map. Otherwise, we will have to harm you, as your people have harmed us."

My heart leaps into my throat. *"There! It's there."*

As I point behind them to the bushes, the witch—queen, whatever she is—and her guards with the big swords turn. I whip around, taking off like Juan—a bat out of hell—hopefully back in the direction from which I came.

I have heard enough to know there is nothing here for me but unthinkable pain or death.

Driven by the mindless mania of pure panic, I fly past a startled peon holding a flaming torch and head into the dark foliage.

Running, stumbling, falling, and getting up again, I hear men thrashing through the bushes behind me. I don't need to turn around to know it's the two with the swords sharp enough to lop off a head.

It doesn't matter who catches me anyway—I would get dragged back to that nightmare of a hag and whatever she had in mind about "harming" me.

My foot catches on something and I go flying forward, taking a dive to the ground. I hit hard, knocking the wind out of me. For a frozen, terrifying moment, I am unable to move and lie sprawled out, paralyzed.

I'm rolling over and trying to get to my knees when the witch's guard, in a jaguar suit, almost runs into me. For a second, he is as startled as I am, but he recovers instantly and, with a snarl, raises his broadsword.

Something whips by me and connects with the man's face with a sickening thump, knocking him backward.

Roger appears beside me, holding a tree branch.

We hear the other jaguar guard breaking through the foliage, coming in our direction.

Roger drops the branch and pulls a pistol out from under his clothes. *"Run!"*

51

W hy did you hit him with a branch rather than shoot him? You have a gun."

We're back, within a short distance of the tents, and my breathing and heart are getting back to normal. But it's dark and I'm still on edge. An oil lamp is burning next to the water barrel in the center of the circle of tents and another in front of the latrine just outside the circle. If I have any calls of nature tonight, they will be held till morning so that I don't have to leave my tent and risk running into two-legged creatures of the night again. I have had enough of them for one night.

"Sorry, but I don't usually kill people. Not strangers at least. Besides, I was carrying the staff to kill a snake if I saw one in the dark, before it got me. Swinging it was the first thing that came to mind."

He stops short of the little tent city and begins packing his pipe. I know what he wants: an explanation. My mind has been churning away since we broke out of the thicket and saw the safety of the tents in the distance. I've been trying to think of a good reason as to why I was being chased by men dressed as jaguars at night in a jungle in Mexico.

Nothing clever comes to mind.

He peers at me as he lights his pipe, and I feel the compulsion to wiggle out of the jam I am in.

"Roger. I'm sure you saved my life tonight. I am forever grateful to you. It was courageous. Thank you." I go up on tiptoe and kiss him on the cheek. I mean every word of it. I am close to tears from the fright I suffered and the gratitude I feel. "Good night."

I take one step before he says "Nellie," and I turn back.

"One more thing," I say, "please don't mention what happened to anyone. It will get back to Don Antonio and he'll ship me home on the grounds that I am out to cast this lovely country in a bad light." I squeeze his arm. "You will promise me not to tell anyone, won't you?"

He shakes his head. "Nope."

Here we go again. "Okay. You deserve an explanation. I saw something in the bushes. I thought it was a cat or dog—"

"I see there is a light on in Don Antonio's tent. We should let him know there is a threat to the camp."

"All right, all right. You really do deserve an explanation. I'm trying to get to the bottom of what happened on the train and to me in Mexico City. That's all there is to it."

"Were-jaguars," he says.

"Were-jaguars, the Cult of the Jaguar, Montezuma's treasure, and a nasty character called La Bruja, a witch who has to do with some or all of it. I don't know. I went to the Aztec museum in the city to learn more about the jaguar legends. When I was there, a young man, the assistant curator, who is the curator's nephew, told me that La Bruja was a good source for information about were-jaguars and dream dust."

"Dream dust?"

I quickly tell him about dream dust.

"So you came to Teo to contact her?"

"Sort of. I actually got invitations to come to Teo from several people. And earlier tonight, when Gertrude and I went to see the ruins, a man suddenly appeared with a note from La Bruja—that note you caught me rereading at dinner."

"The treasure hunt."

"Yes." I go on to tell him about doll man and my brief but explosive meeting with the witch and her bodyguards. "I have no idea how she even knew I would be here in Teo or what I look like."

"She thought you had the map?"

"Have the map or know something about it."

"And you thought she would have the map?"

"No, not the map. I thought she might be the head of the cult or whatever that is sworn to protect the golden disk and that she could provide information about the jaguar figures I've seen. But from the moment she opened her mouth, it was obvious that she only wanted information about the treasure. Which means she's nothing but a treasure hunter herself."

We walk slowly toward our tents.

Roger looks at me. "So, what do you make of it? The attack on the prospector, the vanishing *indio* porter on the train, the stuff called dream dust, Montezuma's treasure?"

What I make of it is a good question, one I can't answer because I just don't know. It is a puzzle surrounded by fog.

"Someone believed the prospector actually had a map," I finally suggest. "No use getting rid of the man if he had only a peso map."

"The cowboys?"

"I'm not sure. They acted like he was a joke to them. But he wasn't a joke to someone. And then there's the mask the person who attacked him wore. It was like the ones those street performers use and that the witch's thugs wore tonight. I believe someone was being clever and wanted to rob the man of the map in a way that he wouldn't be identified."

"Or frighten it out of him," Roger says. "The prospector seemed to be constantly boozed up and believed he was being stalked. Maybe he wasn't imagining it. Somebody could have been wearing a jaguar mask to frighten him into giving up the map."

Roger's theory rings true to me. "What I find most interesting about the jaguar mask I saw on the train is that it was so crude, so much an obvious costume. If I had gotten a good look at it, instead of in the dark through a dirty window, I'm sure I would have thought of it as a clownish mask. And that's another reason La Bruja didn't impress me. The men holding the torches looked like nervous farmers, and the two guards were wearing the crude masks I've seen street entertainers wear in the city."

He shrugs. "What did you expect? Real were-jaguars?"

"Yes."

We stop in front of his tent and I speak so that my words won't carry.

"I saw something in the bushes outside the train that time the train stopped to let Traven load cargo."

I tell him about the thing—creature—I saw in the bushes.

"You think you saw a real were-jaguar?"

"I don't know what I saw, but it was very different from the simple masks that street performers use. It was really creepy." I rub the goose bumps on my arms.

"That is creepy," he says while tapping the stem of his pipe against his teeth. He pulls a face and shakes his head. "You have been a very busy young woman since you crossed the border."

"Don't I know it."

"There's another person who's also been very busy. The prospector, the *indio* porter, the attack tonight. Have you thought about the fact that someone is keeping close track of your movements?"

Licking my dry lips, I give him a forced smile. "Oh yes. That thought has occurred to me."

"They must think you know something about the map. Do you?"

I shake both my fists in frustration. "No, no, no. And I wish I did. I have run every drunken word Howard spoke to me over and over in my mind, looking for something I might have missed. I can't make anything significant out of it. For sure, he never spoke of Teo, a giant golden disk, or anything else that would even be a link to the treasure."

I don't say it aloud, but I am also plagued by whether I missed an important clue from the prospector because his drunkenness reminded me of my stepfather's booze talk. I was just trying to be free of him. I didn't care and wasn't listening to what he was saying. It wasn't important to me—then.

"Well, one thing is for certain," Roger says. "Somebody thinks you know more than you do and thinks that you're just not willing to tell or planning to grab the treasure yourself. They want to know whatever they think you were told by the prospector, and it's a pretty narrow field. It has to be one of your intimates."

"What do you mean?"

"The harassment has followed you from the train to the city and now to Teo. La Bruja didn't invite you here. She wouldn't even know who you are if someone you knew from the train hadn't told her."

"I got invitations to visit Teo from just about everyone."

"Except me."

I hadn't thought of it, but he's right.

"You've gotten a confession from me," I tell him, "but you haven't told me how it happens you were out there."

He turns to go into his tent as he answers. "I was taking my evening constitutional when I saw a dog or cat—"

"No you don't!" I grab his arm to jerk him back to face me.

He spins around, grabs me, and pulls me against him, his lips very close to mine.

I freeze up and then instantly melt, pressing against him, my lips melting with his as they had once before.

He lets go and I step back, flushed.

"If you hear any strange noises tonight," he says, "just pull the blankets up over your head."

As I turn to go to my tent, I find Gertrude standing in the entrance. She gives a smile full of tease. "Just a platonic relationship . . ."

"Oh, be quiet."

52

Isn't the ancient city a marvel?" Gertrude says the next morning.

"Marvelous," I agree. Having made a few more observations about the place that frightened both me and the terrifying Aztecs, I restrain my tongue rather than opening the gates for a barrage of questions.

We are waiting outside Lily's big tent for the grand lady of stage and gossip columns to appear and accompany us to Traven's dig. We have already resolved to look like ugly ducklings with a graceful swan when the three of us walk up the boulevard together.

Juan was waiting outside our tent this morning to "escort" us to the dig—and collect his fee for yesterday and another for today. His disappearing act of yesterday was not mentioned.

"I should add bandido to his job description of street hustler and ragamuffin," I complained to Gertrude after we paid him.

Gertrude is talkative, and I pay only half attention to her. I'm quiet because my head is full of my close encounter with La Bruja and her Jaguar Knights. Last night, I tossed and turned, waking up repeatedly. The realization that I could have been murdered didn't really hit me until I was in bed and tried to sleep.

Howard, the prospector, didn't do me any favors by sharing his drunken mumbo jumbo with me. It sicced a crazy Mexican witch onto me—and who else? That's the question filling my head as Gertrude talks about how exciting it is to be in a city built a couple thousand years ago.

"Marvelous," I repeat again.

Everybody wanted me in Teo; Roger and I had discussed that last night. I exclude Gertrude from the "everybody" category because she is too young and too remotely connected to Mexico to be part of a conspiracy of tomb robbers or whatever.

The best reason I can conjure up for anyone's wanting my presence in Teo is that someone—or maybe a bunch of somebodies—thinks I know more than I do. And it appears that Teo is the place where the treasure hunt is meant to end.

Murder has been on the table since the train, so it's pretty clear that whoever wants me to fess up to knowing the location of the treasure is willing to flay me alive, like that nasty witch would have done, to get a chunk of gold big enough to buy a small country.

An unfortunate part of the human spirit that divides us from the lower beasts is that we all have a miserly desire to gain and hoard wealth. And not even sex or fame fires our souls with the hot passion that a pot of gold does.

And if it means murder and other high crimes and misdemeanors to get it, so be it.

"You are in dreamland," Gertrude says.

"Sorry. I was listening."

"No, you weren't. If you had been, when I mentioned Roger, you would have perked up."

"All right, you win. What about Roger?"

"Not really about Roger, but an observation about the educational system in the colonies." She grins. "That's what my friends at Oxford call your country."

"I won't tell you what my friends in Pittsburgh call Oxford." I rather suspect people in Pittsburgh know almost nothing about Oxford, except maybe that it has a university.

She laughs at my attempt to be witty. "Yesterday, Roger and I spoke briefly when we met at that hub of society here in our tent city, the water barrel. I had a question about the Louisiana Purchase, which added so much territory to your United States. I was surprised that he knew only the basics any schoolboy would know. Frankly, I expect a person planning to teach history at university level would be a lot more knowledgeable about one of the most important events in your country's history."

"Hmm" is the best I can manage. Roger is on my list of favorite persons for saving me last night, but, unfortunately, he is also one of the suspects.

Like Gertrude, I've concluded that there's something unscholarly about him. Most scholars have such an interest in their field of study, they are more than willing, even eager, to talk about it. Not Roger. Plus, those magazines and books he always has his head stuck in—they are not scholarly tomes, but popular pulp. He just doesn't fit the bill. Who is he really? Why is he here? And why is a scholar carrying a gun?

Lily comes out of the tent as bright as another sun in the sky.

Gertrude and I are both dressed sensibly for a trek up the dusty Avenue of the Dead and a climb around Traven's archaeological dig. Lily looks as if she is on her way to high tea with the queen. Her dress is a radiant white cotton one, slim and formfitting, with delicate lace covering her neck. Even though the lace adds an elegant touch to the dress, I would imagine it will be stifling in this heat.

The back of the dress has tiny satin buttons, which must have taken a lifetime to fasten—they go from the bottom of her neck down to almost her bum. The dress stops inches above her ankles, and she is wearing dainty satin green shoes with three-inch heels, which amazes me. How does she plan on climbing steps and maybe even some rubble? Doesn't she realize the dirt will destroy the delicate shoes?

Maybe she doesn't care . . . or maybe dirt parts for her like the Red Sea did for Moses.

I glance down at my clodhoppers. Dirt seems to improve their looks. And they are comfortable and fit for climbing. Gertrude has ones almost the same style as mine, only I'm sure they are one pair of many she brought for her trip. For me, it's my only pair.

Lily's gorgeous hair is up in a bun, I suspect, because she's wearing a big floppy white hat that has a big satin green ribbon around the bottom that matches the color of her shoes.

What I admire most is her skin; it's so white and soft, all she has on is a light pinkish blush and cherry red lipstick, which emphasize her porcelain skin and full lips. All I do is put cream on my face and petroleum jelly on my lips to keep them from chapping.

"Where did you get your parasol?" Gertrude asks Lily. "And your hat? They are both stunning!"

Besides the hat, Lily carries a white parasol—I guess for added protection for her delicate skin—while we are wearing baggy hats that make us look like we are on our way to milk cows.

Lily laughs. "These old things? Paris, I think."

A handsome carriage pulls up and Gertrude and I exchange quick glances. I'm sure she feels the same way I do: We are the ugly stepsisters who are graciously getting a ride to the ruins in Cinderella's carriage.

Oh, well, it's not Lily's fault. It's just the luck of the draw, as the boys in the newsroom would say. Lily got a royal flush, while I was dealt a pair of deuces.

Juan adapts quickly to the presence of the coach. He jumps on the back to ride standing up as a footman.

The ride is short, and once we get there, the boy jumps down and races up a few steps and addresses us after we pile out of the carriage.

"The Temple of the Feathered Serpent"—a swing of his arm encompasses the entire temple ruins—"the mightiest and most bloodthirsty of all the gods." He points at the ferocious figures mounted on the temple wall: large stone heads of a feathered snake with jaws that would scare the skin off a shark.

Then he points up at the sky. "He travels across the sky as Venus, the flaming star."

"Venus is a planet, but they call it the evening star; I guess that's close enough," Gertrude tells me as we clap to show our appreciation.

As we climb the steep steps, Juan repeats pretty much what he told us yesterday about a river of blood flowing down temple stairs during sacrifices while the crowds looked on with glee.

"Similar to what they were doing at the arenas in Rome during the same period of history," Gertrude whispers to us so as not to steal Juan's thunder, "only they had wild animals ripping people apart."

Traven is supervising workers hoisting a large block with ropes. He is coated with as much sweat and dust as his workers. He tells the workers to take a break and brushes himself off as he greets us.

"A dig is a dirty job. And a hard one, but not as difficult as what the original builders suffered. The stone block you see eight men straining to lift with great difficulty is a hundred times smaller than most of the stones that went into building the two great pyramids here at Teo."

He goes on to explain that the ancient Mesoamerican *indios* would have used the same techniques the Egyptians did in transporting stone blocks weighing many tons great distances and hoisting them up to create towering edifices.

"No one knows for certain how it was done, but for sure the *indios* didn't have any beasts of burden to aid them, because there were none in the New World until Europeans began shipping horses, mules, and cattle over."

Moving heavy stones is brutally labor-intensive, he tells us, and he shows how he avoids damaging artifacts by carefully removing them from the places they had rested for perhaps a couple thousand years.

"Things get buried under rubble or so many feet of dirt and sand that it's a major physical task to uncover them. And just as the Egyptians were secretive and careful about hiding their valuables, the ancient *indios* of the New World devised many secret places to hide their treasures from thieves and invaders, making it all the harder to find and recover them intact."

Traven points out that bellows and brushes made from straw are used to carefully remove the dirt on and around an object. "We rarely use a pick or shovel once we have opened a site. We often spend hours blowing off a foot of dirt with a bellows rather than taking it off with a shovel."

He gestures at Juan. "I'm sure your tour guide has told you all about the more gruesome aspects of the city, but you should also be aware that just as it took incredible engineering knowledge to build these pyramids, the city itself is a marvel of skilled contrivance on the scale of how a modern engineer would construct a city. The fact that the ancient and medieval *indios* practiced human sacrifice in no way diminishes the credit due them for the amazing feats of engineering it took to build this great city."

He goes on to tell us that the ceremonial heart of the city, with its great pyramids and temples, is focused north and that all the great *indio* centers that followed over the ages had the same configuration.

"How did the people of Teo know which direction was north?" Gertrude asks.

"The same way ancients around the world did. They knew the sun and the night sky like we know the streets and corners of our hometowns. They found their way on land and water by the stars and planets, taking precise measurements, rather than being directed by the needle of a compass.

"Their astronomers would have known the sky that we see with the naked eye better than astronomers do today, because they didn't just study it; they used it for everything from travel and transporting goods to determining when it was time to plant crops.

"A person making a long journey in ancient times, when Teo was a thriving city, or in Aztec times, when it hadn't much changed over the previous couple thousand years, would not have carried a paper map, but would have read the sun and the stars as we would read a physical map."

"The same way sea voyages were made before the invention of the sextant," Gertrude interjects.

"Exactly. Using a chart of the sky as a road map."

Something pings in my head and I find it crowded with thoughts again that make me deaf to what is being said.

Something very important was just spoken; I know it.

I am on the verge of a sudden intuitive insight, but I can't get my brain to wrap around it.

53

After spending hours exploring the ruins, I am grateful that Lily's "chariot" carries us effortlessly back to the tents.

Lily returns to her tent to freshen up, even though she looks like a blooming daisy next to us withered weeds, and Gertrude is off to find Don Antonio.

Finding the tent too claustrophobic, I splash water on my face, repair my "lipstick" with petroleum jelly, and wander toward the little *indio* village that has been set up by the locals to relieve visitors of some of their money.

The cowboys are no doubt the biggest customers, lining up at a barrel where rotgut, which Don Antonio says is strong enough to strip paint from houses, is poured from a dipper into their tin camp cups. I plan to forgo the paint stripper and find a nice piece of jewelry for my mother.

Still unsettled about the thought that just won't fully coalesce in the space between my ears, I try to break things down—it always seems to help me.

The theory that Howard, the prospector, had a map to Montezuma's treasure is all wrong; at least that's what my brain has been screaming ever since Traven pointed out that the Aztecs would not have used maps. In other words, the people who hid the treasure would not have made a written map that would have been passed on from one protector of the secret to another.

So, if Howard didn't have a map in his back pocket, why has everyone gathered here like the relatives at a rich spinster's wake?

I don't understand it.

If not a map, what did Howard have that people believe I now have?

Then there's the playboy and the actress. They are not here just to buy horseflesh, not when they are camping out in Teo and showing not the slightest interest in finding horses.

The same goes for the rest of them—including Roger, who says he's studying to be a history professor but who apparently doesn't know any more about the Louisiana Purchase than I do.

I still remember my fourth-grade teacher having us all draw a map of what our country acquired from France for about a fifteen-million-dollar purchase price. It was territory constituting nearly a quarter of the present United States, all or part of fifteen states and territories extending from the Gulf of Mexico to the Canadian border, and two areas within Canada. It not only changed the country physically but suddenly opened up a vast region for millions of immigrants to pour into.

Napoléon had sold the land in order to raise money to help finance his wars in Europe.

Thompson suddenly appears in front of me, causing me to stop abruptly, snapping me out of my thoughts. He gives me a big sloppy grin and an exaggerated bow, swinging his big hat in a clownish gesture.

"How ya doin', missy? See any ghosts or goblins down the street of the dead?" He has a toothpick in his mouth that manages to stay planted when he speaks.

I get a whiff of sour whiskey breath, a scent that is always sure to raise my ire, after my dealings with my stepfather.

"Only ones of legend."

I have no desire to make idle conversation with this man, but if my theory is correct that Gebhard and Lily came to Teo for more than horseflesh, then Thompson's calling himself a farm equipment salesman with connections to horse-raising haciendas could be a cover for something else.

It seems unlikely that Gebhard would have hired a farm equipment salesman from El Paso to advise him on the bloodlines of Mexican horses. An expert involved in the trade who knew horses and the territory would be a more likely candidate.

"Well, I can guarantee you they are all exaggerations," Thompson says. "The Indians were all a bunch of ignorant savages who couldn't read or write and went around eating each other. They deserve what they got and continue to get."

"I wouldn't call a civilization that built those giant pyramids ignorant."

What I want to say to him is that only an ignorant person would make such a statement, but I hold my tongue. Everything about this man offends me. He reminds me of corrupt politicians back home.

He leers at me. "You're a spunky one, aren't you? How's about the two of us taking a ride in that fancy carriage tonight? I can take you to places you've never seen."

I see red, but as politely as I can, I reply, "No thank you, Mr. Thompson," and start to step around him.

He blocks my path. "We need to talk."

He pulls back his coat to expose a badge pinned to his shirt.

54

Thompson gives me a wink and jerks his head. "Over there, where we won't have prying eyes."

"Over there" is behind the line of makeshift shacks the villagers had set up to sell their products.

I follow him, flabbergasted and angry. It's not that Thompson wouldn't readily pass for a peace officer; to the contrary, he has that overbearing attitude I'd seen so often in policemen in the small town I grew up in, where the most common path to wearing a badge was being the school bully. But he's a Texan, not a Mexican. So what's he doing flashing a badge in the middle of Mexico?

I really don't like the man, but my reporter instincts are blazing at the prospect that I may get to the bottom of why everyone has gathered in Teo.

He stops and glances around to make sure we're not being watched. "You're a pretty smart young lady, so I'm sure you've already guessed that I don't sell plows and hay balers. This is who I am."

He pulls open his coat again so I can get a good-enough look at his badge to read it. It's shiny brass, with an American flag in the center and writing that identifies the bearer as a United States customs inspector.

"Customs inspector? What's a customs man doing over a thousand miles from the border?"

"We have a long reach. I have some information that will interest you as a reporter." He shifts the toothpick from one side of his mouth to the other. "I'll let you in on something, but you have to promise me you won't write a word about it or say anything to anyone until you're back across the border and I give you the go-ahead. Understand?"

Great. Just what I need—another person who'll give me a story as long as I can't use it anytime soon.

"I give you my word—as long as it's not something I already know."

"I'm pretty sure you're in the dark about what's really going on. I'm working undercover; that's why I know. You heard Gebhard talk about how he's gotten so many valuable horses from Mexico, some of the best horseflesh in the world, from the bloodline of the warhorses of the conquest. Not only that but prize bulls, too."

"We both heard him talk about horses in the carriage. And I've heard he's a collector of Mesoamerican artifacts. What about it? I've also heard he can afford to buy whatever he wants because he's very rich. No law against that, is there?"

"He can also afford to pay customs duties, something he doesn't dig into those deep pockets of his to do. He spends more money for a conquistador bloodline stallion than most men earn in a lifetime. Guess what happens when he gets to the El Paso customs house? The horse gets declared as a work mount at the border and he pays a few measly dollars' worth of duty."

"Don't you border agents require a bill of sale as proof of purchase?"

He lets out a harsh snort. "Hells bells, lady, these Mexs will make out the bill of sale anyway he wants it. They'd say he paid them in Chinese silkworms if he asked them to."

That rings true with me. Most of the farmers I grew up around in Cochran's Mill would do the same if someone asked them to short a bill of sale on a cow. Cheating the government of taxes is not considered a crime by most anyone who isn't employed like Thompson to collect taxes.

"Mr. Thompson, I appreciate your doing your duty, but I'm not sure where I fit in. Other than not running the story until you finish your investigation, what do you want from me? And might I add, you haven't told me anything I don't already know."

"It's pretty obvious that you've gotten in pretty tight with that actress gal. What I want you to do is keep your eyes and ears open when you're around them. Let me know who they're talking to about horses and bulls, so I can gather the evidence against Gebhard."

"What!" I'm outraged. "You're asking me to spy on people who've been kind to me? I'm a newspaper reporter, not a government spy."

"I'm asking you to do your duty as an American citizen."

My blood rises. "Pardon me, but I don't think that there is anywhere in our laws, Constitution, or social rules that says that a citizen should spy on her friends and acquaintances for the tax man. I'm not going to spy for you."

His angry words follow me as I walk away.

"You've been a pain in the ass since you stuck your nose in other people's business in El Paso."

My blood is now boiling over, but I resist the temptation to turn and give him a piece of my mind. After all, I have to go through customs when I return. Despite my dislike for the man, I wouldn't want him to pass the word to his fellow agents to give my customs declaration close scrutiny. I do plan to pick up some Mexican items, perhaps a piece of jewelry or two, nothing too pricey, because I can't afford it, but also nothing I want to pay a tax on just to get it back across the border.

The comment he made about El Paso puzzles me. He didn't say that I'd been a pain since El Paso. Or on the train. He said "in El Paso."

I never ran into Thompson or any of his cohorts in customs in El Paso. At least not that I know of. For sure, I didn't go through U.S. customs when leaving the country. I'll do that when I reenter.

Other than wangling a private compartment at the station with Roger, the only thing out of the ordinary in El Paso arose when Howard, the prospector, staggered, drunk, literally into my arms.

I met Sundance for the first time that night. It seems obvious that Sundance and Thompson have something going. Which makes me wonder if Thompson's comment about my being a pain is related to what passed between me and the prospector. And was observed by Sundance.

I haven't been comfortable with Sundance since I spotted him hanging around the boardinghouse that night. The next day, he used my name when he helped me with my bag. Said he saw my name on the tag, which is there. But it would be a bit hard to read the tag at a casual glance—and that's all he had a chance to do.

What has Sundance got going with Thompson? Could he and the cowboys be helping out a customs agent? I must say, believing that would take a giant leap of faith on my part. I suspected from the first time I set eyes on the cowboy and his sidekicks that they might have something to do with the law—like rustlers have something to do with ranching.

No, Sundance doesn't look like a man who helps collects taxes—or who even pays them. I'm chewing on what connection he might have with Thompson when I see the devil himself.

Sundance is stretched out, lying back against a tree, his tin coffee cup by his side, no doubt recently filled with Mexican rotgut brew. He has a hand-rolled cigarette propped between his grinning lips. The boys in the newsroom call cigarettes "coffin nails" because, unlike cigars and pipe tobacco, they're inhaled.

As far as I'm concerned, cigars and cigarettes stink and are disgusting, but pipes, that's different. I'm sure it's because of memories of walking into my dad's study, with him puffing away, filling the room with a wonderful scent. He let me sit on his lap and tell him all about my day. The best part was that he really listened.

As I come up to Sundance, he looks past me to the retreating figure of Thompson.

"I'd watch out for that dude," he says.

"Why?"

"Not every snake gives a warning before it strikes."

"What do you know about him?"

He grins and shrugs. "Nothing really. He's just one of those people who make my gun hand itch. Back on the train, when he used his deck, he had more luck with playing cards than the Good Lord gave any of us. The more people I talk to, the more I discover nobody is particularly fond of him."

"Then why did you pal around with him in El Paso?"

It is a shot in the dark, and I watch closely for his reaction. I get nothing. He just keeps looking at me deadpan, his perpetual grin almost a smirk.

"I don't know who told you that, but you've been steered wrong. He's no pal of mine."

"Why did you hang around outside the boardinghouse in El Paso after we met on the street?" Another shot in the dark.

His grin gets wider. "Why, girl, I was hoping you would invite me in."

I bite my lip, trying not to laugh, but it doesn't work, and despite myself, I laugh.

"Sundance, Harry, whatever your name is, you are a liar, a scoundrel, and only the good Lord knows what else."

"But you like me anyway, don't you?"

"But I like you anyway, yes. That's my problem and the problem so many women have—there's something about a handsome rogue that makes our hearts flutter. And"—I shake a finger at him—"it will only flutter from afar, because I took one look at you and knew immediately you were born to hang."

"It doesn't matter," he says. "I took one look at you and knew you would never be broken to the saddle. But I'll tell you, Nellie girl, if you were a cowboy, I'd say you were a man to ride the river with."

"Thanks, but what does that mean?"

"The most dangerous job driving cattle is getting 'em across a river. Good chance you'll slip off your horse and get kicked in the head or gored by a panicked steer. You want only the best wranglers riding the river with you. Men you respect and can trust to watch your back when things get down and dirty."

I leave, glowing with pride over the compliment he paid me. I know, of course, that he lied about Thompson and El Paso. The two have something going between them, and they obviously aren't always in agreement.

"Nellie!"

It's Gertrude. She is in front of our tent, staring at me with wide eyes. She looks as if she has been frightened out of her wits, and I run to her as fast as I can.

"What's the matter? What happened? Someone hurt you?"

She shakes her head, unable to speak.

"Gertrude, tell me what happened? I'll get your uncle—"

She lets out a cry.

"He's dead!"

"Oh my God, what happened?"

"His heart."

"He had a heart attack?"

"No! Someone took it, Nellie." She screams, *"They ripped out his heart!"*

55

"They found his body on the pyramid," Gertrude says after I get her calmed down enough so she can speak, "draped backward over the stone where sacrifice victims were taken to be—" She chokes up.

We hurry up the boulevard toward the Pyramid of the Sun, where the body is located. She hasn't seen it and has spoken only to Traven, who came by her tent just long enough to give her the bizarre news.

I wanted her to stay behind because she's in shock and distress, but she wouldn't do it. I think in a way she is fooling herself and hoping that it really isn't Don Antonio who's been murdered.

"Traven told me not to come. He said it's ghastly. But I have to see it and make sure Don Antonio is treated with respect. And witness everything I can. His wife is dead, but he leaves grown children. They will want to know all the details. Some arrangements must also be made for the body. It'll deteriorate quickly in this heat."

She shows amazing knowledge and fortitude for her age. And she's the same as I am when I get orders I don't agree with—told to stay away, she disobeys. She's determined to pay her respects to her uncle and ensure his remains are treated properly. And she wants to get to the bottom of what happened and who did it. Both of us are the type who would whip the horse out from under a man with a rope around his neck if he had harmed someone we cared for.

She goes on, grim but resolved. "Traven told me the workers spotted the body on the pyramid when they were leaving his dig."

I remember the large stone block on top of the pyramid is positioned close to the edge of the steep stairs. The reason for the proximity to the edge is simple: If it wasn't there, people on the ground who gathered by the thousands to watch the sacrifices would not have been able to see the gory, violent act.

"Symbolic," I mutter.

"What?"

"Someone is sending a message."

She stops abruptly and faces me. "You know something. Tell me— *tell me now!*"

Her voice is controlled, but she is close to hysteria.

"It's nothing, Gertrude, just those crazy thoughts I get." I take her arm and continue to walk.

"Nellie, stop it. Please tell me what you know about Don Antonio or who would want to kill him. Something has been going on with you; that's apparent. What you say isn't going to hurt me. He is—was—a lovely man, very kind to me, a friend of my father at university ages ago, but I barely knew him. I met him for the first time in El Paso. I'm grateful for his hospitality and horrified that something terrible has happened to him, but he's not family to me."

That is pretty much how I had sized up her relationship with the consul general. "I don't know anymore about his death than you do, but you're right, it's time I told you what I do know. It all goes back to Howard, the old prospector on the train, who had some sort of map leading to Montezuma's treasure."

"But Don Antonio said the maps are a joke. You can buy them for a peso."

"Well, Howard's wasn't a joke." I stop and lock eyes with her. "Look who has gathered here at Teo. Frederic Gebhard says he's in Mexico to buy horses, but he immediately heads for Teo and doesn't appear to be in any hurry to leave. And the cowboys are definitely the type who rustle more cattle than herd them. They're roughnecks and gunfighters.

"Something else struck me as strange. The cowboys have come here with a heavy-duty hauling wagon drawn by big workhorses—and it's not even half full of their gear, saddles, bedrolls, and the like."

"Things that don't weigh much," she adds. "I saw it, too. Are you suggesting its purpose is to haul away Montezuma's treasure?"

"The notion has occurred to me. Gebhard also has one of the world's finest collections of Aztec artifacts. Can you imagine what a sensation the golden disk would be? The gold value alone would be astronomical."

"That man Thompson." Gertrude gets us walking again. "Do you think he's in on it?"

"I'd bet on it. He claims to be a border patrol agent investigating whether Gebhard is buying expensive horses in Mexico and paying minimum customs fees by calling them workhorses."

Gertrude scoffs. "And he followed Gebhard all the way to Mexico City? And managed to befriend the millionaire and world-famous actress along the way—when Lily and Gebhard weren't even on the train with us? Not to mention Thompson's rather vulgar personality. We'd be ruddy fools to believe that one. They had to have had something going between them before they left El Paso."

"I agree. I think that the prospector had enough proof to interest Gebhard. Whether he went to the rich New Yorker directly or was steered there, I don't know. Considering that the prospector wouldn't have made a good impression, it was probably Thompson who approached Gebhard with the idea of getting the golden disk. It takes money to get everyone to Teo and pave the way for the treasure back across the border, and Gebhard would have it."

"Do you think Don Antonio found out about the scheme and has been murdered because he tried to stop it?"

I avoid her eyes.

"Tell me, Nellie. Please, no secrets."

"Okay, but remember, this is all guesswork. If you're going to take a treasure of historical significance out of Mexico, you would need the help of an influential Mexican official to give you the necessary paperwork."

"So Don Antonio was in on smuggling the treasure out of the country."

I take a deep breath. "Gertrude, I'm just putting two and two together. Thompson's a border agent on the American side. Don Antonio was the consul general at the place where the artifact would most likely have to be slipped through. From what I've heard, the notion of an official being paid for things that are unscrupulous is not unheard of in this country." A polite way of saying her old family friend was a typical bureaucrat collecting "the bite."

"*Mordida.* My father said that Don Antonio bought his position as consul at El Paso. The only reason he would have wanted to leave Mexico City for that miserable little place would have been because it was profitable. You're right. You'd need a Mexican official to provide the export permit and an American customs official to pass it through as something besides a priceless treasure stolen from the Mexican people."

Pieces to the puzzle fit together: the source of the money to finance the scheme, a tough gang to get it to the border, the officials on each side of the border to grease its way across.

We walk in silence until we are nearing a wagon where a group of men have gathered at the foot of the pyramid.

Workers from Traven's dig are carrying down the pyramid steps what appears to be a make-do stretcher composed of long tree limbs tied together to hold a body that is wrapped in a blanket. Their progress is slow because the steps are narrow and steep.

Traven is coming down behind them. He looks in our direction and raises his hand in greeting.

"Why cut out his heart?" Gertrude asks me, choking on her words. "You called it 'symbolic.' What did you mean?"

"Remember what you told me back on the train about the Cult of the Jaguar? How the cult arose after the conquest to protect Aztec treasures and drive out the Spanish?"

"That was hundreds of years ago."

"Look at the villagers we've seen. Off the beaten track, they don't live much differently than their forebears did over the centuries. Most of them still have Aztec looks because their blood is pure. And some of them don't act too different, either."

I tell her about my encounter with La Bruja.

She looks at me in horror. "You think this witch thought Don Antonio knew where the treasure was and tortured it out of him? Or killed him by performing some bizarre ritual? Feeding the gods?"

"La Bruja struck me as a local terror who had the audacity to try to grab me, a foreigner, but I don't see her as trying to intimidate a man of Don Antonio's stature. I have the feeling there is something else going on here. I've sensed an undercurrent of malevolence since I arrived. I think some of it has surfaced."

I tell her about the difference between the jaguar mask on the train and the one I'd seen after confronting Traven over the mule.

"So one looked like a carnival prop and the other looked real?"

"Not real, at least I hope it wasn't. But different. Infinitely more menacing. Much more like the were-jaguar images created during Aztec times and before."

I think about it for a moment, trying to focus my thoughts on what I had seen. "I don't believe there are men who can change into jaguars in Mexico any more than I believe there are European werewolves. But I have to say, there was something truly spooky about the thing in the bush. I felt danger down to a chill in my bones when I saw it."

We close in on the people at the bottom of the pyramid and I whisper to Gertrude. "There's also another possibility we have to consider. If there was a falling-out between Don Antonio and a gang of thieves, his coconspirators might have killed him in a bizarre way to throw suspicion on La Bruja or whoever else is carrying on Aztec traditions in Teo."

She stops and meets my eye. "Nellie, if you are correct, either an ancient cult has started murdering again or one or more of our traveling companions is a murderer. Has it occurred to you that we are a long ways from the city and surrounded by people who are all conspiring to steal a national treasure?"

"It has occurred to me." I just didn't want to think about it.

56

Thompson, Gebhard, his coachmen, and half a dozen other men I take to be local villagers are standing by the wagon that is waiting for the body. Another carriage, which I assume to be Traven's, is also here.

Roger is here, too, off to the side. It strikes me that he never has shown a connection to the other Americans in Teo. I've never seen him speak to any of them.

Maddox, the foreman of the cowboys, comes up from behind us with Sundance. They are on horseback.

"These ladies should be sent back to camp," Maddox says. "This is no business for women."

"This is my business and I'm not leaving," Gertrude says. "Neither is Nellie."

"Suit yourselves." He leans over his horse and spits out an ugly brown wad of chewing tobacco. "But don't expect me to pick you up if you faint."

Sundance gives me a grin. He's chewing on something, too. He maneuvers it to between his front teeth to show it to me: gum.

When the men and stretcher reach the ground, Traven instructs them to put it on the back of the wagon.

"I want to see it," Gertrude says.

"No, you don't," Traven tells her.

"I appreciate your consideration, but it is my duty to identify the body and report to his family. We also have to discuss transportation arrangements. It needs to be transported back immediately. I'll need the coach and a wagon to carry the body."

Gebhard clears his throat. "Actually, *el presidente* loaned Lily and me—"

"Sir, you can come with me, or you will have to make other arrangements. My uncle is a high government official and I'm sure the president would not want his body packed on a donkey."

Good girl! I wonder how Gebhard would like running a donkey back to Mexico City.

Traven addresses both Gebhard and Gertrude: "There are coaches in the area that can be used, including mine."

"Have the police been informed?" Gertrude asks him.

"Not yet. There's a constable about half an hour from here. I'll send a man to notify him."

He pulls down the cover from Don Antonio's face. I take in a sharp breath as Gertrude gasps.

His body is shockingly gray except for blood smears and a gaping wound on his chest—a wound big enough for someone to have stuck their hand in and pulled out his heart while it was still beating.

The body is quickly re-covered.

"Does anyone know how this happened?" I direct my question to Traven. "Any witnesses?"

He shakes his head no. He looks grim, even depressed. No doubt the murder of Don Antonio will probably result in his dig's being shut down.

"A couple of my workers spotted it on their way home from the dig. They never saw anyone around and never went near the body. I went immediately out to investigate and was staggered to find Don Antonio." He wipes sweat off his forehead with his handkerchief. "It's shocking to have found anyone, but seeing someone I know . . ."

"Has it ever happened before? Someone being killed like this?"

"Of course not. It has to be someone insane, and I'm pretty sure I know who's behind it. There's a woman in this area they call a witch. I've heard she's trying to get the locals to return to the old ways. She's even tried to scare off my workers. She probably got some crazies to do it."

"Let me get my boys together and we'll pay this witch a visit and take a look-see around for a bloody knife," Maddox says.

"It wasn't done by her." I surprise myself at my blunt statement, which is based upon thin air. But I don't think La Bruja is capable of this. The murder of the consul is too diabolical. And I had spotted something that is the clincher that the Cult of the Jaguar is alive and well. "For those of you who have come here to steal Montezuma's treasure, this is a warning sent by its protectors to back off.'"

From the looks on the faces around me, I had just fired a shot across their bows.

"You don't know what you're talking about," Thompson snaps. "Accusing us of stealing. You've been speaking bullshit ever since the train. You'd better learn to keep your mouth shut."

"Or what?" Sundance says very bluntly and with a hard edge.

Thompson turns to Maddox. "You'd better remind him what side his bread is buttered on. Besides, this woman's been making up stories and seeing things since she got on the train."

"Did I make this up?" I jerk the cover back enough to expose Don Antonio's chest and point out a pattern on the chest made by blood. "This isn't a blood splatter. It was drawn there for a reason."

One of Traven's men draws back, scared.

"You recognize it, don't you?"

The man shakes his head. "No, señorita, no."

Traven rattles off something to the man in Spanish.

"Sí, señor." The man looks to me and says, "Montezuma."

"What's he talking about?" Gebhard asks me.

"Montezuma's name glyph. The Aztecs wrote in word pictures. Montezuma's name wasn't spelled out in letters, but as a drawing. I saw it at the Aztec museum in the city. These blood streaks are crude, but they get across the point."

"You're right: It's the glyph," Traven says. "I should have spotted it."

I now have their full attention. Maddox has shut his mouth and Roger has moved closer, as if hanging on my every word.

"The message is clear. Someone is willing to protect the treasure by resorting to the old ways."

Everyone stares at me, transfixed, waiting for the next shoe to drop.

"I guess the question is"—I pause and look from one to the other—"who's next?"

57

Gertrude orders the body taken to Don Antonio's tent so it can be properly wrapped for the trip to the city.

She tells me, "I will have to accompany the body back to the city. You can't stay here. Come with me."

"I agree. When are you leaving?"

"Best make it at first light," Traven says. "The road is too dangerous for a four-in-hand coach at night, even without bandidos. Good chance you'll break an axle or a horse's leg."

"He's right," Sundance says. "The road back to the city ain't nothing to brag about even in broad daylight." He gives me a nod and I smile my thanks for his help in putting Thompson in his place.

People fade away: Gertrude escorting the body, the cowboys heading back to the tent city on horseback, and the others walking or piling into the carriage, with the wagon carrying Don Antonio's body bringing up the rear.

Everyone leaves but me and Roger.

"Let me guess," he says. "You want to see the scene of the crime."

"And you're coming with me. I hope you have your gun. Night is falling and there are some creatures that come out around here at night that I'd prefer seeing over the barrel of a six-shooter."

He pats a bulge in his coat.

To beat the darkness, we go up the steps as quickly as we can, leaving us both a bit breathless.

The only evidence of the terrible assault on the man are the bloodstains on the sacrificial block. But I'm glad I came anyway. We're only a couple hundred feet above the ground, but the darkening night sky already looks different.

"Did you know that the ancients used the sky as their map?" I ask Roger. "Traven told us that."

He grunts. "Very interesting. I listened to your dissertation about ancient evil. But I'm not convinced we don't have a copycat—a falling-out among thieves and someone throwing the suspicion away from themselves."

"Maybe. But I doubt it. The glyph is too . . . too Aztec." At the moment, I am too fascinated by the sky to argue the point. It is astonishing. I never really looked at the sky before as something other than a black field with a shiny moon and stars, meaningless except as pretty objects. Now I see it in a different way—the way that Howard, the prospector, meant when he rambled on in a drunken state.

Like he said, the answer is in the stars.

I wondered what I would do if I had to follow the stars and planets to get somewhere. It doesn't look easy. It's even a little hard to tell the difference between planets and stars unless you keep staring at them. The planets, of course, are the lights that don't sparkle.

"Did you know that planets don't twinkle?" I ask Roger.

"Everybody knows that."

"What would we do if we had no map and you had to get back to New York and I had to get back to Pittsburgh by following what we see in the sky? Like Christopher Columbus crossing the ocean."

"I think you've gotten dizzy from the altitude."

"No, for the first time on this trip, I'm thinking clear. You know what, Roger, it's all in the stars. That's the answer."

I lean up and give him a kiss.

"What was that for?"

"For bringing me up here so I could see the stars."

"Let's get going down. If we manage to reach the bottom without breaking our necks, you owe me another kiss."

Going up the steps was challenging. Going down them in the dark is a hair-raising experience. Like climbing a tree or a mountain, getting back down is the biggest challenge.

We are about a third of the way down when Roger says, "You know something."

"I know lots of things." I laugh at my bold statement.

"No, I mean you know something important. I've been thinking about your voice back there. It was like you'd had an epiphany. Spoken to God or something. Tell me what you've figured out."

"Smart man. Okay. I'll tell you if you tell me what you know about the Louisiana Purchase."

"What? What's the matter with you? And Gertrude. She also asked me about that."

I pause and sit down. My heart is pounding a bit. Getting down the steps is scary. Roger sits beside me.

"Both of us wondered why a soon-to-be history professor would not know any more about the biggest land purchase in the history of our country than a schoolboy."

"Hmm. I know we bought it from Napoléon. He was trying to conquer Europe and needed the money. Is that good enough for you?"

"Not even close. I know that much, and I'm no professor."

"What if I told you I wasn't a college guy?"

"I'd say you are finally telling the truth."

He pulls something out of his pocket and then strikes a match to show me a badge.

"Oh no, not another badge. Thompson has one, too."

"Not like mine. Thompson's a customs inspector."

I take a closer look at Roger's silver badge as I get up to continue the climb down. It reads *United States Secret Service.*

"What is the Secret Service—"

"Doing in Mexico—"

"Along with a customs agent," I finish. "Is Thompson's badge a phony?"

"His is as genuine as mine. The difference is, he's dishonored his. He's been running a racket with Don Antonio for years. Antonio provides Thompson with bills of sale that reflect a fraction of the true value of goods being exported from Mexico to the States, and Thompson passes them through customs, pocketing a pretty penny for doing it."

"Like passing off expensive Thoroughbreds as workhorses?"

"Yes, but that's chicken feed compared to say a thousand head of cattle at a time or a priceless ancient artifact."

"So where do you fit in?"

"The Secret Service and customs are both part of the Department of the Treasury. Customs collects money and we investigate when we get suspicious that there's monkey business."

"So what are Thompson, Gebhard, and the rest of the cowboys up to?"

"I didn't know when I jumped on that train out of El Paso at the last minute with a rather pretty traveling companion. We've been watching Thompson and Castillo. We know that Aztec and Mayan pieces have made their way across the border and through customs labeled as pottery in the past."

"And ultimately to Gebhard?"

"Yes. So when the whole bunch of them headed out for Mexico at the same time with an outlaw gang—"

"I figured they were gunfighters."

We finally step onto solid ground, to my relief. It's dark, but there is a bright moon, which brings light and shadows along the Avenue of the Dead.

"You figured right. They all headed for Teo, bringing along Lily Langtry, who, I suspect, just wants to see Mexico and isn't part of the customs fraud."

"They gathered here because the prospector had discovered—"

"¡Señor!"

The voice comes out of the dark shadows and Roger turns to it. A man is suddenly there with an object that looks like a piece of pipe poking from his mouth. Roger steps back and reaches for his gun as the man blows dust in his face from the pipe.

"Dream dust!" comes from me. I hold my breath, determined not to have the substance capture my mind.

More men emerge. I drop to my knees, clutching for Roger's gun under his coat, but someone grabs my hair and jerks me back.

My screams get smothered as they grab me and gag me.

A blindfold goes over my eyes as my heart ricochets in my throat.

58

C offin black.

I can't see anything. It's pitch-black, without a speck of light, not even the twinkle of a star. And it is dead still.

I'm alone.

My hands are no longer tied and the blindfold has been taken off by the men who brought me here. They disappeared like wraiths as soon as they untied me, leaving me standing alone, surrounded by dark and silence.

I'm afraid to move.

Brought from the tepid night outside to a cool place that smells like earth, I feel like I am in a cave. I'm sure of it. But I still fear taking a step because I don't know what is around me. It's too dark to see anything— not even my hand in front of my face. Am I at the edge of a cliff? Where would a step take me?

I feel as if I'm suspended in midair, but my feet tell me I'm on solid ground. I put my hands out to see if I can feel a wall, but I feel nothing.

All I can do is wait in a place darker than night and quieter than a crypt.

The queasy feeling I'm experiencing—my heart in my throat, my mouth dry, my breathing shallow, the strange sensation of my mind being detached from my body—is much like I had when I awoke in the culvert in Mexico City. But this time, they didn't attack me with dream dust, and I'd only gotten a whiff of what Roger was hit with. It's my panic that's creating a sensation of déjà vu.

Poor Roger. I hope he is okay, that he wasn't harmed. The fear that they might have ripped out his heart is petrifying.

While the air in Mexico City has the foul taste that only humans can create, this air smells as if it has not been stirred in an eon. Is it a cave underneath the city? Why not? The ancients built incredible edifices aboveground, so there's no reason to believe they didn't put tunnels under their city.

A light appears. A small light, not much more than how a match would appear dozens of feet away. Like a star. Or a planet—it's not twinkling.

It's something for me to move toward. Maybe it's beckoning me.

I carefully feel around me, moving very cautiously to the side until I feel a wall. Dry earth surrounds me completely. For sure I'm in a cave.

I slowly take a step toward the light, making sure my feet are planted on solid ground, worried that the star might be luring me to something evil or deadly. I suddenly get an image of stepping into a hole and falling face-first down it, flying downward, to be impaled by spears that savages have rigged to kill big game.

Why did they leave me like this, disorientated and helpless?

"Help." I mutter the word, not shouting it, but then clamp my mouth shut. Never show fear to a dangerous animal. Who would help me down here anyway?

A door flies open for a second and *a ball of fire flies at me.*

I stumble backward as it falls and hits the dirt floor in front of me, sending off a spray of sparks. A torch. It lies there, burning and smothering. I stand frozen, staring at it, unable to move my arms and legs.

There is no more movement. No more flaming torches. Nothing. I've been thrown a torch. Why? What in the name of God is going on?

Gathering my courage, I bend down and pick up the torch. Raising it to chest level, I confirm in the sudden light that I am in a dirt tunnel—*and that I am not alone.*

They're present, on both sides of me—lifeless forms.

Not statues of stone, but costumed figures, as if I'm in a wax museum. *A museum of horror.* Bizarre figures that I realize I've seen before—they look like the wall paintings I saw at the Aztec museum and here at Teo. Not the exact ones, but drawn by ancient hands with the same technique.

Aztec gods with huge eyes, gaping jaws, ugly, twisted, even demented features stand erect and glare at me. Each one is adorned in its own tall headpiece, cloaks of bright feathers, and shields befitting Aztec warrior kings. The feathers are long and brilliantly colored: reds, greens, yellows, purples, oranges.

Only one of the inanimate creatures is not bedecked in feathers, and I stare at him, my heart racing. His back is to me, but I can still tell it is a man, not a god. He's almost naked and has that strange gray skin that strikes me as *dead*—cold dead as gray marble, but without the shine and luster of polished stone.

He turns and looks at me as I scream and scream.

It's Howard, the prospector.

I back up as he comes toward me.

His face is distorted; his skin is . . . is . . . *stretched.*

It hits me like a blow to the chest, knocking the wind from me, startling me so much, I freeze in place.

Howard's skin is stretched.

It's someone wearing his skin. What was I told at the museum? Xipe, the flay god, skinned people alive, removing the skin whole and then stretching it over his whole body?

Howard had jumped from the train and made his way to Teo. And into the arms of those who feared he had uncovered their secrets. He'd been flayed, skinned alive. And now someone is wearing his skin.

A door flies open, the same opening that the torch was flung out of.

A man—a beast—*a were-jaguar*—is standing in the doorway.

A creature of the night with the body of a man but facial features that have some of the shape of the jungle beast guards the door, preventing me from any escape.

A beast I have seen before.

59

In front of me, seemingly materializing out of nowhere in the darkness, is the creature I saw outside the train after I argued with Traven. The thing is naked except for the sort of short skirt ancient *indios* wore.

My heart jumps back into my throat. I don't know what it is. Man? Beast? An Aztec magician who inhales magic mushrooms and changes shape?

I can see for sure now that it is not wearing a mask, but I don't know if the animalistic features of its face are formed by the hands of the gods or by a good artist.

It turns away from me and goes deeper into the cavern. Its intent seems to be that I am to follow. There is nothing behind me but an otherworldly darkness, so I follow, passing the thing in a dead man's skin, staying behind the were-jaguar for want of any place to hide.

My knees are weak and my courage is waning. I want to cry and flee at the same time, but I have nowhere to flee. And I'm afraid to show fear, to turn tail and run, sure that the creature will chase me down and rip my flesh to pieces if I try to flee or expose the terror I feel.

I follow the thing into a larger cavern lit by torches. There are more things in the room, more creatures from nightmares. All appear lifeless, statues of stone, until one of them speaks.

"Do you know where you are?" it asks.

It takes a second to recognize the voice, to realize where I have heard it before—the curator at the Aztec museum in Mexico City. His name is Torres.

Then I see him. He is on an elevated throne in front of me. He's dressed as an Aztec nobleman, with robe, tunic, and the brilliant headdress made of the dazzling feathers of rare tropical birds. His features are concealed by a golden jaguar mask.

Do I know where I am? In the caverns of a netherworld? I hope it's not hell. I'm not ready for that place, yet.

"Under the city," I say. "Somewhere. The Pyramid of the Sun, Moon, or one of the other ruins?"

"The archaeologist told you there were secret places."

How did he know that? From Traven? Or his workers?

"Yes. He said he believed there were passageways and chambers but that they would be difficult to find and access."

"Do you know why you are still alive?"

I find this a strange question even in these peculiar circumstances.

"The Good Lord has spared me. So have you." *So far.* "Besides, I've done nothing to deserve to have my life taken. And enough blood's already been shed."

"Don Antonio used his position of trust to permit foreigners to rob Mexico of priceless and irreplaceable antiquities. There are museums in your country and Europe that have finer collections of our art than our own museums. He paid with his life for his crimes against our history."

"I've done nothing to hurt your country."

"Sometimes a life must be sacrificed to save something much more important. You've trespassed. You came to the City of the Gods to find the golden disk of the sun god."

"No, that's not true. I came to Mexico to write entertaining stories about the people and the food. I got involved innocently because people believed the drunken old prospector had passed me information. I was lured here by others who are trying to find the treasure. I don't have any interest in treasure. I came to Teo only to find out what was going on."

"Why? So you can also expose the location of the disk in a newspaper story?"

"I'm not a treasure hunter. I don't care about the disk. I came here in the name of justice, to find out why two men were killed on the train. At least I thought I saw two killed. But back there . . ."

"You saw the skin of the prospector. He didn't die on the train. He had arranged with two conspirators to pretend to be killed so they could get to the treasure first and not split it with so many others. The porter on the train was one of us, sent to watch those we knew were seeking the artifacts that we have sworn to guard.

"In terms of the justice you mention, the prospector received what he deserved. Following the conquest, the Spanish conquistadors tortured the native people to get them to reveal where they hid their valuables. Their favorite method was to roast the feet of people over a blazing fire until the information was revealed or they died from the pain.

"The prospector was a cruel demon who learned the secret to where the golden disk of the sun god was hidden by torturing one of our members in the same way until the man revealed the map. But he paid for his crimes and atrocities when he returned here. Before our man on the train was killed, he sent a message, telling us that the prospector had faked his own death. We were waiting for the prospector when he arrived here."

"Are all these deaths and horrors necessary? Why don't you just turn your golden disk over to the Mexican government and let them put it in your museum?"

I already knew why. The government is unstable at best, with veins of corruption running deep. As Torres told me at the museum, the artifact he saved from being exported ended up at *el presidente*'s house rather than in a museum.

I lamely answer my own question. "You don't trust the government."

"I trust no one but a few like myself who have devoted their lives to the sacred duty. Don Antonio was a good example of how faithful to historical treasures our government will be."

"But you can't kill everyone who seeks your treasure. There are a lot of them in Teo right now and they have guns. And even if you did, more would come."

"They will come as long as they believe there is treasure here. That is why we have brought you here."

"What do mean?"

"There is no treasure, no golden disk. It is true that a golden calendar that is round and as tall as a man once stood atop the sun god's pyramid, but that disk was moved centuries ago, after its location was revealed under another torture. Where it is stored"—he shakes his head—"is a secret taken to the grave by those who hid it. They knew that where it rests could be again revealed by torture and thus they allowed the secret to die with them rather than passing down its location."

"You want me to tell the others this? They won't believe me."

Oh my God, did I say that? As soon as the words were out of my mouth, I wished I could grab them and pull them back.

"You're correct. They won't believe the truth. So you must tell them a lie."

"A lie? What lie?"

"That you met the leader of the Cult of the Jaguar and he told you that the disk was moved after we discovered that the prospector had obtained the location."

"I'm confused. You told me that long ago the disk was taken from Teo and put somewhere no one living knows. Now you want me to say that it was actually here and you moved it after you found out the location, this place, was compromised?"

"As you said, no one will believe we don't have the disk, so they will keep looking. And if not these men, then the next seekers, and sooner or later, one of them will find these caverns. When they do, they will discover the true treasures hidden by my forefathers—codices that are irreplaceable works of arts and literature, murals so well preserved that they are as beautiful as at the moment the artist finished them.

"These are the treasures my ancestors hid and that I am sworn to protect with my life. Those with lust for treasures will take these artifacts when they discover there is no disk of gold, and they will sell them to the highest bidder in New York, London, or Berlin."

I understand his concern. But some sense of justice in me will not let a hole in his theory be passed over.

"I want to help. I sincerely do. You should keep the historical pieces of your history safe until they can be displayed for everyone, but I just don't see how those people out there will believe me. They already think that I am imagining things. Don't you see," I pled, "I don't have any proof. They just aren't going to buy the story."

"Once again, you are correct. So I am sending you back with proof that you have met with the Cult of the Jaguar. This will go with you."

A round bundle comes flying out of the darkness. It hits the cavern floor and rolls up to my leg. In the dim light, it appears to be a bundle of cloth.

"What the . . ." I stare down at the bundle, wondering how a bundle of cloth is going to convince people I have met with the leader of the cult.

I lean down to get a closer look at the bundle.

Oh . . . my . . . God!

60

Well, I think it gets across the point nicely."

That is from Gertrude.

We are in the dining tent, all of us who were drawn one way or another to the City of the Gods by the legend of its golden treasure. Besides Gertrude and me, Roger, Traven, Thompson, Maddox, Sundance, Gebhard, and Lily are here. Maddox's cowboys are outside somewhere, probably still fraternizing with the señoritas at the makeshift cantina.

Oh, and the guest of honor: Howard, the prospector. At least at the pile of skin that was left of the man. Before I began my explanation, I put the bundle that had been thrown to me in the caverns on the table, then opened it.

He had been nicely folded, so his startled face was up. The sad, pale face, flattened as if it had been a balloon that the air was let out of, is not one that would be recognized by his mother, but I don't think anyone present doubts that it is his. The bushy hair, beard, and eyebrows are recognizable features that would be hard to duplicate.

"Howard left the train, came here, and ran afoul of the cult, which have taken on the task of protecting Aztec artifacts," I tell them, deliberately avoiding the word *treasure,* at least for the moment. "It got him skinned. Some sort of ritual for those who offend the Aztec gods."

"Xipe," Traven says. "The flay god. Aztecs worshiped him as a god of life, death, and rebirth. Priests flayed the skin whole from people and wore it as a symbol of rebirth."

"That double-crossing, two-timing bastard will be reborn in hell," Maddox says.

Hopefully, Maddox will meet him there one day . . . soon. Running an outlaw gang isn't going to be ticket through the pearly gates.

Traven's explanation helps me catch my breath. I am so mentally drained and numb that I was able to flop Howard down and open the bundle without fainting or vomiting—I didn't have the strength to get nauseated.

Howard went on the table, faceup, for the exact reason that Gertrude had guessed: He gets the point across nicely. Now I had to drive it home.

No one seems to have much to say. More likely, they don't know what to say. Me, either. I'd been blindfolded again while in the caverns and taken on a circuitous route before being released about half a mile north of the Pyramid of the Moon.

The first person I saw was Roger, who had a genuine expression of relief when he saw me. I led Roger, Gertrude, and the others who had been out looking for me down the Avenue of the Dead, refusing to answers questions or tell them what was in the bundle I was lugging from a piece of rope tied around it until I had had a glass of water and the undivided attention of everyone.

After I had Howard on the table and we got past the gasps, mutterings, and quite a bit of profanity that was new to me, I told them the truth, the whole truth, and nothing but the truth—except for the part the cult leader had told me to lie about.

No one said much as I laid out the fact that the disk had been moved from Teo to a secret place far away. Not that I had their undivided attention. I'm not certain which of them really listened. For sure, the ones who had come here to find the treasure didn't hear what they most wanted—some clue from me as to where it is.

I looked around as I told them what I had been through and learned, hoping that I'd get some clue as to who lusted the most for the treasure and may have been capable of murder to find it, but mostly they just stood quietly and stared at Howard, as if he had the answers.

I finished talking and there was an awkward silence, the kind you get when you tell a joke that falls flat. That's when Gertrude piped up about Howard getting the point across.

It certainly does make the situation clear, at least to me. If they had the time to catch and skin Howard before the pack of us even arrived, then it's obvious that the protectors of the sun god's gold disk knew treasure seekers were coming and would have had both the time and inclination to move the disk to a safe place. And they could do it faster than their ancestors did because it could be loaded on a wagon.

But logic and reason doesn't count for much when you trample someone's dream of getting rich fast.

"That's all I know," I tell them. "The treasure's been moved somewhere else and you all might as well go back to whatever you were doing before you got involved in this wild-goose chase."

"Bullshit!" Thompson snaps.

I give him a polite smile. I'm calm and even a bit at peace. I think all my energy to do anything more than just keep my eyes open and breathe has been burned up.

"And which part of the situation do you find analogous to cow droppings, Mr. Thompson?"

"All of it!" He slams his fist on the table.

I'm sure he would have been delighted if my face had been there.

"Don't blame her for the message," Roger says.

"It's all a bunch of crap," Thompson says to me. "You're in cahoots with others seeking the treasure."

"Why don't you point out whom I'm scheming with? Sundance? Mr. Gebhard? Lily, did you come to Mexico to steal Aztec treasures? I guess Mr. Thompson suspects you of helping me skin poor Howard."

"Ridiculous," Gebhard says.

Poor Lily just stares with wide eyes filled with horror that comes from her heart, not her acting ability. I will have to apologize to her later. It's just that I am trying to get a point across to Thompson. But I don't think it's working.

"None of you are foolin' me." Thompson is boiling over, ready to blow his stack.

Maddox's hand stays close to his gun as Thompson continues ranting.

"There's gotta be a hidden door out there leading to the gold. I learned tracking from a Comanche chief. I'm going out to the ruins and follow your tracks back to where you were taken to." He jerks his head at Sundance. "Let's go, cowboy."

As Sundance follows Thompson, Maddox says, "Sundance, you're with us. You, too, Thompson."

Sundance shrugs and leaves with Thompson.

I could have told his boss that Sundance is with Thompson. It was

Sundance who was supposed to have seen Howard killed and thrown from the train. And Thompson was playing the were-jaguar who threw him off.

Maddox suddenly seems like he has ants in his pants. "I'm not letting them get away with the treasure," he tells Gebhard. "I'm getting my boys and cutting ourselves in. Maybe for all of it."

Gebhard shakes his head. "You're on your own. Lily and I are leaving."

To my surprise, Roger follows Maddox and the others out, avoiding looking at me as he goes.

Gertrude and I are suddenly alone with Howard.

"Do you think they'll find the tracks?" she asks.

"I don't know. I have no idea where they took me except that it was underground. It may have even been beyond the ruins. And I'm positive they covered their tracks, assuming the ground was soft enough to even leave tracks. I guess in a sense, the members of the cult have been covering their tracks for hundreds of years, so they must be good at it."

"It's barbaric what the cult did to Don Antonio," she says. "If it's true that he permitted Aztec art objects to be taken out of the country, he should have been prosecuted, but not murdered. At least with the prospector, they told you he had tortured one of their people. It's like the Bible says, live by the sword, die by the sword. Are we supposed to, uh, bury . . . it?"

"I think we'd better leave that for the Mexican police, constable, or whoever is coming. If anyone has actually sent for them."

"I don't quite get how the cast of characters in this treasure hunt line up. They don't seem to all be on the same side."

"I'm sure Thompson, Sundance, and Howard double-crossed the others and faked Howard's death to get the treasure for themselves. Why Thompson came up with a reason to throw doubt on the fact I had seen the were-jaguar stumped me, but then I realized it was because I had pretty much described the were-jaguar I saw on the train as someone wearing a mask.

"That would have caused suspicion among Maddox and the others. Sundance wouldn't have mentioned the mask if he had been the sole witness. Instead, he would have claimed that the prospector was attacked by what appeared to be a were-jaguar—not something with a simple mask, but made up like the person I saw after arguing with Traven over the donkey.

"With the plan devised by Thompson, Sundance, and Howard to cut out the rest of the conspirators going down the drain, Thompson and Sundance protected themselves by claiming Howard had jumped ship to cut everyone else out of the treasure. And they came up with a reason for the jaguar mask I saw, not so much to discredit me, but so Don Antonio would believe Howard had jumped ship by himself."

Gertrude shakes her head. "Greed has no limits, does it? A man like Thompson and the cowboys who aren't rich hunger for wealth. Don Antonio had plenty but wanted more. Gebhard, who has great wealth, wants to have something no one else has. Rich or poor, each of them will do anything to get what he lusts for."

"I'm—I'm shocked Roger is part of it."

She gives me a look of sympathy. "I saw your face when Roger followed the others out."

I sigh. It's not a subject I want to talk about. And I'm very tired, worn to the bone, and my brains have turned into scrambled eggs.

"Why don't you take a nap while I get the carriage and our things ready to go," she says. "I have to find the coachmen. Last time I saw them, they were talking to women at the *indio* village."

We part outside the tent, Gertrude to find the coachmen, and I to wander wearily to the tent.

As I enter the dark tent, I'm grabbed from behind and a hand grips my throat.

61

S cream and I'll kill you."

Thompson is behind me, his hand a steel vise gripping my throat. I try to pull his hand off my throat, but he is so much bigger and more powerful, I'm like a child in his grasp.

He tightens his grip and jerks me up off my feet. Strength I didn't think I had left erupts in me as I panic and struggle, kicking and twisting as my windpipe closes and I can't get air into my lungs.

"Hold still."

He lets up on the pressure but still has a hold on me as I take in a gasp of air.

"Listen to me—I'm going to let you go."

His mouth is next to my ear and I can feel his hot breath.

"You make a sound and I'll break your neck."

He removes his hand from my throat and grabs me by the shoulders, turning me to face him.

"Tell me where the treasure's at and I won't hurt you."

He grabs my throat again and lifts me up on tiptoe.

"Lie to me and you're dead meat. You understand, bitch?"

The only understanding I can convey is a gurgle, which I hope he understands is my agreement to his terms.

He slowly relaxes his grip on my neck and I cough and gasp as I take in air, my chest heaving. I push his hand away from me as I try to get my breathing under control.

"I know you lied back there. You've made a deal with the *indios*, haven't you? A deal for you to get something."

My agreement is what he wants to hear and nothing short of that will keep him from wringing my neck again, so I give it, gurgling out a yes as best I can and nodding my head.

"What did they give you? The gold disk?"

Trick question. I can see it in his eyes. He knows they would never give me the sun god's treasure. I vigorously shake my head.

"But they gave you something, didn't they?"

More nodding of my head as I jerk it up and down like a pump handle.

"Tell me," he says, his voice so excited, he sounds hoarse. "We'll take it and get the rest of the treasure, and I'll split it all with you."

I try to speak and touch my throat, shaking my head. I gesture for him to come closer so he can hear me. He leans down and I do what comes naturally to me, a move taught to me by my brothers to use after I got the worst of it at school when I tangled with a bully.

"At the side of the pyramid." I speak so hoarsely and softly that I'm sure he can't make out my words.

"What'd you say?"

He bends down even closer to hear, and I go up on my toes and butt him in the nose with my head.

He takes a step backward and I slip around him as he grabs at me. I go through the tent opening, more in a dive than a run, and go down, hitting the ground facedown.

I scream, but it comes out as a hoarse yelp.

He flies out behind me and grabs my left foot to drag me back inside. I kick at him with my other foot and pull out of his grip.

Getting on my hands and knees, I start to crawl, but he grabs me by the back of my head.

"Let her go!"

It's Roger. He comes running up and flies at Thompson, slamming into him, knocking the man back, both of them hitting the ground.

Roger rolls over and is up on his feet first. I scramble away in a crawl as he goes at Thompson, who is trying to get up. He swings at Thompson and connects, hitting him in the side of the face. The man falls back again, going down as he avoids another punch from Roger.

As Thompson hits the ground, he draws his six-shooter and brings it up, sending off a shot.

Roger spins around and staggers backward, losing his balance and dropping to one knee.

Thompson turns to me, taking aim, when I hear Sundance shout, "Thompson!"

Thompson looks to the cowboy, who is fifty feet away. He raises his gun and gets off a shot.

Sundance's movements are a blur as his gun comes out of its holster and a shot is fired.

Thompson grunts and falls back for a second, but he comes back around, raising his gun as Sundance fires again.

The bullet strikes Thompson and the man is slammed back, his gun flying out of his hand. He lets out a gurgling gasp and then lies still.

Roger is suddenly hovering over me.

"Damn." Roger shakes his head. "I forgot I have a gun."

62

Sundance gives me a sour grin.

We're standing by the rain barrel, where I've dipped a handkerchief Gertrude gave me to take some of the raw burn from my bruised throat.

She and Roger had backed off after workers carried Thompson's body into his tent, giving me a chance to thank Sundance in private.

He's taken off his hat and is shuffling it through his fingers nervously as he talks. Tough guy that he is, he's more comfortable with other men and guns than he is with a woman.

"Things just would never work out between us," he says. "Sure would have been nice to have met you in another time, maybe in that other life when I lived in Pennsylvania and still stood in good favor with John Law."

How he had fallen from the grace of the law is not a concern for me except that his being an outlaw, which he has admitted to me that he is, makes me worry that he will someday get his neck stretched by a posse's rope.

He set a path for himself when he left small-town Pennsylvania, and for whatever reason, he has made it a crooked one.

"I'm heading back with the boys," he says.

He hasn't volunteered that he and Thompson schemed with Howard, the prospector, to get the treasure for themselves, but I'm certain that was the case. At this point, I'm just grateful he has decided to take my side instead of Thompson's.

And I'm grateful for the fact he has not questioned me about the treasure. How successful I would have been lying to him with a straight face after he saved Roger and me is doubtful.

I give him a kiss on the cheek. I cried earlier when I thanked him for saving our lives. Roger thanked him, too, looking a bit sheepish when Sundance told him he shouldn't pack a gun if he's not going to use it.

"Please tell your friends that I really don't know where the treasure is or even if it exists."

He chuckles. "I know that, Nellie. Those bloodthirsty Aztec warriors would have sent you back as a sackful of skin, like they did Howard, if you knew where they're sitting on their gold."

"Are you going to be okay with your, uh, pals?"

I posed the question because he had schemed to double-cross them, and regardless of how much they fear his prowess with a gun, there are too many of them for him to take on.

"Yeah, don't you worry about it; we're tight. None of us trusted Thompson, so when he approached me with the notion of going it alone with Howard, the boys all agreed that I would play that hand. In the end, it would have been Thompson who got cut out."

He gives me a big hug and I hold him tightly. I know that there is something about that big grin and eyes that tease and tempt a woman that I will not soon forget.

"Sundance, do me a big favor."

"Anything you want."

"Stay out of trouble. If you want to go into banks, get a job in one rather than robbing them."

ROGER IS WAITING UNDER THE SHADE of a tree. Thompson's shot did not hit him, but getting out of the way had sent him sprawling.

"You planning on riding off into the sunset with that cowboy? I saw the way you were looking at each other."

"I'm not planning on running off with anyone. I'm married to a job as a newspaperwoman. I'm just grateful for his help."

"I suppose you think he would have let you have the lower berth."

"Oh, Roger, I don't just think that; I know it. Sundance may have his faults, and he may end up on the wrong end of a rope someday, but he is a gentleman and knows how to treat a lady."

He gives me one of his big sardonic grins. "I just treated you like the independent woman you are."

Touché. "You'd be surprised how much an independent woman ap-

NO JOB FOR A LADY 285

preciates a man's help when she's attacked by a were-jaguar and a treasure-hunting thug."

He beams with pride. "Well, the two men I came here to bring to justice back home, Thompson and Don Antonio, are now dead. Guess that's for the best. Saves taxpayers the cost of a trial, not to mention that I would never have managed to get Don Antonio out of the country." He grins. "I think you know I'm not very good at pretending to be a historian."

You're not very good at remembering you carry a gun, either, I think but I let that pass. "You truly need a different undercover identity; your history skills are shaky. You dodged the question about Cortés's last big battle by passing it to Gertrude and flubbed when she asked you about the Louisiana Purchase."

"I think Don Antonio was testing me, wondering if I really was a student of Mexican history. He was suspicious of me from the start. But I think he finally accepted me at face value when he found out we were sharing a compartment. It wasn't something an investigator would do."

Nor a lady.

"Are you coming back to the city with us? Gertrude is waiting with the carriage."

"No, I'm going to stick around and speak to whatever Mexican policeman shows up. Let them know what happened, so everything dies here. You realize you'll be contacted by them when you get to Mexico City."

I had already thought about that, and I knew that I would be exported pronto if I didn't agree not to use the story in a dispatch home.

"I'm going to miss you, Nellie Bly. I don't know what I will do when I don't have you picking on me."

"Oh, you'll find someone. A handsome man like you won't have any trouble finding a woman who wants to order him around."

"You were right, by the way. I almost had one up to the altar, before she got scared and ran. Or came to her senses. How about you? When will you be ready to settle down and marry?"

"As my brothers would say about themselves, after I sow my oats. But in my case, it doesn't mean being wild, but carving out a career for myself in this man's world."

"Not to worry, Nellie Bly, you'll succeed."

And then he does something I'm not expecting: He gives me his book by Edgar Allan Poe.

"I marked a poem for you so that you won't forget me."

JOINING GERTRUDE IN THE CARRIAGE, my eyes are a bit misty. I will miss Roger and always wonder what might have been.

Gertrude hands me a handkerchief.

"There's a poem, Nellie dear, one that I love dearly. It's relates how a young judge stops to ask a farm girl for a drink of water. Both the judge and the girl are smitten with each other, but they go on with their lives, he marrying a socially prominent woman who loves him only for his money and power, and she marrying a simple farmer and living a life of drudgery.

"The poem has one of the most telling and poignant lines in our English language. It goes like this." She looks up at the sky as she says:

> "For of all sad words of tongue or pen,
> The saddest are these: 'It might have been.'"*

I make good use of her handkerchief.

WHEN WE REACH MY HOTEL ENTRANCE, Gertrude and I part with hugs and promises to keep in touch. She is returning immediately to Oxford.

"I would have had to anyway," she tells me, "but now that poor Don Antonio died so horribly, I can't stand to stay a moment longer."

As for me, my next quest will be off to Puebla, a large city southeast of the capital, and a visit to Cholula, which is near Puebla. Cholula is the largest pyramid in the world and I want to report about it.

I am halfway across the lobby when I hear an exclamation. "Well! It's about time!"

"Mother!"

"Oh, you remember me? The old woman you abandoned when she fell weak and sick?"

That isn't exactly true, but I don't care. I'm just happy to see her.

Nellie Bly

---

* The poem is "Maud Muller," written by John Greenleaf Whittier in 1856.

CAST OF CHARACTERS

ARCHAEOLOGIST, SPY, WRITER, explorer, and adventure traveler are just some of the labels pinned on this incredible woman.

Born Gertrude Margaret Lowthian Bell in 1868, she grew up headstrong, with a willful desire for independence and obtaining knowledge. After graduating from Oxford, she just didn't go into the world, a "man's world"; she charged into it. Like Nellie, she gave no quarter in the battle to succeed in a man's world.

GERTRUDE BELL VISITING ARCHAEOLOGICAL
EXCAVATIONS IN BABYLON, 1909.
(Wikipedia Commons)

She took on challenges and achieved accomplishments that few men had. She went to Egypt and Arabia, learned the languages, and traveled by camel to places no Westerner had set foot upon. She spoke Arabic, Persian, French, German, Italian, and Turkish.

During World War I, she used her knowledge of the deserts to guide British troop movements in battles taking place in the Middle East.

After the war, she and T. E. Lawrence (Lawrence of Arabia) were instrumental in the creation of the present-day countries of Iraq and Jordan. She was also the driving force behind the creation of the great archaeological museum in Baghdad.

People described her as a woman with loads of energy—too much; very intellectual, with a lot of drive and determination; arrogant; imperious; ruthlessly ambitious; sharp-tongued; someone who expressed authority in her manners and voice; high-spirited and possessing extraordinary self-confidence and an urge to debate. However, there were three things she did not excel in—spelling, music, and cooking; and it was because these were of no interest to her that she didn't see the importance of them.

But Gertrude had a love for clothing. She dressed extravagantly, and when meeting her for the first time, people would comment on her "Mayfair manners and Paris frocks."

Another of her great loves was reading. Her nose was never out of a book, and she said she escaped through them. "They are my magic carpet."

While in college, she liked going places alone and thought it extremely unfair that boys could go without a chaperone. Not only was this frustrating but it angered her, as well. Given that even a museum visit required an escort, she complained, "I wish I could go to the National, but you see there is no one to take me. If I were a boy, I should go to that incomparable place every week, but being a girl to see lovely things is denied me!"

Unlike Nellie, Gertrude never married. Instead, she had an unconsummated affair with Maj. Charles Doughy-Wylie, a married man, with whom she exchanged love letters.

On July, 12, 1926, she died. She was fifty-seven, the same age that Nellie Bly was when she died.

She had been born wealthy, but after her father passed away, there were family money problems. In Baghdad, ill from pleurisy, she took an overdose of sleeping pills. No one knows if it was accidental or intentional, because the night she took the pills, she asked her maid to wake her up at a certain time the next morning.

POOR NELLIE! SHE THOUGHT Lily was a beautiful swan and that she was an ugly duckling. And as the world judged beauty, a woman who cap-

LILY LANGTRY, 1885 (National Archives)

tured the hearts of audiences on the stage and the beds of princes offstage outranked a wannabe foreign correspondent who traveled across a continent (and eventually around the world) carrying a single carpetbag.

Lily was born Emilie Charlotte Le Breton in 1853, on Jersey, a British island in the English Channel.

She had a number of prominent lovers, including the future king of the United Kingdom, Edward VII. In 1877, when he was the Prince of Wales, he arranged it so that he could sit next to Langtry at a dinner party given by Sir Allen Young May. Her husband was conveniently placed at the other end of the table.

Their affair lasted from late 1877 to June 1880. Some say it was because of Lily's spending habits. Edward once complained to her, "I've spent enough on you to build a battleship," whereupon she tartly replied, "And you've spent enough in me to float one."

Being brought up with six brothers, just like Nellie, Lily had no problem speaking her mind to anyone. Because she was a challenge for her French governess, Lily was put with her brothers' tutor and became better educated than most women of her time.

At twenty, she married Edward Langtry, an Irish landowner and widower. They knew each other because his wife had been the sister of the wife of one of Lily's brothers. It was not the happiest of marriages, and Lily went on to have numerous affairs.

Like Gertrude Bell, Lily loved fine clothes, but she preferred to wear a simple black dress. She didn't need anything else—her beauty outshined anything she wore.

She soon became close friends with Oscar Wilde and Sarah Bernhardt, and it was because of their encouragement that she embarked upon a stage career. Her debut was in London at the Haymarket Theatre, in a play called *She Stoops to Conquer*.

It is no coincidence that Nellie knew about Lily. Lily toured the United States many times, first in 1882, and even though the critics didn't give her the best of reviews, the audiences loved her. The roles she appeared in included Pauline in *The Lady of Lyons* and Rosalind in *As You Like It*.

It wasn't until 1882 that Lily became involved with Frederic Gebhard, who was a well-known New York City millionaire. He introduced her to the sport of Thoroughbred horse racing, which Lily embraced so wholeheartedly that together they took a stableful of American horses to race in England. Their relationship lasted nine years.

When Nellie mentioned to Lily that a town in Texas was named after her, Nellie was not correct. The town of Langtry was named for a railroad supervisor. However, Judge Roy Bean, a notorious hanging judge of the Old West, lived there and was in love with Lily from afar. He even built an opera house in hopes that one day she would perform in it.

Of the three women in the book, Lily, Gertrude, and Nellie, Lily lived the longest. She died in 1929, at the age of seventy-five. However, before her death she basically was a lonely woman. She had married a man much younger than she and he lived in another house. They would see each other occasionally, but her closest companion was her maid.

HISTORY HAS GIVEN LILY LANGTRY many more pages than her lover Frederic Gebhard, but in his day he was a wealthy, well-known playboy and owner of some of the best racehorses in the country. He also had a deep interest in Mexico and in encouraging U.S. trade with that country.

His obituary in *The New York Times*, September 9, 1910, summarizes a life of luxury and leisure, his every whim satisfied . . . until it caught up with him:

FREDERIC GEBHARD DIES IN GARDEN CITY

———

One of Best Known Men in New York 15
Years Ago—Suffered Breakdown Last Spring.

———

HIS INCOME ONCE $80,000

Racing and Yachting enthusiast and Member
of Many Clubs—Former Friend of Mrs. Langtry.

Frederic Gebhard, fifty years old, one of the best known men in New York some fifteen years ago, the uncle of Mrs. Reginald C. Vanderbilt and the brother of Mrs. Frederick Neilson, died yesterday morning at 8 o'clock in the Garden City Hotel, in Garden City, L.I. Early in the year Mr. Gebhard suffered a breakdown that developed into a dangerous case of pleurisy. In April, with two doctors and two nurses attending him at the Stratford House, 11 East Thirty-second street, where he had been living for some time, his friends did not expect him to live ten days.

He recovered strength, however, and two months ago was moved to Garden City, on the advice of his doctors. His sister hurried to his bedside three days ago from Sandy Point Farm, near Newport, and Mrs. Vanderbilt started for Garden City Wednesday night. His second wife, who was Marie L. Gamble, had been in constant attendance at his bedside since early in the Spring.

Mr. Gebhard's father left, upon his death, an estate valued at $5,000,000. Frederic Gebhard early came into an income of about $80,000 a year. The newspapers of many years ago said that he was the best-dressed man of the times. He gave himself up to answering the calls of society, went in for racing and yachting, and lived generally the life of the accomplished, leisurely man about town.

One of his earliest interests outside of ballroom and clubs was horse racing. He owned the famous runner Eole, and paid $10,000 for the filly Experiment,

FREDERIC GEBHARD
(Library of Congress)

which he renamed Louise in honor of his first wife. Volunteer II, and Olinda, the famous high jumper, were also property of his. For a while he was in partnership with A. W. Hunter in the management of a string of racers.

For several years after he met Lily Langtry, the famous beauty, who was termed the "Jersey Lily." It was reported that they were to be married. They bought adjoining ranches in the West, both giving it out that they were going to lead simple lives. The stage called her back, and he could not escape Broadway and Fifth Avenue. They drifted apart in 1893.

The following year he became engaged to Miss Louise Hollingsworth Morris, then perhaps the best-known beauty in Baltimore. The wedding was on an elaborate scale. Friends of the two families came from all parts of the world to attend it. The couple were divorced in 1901 in South Dakota, Mrs. Gebhard later marrying Henry Clews, Jr.

Again free, he took up the old life that he had followed years before. In the latter part of 1906 it was announced that in January of that year he had married Marie L. Gamble, an actress. The Rev. Henry Marsh Warren performed the ceremony at his home, 48 West Ninety-fourth Street, and kept it a secret until the end of the year. It was said at the time that Mrs. Gebhard before her marriage had speculated luckily in Wall Street and had made $750,000.

She was the daughter of a Washington business man. At the age of sixteen she eloped with a clerk named Urimstatt in the Government Printing Office, but the marriage was unhappy and they were divorced.

The year after his second marriage it was said that at last Mr. Gebhard had come to the end of his resources. Mrs. Neilson, his sister, obtained a judgment against him for $72,159, which he had borrowed, it was alleged, in 1905. He paid the judgment in January of 1907. In July of that year he and Waldo Story, a sculptor, went into trade at 547 Fifth Avenue under the name of the Ritz Importation Company of America, Canada, and Cuba, selling wines, coffees, and spices.

Mr. Gebhard was born in this city. He belonged to nearly every club in the city at one time and another, including the Metropolitan, Union, Coaching, Knickerbocker, Racquet, New York Yacht, Larchmont Yacht, Tuxedo, and the Westminster Kennel.

WHEN NELLIE CONCLUDED that Sundance was born to hang, she was right.

Harry Alonzo Longabaugh, alias the Sundance Kid, went west from Pennsylvania on a wagon train when he was just fifteen years old, in 1882. He soon earned his outlaw handle by stealing a horse, saddle, and gun from a ranch in Sundance, Wyoming.

Sundance was fast with a gun and became known as a gunslinger. He eventually became a member of the Wild Bunch gang with Butch Cassidy and pulled off the longest series of successful bank and train robberies the country has ever seen.

He and Butch are the best-known outlaws in American history, thanks to the 1969 movie *Butch Cassidy and the Sundance Kid,* starring Paul Newman and Robert Redford. The film was selected for preservation in the United States National Film Registry by the Library of Congress as being "culturally, historically, or aesthetically significant."

It is believed that in 1908, Sundance and Butch Cassidy (his real

FRONT ROW LEFT TO RIGHT: HARRY A. LONGABAUGH (ALIAS THE SUNDANCE KID); BEN KILPATRICK (ALIAS THE TALL TEXAN); ROBERT LEROY PARKER (ALIAS BUTCH CASSIDY). STANDING: WILL CARVER AND HARVEY LOGAN (ALIAS KID CURRY). (Photographed by John Schwartz, Fort Worth, Texas, 1900)

name was Robert Leroy Parker) were killed in a shoot-out with the law in the South American country of Bolivia. However, no one knows for sure if they were killed. Modern DNA tests were conducted on bodies interred after the fight, but these DNA samples did not match the DNA of either man's descendants.

So whether Sundance and Butch bit the dust in a gun battle over a mule train of gold or died with their boots on in some luxurious tropical paradise paid for with ill-gotten gains is a mystery covered by the dust of history.

NOTE

FROM

The Editors

IN REGARD TO *No Job for a Lady,* we are once again forced to defend against accusations that real-life events in Nellie's life were merged with a fictional story that was concocted. It's true that Nellie's 1888 book, *Six Months in Mexico,* does not include the murders, treasure hunt, were-jaguars, or the other mysteries and adventures recounted here, but that's because Nellie was forced by the Mexican government to omit from her own book all the facts concerning Montezuma's treasure.

As we have with the other books in the series, we want the reader to rest assured that they may compare the truth and veracity about the series to that attributed to the lioness of literature, Lillian Hellman, by none other than Mary McCarthy.

Nellie's book about her trip to Mexico was not published until 1888, two years after her attempt to establish herself as a foreign correspondent by running off to Mexico. When she did return to Pittsburgh, she believed that because her articles sent to *The Pittsburgh Dispatch* were so well received and enjoyed by readers, she would be officially appointed a foreign correspondent.

Instead, Mr. Madden, the managing editor, thought Nellie was very lucky not to have been kidnapped, raped, or killed. He said she could have her previous job back, writing society twaddle—and nothing more.

Angered, Nellie headed for New York. Publication of her Mexico experiences (those she was able to share with the public) had to wait until her spectacular ten days in a madhouse caper, which we shared with readers in *The Alchemy of Murder*.

The following are excerpts from the 1888 publication of *Six Months in Mexico*. Her opening paragraph reveals in an understated manner that she had left the reporter's job "usually assigned women on newspapers" and headed for Mexico to become a foreign correspondent, with her mother tagging along.

ONE WINTRY NIGHT I bade my few journalistic friends adieu, and, accompanied by my mother, started on my way to Mexico. Only a few months previous I had become a newspaperwoman. I was too impatient to work along at the usual duties assigned women on newspapers, so I conceived the idea of going away as a correspondent.

Three days after leaving Pittsburgh we awoke one morning to find ourselves in the lap of summer. For a moment it seemed a dream. When the porter had made up our bunks the evening previous, the surrounding country had been covered with a snowy blanket. When we awoke the trees were in leaf and the balmy breeze mocked our wraps.

The land was so beautiful. We gazed in wonder on the cotton-fields, which looked, when moved by the breezes, like huge, foaming breakers in their mad rush for the shore. And the cowboys! I shall never forget the first real, live cowboy I saw on the plains. The train was moving at a "putting-in-time" pace, as we came up to two horsemen. They wore immense sombreros, huge spurs, and had lassos hanging to the side of their saddles. I knew they were cowboys, so, jerking off a red scarf I waved it to them.

I was not quite sure how they would respond. From the thrilling and wicked stories I had read, I fancied they might begin shooting at me as quickly as anything else. However, I was surprised and delighted to see them lift their sombreros, in a manner not excelled by a New York exquisite, and urge their horses into a mad run after us.

Such a ride! The feet of the horses never seemed to touch the ground. By this time nearly all the passengers were watching the race between horse and steam. At last we gradually left them behind. I waved my scarf sadly in farewell, and they responded with their sombreros. I never felt as much reluctance for leaving a man behind as I did to leave those cowboys.

I shall never forget the sight of that waiting-room [at the El Paso, Texas, train station]. Men, women, and children, dogs and baggage, in one promiscuous mass. The dim light of an oil-lamp fell with dreary effect on the scene. Some were sleeping, lost for awhile to all the cares of life; some were eating; some were smoking, and a group of men were passing around a bottle occasionally as they dealt out a greasy pack of cards.

It was evident that we could not wait the glimpse of dawn 'mid these surroundings. With my mother's arm still tightly clasped in mine, we again sought the outer darkness. I saw a man with a lantern on his arm, and went to him and asked directions to a hotel. He replied that they were all closed at this hour, but if I could be satisfied with a second-class house, he would conduct us to where he lived. We were only too glad for any shelter, so without one thought of where he might take us, we followed the light of his lantern as he went ahead.

El Paso, the American town, and El Paso del Norte (the pass to the north), the Mexican town, are separated, as New York from Brooklyn, as Pittsburgh from Allegheny. The Rio Grande, running swiftly between its low banks, its waves muddy and angry, or sometimes so low and still that one would think it had fallen asleep from too long duty, divides the two towns.

Communication is open between them by a ferryboat, which will carry you across for two and one half cents, by hack, buggies, and saddle horses, by the Mexican Central Railway, which transports its passengers from one town to the other, and a street-car line, the only international street-car line in the world, for which it has to thank Texas capitalists.

It is not possible to find a greater contrast than these two cities form, side by side. El Paso is a progressive, lively, American town; El Paso del Norte is as far back in the Middle Ages, and as slow as it was when the first adobe hut was executed in 1680. It is rich with grass and shade trees, while El Paso is as spare of grass as a twenty-year-old youth is of beard.

At every station we obtained views of the Mexicans. As the train drew in, the natives, of whom the majority still retain the fashion of Adam, minus fig leaves, would rush up and gaze on the travelers in breathless wonder, and continue to look after the train as if it was the one event of their lives.

As we came to larger towns we could see armed horsemen riding at a 2:09 speed, leaving a cloud of dust in their wake, to the stations. When the train stopped they formed in a decorous line before it, and so remained until the train started again on its journey. I learned that they were a government guard. They do this so, if there is any trouble on the train or any raised at the station during their stop, they could quell it.

Hucksters and beggars constitute most of the crowd that welcomes the train. From the former we bought flowers, native fruit, eggs, goat milk, and strange Mexican food. The pear cacti, which is nursed in greenhouses in the States, grows wild on the plains to a height of twenty feet, and its great green lobes, or leaves, covered thickly with thorns, are frequently three feet in diameter. . . . It has a very cool and pleasing taste.

At larger towns a change for the better was noticeable in the clothing of the people. The most fashionable dress for the Mexican Indian was white muslin panteloons, twice as wide as those worn by the dudes last summer; a *serape,* as often cotton as wool, wrapped around the shoulders; a straw sombrero, and sometimes leather sandals bound to the feet with leather cords.

The women wear loose sleeveless waists with a straight piece of cloth pinned around them for skirts, and the habitual *rebozo* wrapped about the head and holding the equally habitual baby. No difference how cold or warm the day, nor how scant the lower garments, the *serape* and *rebozo* are never laid aside, and none seem too poor to own one. Apparently the natives do not believe much in standing, for the moment they stop walking they "hunker" down on the ground.

Never once during the three days did we think of getting tired, and it was with a little regret mingled with a desire to see more, that we knew when we awoke in the morning we would be in the City of Mexico.

"THE City of Mexico," they had called. We got off, but we saw no city. We soon learned that the train did not go further, and that we would have to take a carriage to convey us the rest of the way.

Carriages lined the entrance to the station, and the cab-men were, apparently from their actions, just like those of the States. When they procure a permit for a carriage in Mexico, it is graded and marked. A first-class carriage carries a white flag, a second-class a blue flag, and a third-class a red flag. The prices are respectively, per hour: one dollar, seventy-five cents, and fifty cents. This is meant for a protection to travelers, but the drivers are very cunning. Often at night they will remove the flag and charge double prices, but they can be punished for it.

We soon arrived at the Hotel Yturbide, and were assigned rooms by the affable clerk. The hotel was once the home of the Emperor Yturbide. It is a large building of the Mexican style. The entrance takes one into a large, open court or square. All the rooms are arranged around this court, opening out into a circle of balconies.

The lowest floor in Mexico is the cheapest. The higher up one goes the higher they find the price. The reason of this is that at the top one escapes any possible dampness, and can get the light and sun.

Our room had a red brick floor. It was large, but had no ventilation except the glass doors which opened onto the balcony. There was a little iron cot in each corner of the room, a table, washstand, and wardrobe.

It all looked so miserable—like a prisoner's cell—that I began to wish I was at home.

One continually sees poverty and wealth side by side in Mexico, and they don't turn up their noses at each other either; the half-clad Indian has as much room on the Fifth Avenue of Mexico as the millionaire's wife—not but what that land, as this, bows to wealth.

Policemen occupy the center of the street at every termination of a block, reminding one, as they look down the streets, of so many posts. They wear white caps with numbers on, blue suits, and nickel buttons. A mace now takes the place of the sword of former days. At night they don an overcoat and hood, which makes them look just like the pictures of veiled knights. Red lanterns are left in the street where the policemen stood during the daytime, while they retire to some doorway where, it is said, they sleep as soundly as their brethren in the States.

Among the most interesting things in Mexico are the customs followed by the people, which are quaint, and, in many cases, pretty and pleasing. Mexican politeness, while not always sincere, is vastly more agreeable than the courtesy current among Americans. Their pleasing manners seem to be inborn, yet the Mexican of Spanish descent cannot excel the Indian in courtesy, who, though ignorant, unable to

read or write, could teach politeness to a Chesterfield. The moment
they are addressed their hat is in hand. If they wish to pass they first
beg your permission. Even a child, when learning to talk is the perfec-
tion of courtesy. If you ask one its name it will tell you, and immediately add, "I am your servant" or "Your servant to command." This
grows with them, and when past childhood they are as near perfec-
tion in this line as it is possible to be.

When woman meets woman then doesn't come "the tug of war,"
but instead the "hug and kissing;" the kissing is never on the lips, but
while one kisses a friend on the right cheek, she is being kissed on the
left, and then they change off and kiss the other side. Both sides must
be kissed; this is repeated according to the familiarity existing between them, but never on the lips, although with an introduction the
lips are touched. The hug—well, it is given in the same place as it is in
other countries, and in a right tight and wholly earnest manner. From
the first moment they are expected to address each other only by their
Christian names, the family name never being used.

There are some really beautiful girls among this low class of people. Hair three quarters the length of the women, and of wonderful
thickness, is common. It is often worn loose, but more frequently in
two long plaits. Wigmakers find no employment here. The men wear
long, heavy bangs.

Nine women out of ten in Mexico have babies. When at a very
tender age, so young as five days, the babies are completely hidden in
the folds of the *rebozo* and strung to the mother's back, in close proximity to the mammoth baskets of vegetables on her head and suspended on either side of the human freight. When the babies get older
their heads and feet appear, and soon they give their place to another
or share their quarters, as it is no unusual sight to see a woman carry
three babies at one time in her *rebozo*. They are always good. Their
little coal-black eyes gaze out on what is to be their world, in solemn
wonder. No baby smiles or babyish tears are ever seen on their faces. At
the earliest date they are old, and appear to view life just as it is to them
in all its blackness. They know no home, they have no school, and before they are able to talk they are taught to carry bundles on their heads
or backs, or pack a younger member of the family while the mother carries merchandise, by which she gains a living. Their living is scarcely
worth such a title. They merely exist. Thousands of them are born

and raised on the streets. They have no home and were never in a bed. Going along the streets of the city late at night, you will find dark groups huddled in the shadows, which, on investigation, will turn out to be whole families gone to bed. They never lie down, but sit with their heads on their knees, and so pass the night.

. . . The Mexicans are certainly misrepresented, most wrongfully so. They are not lazy, but just the opposite. From early dawn until late at night they can be seen filling their different occupations.

On the street a woman is not permitted to recognize a man first. She must wait until he lifts his shining silk hat; then she raises her hand until on a level with her face, turns the palm inward, with the fingers pointing toward the face, then holds the first and fourth fingers still, and moves the two center ones in a quick motion; the action is very pretty, and the picture of grace when done by a Mexican senora, but is inclined to deceive the green American, and lead him to believe it is a gesture calling him to her side. When two women walk along together the youngest is always given the inside of the pavement, or if the younger happens to be married, she gets the outside—they are quite strict about this; also, if a gentleman is with a mother and daughters, he must walk with the mother and the girls must walk before them.

Tortillas is not only one of the great Mexican dishes but one of the women's chief industries. In almost any street there can be seen women on their knees mashing corn between smooth stones, making it into a batter, and finally shaping it into round, flat cakes. They spit on their hands to keep the dough from sticking, and bake in a pan of hot grease, kept boiling by a few lumps of charcoal. Rich and poor buy and eat them, apparently unmindful of the way they are made. But it is a bread that Americans must be educated to. Many surprise the Mexicans by refusing even a taste after they see the bakers.

The frijoles, or beans, are served on a tortilla, a sort of corn-cake baked in the shape of a buckwheat cake. Another tortilla is folded together, and answers for a spoon. After finishing the beans it is not considered proper or polite unless you eat your spoon and plate.

The meat express does not, by any means, serve to make the meat more palatable. Generally an old mule or horse that has reached its second childhood serves for the express. A long, iron rod, from which hooks project, is fastened on the back of the beast by means of straps.

The meat is hung on these hooks, where it is exposed to the mud and dirt of the streets as well as the hair of the animal. Men with two large baskets, one in front, one behind, filled with the refuse of meat, follow near by. If they wear trousers they have them rolled up high so the blood from the dripping meat will not soil them, but run down their bare legs and be absorbed in the sand. It is asserted that the poor do not allow this mixture in the basket to go to waste, but are as glad to get it as we are to get sirloin steak.

As a people they do not seem malicious, quarrelsome, unkind or evil-disposed. Drunkenness does not seem to be frequent, and the men, in their uncouth way, are more thoughtful of the women than many who belong to a higher class. The women, like other women, sometimes cry, doubtless for very good cause, and then the men stop to console them, patting them on the head, smoothing back their hair, gently wrapping them tighter in their *rebozo*. Late one night, when the weather was so cold, a young fellow sat on the curbstone and kept his arm around a pretty young girl. He had taken off his ragged *serape* and folded it around her shoulders, and as the tears ran down her face and she complained of the cold, he tried to comfort her, and that without a complaint of his own condition, being clad only in muslin trowsers and waist, which hung in shreds from his body.

OF course, everybody has heard of the famous floating gardens of Mexico, and naturally when one reaches this lovely clime their first desire is to go up to La Viga. I wanted to visit the gardens, and with a friend, who put up a nice lunch, started out to spend the day on the water.

When the car reached its destination we alighted, and were instantly surrounded with boatmen, neatly clad in suits consisting of white linen blouse and pants. Everyone clamored for us to try his boat, and the crowd was so dense that it was impossible to move. As there is no regular price, we had to make a bargain, so we selected a strong, brown fellow, who, although he pressed close up to us, had not uttered a word while the rest had been dwelling on the merits of their boats. We went with him to the edge of the canal and looked at his little flat, covered with a tin roof. White linen kept out the sun at the sides, and pink calico, edged with red and green fringe, covered the seats. The bottom was scrubbed very white and the Mexican colors floated from the pole at the end. We asked his price. "Six dollars," he answered. "No," we said; "it's too much." After more debating and deliberating he set his price at one dollar, which we accepted.

In blocks of fifteen by thirty feet nestle the gardens surrounded by water and rising two feet above its surface. The ground is fertile and rich and will grow anything. Some have fruit trees, others vegetables and some look like one bed of flowers suspended in the water. Around in the little canals through which we drifted, were hundreds of elegant water-lilies. Eagerly we gathered them with a desire which seemed never to be satisfied, and even when our boat was full we still clutched ones which were the prettiest yet.

The people who give the natives the worst name are those who treat them the meanest. I have heard men who received some kindness address the donor as thief, scoundrel, and many times worse. I have heard American women address their faithful servants as beasts and fools. One woman, who has a man-nurse so faithful that he would sacrifice his life any moment for his little charge, addressed him in my presence as: "You dirty brute, where did you stay so long?" They are very quick to appreciate a kindness and are sensitive to an insult.

Thus we leave the largest part of the population of Mexico. Their condition is most touching. Homeless, poor, uncared for, untaught, they live and they die. They are worse off by thousands of times than were the slaves of the United States. Their lives are hopeless, and they know it. That they are capable of learning is proven by their work, and by their intelligence in other matters. They have a desire to gain book knowledge, or at least so says a servant who was taken from the streets, who now spends every nickel and every leisure moment in trying to learn wisdom from books.